Avail
from

Fast, Furious and Forbidden
by Alison Kent
&
Hard To Resist
by Samantha Hunter

★

Ready For Action
by Karen Foley

Ms. Match
by Jo Leigh

FAST, FURIOUS AND FORBIDDEN

His hands holding hers above her head were possessive and strong, and being his captive thrilled her.

He angled his head in one direction, she angled hers the other, fitting against him to deepen the tangle of their tongues, the crush of their lips. The heat deepened, too, as did the beating of hummingbird wings in her belly.

He saw to the close fit of everything else; the threading of their fingers, her hands pressed to the wall, the in and out weaving of their thighs, their flush torsos. She felt as if she was the tiniest thing beneath him, hiding in the shadow of his shoulders, disappearing behind his breadth.

HARD TO RESIST

"When do we start doing this for real?"

"Tomorrow."

"Do I get to keep my clothes on?" Jarod asked cheekily with a naughty sparkle in his eyes. Lacey fumbled the camera.

"Depends on whether you mean during or after the shoot," she said off the cuff, shocking herself – it was something the "old" her would have said without a second thought, and she couldn't stop a smile as she watched his shocked reaction.

Score one for Lacey. She could still come out and play, apparently.

He didn't say anything else, and she finished the last roll of film, pleased with herself for the shots and for finding a little of her own spark. Temptation quelled doubt for the moment.

Lieutenant Wyatt had something special, a mysterious quality that reached past her fears and made her see what she'd been missing out on for some time. This tall Texas cop might be good for her, after all.

Did she dare?

First published in Great Britain 2010
Harlequin Mills & Boon Limited,
Eton House, 18-24 Paradise Road, Richmond, Surrey TW9 1SR

Fast, Furious and Forbidden © Mica Stone 2009
(Original title: *A Long, Hard Ride*)
Hard To Resist © Samantha Hunter 2009

ISBN: 978 0 263 88121 9

14-0210

Harlequin Mills & Boon policy is to use papers that are natural, renewable and recyclable products and made from wood grown in sustainable forests. The logging and manufacturing processes conform to the legal environmental regulations of the country of origin.

Printed and bound in Spain
by Litografia Rosés S.A., Barcelona

FAST, FURIOUS AND FORBIDDEN
BY
ALISON KENT

HARD TO RESIST
BY
SAMANTHA HUNTER

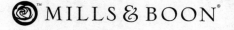
MILLS & BOON®

FAST, FURIOUS AND FORBIDDEN

BY
ALISON KENT

Alison Kent is the author of several steamy books for Mills & Boon, as well as a handful of fun and sassy stories for other imprints. She is also the author of *The Complete Idiot's Guide to Writing Erotic Romance*. Alison lives in a Houston, Texas, suburb with her own romance hero.

To Lori, Julie and Jennifer for making sure a good time was had by all of us in Dahlia.

And for Jennifer especially, for knowing Outlaw 10.5 racing and understanding insanity.

1

"WHIP! I GOTTA HAVE THAT torque wrench or I ain't never gonna get this done."

"Take a look in the far chest, Sunshine. The second drawer. I got it out of there earlier."

"Well, it ain't in there now. It ain't in any of 'em. Drawers or chests. I done looked."

Hunkered down outside the Corley Motors rig, the tractor-trailer used to haul "Bad Dog" Butch Corley's dragster to National Hot Rod Association events, Trey "Whip" Davis straightened from where he'd been securing an extension cord against the movable race pit flooring, and mentally retraced the day's steps.

He'd had the torque wrench with him when he'd grabbed for his BlackBerry to call Butch—the driver had been enjoying a late breakfast with his wife and son—only to realize he'd left the PDA on a shelf in the hauler's workshop. He'd obviously set down the tool when he'd picked up the phone, but—crap on a cracker.

What was wrong with his head?

This wasn't like him, being off kilter, disorganized, careless. He was making stupid mistakes. It had to stop. And it had to stop now. He headed for the racing trailer's open door. "Take a break, guy. Grab a corndog. Get a cup of coffee. I'll rustle it up."

Sunshine got to his feet, twisted and stretched his stocky five-foot-seven frame, and gave Trey his trademark sunny smile—one that reddened his already ruddy complexion, which in turn made his blond eyebrows appear to have been bleached within an inch of their life. "Can't turn down that million-dollar offer. See ya in a bit, Boss."

Trey watched his assistant crew chief make his way toward the concession stands, zigzagging through the haulers, pop-ups and motor homes turning the Dahlia Speedway pits into a virtual campground.

The late morning sun shone off the reds and greens, and the blues and yellows of hundreds of logos decorating everything from trucks and T-shirts to ball caps and tattoos. Behind him, Trey knew, the snarling Corley bulldog, with its spiked silver collar, would be gleaming bright white against the backdrop of the team's black trailer.

The vibrant colors, the beehive activity, the smells of exhaust and fuel as mechanics test-fired engines, the din of the fans whooping and hollering along with the jetlike roar—he would never tire of witnessing a dragstrip coming to life and was, in fact, going to miss it like hell while away.

When Corley Motors pulled out early Monday morning following this weekend's Farron Fuel Spring Nationals, Sunshine would be taking over Trey's crew chief duties—working with Butch on developing racing strategies and supervising the crew of mechanics who precision-tuned the engine for optimum performance.

It was a temporary arrangement only; Trey had made sure his crew and his driver understood he would be back. For now, however, he was staying in Dahlia—the town where he'd lived the first twenty years of his life. It was long past time to go through the paperwork and personal belongings he hadn't touched in the six months since his father's death from heart failure.

And since he rarely visited, he'd decided there was no reason to keep the house or the property he owned here. It held memories, sure, but he wasn't the sentimental type that attached them to a place. He could think back to his childhood anytime he wanted to remember the past.

Unfortunately, getting the place fit for a buyer was going to require a hell of a lot of manual labor, and most of it would have to be his. He was the only one who would know what to keep, what to toss, what to store until he could make arrangements to sell or give away.

All that weight pressing down had everything to do with his mind being on the fritz. But clearing away those obligations was only one part of it. Solving the puzzle of why the hell, shortly before his death, his father had taken a swing at a pillar of the Dahlia community and nearly killed the older man's son when he'd come to his defense was another.

Both had to be done if he intended to remain in the top fuel game. He did—leaving him no choice but to take this sabbatical.

It was either do so, or find himself canned as Butch Corley's tuning boss, and he'd worked too hard to let that come to pass. No mechanic with a lick of sense wanted to work for a screwup. No driver worth his salt would let one near his car.

Knowing Sunshine couldn't resist a conversation anymore than he could a corndog, Trey stepped up into the hauler's workshop, figuring he had a free thirty minutes while the other man schmoozed the vendors setting up around the track.

The rest of the crew would be rolling in throughout the day to prepare for Friday's first round of qualifying. There would be no downtime over the weekend; work would continue from dawn to dusk to dawn again, the team tweaking their formula to guarantee a "Bad Dog" performance the Corley fans wouldn't forget.

This breather was the last one Trey figured he'd have until at least Sunday night. By the time Sunshine got back, all hands would be required on deck and—

"You know, the last time I saw you standing still, you had your pants around your ankles."

What the hell?

"And it's nice to see my memory hasn't failed me. You do have a fantastic ass."

Glowering, Trey turned. The woman in the doorway had the sun at her back, which put her face in shadow. It didn't matter. He knew without question who it was standing there giving him the eye. Had known who was speaking the moment he'd first heard her voice.

That didn't mean he was able to answer without taking a deep breath first. Seven years had done nothing to dull his body's response to having her within reach. "Cardin Worth. It's been a while."

She wore black Converse sneakers, low-riding jeans, and a black Dahlia Speedway logo T-shirt. His pulse began to hum, but not because of the way she looked in her clothes.

Humming was what it had always done when she was around. What it had done even before the pants-around-his-ankles incident all those years ago. What it had done anytime he'd thought of her since.

He'd thought of her a lot. A whole hell of a lot. "How are you?"

Pulling off her sunglasses, she came further into the trailer, her long black ponytail swinging, her cheekbones more defined than he recalled. "I'm good, Trey. You?"

"The same." He looked on as she laid down the glasses,

as she picked up and fondled the wrench he'd come for. He'd always thought she had the most graceful hands, had always wanted her to touch him more than she had the night she'd caught him bare-assed. "What brings you out here so early on race weekend?"

"I'm actually looking for my grandfather." Her gaze came up, intense, searching. "Have you seen him?"

"Jeb? No." Trey shook his head. He hadn't remembered her eyes being so blue. Her body being so…fine. But he finally did remember his manners. It didn't matter that her grandfather was someone he really didn't care to see. "Is he doing okay?"

A comma of a dimple teased one side of her mouth. "Flying as right as ever, thanks."

"And you? You're doing okay?" Because he sure as hell wasn't.

Her smile took pity, her gaze softened. "We already did that part."

"Right. Sorry. My mind's—"

"On the race?"

Actually, it had gone back seven years to the night of the kegger celebrating her class's high school graduation. The night of the pants-around-his-ankles incident. The night he'd backed her into the wall and listened to her breathe.

He still wondered how long she'd been standing there, why she'd stayed and watched instead of skittering away. If she'd been as turned on as he'd thought. If she dreamed about that night the way he did, for no reason that made any sense.

He cleared his throat, went back to what she'd asked him. "Yeah. Farron Fuels is always a big one for Butch."

"For all of Dahlia," she reminded him sagely, her home-town pride strong.

He nodded in response, knowing her family, along with the others whose businesses thrived on the income generated by visitors who'd come to the spring drag racing series to see "Bad Dog" Butch, would get the bad news soon enough.

Thanks to one Artie Buell, son of the local sheriff, who'd messed with Butch's wife at a local watering hole where she'd stopped for a drink with Sunshine's wife last night, this weekend's Farron Fuels was the last one for Butch—who would've landed behind bars and had to forfeit the race if Trey and the others hadn't kept him from kicking Artie's ass.

Butch had no use for a town where a supposed upstanding citizen, one related to what passed for the law, didn't know that a married woman's no meant no. So this year's race was it. Corley Motors, one of the biggest outfits in top fuel dragster racing, wouldn't be coming back to the Dahlia Speedway.

And once he'd finished his business here and cut his personal ties with the town, that meant neither would Trey.

Cardin turned the torque wrench over in her hands, a thoughtful crease appearing between her arched brows. "It has to be strange to have grown up here, yet never visit. Except during the Farron Fuels."

He wanted to tell her it wasn't strange at all. That these days he didn't think of Dahlia as anything more than another quarter mile strip of asphalt he needed to get his driver down as fast as he could. But he didn't say anything, just waited for her to dig deeper for whatever it was she wanted.

She did, switching from a gentle trowel to a more painful pick. "Surely you miss seeing old friends? Spending time at home? Hanging out with Tater, as inseparable as you two were?"

He missed Tater, sure. They'd been best friends before either of them could spell his name. But the only thing that would've kept Trey here had never been his to come home to—even though she'd sought him out and was standing in front of him now.

And so he shook his head.

"Really?"

"Really."

"Hmm." Her tone said she didn't believe him. "There's not anything about Dahlia you miss?"

"Nope," he said, and knew he lied.

"Or anyone?"

"Nope." Another lie.

"Not even Kim Halton?"

Kim Halton had been the girl on her knees when his pants had been around his ankles. The girl who'd finished what she'd started, then left Trey alone to pull up, zip up and deal with the girl who had watched.

"There is one thing."

"What's that?"

"I miss seeing you."

"Pfft." She fluffed her fingers through her bangs, hiding behind her hair and her hand. "When did you ever see me before?"

He wondered if her refusal to look him in the eye meant her cool was all a ploy. Then he wondered how much of the truth she really wanted.

He went for broke. "You mean besides the time you stood there and watched Kim blow me?"

Color rose to bloom on her cheeks, but it was her only response until she gave a single nod.

That one was easy. "I saw you at school, in the halls, shaking your ass on the football field. I saw you every time I came into your family's place for a burger or a beer."

"That was a long time ago, Trey," she said, her voice broadcasting her bafflement. "At least—"

"Seven years," he finished for her.

Her frown was baffled, too. "You say that like you've kept track."

"I have." He knew exactly when he'd moved away from Dahlia. When he'd last seen her except in passing at the annual Farron Fuels.

"I don't get it. You were two years ahead of me in school. We didn't exchange more than a couple dozen words."

Words had nothing to with the heat she'd stirred in him then. That she still stirred now, a stirring he felt as his blood flowed south. "So?"

"So, there's no reason for you to miss seeing me."

"None you can think of, you mean."

"Whip—"

"Hold up." He lifted a hand. "Forget about me missing you. Let's talk about the nickname instead."

That got her to laughing, a throaty, bluesy sound that tightened him up. "Hey, I had no idea it would stick. You can blame that on Tater."

She returned the wrench to the shelf, her fingers lingering, her lashes as thick and dark as the bristles of an engine brush as she lifted her gaze coyly to his. "At least most people think it's about you cracking the whip over your team."

That was because most people hadn't been there to hear the gossip about him whipping it out for Kim Halton.

He was lucky their secret had stayed close. That no one knew he couldn't have cared less about Kim. That, instead, he'd wanted the girl watching from the doorway as Kim stroked him. The one too close to his doorway now.

He moved to block it. "I suppose it could've been worse."

"You're right." She paused, added, "I could've called you... Speedy."

Ouch. But he grinned. "Maybe I was wrong when I thought I'd missed seeing you."

"I'd say that's a distinct possibility." Coy was gone, a

come-on in its place. "Especially since I'm right here, and you're still missing seeing me."

He was pretty sure his definition of missing and hers of the same word were two different things. That didn't mean she wasn't right. That he wasn't overlooking something vital.

He crossed his arms and widened his stance, furrowing his brow as he gave her an obvious once-over. "I'm seeing you now."

Her tongue slicked quickly over her lips. "You're too far away to see much of anything."

There were less than three feet between them. He came closer, backing her into a waist-high storage locker. "Is this better?"

"You tell me," she said.

He leaned in, flattened his palms on the stainless steel surface, one on either side of her hips, and hovered, her body heat rising, his breathing labored and giving him away. "Not as better as it needs to be."

Her hesitation in replying wasn't about uncertainty, or impropriety, but about making him sweat, making him wait, making him want and ache. He was doing all of those things, strangling on the tension that was thick in the trailer around them, and robbing him of his air.

Finally, she moved, her hands coming up, her palms pressing to his chest, her fingertips finding his nipples and rubbing circles where they dotted his shirt. He shuddered, and she tipped forward, nuzzling her nose to the hollow of his throat.

He closed his eyes, inhaled, caught the scent of her shampoo, of her sun-heated skin, of her perspiration that was sweet, a damp sheen. Keeping his hands to himself had seemed smart, but she made him too stupid to care about anything but taking up where seven years ago, they'd left off because they were too young to know better.

He held her upper arms, her shoulders, sliding his hands up her neck to cup her face, her cheeks, her jaw, sliding them down to her ribcage and over the sides of her breasts.

There was no sense in any of this, no reason, no rhyme. They hadn't kept in touch since he'd pressed her into the wall with his body. They'd never talked about how close they'd come that night to tumbling into bed. He had no idea what had driven her here, and the climb of his temperature left him unable to figure it out, to do anything but feel.

She met his gaze, parted her lips, pushed up on her sneakered tiptoes to find his mouth. He bent to make it easy for her, but mostly he bent for himself. Her tongue slipped between his lips to tease and seduce and show him the years he'd missed out on.

He couldn't let himself wonder about or regret any of that now because she was here, and he didn't want to miss any of what was happening. Her hunger was that of a long separation, a desperation, neither which he understood or which fit.

What he did understand were her hands at his waist, tugging up his T-shirt, slipping beneath. Her fingers threaded into the hair on his belly, then through that on his chest. She toyed with his nipples, and drove him mad with wanting her.

He broke the kiss because he had to, and rested his mouth at the corner of hers to catch his breath, his control. Her lips parted. He felt the urgent beat of her heart all over. "Cardin, why are you here?"

She shook her head. "I don't know. It's been so long. I wasn't sure. I need—"

"Yo! Whip! Where you at? You'll never guess who I found holding a corndog in each hand."

Sunshine was back, and Trey had no choice but to set Cardin away, his question unanswered, her reply incomplete. He looked down, trying to find something to clue him into the truth, seeing only the flush of her arousal.

His own strained obviously and would take time to calm. "We'll finish this later."

"Yo! Whip!"

"Be right there," he called toward the still open door, smoothing down his shirt as Cardin checked that nothing was out of order. "You heard me, right?"

"That we'll finish this later?" She nodded.

Good. But also... "And you'll tell me then what you need?"

She didn't answer. She brushed her mouth one last time against his before turning, snagging her sunglasses and hopping from the trailer to the ground.

Trey took another few seconds to gather himself, grabbed for the torque wrench and walked from the rig's interior into the white-hot light of the sun.

He squinted, then shook his head at the irony of the interruption as he recognized Jeb Worth standing beside the four-wheeler with Sunshine. That settled one thing at least.

Cardin looking for her grandfather was not as far-fetched as Trey had thought. Whether or not finding Jeb was what had brought her to the Corley hauler was yet to be seen.

Trey had a feeling it was something a whole lot bigger—and with a whole lot more baggage—than that.

2

CARDIN SERENITY WORTH had lived her entire life in Dahlia,
Tennessee. She'd sold Dixie cups of lemonade and Girl Scout
cookies and fund-raising candy, tchotchkes and Christmas
paper to half the folks in town.

She'd been a member of the Dahlia High School Darlings,
high-kicking her way across the football field during three
years of half-time shows, and a member of the local FFA,
raising rabbits to show at county fairs.

She'd worked at Headlights, her family's ice house, since
she was old enough to pay taxes and social security on her
wages, but had earned her allowance busing tables and
sweeping peanut hulls from the floor before that.

She was twenty-five years old, a hometown girl known to
one and all, and well aware that two decades from now, she
would still be thought of as her father Eddie's shadow, her
mother Delta's princess, and her grandpa Jeb's pride and joy.

It came with being a Worth, a family that was as much a
local fixture as the Dahlia Speedway, the drag-racing track
where in less than two weeks, the whole town would switch
gears from this weekend's NHRA race to Dahlia's annual
Moonshine Run.

The midnight race was the only event in which Jeb still

entered the car he called "White Lightning"—a nod to the years of Prohibition when her great-grandpa Orin's moonshine had kept the folks in three counties from feeling any pain, while keeping his own family out of the poor house.

Right now, however, the race still on everyone's mind— Cardin's included—had featured top fuel dragsters: long, narrow purpose-built race cars with thin front tires that tore in a straight line down a length of the quarter mile track in under five seconds and at over three hundred miles an hour.

The Farron Fuel Spring Nationals had wrapped up earlier in the day, and the entire Corley Motors crew—"Bad Dog" Butch Corley having taken top honors again this year—was chowing down and raising hell at two of Headlights' tables not fifteen feet from where she stood scooping crushed ice into red plastic tumblers for cokes and sweet tea.

Except it wasn't the whole team causing her mouth to go dry, her palms to grow damp, her nape to tingle from the heat. It was one member, one man.

The man sitting at the far corner of the second table, the garage door style wall behind him rolled open to the early evening breeze.

The man polishing off the last ear of corn from the platter the group had ordered to go with their burgers, hot wings and pitchers of beer.

The man she'd thrown herself at three days ago and kissed with unheard of abandon as if she were a woman in love.

Trey Davis was the crew chief for Corley Motors. He was also Cardin's counterpart: a hometown Dahlia boy. Granted, he hadn't stayed in Dahlia the way she had; though he still owned property here, he only managed to visit during the spring drag racing series.

She liked to think his growing up here connected them. Trey knew what it was like to have sprouted from small town

Tennessee roots, to be saddled with the stereotypes, the prejudices, the accent…the family that could drive a person mad.

And then there was that woman in love thing, and the possibility that what she felt for him wasn't an "if". The high school crush. The continuing infatuation. The way March roared in every year, a lion bringing with it the Farron Fuels and a chance to see him.

The way she felt like a lamb once he was gone—a victim of her own weakness because she'd been afraid to seek him out and talk to him about that night seven years ago…what they'd almost done, how the things he'd whispered had made her feel, the way she'd been unable to get him out of her mind since.

Because of all that, and because of their families' shared history—Trey's great-grandfather Emmett had been her great-grandfather Orin's partner in the moonshine biz—she trusted him, and hoped his instincts could help her put an end to the Worth family feud.

It was obvious she couldn't do it alone; Lord knew she'd tried to patch things up between her parents, to no avail. Eddie and Delta were now estranged. She'd tried, too, to smooth things over between her father and her grandpa Jeb, who'd stopped speaking to Eddie when he wouldn't shut up about the fight that had nearly cost her father his life.

For a year she'd played the part of peacemaker, insisting her mother be understanding of her father's moods; they'd come so close to losing him, after all. Insisting her father be patient, that his recovery would be a long process, not one with the overnight results he expected from his doctors and himself.

Insisting her grandpa cut his son a break and answer Eddie's questions; he'd been the one to break up the fight before either of the other men got hurt…so, yes. He did have a right to know why Aubrey Davis had taken a swing at Jeb. And since that blow-up twelve months ago that sent Eddie to the hospital had involved Trey's father, well, Cardin figured he owed her.

Of course, he was totally unaware of her plans to use him. And she still wasn't sure how to go about her…proposal.

During her Thursday visit to the Dahlia Speedway, she'd had no time to lay out for him her thoughts. All she'd managed to do was test the waters, see if the electricity that had always crackled between them was still there.

It was, burning as hot as the night his unyielding body pressed hers into the bedroom wall, trapping her, molded to her, an imprint she felt always and would never forget.

She shivered, silenced a moan. This was not a good time to be remembering the bristly sensation of his beard against her cheek, or the hardness of his bare chest beneath her hands.

But that was the direction her mind had decided to travel, following a map that took her imagination into territory that had her pulse thumping, her breath quickening, her belly growing taut…

"Cardin?"

"Hmm?"

"You didn't leave any room for the drinks."

"What?"

"The drinks. The ice. Cardin!"

Cardin pulled her attention from the hands holding the corn that she wished were holding her, and turned toward the biting voice and the woman with the teeth.

Sandy Larabie had been working at Headlights as long as Cardin. She was six years older, had two divorces under her belt, and was both the most caustic and well-tipped of all the ice house's serving staff.

She nodded at the tumblers Cardin held, not a hair out of

place in her big brassy 'do. "Get your head in the game. It's hopping like hell bunnies in here."

Cardin's head was in the game. Just not the game Sandy was talking about. "Sorry. I got…distracted."

Sandy scooped ice for her own drink order, following the direction of Cardin's gaze. "You know he's staying behind when the team checks out tomorrow, right?"

She did know. She'd even heard it earlier than most; as Dahlia's unofficial herald, Jeb had his ear to the ground. She'd been surprised by the news, as had everyone, but the lead she'd gained from her grandpa's announcement had given her time to put together her plan.

Too bad she'd got caught up in kissing Trey before she could explain it to him. Just seeing him again had unraveled her to the point of barely being able to think.

She turned to Sandy. "So I've heard. Hard to believe, isn't it?"

Pop, pop went Sandy's gum as she nodded. "Tater told me Whip's taking a few months to get his place cleaned up and sold." Winston Tate "Tater" Rawls, a mechanic at Morgan and Son Garage, had been Trey's best friend in high school, and was Sandy's newest boy toy.

"I don't think Trey's set foot on the property in a year, at least. I wonder how long he'll be here." Might as well see what else Sandy-by-way-of-Tater knew. The more information Cardin could sock away, the more convincing she'd be when she finally talked to Trey.

"According to Tater," Sandy said, "Whip's gonna join back up with the Corley team later this season. But since they've put the kibosh on coming back to the Speedway, I'd say this might be the last time we see him around here."

Sandy spun away at the sound of the order bell, while Cardin just spun. She'd heard the rumors of Corley Motors blacklisting the Dahlia Speedway. The winning team was a Dahlia favorite and a huge draw; having one of their own working as crew chief was a highly prized bragging right.

But now with that moron Artie Buell having put the moves on Butch Corley's wife, "Bad Dog" Butch was done with Dahlia. A shame, too, because the town needed the income generated by the big boys. Big boys like the team that employed the man she was about to ask to pose as her fiancé.

Both her parents and her grandpa Jeb needed to move beyond the hell of the last year, and get back to acting like a family. Her thinking was that introducing Trey as her fiancé would shake them out of their funk, would give them a new outlet for their focus, a common goal toward which they could pour their combined energies—that of doing all they could to break up the engagement.

Trey was Aubrey's son. Aubrey who had taken a swing at Jeb. Aubrey who had sent Eddie to the hospital. Aubrey who had instigated a fight with an elderly man, and taken the genesis of his beef with Cardin's grandpa to his grave. If the thought of her marrying Aubrey's son didn't shake them out of their blind self-absorption, she knew nothing ever would. This was a last-ditch effort, and an admittedly desperate one.

But there was more to her choice, to her plan. Trey was also the man Cardin hadn't been able to get over in seven long years. She had to find out if what she felt for him was as real as her heart insisted it was, as real as her head told her every time she thought of him.

He'd been two years ahead of her in school, but since the teen crowd in Dahlia was small, they'd crossed paths regularly. At school functions. At sporting events. At parties classmates threw behind their parents' backs.

Like Tater's post-graduation kegger. Where Cardin had

opened what she'd drunkenly mistaken for the bathroom door only to find herself looking into the master bedroom, and into Trey's eyes. His pants had been around his ankles. And Kim Halton had been kneeling open-mouthed in front of him.

Cardin had been more tipsy than not, but Trey had been one-hundred percent sober. She'd seen it in his face when the light shining from the hallway spilled into the darkened room; it had exposed his raw emotions as fully as the part of his body she'd been certain he'd wanted her—and not Kim—to take care of.

She was twenty-five now, not eighteen, but she had yet to forget the way their eyes had connected, the intensity in his craving, the look that had beckoned her to wait, to stay, to want him the way he wanted her. She had waited. Wanted. Watched him while he'd come, knowing all the while he was imagining it was her hand stroking him, her lips sucking him, her tongue slicking over the head of his cock.

Kim had finished her, uh, service, caught sight of Cardin in the shadows, and smirked as she'd stormed out of the room, leaving Trey halfway dressed and Cardin's cheeks to flame while she watched him tuck himself into his pants, while she listened to him curse in a voice harsh with anger.

Once he'd caught his breath and his composure, he'd come for her, swiftly, pressed the length of his body to the length of hers and told her to forget what she'd seen.

He'd toyed with a lock of her hair and asked her how she could smell like sunshine in the middle of the night. He'd stroked her throat from her chin to the hollow and told her she was softer than down. She'd stayed silent, shaken her head at his words, given in to a longing she didn't understand and laid her hands on his chest.

His heart had pounded, a match to hers. His breathing had grown ragged and rushed. She had barely been able to think, or to swallow, or do more than chew at her bottom lip. He'd stopped her with his thumb, and the contact had sent her belly falling to her feet.

She'd moved one hand to hold his wrist, but her fingers didn't fit around it. She felt his skin, his bones, the crisp hairs there, wondering at how human he felt to her touch. And so she'd touched more. The back of his hand, his nails, the pads of his fingertips, the dip between his forefinger and thumb.

She'd touched his face, found the bump where he'd broken his nose during football, learned the arch of his brows, his right that was especially wicked, the thickness of his lashes, the way his dimples deepened when he smiled. She'd threaded her fingers into his hair, and he'd turned his face to kiss her palm, holding her gaze while his tongue circled around and around on her skin, while his teeth took hold and marked her.

Nothing had been the same for her since.

Ridding herself of the disturbing musings with a very deep breath, on shaky legs Cardin delivered the drinks she'd taken too long to serve, apologizing to the family of four who were long past ready to eat. Once she had their order, she made a beeline for the kitchen and entered the menu items into the system that would queue them up for Eddie and his staff.

That done, she slipped away to the ladies' room to check her face and hair. She needed to know if she looked the harried mess she felt before heading over to finish her business with Trey. He was here. She was here. Why wait?

Surprisingly, the reflection staring back at her wasn't a harried mess at all. Yes, flyaway wisps of hair had escaped her ponytail to frame her face, and her cheeks were understandably flushed, but it was a sexy rather than flustered look, if she did say so herself.

The loosely rolled neckline of her Headlights T-shirt revealed her collarbone from shoulder to shoulder. The big, round lights of the truck-grill logo were strategically screen-printed to outline her breasts. It was cheesy, sure, but since this was Trey and her quest so important, Cardin was not above using her arsenal of female ammunition.

And with her long bare legs beneath her short denim skirt, her big baby blues and her 34Bs looking like Cs with help from Victoria's Secret, she figured all angles—and curves—were covered.

Another steadying breath, and she headed back to the kitchen, bypassing the service window where orders sat waiting. Grabbing a clean platter, she ducked around the two high school kids who worked as dishwashers, and dodged Albert, the second shift cook, who was carting a tub of freshly ground beef from the walk-in refrigerator to his station.

With Albert's hands full, Cardin didn't have to worry about the retired and grizzled military man slapping her on the ass, and she reached her father unscathed. Holding out the platter for him to fill, she got straight to the point. "I need a half dozen ears of corn."

Eddie Worth had been only eighteen when Cardin was born. Now separated from her mother, he was considered a very hot property by single women of all ages. He turned from stirring a big pot of chili, his blue eyes that he'd passed to his daughter twinkling. "This corn's going out free of charge, I'm guessing? Since you're back here after it yourself?"

"It is, yes. Compliments of the house."

"Who are we complimenting this time?"

Cardin stuck out her tongue. "You say that like I give away food on a regular basis."

"You do give away food on a regular basis." He reached for a pair of heavy duty tongs, steam from the boiling vat clouding around his face and his already sweaty forehead. "I just like to know the who so I can puzzle out the why."

Hmm. She didn't really like the idea of her father puzzling out anything about her plans for Trey. "It's for the Corley Motors table. They finished what they ordered, and I thought it would be nice to toss another platter their way. Butch won today, you know."

Eddie dropped the sixth ear on the pile Cardin held and looked up at her from beneath his narrowed black brows. "Something tells me you're not tossing anything at the whole team. And that Butch winning doesn't matter to you any more than it does to me."

And to Eddie, she knew, it didn't matter at all. He'd gotten over racing when his accident left him unable to drive Jeb's car. He'd gotten over Corley Motors at the same time because the team's crew chief was the son of the man who'd almost killed him. "Okay. It's for Trey. Happy now?"

"Happy that you're singling out Whip? No." He shook his head. "Not really."

Cardin sighed her frustration. Her father could hold a grudge longer than anyone she knew. And a stupid grudge at that, since it had been Aubrey Davis—not Trey—who had put Eddie in the hospital. "Even if I were singling him out for more than a few ears of corn, you don't have anything to worry about."

Eddie went back to stirring the chili. "What part of that is supposed to make me feel better?"

It was hard, but Cardin managed not to strangle him. "The part where you remember all the things you taught me about dealing with men. The part where you remember that I can take care of myself. You can trust me, okay?"

The spoon stopped. The chili bubbled around it. "My trusting you doesn't mean he won't break your heart."

"Oh, Daddy." Cardin rubbed her cheek against her father's shoulder as he stared down, reducing the fire on the stove when the chili started getting too hot. "No one is going to break my heart. I won't let them. And that includes Trey Davis."

Eddie took a minute to shake it off, then he banged the spoon against the side of the pot and used it instead of his finger to point. "I'm going to remind you of that when you come to me with tears in your eyes because he has. Now get that corn out there before it's too cold to melt butter."

With a quick kiss to Eddie's stubble-covered cheek, Cardin was off, dodging Albert's hands, the dishwashers' sudsy puddles, and Sandy's biting tongue—the other woman snapping about Cardin expecting her tables to be covered while she was off doing God knew what.

It hadn't been that long, and Cardin was well aware that she needed to get back to work, but if she didn't snag Trey's attention now, she'd have to hope for—or manufacture—another opportunity. Waiting would be a waste of the time he would be in Dahlia, and this trip would very likely be his last.

She was only halfway there when he saw her coming. He was leaning on one elbow, his beer mug palmed in his hand, listening to one of his tablemates tell a whopper of a story when he caught her eye. It was a live-wire jolt, the way their gazes fused, and she had to step carefully since she couldn't see a thing in her path.

Reaching the end of the row of tables, she turned the corner, vaguely aware that the men had gone silent and all eyes were on her. She couldn't let herself wonder what they were thinking or care about that now. Trey was waiting, his dark eyes broadcasting his curiosity and a much more personal interest.

Good. That's what she wanted. To see she wasn't alone in feeling this connection, the one driving her impulsive actions and the staccato beat of her heart.

With the television mounted high in the corner playing clips from today's Farron Fuels, she stopped at his side, set the platter of still steaming and sweet smelling corn in front of him, reached across him for the salt, pepper, and bowl of softened butter balls, pulling them close.

And then with a tingling rush of heat tightening her to the core, she leaned in, her breasts brushing his shoulder as she whispered for his hearing alone, "I'm ready to tell you what I need."

She didn't wait for him to respond, but walked away, smiling to herself at the catcalls and raucous whooping-it-up that erupted at the table behind her.

3

"C'MON, WHIP. What did she say?"

"Yeah, man. Don't leave us hanging."

"I tell ya. That little gal can whisper sweet nothings in my ear anytime she wants. 'Course I'd have to explain to the wife that whispering was the only thing going on."

"Look at yourself, Sunshine. Now look at that little gal. You'd have a hard time convincing anybody that something more was."

While the wolf whistles accompanied Cardin to the kitchen, the digs, jabs and good ol' boy ridicule continued around the table. Ignoring the noise, Trey watched over the heads of dozens of customers, his gaze following her until she pushed through the swinging saloon doors, her dark ponytail bobbing as she crossed behind the order window and disappeared from sight.

Only then did he think about breathing again, or respond to the ribbing his crew members were killing themselves over. The group of men he worked with were also his friends. He could take whatever they dished out, could dish it right back, tit for tat.

But he had absolutely no intention of repeating what Cardin had said to anyone, dead or alive. Not when he was about to find out why she'd come to see him the other day at the hauler.

He set down his beer mug, wiped his mouth and hands on

one of the towelettes Headlights provided, then slapped the table and got to his feet. "If you boys will 'scuse me, some unexpected business has just come up. I'll catch up with y'all later."

"What kind of business would that be, coming up?"

"Sure you don't need some help with whatever it is?"

"Holler if you do. The wife's pretty understanding when it comes to helping out a friend."

"I know your wife, Sunshine. I don't think she'd be anything close to understanding about you helping out yourself."

Trey waved one hand and ignored the lot of 'em, winding his way through the tables, dodging serving trays and customers and kids running wild. Kenny Chesney on the jukebox singing about his sexy tractor added to the din. He wanted to catch Cardin before she ditched him for work; with a crowd this rowdy, he figured that scenario was seconds from coming to pass.

At the swinging doors, he gave a smile to the waitress with the big mouth and big hair who told him he wasn't allowed in the kitchen. He looked toward the grill, the fryers, the freezer, the fridge, searching for Cardin…nothing. Staff scurried like ants on a hill, but she was nowhere to be seen.

Her father was, however.

"Hello, Whip." Eddie Worth was as tall as Trey, as strong as Trey, and sixteen years more clever. His eyes saw all. His keen wit missed nothing. He wasn't anyone a smart man messed with.

"Hello, Eddie." Trey shook Cardin's father's hand. It was hard to know what else to say when Eddie was obviously well aware of what had brought Trey into the back. "How've you been?"

"I've been fine." He held on to Trey's hand as he added, "Sorry to hear about your dad."

Though his dad was the one who'd put Eddie in the hospital and there wasn't any love there lost, Trey acknowledged the condolence with a nod. He'd had six months to put it behind him. "Thanks. It was, uh, rough there for a bit, dealing with the funeral and all."

"But things are better now?"

Another nod. It was an easier response than explaining what he needed to make things even better than they were.

"That's good. That's good." Eddie crossed his arms, a dish towel slung over one shoulder. "And I hear you're going to get your place ready to sell?"

Another something Eddie no doubt thought was good. Trey stood his ground. "This economy, it might take awhile, but holding on to it doesn't make much sense considering I'm never here."

He imagined his never being here was also to Eddie's liking. Trey was his father's son after all.

"Well, I hope it all works out," Eddie said, stepping back, but adding before he turned to go, "I guess you're looking for Cardin?"

"I am. Yes, sir."

"She's out back." Eddie gestured toward the door. "Took a load of trash to the Dumpster."

"Thank you, sir. Good to see you again," Trey said, then made his way to the exit, feeling the heat of Eddie's gaze boring into his back. He'd deal with Eddie and Jeb and the cause of the fight with his father later. Right now, he had other things on his mind.

Outside, he found Cardin wrestling a huge black trash bag out of an equally huge gray plastic can. She didn't notice him there, and as much as he wanted to help, he waited, looking on as she scrunched up her face and rocked the bag side to side, working to dislodge the items wedged against the sides of the container.

He watched the flex of muscles in her arms and shoulders, the tendons in her neck as she tugged. He watched her frustration mount, her frown deepen, her aggravation grow until disgust took its place.

She stopped then, blew a puff of air up at her bangs, stretched her back and groaned. She was still unaware of his presence. He knew that because when she swiped her wrist across her forehead and saw him leaning against the building, she straightened, stiffened and glared.

"How long have you been standing there?"

He liked that she wasn't wearing her sunglasses this time. Her eyes were so blue, full of such life, and though he'd expected to see anger, he hadn't been ready for the thrill he saw in them. He wondered if it was a reflection of his own.

"Well?" she prompted.

He pushed away from his perch. "Long enough to see that you could use some help."

"Just not to offer it?" When he shrugged, she added, "In that case, I'm sorry I wasted the corn."

"Trust me. The corn was no waste," he said, making his way slowly to where she stood.

She watched him approach, her fingers tightening on the bag, crinkling the plastic, stretching it, piercing through. The set of her shoulders grew taut as he neared. Her pulse was visible in her throat. "Then brace this here so I can get the trash out and get back to work."

He stopped in front of her, planted his palms on the can's rim and used his weight as an anchor, leaning forward into her space. He smelled sunshine, sweat and cooking smoke, and wanted to be closer still. "This is certainly not the reception I was expecting."

"Sorry." She jerked the bag free, and hauled it toward her. "I'm not my best when surrounded by garbage."

The trash in one hand, she climbed onto an empty crate, lifting the Dumpster lid and tossing the bag inside. Once again on the ground, she dusted her hands together, keeping the can between them as a buffer. "Thank you."

Trey took a minute, cleared his throat. His mind's eye was still looking up her short skirt and at her black panties. "Can we get to what you need now?"

He could've stepped around the can, shoved it to the side and out of the way. He could've reached for her the way she'd reached for him that day in the hauler, wrapped her close and finished what they'd left undone that night he'd pinned her against him as long as he could. But this ball was in her court, and he would play by her rules for now.

She considered him closely, dodging his question as if not sure how to answer, and asked him one of her own. "What made you decide to sell your place?"

He pushed up from the can to stand straight. "You heard about that, did you?"

"Everyone in town has heard about it. You know how Dahlia is."

He knew well, and that was part of the reason he was cutting his ties. He was tired of everyone being in his business. "Dad's gone now, and I spend most of my time on the road. I figured it was the best solution."

"But then you won't have a home."

He ignored what looked like sadness—was it sympathy? Pity maybe?—in her eyes. He crossed his arms over his chest. "Home is where the heart is. Isn't that what they say?"

"Do you need help?"

He frowned. "What?"

"I'm happy to give you a hand. Packing, organizing,

tossing out trash." Her mouth twisted as she gestured over her shoulder with her thumb. "I'm good with trash."

Huh. This wasn't what he'd expected to hear when he'd decided to hunt her down. "Is that why you came to see me the other day? You're offering to help me get things ready to sell?"

Again she avoided a straight answer. "I've seen your family's place, Trey. That's a lot of work for one person."

She was right. Making order out of the chaos left behind at his childhood home was not a one-man job—not if that man didn't want to spend an eternity living in his past. Not that it was such a bad place to be. He just liked the here and now a whole lot more.

As an only child with two working parents, he'd spent a lot of time with a sitter until he'd been old enough to stay alone. By the time he was twelve, his mother had split, leaving him and his father in each other's care. He'd hated her for leaving, until he'd learned of his father's indiscretion. Then he'd decided the hate was a waste since both of his parents had done wrong.

But he didn't believe for a moment Cardin had him out here to talk about his plans for his property. "You're welcome to help, but I gotta know. What's behind the offer?"

"What do you mean?" she asked, affecting a frown that raised his suspicions not already at full mast.

"What do you want from me, Cardin?" he asked, taking hold of the lip of the can and spinning it out of the way, leaving the space between them filled only with a tension that lived and breathed. "Because I can't imagine it's the same thing I want from you—no matter the message you delivered with the corn."

She licked her lips as she looked away, lifted her chin as she looked back. "If you take me up on my offer, you'll find out, won't you?"

Trey pulled in a deep breath, blew out a sigh. Her rules, he reminded himself. Her rules. And since he wasn't getting anywhere today… "What about your hours here? Don't you work pretty much full time?"

"I do, but I have connections." Her smile punched him in the gut, and he was already aching. "The boss won't mind scheduling around me."

In that case, he wasn't going to say no. "You wanna start tomorrow? I figured I'd tackle the outbuildings first. See what's worth selling. Burn the rest, and haul what won't burn to the dump."

"Sure. I'll talk to Jeb about using his truck. He gets a kick out of driving my Mini."

Trey tried to picture the wide shoulders, six feet two inches, and prominent paunch of Cardin's grandfather behind the wheel of her red Mini Cooper convertible and had not a bit of luck. "That I'd pay to see."

"Then I'll get him to quote you a price."

Funny girl. He took a step toward her. "Say eight o'clock then? Or do you need more beauty sleep than that?"

"I'm okay on the beauty sleep, don't you think?"

Cocky girl. A second step. "Could be you've had too much already. Could be an early morning would be good for you. Say…seven?"

"If I didn't have so far to drive, we could get started at six."

Brave girl. He took a third. "You looking to spend the night?"

"I might consider it," she said, wetting her lips—and causing his head to blow a fuse.

Fuses elsewhere were inches from overload. "I've been at the track since I got here. I'm not sure there's a mattress worth sleeping on at the house, but I do have a second sleeping bag in my gear."

"Sounds great. We can stack them and spread them out. Or even zip them together."

"Don't toy with me, sweetheart." Another step, and their thighs brushed. "I might think you're actually of a mind to see to our unfinished business."

"Do we have unfinished business?" she asked, backing away.

He followed. She stayed. "Cardin? Toying?"

"Now that you mention it, there is something I've always wanted to ask you."

"So ask me." He was willing to give her any answer she wanted as long as it meant he could touch more of her, and do so with something other than his denim-covered thighs.

"It's about Tater's kegger."

"What about it?" As if he didn't know.

"When I saw you…" She let the sentence trail and backed into the rear wall of the ice house.

"With Kim?"

She nodded. "What were you thinking?"

Hands at his hips, he snorted. "There wasn't much thinking going on there."

"I know that, but I've always wondered if your mind wasn't on me…instead of Kim."

What was he supposed to say to that? Admit the truth? Tell her that he had trouble remembering that Kim had been there at all? That his mind saw only the look of fascination that had been on her face? That even now he could feel how firm her breasts, how hard her nipples had felt against his chest?

"I'm thinking about you now. That's all that matters." He pressed his body to hers finally—finally!—raising her hands and pinning them to the wall. Then he lowered his head and nuzzled his cheek to her jaw, finding her earlobe and nipping it, nipping it again when she groaned.

"It's softer than I thought it would be. Your beard stubble."

The last time they'd been this close, he'd been fresh from the shower. "I need to shave."

"No. Don't. Not until I get a chance to feel more."

This time Trey was the one to groan. Two sleeping bags zipped together. Her skin smelling like the sun. *Crap on a pinhead,* and he was supposed to wait? "Are you talking about now? Or are you talking about tonight?"

"I'm talking about anytime you want me."

4
———

IF CARDIN WASN'T CAREFUL, kissing Trey Davis was going to become her favorite pastime, and she would forget all the other things she needed his help to accomplish. But right now? All she wanted was this kiss.

Like the one in the Corley trailer, this one wasn't perfect. It couldn't be; it was stolen, desperate, next to a Dumpster against the ice house's back wall. Anyone could come along at any moment…

She increased the pressure of her lips on his, pulling him in, needing him nearer to have her way. His mouth was warm, tasting of butter and salt and yeasty beer. His hands holding hers above her head were possessive and strong, and being his captive thrilled her.

He angled his head in one direction, she angled hers the other, fitting against him to deepen the tangle of their tongues, the crush of their lips. The heat deepened, too, as did the beating of hummingbird wings in her belly.

He saw to the close fit of everything else; the threading of their fingers, her hands pressed to the wall, the in and out weaving of their thighs, their flush torsos. She felt as if she was the tiniest thing beneath him, hiding in the shadow of his shoulders, disappearing behind his breadth.

He felt like hard work, and smelled like clean clothes and fresh country air. He was everything a girl could want in a guy, and more than most would get. He was decent, honest, a good man. She'd wanted him since high school, and was close to admitting she had been a little in love with him all this time.

She nuzzled his ear, whispered, "Trey?"

"Hmm?"

"Will you marry me?"

TREY JUMPED BACK AS IF Cardin had jabbed him with a cattle prod. Not exactly the response she'd hoped for, but then he hadn't given her time to explain.

"That didn't come out exactly right," she heard herself saying, though she supposed even had she used the words she'd carefully thought through and planned for her proposal, it would still have been an unexpected shock.

"I goddamn hope not," Trey said, his hands at his hips, the furrow of his frown deep enough to get lost in. "Marriage is the last thing I'm looking for."

"Oh, me either," she hurried to assure him, thinking the frown and the "goddamn" were a little over the top.

He blinked, blinked again. Shook his head. "You just proposed."

"You're right. I did." She held up one hand, then rolled her fingers into a fist of frustration, wondering if punching herself would help. She didn't want to screw this up any more than she already had. "But it's not what you're thinking."

"So you didn't mean it?" Trey rubbed a hand over the back of his neck. "It just…slipped out?"

Oh, yeah. This was going just great. She blew air up into her bangs. "Let me try this again. Trey, how would you feel about posing as my fiancé while you're here? No permanent strings. No hard feelings when you leave."

He was looking at her as if she'd grown a second head. "I'm going to need a whole lot more than that before I can figure out what you're asking here, much less give you an answer. Is there a beginning where you can start? I mean, with our families' history, who would believe for a minute that you and I were engaged?"

Their families' recent history was at the root of as many of his problems as her own. She was Juliet to his Romeo. A Hatfield to his McCoy. But right now, her family was at risk of imploding. "If I start at the beginning, I'll have to go back to the days when our great-grandfathers ran moonshine, so why don't I start with the fight between your father and mine?"

Trey's scowl darkened. "The one where Eddie got all busted up?"

"Exactly," Cardin said. "A broken hip, a broken leg. Pins holding him together."

Trey went on the defensive. "Even Eddie said that was an accident."

"Guess what? I don't care. All I know is my family went nuts after the fight. No one talks about anything except work, and they only do that while *at* work." She pressed the heels of her palms to her eyes for a moment, hoping to stave off the stress headache bearing down.

It didn't work. Surprise, surprise. Her temples pounding, she went on. "It's like Headlights is one big eggshell now, and I can't deal with it anymore. I just can't. If things don't get back to some semblance of normal, I'll have to leave town before I lose what's left of my mind. Seriously."

"And since my father was involved, you want me to help you settle your family's feud?"

"Give the man a cigar," she said, and punched him in the shoulder.

Frowning, he rubbed at the injury that really wasn't one. "How long is this engagement thing going to take you to explain? I've got to get back to the Speedway and pack up the hauler. The team's hitting the road at first light."

Wow. He hadn't said no. Initial hurdle cleared. "It'll take longer than either one of us has now, that's for sure."

"My place tonight, then?" he asked after studying her for several long seconds, the light returning to his eyes, the dimples to his cheeks. "Or was the offer to help me mock foreplay? You know, to get me on board with the mock engagement?"

"What time do you want me there?" was her only response. She didn't think it would be a very good idea to talk about foreplay when they were only minutes separated from that kiss.

He grabbed his BlackBerry from his waist and glanced at the screen. "It's already six. I might not get out there till ten."

"Then I'll be there at ten. With Jeb's truck, if I can get it." She waited for him to come back with something about sleeping arrangements, the lack of mattresses, his camping gear, her suggestion that they zip two bags into one.

But he didn't. He just nodded, contemplating something she was certain had to do with her, but keeping his thoughts to himself.

She stared into his eyes, and realized she didn't need to hear him say anything at all. She could see the way he wanted her in his expression. Could read the story of his desire in the language of his body.

He hovered close, his chest rising and falling more rapidly than just moments ago. She expected him to lean in and continue the kiss, to lift her short skirt and explore.

He did neither, smiling as he took a step back, as he raised one hand, a temporary farewell to hold them until later. It made her stomach flip, that smile, so lazy, so sure.

She leaned against the wall of the ice house and watched him go, wondering if she'd bitten off more than she could chew—and if she'd come out the other side of this adventure the same person she was now.

TREY DIDN'T THINK HE WOULD ever finish closing up shop and making his escape from the Speedway. Sales by the track vendors were winding down, and most were engaged in the same sort of packing up as the Corley team. That didn't mean there wasn't plenty of action happening all around.

Smoke from charcoal fires lifted the aromas of bratwurst and burgers into the air, and the same wind carried the music of slide guitars, fiddles and accordions to appreciative ears. Monday morning was going to come a whole lot earlier than a lot of the beer-drinking, barbecue-eating, hard-partying folks in the pits would be ready for.

Trey couldn't have cared less about Monday morning. He was waiting for ten o'clock tonight, the hour he'd finally get Cardin Worth alone. No pit crew to interrupt. No family hovering. No one but the two of them. Just him. Just her. Just like it had been seven years ago the night she'd left an imprint he'd never been able to shake.

But as ready as he was to have Cardin to himself, this trip was about more than getting laid. A big part of Trey's temporary homecoming was to dig into the fight between his father and Jeb. The one that had sent Eddie Worth to the hospital after being slammed to the floor of the slicker hole—the oil changing pit in Morgan and Son's garage.

The same fight Cardin had said made everything in her life go wrong.

He couldn't say his life had been left unchanged, either.

A year ago this month, the fight had brought him back to Dahlia. When he'd left a week later, he'd owned his family's home, buying the place from his father for the price of a beer, and paying off the huge gambling debt Aubrey had racked up in the years since Trey had hired on as a mechanic for Butch Corley and split.

Trey hadn't even known about the gambling debt when the

sheriff's office had called to let him know about Aubrey's arrest for assault. It had been after he'd settled things and was on his way out of town that he'd learned the full truth of the trouble his father was in. He'd stopped by the track to see Tater, who worked on site there with Trey's father at Morgan and Son's garage, and heard the story straight from his best friend's mouth.

Trey hadn't even hesitated, but turned and driven straight back to the house, striking a deal with his dad: Aubrey turned over the house, the barn, the five acres to Trey, and Trey paid off the damage Aubrey had done—as long as Aubrey left Dahlia and found a job in a town without the temptation of a track.

Sure, Trey's father could've gone to Vegas, gambled online, found bookies anywhere to take a bet. But looking like a broken man, Aubrey had sworn he would do what Trey asked, thanking his son for having faith and staying true, for helping him in his time of need.

All of that had happened almost a year ago. Even so, Trey couldn't help wonder if Aubrey losing everything he had left and being forced to move on hadn't contributed to his decline, and six months later, his death. Or if the damage to his heart had been years in the making, and it simply his time to go.

Shaking off thoughts of his loss, Trey unlocked his pickup's retracting bed cover and started sorting through his supplies. Knowing he could pick up what he needed in the way of tools, building materials, fuel and food in town, he'd packed only his laptop, his camping gear, his clothes and essentials.

No one had been living in the house for a year, and though he'd hired Beau Stillwell to keep the place from falling down, he had no idea what condition it was in. It didn't matter. He wanted to stay on site. And if he had to camp out to do it, he was ready.

"Looks like you're set for some kind of vacation."

Trey looked up, and saw Jeb Worth standing a couple of feet away in the shadows cast by the truck that pulled the Corley hauler. "A change of scenery. A temporary change of vocation. But not much in the way of relaxation or time off."

"You don't have to stay out at your place." Even at this late hour, Jeb's crisp white shirt tucked into khaki pants worn with a cowboy hat and boots painted a picture of the lawman he should have been. "You're welcome to stay at the house. We've got plenty of room."

Trey wanted to sleep with this man's granddaughter. There was no way he was going to stay at his house. He turned around, leaned against the open tailgate, the heels of his hands curled over the cool metal at his hips. "It'll be easier if I stay out there. I'll save gas and time not having to drive back and forth."

Jeb nodded. "Any idea how long you'll be in Dahlia?"

"As long as it takes to get the place ready to sell. Since I'm doing most of it on my own…" Trey stopped, wondering what Cardin's grandfather would think were he to learn of her offer to help. Wondered, too, if the older man secretly harbored any hard feelings toward him because of the fight his father had started, a fight that had seriously injured Jeb's son. "It'll take as long as it takes, I guess. Depends on how fast I do the work."

"So you'll still be here in a couple of weeks."

"Yeah, I'm not that fast," Trey said, hoping he hadn't read Cardin wrong and that he'd be spending a lot of what he'd planned as work hours otherwise engaged.

Jeb glanced toward the racing rig where Sunshine was dismantling the pop-up under which the crew worked on the car between heats. "I've got a '69 Chevy Nova SS with Crane lifters, an Eagle 4340 Nitrated Pro Crank, and more goodies than you can shake a stick at sitting in the garage behind my house."

Interesting. Trey crossed his feet at the ankles. "That so."

Jeb nodded, still looking away. "Eddie's always driven it for me in the Moonshine Run. Doesn't look like he's going to be doing that anymore."

Was Jeb here to blame Trey for what Aubrey had done? Putting Eddie out of commission and leaving Jeb without a driver for the annual event? He kept silent rather than broach a subject he wasn't sure was on the other man's mind.

"The car's won the last six out of seven years. It would be a shame not to run it this one."

Trey knew the legend of the Moonshine Run. Hell, his great-grandfather, Emmett Davis, had been one of the moonshiners to draw the attention of the gangster Diamond Dutch Boyle. Jeb's father, Orin Worth, had been Emmett's partner in crime, and Boyle had hunted the two of them like dogs in his effort to put an end to their enterprise that had encroached on his.

The whole town knew that Jeb, at fourteen, had found the gangster's '32 Plymouth at the bottom of the LaBrecque ravine. The car had been there since before he was born, having crashed down the mountain during a wild and wooly midnight chase. Rumors that a fortune in diamonds were lost along with the car and Dutch Boyle had been circulating just as long.

Jeb had sworn since being told the story of the gangster's disappearance that he'd find it. He had. And brought up the car's two headlights from the bottom of the ravine as proof. Those same two headlights now hung on the plaque in the entryway of their namesake ice house, the inscription between them reading, "A wrong turn can be the downfall of anyone."

Trey had always wondered if the epitaph meant something special to Jeb.

"I was going to ask you about it the other morning in the pits. But never got the chance."

Trey frowned. What had he missed? "You were going to ask me what?"

"About driving White Lightning in the Moonshine Run." Jeb turned toward him, pushing his hat a couple of inches up his forehead.

Ah, finally. The point. "I don't know. I'm not a driver."

"You know how to drive. You know cars."

He knew both, had driven more cars than Butch Corley's in his time. He just didn't know why Jeb would ask him of all people. "Why not get Tater to drive?"

"Because I want you."

A loud crash came from the other side of the hauler, followed by Sunshine yelling at someone to watch the hell where he was going. "I don't know your car. I'd have to look it over. Take it down the track first."

"You'll do it then."

Trey laughed. "Now, I didn't say that. But I will think about it."

Jeb nodded as if that was good enough. "Don't be a stranger while you're in town. As many meals as you can eat are on the house at Headlights."

"Thank you, sir. I'll definitely take you up on that."

"Good showin' today, by the way. I never thought Bad Dog would hit three-twenty on that track."

"The amount of time I've spent on that engine? I was hoping for better," Trey said, thinking he should grab his fire-proof driving gear before the hauler pulled out, just in case.

"I knew you were the right man for the job," Jeb said, patting Trey's shoulder before walking away, leaving Trey to wonder if Cardin's grandfather wanted more from him than his skills as a mechanic—and what the hell it could be?

5

DELTA WORTH DIDN'T THINK there WAS any job in the world more boring than keeping a business's books, and she'd been doing Headlights' accounting long enough to hold stock in her own opinion.

Oh, she took the occasional break to schedule employee work hours and meet with restaurant vendors hawking their wares. But since she did it all from her small windowless office tucked between the kitchen and the restrooms, the breaks in her routine didn't feel like breaks at all.

And it didn't help that she was still working up to seven days a week with her estranged husband a closed door away.

Pushing out of her chair, she circled the desk to the corner file cabinet where she jammed the folder of reconciled bank statements into its top drawer slot, breaking one of the nails she'd just had done at Lila's in the process. She and Eddie were going to have to resolve this thing between them—and soon.

Not only could she not afford the abuse to her manicure, she didn't want to spend more time than she had to living in her daughter's apartment—and she was quite sure Cardin was ready to get away from the house she'd already moved out of once.

Living with Eddie and Jeb for eighteen years would be enough for any young girl. Delta had made it twenty-six years before she couldn't take it anymore—though if Aubrey Davis hadn't turned her whole family end over end, she would likely have stayed until the Mississippi ran dry. And probably to her own detriment, she mused with no small amount of self-deprecation.

Grabbing their produce supplier's vendor file and returning to her chair, she forced herself to admit she was as set in her ways as the men in her family; more than once she'd wondered how much of the trait was inherent personality, and how much she could blame on having married into the Worths.

A knock on her door stopped her from doing more with the folder than setting it on her desk. "Come in."

Ah, Eddie. The last person she wanted to see. He tossed his hand towel over his shoulder, and leaned against her door jamb, arms and ankles crossed. The noise from the dining room flooded her small office, but asking Eddie to close the door meant he would have to move.

And she'd been lying to herself when she said he was the last person she wanted to see.

Looking at him now—his blue eyes bright, his black hair too long, his beard stubble way too sexy—had her stomach tumbling just as powerfully as it had the day he'd walked up to her at the Speedway, and licked her cone's melted ice cream from her thumb.

She dropped into her chair, hating that he was her weakness. "Why are you here, D? It's Sunday. Your day off."

Thanks. Way to rub salt in the wound of her having no life since she'd left him. "I had a few things I wanted to catch up on before tomorrow."

Eddie frowned, the lines at the corners of his eyes deepening. "What's going on tomorrow?"

"It's Monday," she reminded him, resisting the urge to get

up and smooth her thumb from the fringe of his lashes to his temple. "Monday's always insane. You know that."

"I do," he said, pushing away from the door and closing it behind him. The chatter from outside was silenced, and the room became a cocoon. "I also know you've been here too many weekends lately. What gives?"

He grabbed for the only other chair in the office—a molded plastic waiting room number—stepped around it, straddled the seat, and took it over. That's what had gotten to her all those years ago. The way he took over. A chair, a conversation, an ice cream cone.

There was no way she was going to tell him she was here because he was. He'd take over then and demand she come home.

"Am I hearing you right? Eddie Worth questioning an employee for putting in extra hours?" She crossed her arms, crossed her legs, sat stiffly in her seat.

Eddie spread his legs and slouched farther in his. "You're not an employee, D. You're family, and you know it."

She was a Worth in name only, one who had moved out and left her husband because she couldn't take his silences—or his rage—anymore.

"Did you want something, Eddie?" *Besides to sit there and make it hard to remember how bad things were?*

"Yeah, actually. It's Cardin. She's out back."

He wasn't worried, so Delta knew there was no reason for her to be. "And?"

"With Whip Davis."

Ah, well, now she understood why Eddie was here. God forbid their daughter become involved with a Davis. Though to be honest, Delta wasn't overjoyed with the news. She wanted better for Cardin than a life spent on the road, a life not her own, but Whip's.

"If you're worried, why aren't you out there playing chaperone?" she finally asked, realizing she'd been lost in thought way too long, and Eddie had been staring at her all the while.

"Because Cardin's twenty-five, making Whip twenty-seven, and I remember being that age."

What he meant was he remembered being seventeen and not even out of high school, and then by eighteen, both a husband and a father. "Are you more concerned with their privacy, or with the embarrassment of catching your daughter in flagrante delicto?"

"Up against the Dumpster in broad daylight?" Eddie shook his head, snorting an incredulity Delta didn't buy. "I hope we taught her better than that."

"Oh, Eddie." Frustration squeezed her like a too tight belt. "It doesn't matter what we taught her. Hell, if kids listened to what their parents said, Cardin wouldn't even be here." She paused, added, "Or maybe your memory of being that age isn't so great after all?"

His eyes flared with heat, then grew smoky, smoldering as he leaned forward, his elbows on his knees, his fists bracing his chin. "I have the memory of ten thousand elephants, D. I haven't forgotten a thing."

That made two of them, and was the reason this conversation was now at an end.

She looked down at the folder she'd completely mangled, and at a second fingernail that was now a mess, and tried to find a thought that didn't have the remembered imprint of Eddie's hands and mouth all over it.

She had absolutely zero luck, so couldn't have been more appreciative of the interruption when Cardin opened the door.

"Mom, I need to change my schedule—" Cardin cut herself off and careened to a stop, her ponytail flying, her face flushed. "Dad. What're you doing here?"

"He's worried about the company you're keeping," Delta answered before Eddie could say a word.

Cardin looked at her father and frowned, her black hair and blue eyes so similar to his that Delta couldn't breathe for the crushing ache in her chest. How had things gone so wrong?

"What company?" Cardin asked Eddie. "You mean Trey? Are you kidding me? Why in the world would you worry about me talking to Trey?"

"I'm worried that you're not just talking," he told her, delivering the words as he would a reprimand.

Cardin rolled her eyes. "Is this more of that broken-heart crap?"

Delta raised a brow at that. "What broken-heart crap?"

Spinning away from her father, Cardin pushed up her bangs with one hand, parked her other at her hip. "He told me earlier he doesn't want Trey to break my heart, and I told him it's not going to happen."

Oh, to be young and certain and naive. Delta sighed, choosing her words carefully. "His breaking your heart would imply there's something going on between you two."

Cardin didn't answer. She faced the room's small air conditioner instead, the refrigerated breeze blowing her hair here and there. Delta switched her gaze to her husband. All Eddie did was shrug and drape himself at an angle in the chair.

That left Delta to do the dirty work. Hardly a surprise. She'd been doing it all this last year. "Cardin? Is there something going on with you and Whip?"

Their daughter's shoulders stiffened before she turned, her expression bright and wary, the color in her cheeks giving her away. Delta stifled a groan, and barely managed to keep herself from looking toward Eddie, from telling him silently that they did, indeed, have cause for concern.

If Delta knew anything about her daughter, it was how

much Cardin hated the way her parents could talk without saying a word. "Is that a yes or a no?"

"I don't want to talk about Trey. I want to talk about my schedule."

"What about it?"

"I need to cut my shifts in half for a few months."

"For however long Whip's here, you mean," Eddie said, getting to his feet.

Cardin stared him down. "Yes. For as long as Trey-who-I-will-not-let-break-my-heart is here. Happy now?"

Eddie didn't snap back as he would've done in the past, but pushed aside the chair and slammed out of the room. Delta stared at the door as it bounced back open, and Cardin could only say, "Guess not."

Delta felt as if she were caught in a war with too many battles to fight, and too many sides to take. She loved her daughter, but Cardin could be as hardheaded as her father, and Delta was lost when it came to understanding her feelings for him these days. And so she did the only thing she could think to do.

She dug into her lower file drawer and pulled out the folder of timesheets and schedules. Once it was open on her desk, she laced her hands on top and looked at her daughter. "If you want four-hour shifts, you have to take the dinner rush with Megan, Holly and Taylor. I'll split Sandy between lunch and late nights."

Cardin cringed. "She's not going to be happy about that."

"And it's going to be up to you to give her the bad news."

"That's fine," Cardin said, waving her hand as if now it were nothing. "I'm sure she'll need me to accommodate her at some point."

"Just be sure you remember this when she does." Delta marked the changes, then shut the folder and shoved it back in the drawer.

"Are you mad at me?"

"Why would I be mad at you?" Delta asked in return, never looking up as she turned her attention to the produce supplier's file. "Schedule changes happen."

"Not about the schedule," Cardin said, sitting in the chair Eddie had abandoned. "Well, yes, the schedule, but not so much about changing it as why I want the change."

"Am I mad that you have your sights set on Whip?"

"I didn't say I had my sights set on him—"

Delta held up one hand. "Whip's a great guy. One of the best of all the boys I watched you grow up with. He and Tater both are men any parent would be happy to see their daughter choose."

"And yet you're not any happier than Dad." Cardin slumped, her posture the identical twin of her father's.

"My being unhappy is not about Whip."

"Then what? What else is there?"

There was so much, Delta didn't know she could do justice to her concerns. "I want you to have a home, Cardin. And if it's in your plans, one day, a faraway day, I would love for you to make me a grandmother."

Cardin dropped her head back on her shoulders. "Jesus, Mom—"

"I'm not finished. I don't want to get a call in the middle of the night that you've had to stop on the side of the road to give birth between races. You're the love of my life, and I want better for you than that."

"You mean you want me to stay here. To live the rest of my life in Dahlia."

"That's not what I said." They were going to have to table this discussion for a time when emotions weren't running so high. Delta didn't want to say something she would never be able to retract. "And once you give it some time, I think you'll realize that. Right now, however, we both need to follow your father's example and get back to work."

And as much as Delta hated to admit it, she breathed a sigh of relief when her only child left the room and closed the door behind her.

6

BY THE TIME CARDIN SAW the lights of Trey's pickup bouncing off the trees at the end of his drive, she was over her aggravation and had managed to cool down. She couldn't believe a day that had started out to be just about perfect had gone downhill so fast.

Lately, it took next to nothing to trigger a family flare-up. The resulting stress drained her as completely as an eight hour shift—part of the reason she'd cut out early tonight.

After talking to her parents, she'd been in no mood to work. She'd stayed anyway—at least until Sandy told her to get the hell outta town if she was going to act like a princess who had fallen off her pony and smashed her frog prince flat.

Sitting on Trey's front porch, her legs dangling and her feet swinging above the square of bare earth where azalea bushes used to grow, Cardin allowed herself a disparaging smile. She'd be the first to own her bratty behavior, and tomorrow she'd be back on her game.

Right now, however, she didn't want to do anything but give her full attention to Trey.

The moon shone down like a spotlight. It was the only illumination Cardin had by which to watch as he braked his truck to a stop. She couldn't see him at all until he opened the door and the cab's overhead light came on, glowing behind him, putting him in silhouette, leaving her to wonder about his expression…

If he was happy to find her waiting, if he was irritated that she'd trespassed. If he was filled with the same anticipation twisting knots in her belly and zinging in the small of her back. She'd been imagining his two sleeping bags in all possible configurations…stacked as one, zipped together, unrolled side by side.

He held nothing in his hands when he walked toward her, not one sleeping bag, not two. She curled her fingers over the lip of the porch, kicked out with one leg, then the other, watching the roll of his hips and shoulders, the ground-eating strides of his legs.

Ignoring the path leading to the front steps, he hopped a mangled strip of garden lattice to reach her. She stayed where she was, her heart urging her to scoot away from the precipice and onto the safe surface behind. What she felt for him frightened her, all of it right, and real. But then she couldn't move because he was there, stepping between her legs.

"You look good in moonlight," was all he said, reaching up to tuck her hair behind her ear.

She'd left it loose after her shower, and though she'd told herself her scalp needed a break from her ponytail, she knew that she'd done it for him.

"Is that a pick-up line?" she asked, feeling the tingle of her nipples growing taut.

"Why would I need a pick-up line? You're already here."

He was too confident, cocky. She loved it, but she wasn't that easy. "Don't make more of it than it is. I'm already here because you said ten."

"It's a quarter till."

"Call me punctual."

"I'd rather kiss you," he said, and threaded his fingers into her hair at her nape, lowering his head.

She met him halfway, no hesitation just desire, parting her lips before he asked, and offering him her tongue. He took it, slid his against it with a tender aggression. He made a hungry sound low in his throat. She moved her hands to his chest, took the measure of the vibration there, remembered the way he'd felt the first time she'd touched him so long ago.

When she curled her fingers into the fabric of his shirt, he leaned forward, pushing her back. Needing her elbows to brace herself, she let him go. His lips drifted to her throat, the hollow there, the ribbed neckline of the Corley Motors T-shirt she wore, the fabric covering her breasts.

He nuzzled between them, making his way to her shirt's hem, pushing it up to reveal her belly where he settled his lips. She closed her eyes, and lay flat on the porch, her arms stretched out to the side. What he was doing was magic, and she wanted nothing to break the spell.

His fingers were like matches on her skin, his lips and tongue like flames. He burned her, consumed her. She was willing kindle for his fire, and she wanted to be naked beneath him, not clothed and unable to fully realize all these things he made her feel.

His mouth was a wicked warmth, wet and wild as he tasted her, kissing from her sternum to her navel, leaving a long damp trail that the night breeze cooled. She shivered, wanted to squirm, but stayed perfectly still, the porch hard under her back, rough beneath her elbows. She scraped her fingernails over the wood, spreading out her hands as if to hold on.

Trey was toying with the buttons of her jeans, his fingers slipping beneath the waistband to find the elastic edge of her panties. When he freed the first, her eyes popped open. When the second followed, she felt the night's air low on her belly.

When he reached the third, she shook off the sex daze he'd lulled her into and pushed up.

"Stop."

He raised his head, met her gaze, his eyes bright and full of the same confusion she was feeling. "Okay."

"What are we doing here, Trey?"

He stood then, moving his hands from her hips to his own. "Taking care of unfinished business?"

She sat up, tucked her crossed legs beneath her. The top two buttons of her jeans remained undone, and she swore she could still feel his touch where the fabric gaped. "Maybe we should talk about my proposal first."

"You want to talk?"

The light from the moon was enough for her to see the sarcastic arch of his brow. "I don't mean idle chitchat. But we did agree I'd explain things tonight."

He didn't say anything for several seconds, staring at her as his breathing settled, giving her time to gather her scattered emotions close. She couldn't tell what he was thinking. His face was unreadable, shadowed by the big oak behind him, the tree's limbs spreading over what had once been a lush green yard, but was now dirt and hardscrabble weeds.

She'd come here a few times in high school, a passenger in a friend's car giving Trey a ride home, but she'd never been inside the house to see how he lived. She wondered if he didn't want to go inside at all. He'd been in Dahlia four days and tonight was the first time he'd set foot on the property where he'd lived for twenty years. Or maybe, as he'd said, he'd just been too busy to come out here and open the door.

He finally moved, scrubbing his hands down his face. "Let me get my things then. Unless you've changed your mind about staying."

She hadn't, but there was no reason for him to if the memories he had of living here weren't ones he wanted to face in the dark. "If you don't want to stay here, we've got an extra room at home. We can sleep there and come back here in the morning."

"Yeah," he said, with a huff. "I can see that going over well with Eddie. The son of the man who nearly killed him under his roof."

The conversation about their fathers was one she wasn't going to have until they'd said and settled a lot of other things first. She scooted to the edge of the porch and hopped down, dusting the dirt and grit from her backside. "I'll grab my backpack."

"I've got it," he said, turning and walking away.

She followed. "I can get it. You have all your own things to get."

"If that's your way of asking if I brought both sleeping bags—"

"I was just offering to help."

"If you say so," he said, lowering his pickup's tailgate and retracting the bed cover part way to slide out a box of supplies.

Cardin grabbed his arm and spun him to face her. "If you don't want me here, Trey, say the word and I'll go."

"And do what?" He towered over her, a dark shadow, a menace. "Find someone else to play your fiancé?"

She felt his hard-beating heart where she held him. "No, I'll find another solution."

"Why not another guy?"

"Because no other guy will work," she said, and let him go, stunned by her own words. No other guy *would* do; only Trey. Her feelings for him had never lessened, but changed, and grown, deepening into something she'd been afraid to let herself see.

He looked down at her then, his gaze searching, and she was the first to look away. She'd been so sure this would work, that he'd go along because of the connection she'd imagined between them. It was obviously the only part he had interest in pursuing was the physical.

Talk about naive. What had she been thinking? This man was not the boy she'd had a crush on in high school. He was bigger, larger than life, a man who could have any woman he wanted.

She sighed, turned and leaned against the truck, the tailgate cutting into her back. "I must've been insane. Seriously. I'm going to go home now, you're going to go inside, and we're both going to forget I proposed."

He left the box where it was and moved to stand in front of her, lifting her chin with the edge of one finger when she refused to look into his eyes. They were calmer now, sweet and understanding. And it nearly broke her heart when he smiled and told her, "I'll never forget you proposed."

"Well you should," she said, pulling free of his touch. She couldn't let herself get sucked further into a fantasy that had nothing to do with real life. "My family needs a wake-up call, but this engagement isn't it. Trust me."

"No."

She frowned, looked back. "No, what?"

"No, I'm not going to trust you. I'll make up my own mind once you spell out your plan."

"I have no plan."

"You did. You do. It involves me posing as your fiancé. But I don't know what you're trying to accomplish or why."

"I told you—"

"You told me your life has gone to hell. And it happened after the fight. Well, things for me haven't been all puppies and rainbows since then, either, so why don't we unload our gear, go inside and compare notes?"

His life had gone to hell? Seriously? Or was he trying to

placate her, make her feel like less of a fool for going to desperate lengths to make things better?

Her plan stunk, but she supposed it couldn't hurt to talk. Maybe she'd come up with another idea, because this one? She had a feeling things would end up just as her father had predicted.

Trey Davis was going to break her heart.

IT WASN'T HARD FOR TREY to recognize that he was using Cardin as a punching bag to rid himself of more than sexual frustration. There was that, true. And Cardin being the one he wanted to sleep with pretty much sent his frustration through the roof. But when it came down to the nitty gritty, his frustration was with himself for not having done what he should have by now.

Standing on the porch, his arms wrapped around a stack of three boxes, both shoulders weighted down with duffel bags, and Cardin equally burdened at his side, he stared at the front door to his childhood home and admitted he was an ass for avoiding his responsibilities here.

He'd grown up in this house, he'd enjoyed the good times and suffered the bad. Hell, he owned the place outright and had for a year. Yet he hadn't once stepped through the door since signing the final papers at close. He didn't want to step through now. There was too much work waiting for him, too much guilt that he hadn't done anything to stop his father's death.

Not being alone made it easier.

Being with Cardin made it easier still.

"Trey? My arms are breaking here."

"Yeah, hang on." He braced the boxes against the wall with his hip and dug into his pocket for his keys. He hadn't tested the door to see if it was locked; he'd just assumed Beau Stillwell made sure it was.

Whatever growth and change Dahlia had experienced in

the years since Trey had moved on, the town had retained its innocence. Both privacy and property were respected by all but a bad apple few.

The door squeaked just as he remembered, though the smell that first reached his nose was musty and stale, not that of newspapers and diesel fuel and dirty socks. His father's smells. Ones imprinted forever in his mind.

He stepped back, holding open the screen door with one shoulder and making room for Cardin to pass. "The electricity should be on, and there's a lamp—"

"Oomph."

"—on the table to your right," he finished too late. "Sorry about that."

She dropped her boxes, found the switch. He heard the *click-click* as she turned it twice before it came on. "It's okay. I have another shin."

"Yeah. I forgot you've never been inside." He set his boxes beside hers, dropped his duffels as she swung her backpack around and put it beside the lamp on the table.

She looked over at him, using the back of her hand to push her bangs from her forehead. "The only person I ever knew to come here was Tater."

After his mother was gone, he and his dad never had been much for entertaining. Tater had been the exception. Aubrey had considered Trey's best friend to be a second son. "I need to give the boy a call. I saw him at the Speedway a couple of times this weekend, but didn't have time to do more than wave."

"You need to make time. You have no idea how much he talks about you every year before the Farron Fuels."

"You hang with Tater now?"

She gave him a look. "We're not in high school anymore, Trey. Everyone hangs with everyone. He's in Headlights a lot these days. He's dating Sandy Larabie."

No way. "The waitress? You're screwing with me, right?"

"I'm not, no. Is it so hard to believe?"

"From what I saw of her today? Yeah."

"Jumping to conclusions?" she asked, cocking her head.

He rubbed the back of his neck. "Only because it's been a hell of a long four days."

He was beat, beyond exhausted. The Farron Fuels had eaten up every hour between Thursday and Sunday with the qualifying heats before this afternoon's finals. It had passed in a blur of engine work and catnaps and studying the competition's runs.

He didn't have the energy tonight to care if Tater Rawls was dating the waitress or his own right hand. All he cared about was getting to the bottom of Cardin and her proposal, and checking out the house so they could both get some sleep.

He ran a hand through his hair and turned to take in the living room. Nothing much had changed since the last time he'd been here, except his father's chair sat empty because he'd forced Aubrey to leave his own home six months before he had died.

Choking back the lump in his throat, Trey walked the length of the narrow room, entered the kitchen and felt for the wall switch just inside the door. The single bulb in the fixture on the ceiling burst to life, giving up the ghost seconds later with a sizzling pop.

"You didn't happen to bring light bulbs, did you?" Cardin asked from behind him.

"I imagine there are still extras in the cabinet above the sink."

"Same vintage as the one that just blew?"

Yeah, that could be a problem. He headed back for his gear, leaving Cardin standing in the kitchen doorway as he dug for a flashlight in the box on the top of the stack. He found what he was searching for, and with the beam to guide him, located the bulbs.

Once the light was back on, Cardin came into the small kitchen and looked around. "This is…cozy."

Cozy? It was cold and lifeless, and the workshop in the Corley hauler would hold it twice over. It was also the room where Trey and his father had done most of their talking. They'd just never talked about a lot of what they should have. Things that would've had Trey visiting more than once a year if he'd known they were going on.

Spilled milk, but it still caused a hitch near his heart. "There probably wasn't a single day that my dad and I didn't trip over each other in here. He finally gave up and let me do the cooking."

"You cook?" she asked, wiggling her brows as she pulled a chair from beneath the kitchen table, the yellow plastic tablecloth covering it long since faded to white, and sat.

He leaned against the sink, crossing his arms over his chest. "Don't be getting any ideas. The stove was dicey when I left home. I wouldn't trust it to boil an egg."

"I only eat mine scrambled, so that's okay."

"Are we going to have to have meals catered?"

"I'm not that picky, but I can pack carry-out from work for dinner."

"What time do you work?"

"I've got the four-to-eight dinner shift. Think you can survive without my help for that long?"

It wasn't her help he cared about. He wanted her company, and the chance to find out what she knew. "I'll do my best."

"I don't know about you, but my best is going to require sleep."

"Then we need to figure out where to do it."

"And where to go to the bathroom."

He inclined his head to the left. "Through the laundry room to the left."

She didn't move, just gave him a look from beneath her long lashes and fringed bangs—a look that said she wasn't budging until he'd given the room his okay.

He smiled and pushed away from the sink, grabbing his flashlight from the countertop where he'd left it. "You know I pay Beau Stillwell to keep things working around here."

"Just not to change light bulbs. Or keep out six-legged inhabitants."

He laughed, and walked away.

7

LEAVING CARDIN TO DO her thing, Trey returned to the front of the house. Though he'd paid off his father's gambling debts in exchange for the title to the property, he'd never had any intention of coming here to live. Paying Stillwell Construction to keep the place from falling apart was just Trey being a responsible owner.

Standing in the center of the living room, he gave the space more than the cursory glance he'd afforded it when he'd first walked in. Coming back here now, a year after the showdown with his father, six months after his father's death, left Trey feeling, well, guilty. None of the arguments he'd had with himself that he couldn't have changed a thing made a difference.

He was still convinced that while on the road, had he paid attention to what was going on with his father, if he'd been around to keep Aubrey from gambling away most of his money and drinking away the rest, he wouldn't be the only member of the Davis family left in town. The only member of the Davis family left at all.

Once the house was emptied of his past, the property cleaned up and on the market, Trey would finally be freed from his ties to Dahlia, Tennessee. It wasn't that his years here had been bad—there just wasn't anything from them he wanted to keep. The life he'd built for himself once he'd moved on was where his best memories had been made.

He'd worked his way up in the Corley organization, learning the ropes while plying the trade he'd studied both in high school and at his father's feet. His work ethic and initiative had caught Butch's eye. His instincts had earned him the crew chief position. He loved the traveling, he loved the work, and was already looking forward to being done with things here and getting back to that life.

The only reason he'd decided to prep the place for selling himself instead of hiring out the job was the fight. He could walk away from Dahlia, sure, but he would always be looking back and wondering what had driven his normally mellow father to use his fists against a pillar of the Dahlia community who was nearly eighty years old.

"All done," Cardin said from behind him, bringing him back to the present. He'd been staring at his father's chair this entire time.

Turning to face her, and without preamble, he asked, "Do you have any idea what the fight was about?"

She shook her head, knowing right away what he meant. "Not a clue. And Jeb is the last person I would ever expect to punch anyone. He's too…"

"Old?"

"Old, yes," she said, walking by him on her way to their gear. "But I was thinking more…law and order. Jeb's not one to duke things out."

"My father wasn't, either," Trey reminded her.

"I know. That's what makes it so weird." She reached over the stacked boxes for the sleeping bags. "Eddie stepping in the way he did I can see. He didn't inherit his father's straight and narrow nature. But Jeb and your dad trading swings? It had to be something huge."

"And yet not a word about it from anyone." He moved the

boxes out of her way. "Was Eddie there for the whole thing? Does he know what happened?"

"He hasn't said a word about it since he got out of the hospital. I think his silence is a big part of why my mom left."

"What? Your folks split?"

"About four months ago." She tossed the first of the two bags out in front of her to unroll. "Delta moved into my apartment, and I moved back with Eddie and Jeb. I've got the whole second floor to myself, rather than having to fight my mother over bathroom time at my place."

Trey was confused. "Why switch with you? Why not get her own apartment or whatever?"

"It's a temporary arrangement until she and my dad settle things permanently."

"So they're not divorced."

"Nope. And nothing legal in the works, thank God."

"You think they'll patch things up, then? Get back together?"

She finished unrolling the second sleeping bag alongside the first before she answered. "That marriage thing about two becoming one? They took that to heart. I've never in my life known any couple better suited. But then Eddie became all emo one minute, PMSy the next... It was too much for my mother to deal with. Which tells me this fight between Jeb and your father was something big."

"Then you've got as much reason to get to the bottom of it as I do."

She shook her head. "I don't want to get to the bottom of it at all. All I want is for my parents to wake up before it's too late to put Humpty Dumpty back together again."

Leaning against the front door, Trey grinned. "And you think our fairy-tale engagement will do that."

"It's the sort of shock that's worth a shot. I've tried everything else I can think of. And their reaction when I asked for the schedule change to spend time with you said a lot."

"What was it? Their reaction?"

Cardin fought a smile and considered him closely. "Eddie's afraid you'll break my heart. Delta's afraid you'll make me live in cheap motels and have babies on the side of the road between races."

What a bunch of unflattering crap. "Then you've already told them we're together?"

She hesitated, and even in the dimly lit room, he could see her face color. "No. The only thing I told them was that my heart would not get broken."

"Then I'll have to be sure I don't break it."

"It's not up to you. I'd have to let it happen."

"And my heart?" he queried, expecting her to tease him in return and ask if he had one.

But she didn't. She grew serious, pensive, then sat cross-legged on the sleeping bag she couldn't know was his. She ran her palms over her thighs, looking down instead of at him. "Does that mean you'll do it?"

He moved closer, dropped down beside her, leaning on one elbow with one knee raised. "I'm going to guess you've thought this through, so you have answers to the questions people will ask?"

"Such as?"

Was she kidding him? "How long have we been engaged, for one? Except to bail out my dad, I haven't been to Dahlia since last year's Farron Fuels. You think folks are going to buy a long-distance hookup?"

"We've known each other all our lives—"

He waved a hand, cut her off. "We lived in the same town. We went to school together. The day you showed up at the hauler was the first conversation I think we ever had."

"It wasn't the first, Trey." She said it quickly. Almost before he'd finished speaking.

She thought he'd forgotten, did she? She thought that night at Tater's kegger hadn't meant anything to him but a blowjob. And why shouldn't she? She couldn't know that the feel of her body had lived with him since, had caused him to lose sleep, had kept him from any serious dating.

She couldn't know that he felt more for her than what she'd seen as desire because he'd never said a word. "That night…what I said to you…those words. That isn't what I think of as a conversation."

Her head bobbed, a quick nod of acknowledgment, and her shoulders seemed to relax, as if the tension of wondering had been keeping them tight. He should've told her sooner. He should've stayed in touch.

He should have never let her get away. "So, then, I guess we could say we've been pining after one another all the time I've been gone?"

Her mouth quirked. "Or we could've started pining this past year."

"It's more believable the pining started after Tater's kegger."

"Believable to who?" Her gaze whipped sharply to his, her pulse visible at the base of her throat. "Unless you told someone else, then you're the only one who knows I was there."

Hmm. He wondered what prompted her hand-in-the-cookie-jar reaction. "Kim didn't say anything?"

"Not that I've heard."

He supposed that made sense. Kim wouldn't have wanted anyone to know that his pants weren't even zipped before his attention had turned to Cardin. Cardin, who was still looking like she'd almost been caught doing…something.

He was curious, and only one thing came to mind. "So you haven't been pining then?"

"Have you?"

"I told you the other day that I missed seeing you."

"I'm not sure that's the same thing as pining."

She clearly didn't want to go down that road right now. "Maybe not, but it's close enough for a fake engagement."

She exhaled heavily, as if relieved that he hadn't pressed harder. "Then we say we hooked up last year? And we've had a long-distance relationship since?"

He nodded. It should work. And eventually, he would come back and press. "We'll need to figure out the details, like why we kept it secret, but sure. That'll do. And now that we've got that settled…" He reached for her hand, stroking his thumb along her fingers. "Tell me why you think defibrillating your family is going to fix things."

CARDIN STARED AT HER HAND where Trey held it. "I don't know if I can find a way for it to make sense to you. I mean, it makes sense to me, but they're my family, and I know what makes them tick."

Not to mention that expressing her thoughts with any coherence was going to be impossible sitting with him in the dark.

There was no question that Trey was hot. He had every physical attribute going for him a woman could want in a man. The height, the build, the hair and the eyes, and she couldn't forget his mouth. Or his hands.

What she hadn't anticipated was the up close and personal impact his hotness would have—especially when it wasn't just his appearance getting to her.

It was the intensity of his gaze, the way he devoured her with a look, eating her up as if he were starving and she the only meal that would do.

Breathing naturally was out of the question. Her heart filled her chest as it raced. Pulling off this mock engagement was the least of her worries.

She was beginning to wonder if she would make it through the night. "I mean, I can try…"

"Then try," he said, and smiled until she thought his dimples would kill her. "You said your father's afraid I'll break your heart, and your mother's afraid our babies will be born on the side of the road."

It sounded so lame when he said it. "Crazy, huh? But you should've seen them banding together over something as small as me asking for a schedule change."

"So, this engagement will have them teaming up and siding against our nuptials, and you're hoping once they remember how well they work, they'll patch things up for good."

"Exactly."

"What about your grandfather? How would he feel about our getting together?"

Cardin stared at the zipper on her sleeping bag. "Jeb's his own man. He may be at odds with my father, but as far as you and me? He would think he'd died and gone to heaven if I were to marry into the Corley Motors family. He's the team's biggest cheerleader."

She smiled as she slid her hand from Trey's, reached for the zipper pull and tugged. "From day one, Headlights was about the cars and the drivers and the crews even more so than the fans. If not for the shrapnel hit he took in Korea, he'd probably be doing what you do. It's hard for him to be on his feet any length of time, but he tinkers an hour or two every day on his Nova, out in the garage behind the house."

"He asked me about driving it for him in the Moonshine Run. Since your father can't do it."

That brought her gaze up. "Are you going to?"

"Anything to make my future grandfather-in-law happy," he said with a wink, killing her again.

"You know, when we break up, I think Jeb's going to take it harder than anyone. My parents will both be relieved, but Jeb's going to be so disappointed."

"Disappointed for you, or for himself?"

"Oh, himself, definitely," she said laughing. "But I'll still hate seeing him hurt."

"This breakup. Have you given any thought to that?"

She shrugged. "I just assumed you'd leave to join your team, and I'd stay here because this is where I belong."

"Staying in Dahlia with a broken heart. Your father's prediction come true."

She didn't care. "All I want is for them to talk. To fix things between them, or to move on. As long as that happens, I can deal with their I-told-you-so's."

He seemed to give that consideration. "Are you going to tell them? When all is said and done?"

"What, that we were faking it?" When he nodded, she said, "I guess I'll play it by ear."

"What if I finish here and leave before they settle things?"

Judging by her parents' earlier reaction, she hoped things would move quickly. Still… "How long are you planning to stay?"

"As long as it takes, but no longer than I have to."

"Then we'll have to make sure our act is convincing," she said before she could stop herself.

"You want to explain that? Because I could take it to mean…wait a minute." He swung up to a sitting position, his frown ruthless. "This convincing thing. Is that why you came to see me at the pits? Why you kissed me in the hauler? Were you auditioning me for the part of your fiancé?"

She swallowed what remained of her nerves. "Yes and no."

"What's that supposed to mean?" He got to his feet, and started pacing the room, stopping with each pass to look at her.

"It was more about auditioning me."

"Auditioning you."

She nodded. "It's why I brought up what happened at Tater's kegger. To see if you remembered."

"You think I would've forgotten?"

"I don't know. We never talked about it, and you left Dahlia that summer."

Every move he made radiated frustration, as did the hitch in his voice. "Cardin, Jesus. You were there—"

"And I was drunk," she reminded him.

"Even so, you had to know I wanted you. That Kim was nothing but a means to an end." He quit pacing. "I'm not particularly proud of how that night went down, but seven years was a long time ago. I've done some growing up since then."

"That's what I thought. What I hoped I hadn't imagined." She paused. She could barely breathe. Barely think. Barely find the words she needed to say. "Especially after what happened the other day."

He hunkered down in front of her then, desperate. "Tell me what you hoped, Cardin. Tell me before I burst a blood vessel here trying to figure it out."

"That I wasn't the only one who'd been turned on…and that I'm not the only one still wanting." Admitting those things to herself had been easy. Admitting them now to Trey, not so much. The look in his eyes had her struggling to catch a breath.

And when he came for her, she thought she would die.

8

WANTING.

It was a word with which Trey was intimately familiar when it came to his feelings for Cardin. And with her gaze—fear and hope tied into her longing—pulling him in, it was the only emotion he knew…his heart racing, his body growing hard. His skin tingling and hot.

He sat back on his heels, his hands on his thighs. He wanted to reach for her, he wanted to speak. He couldn't move his fingers any more than he could work his tongue. She did this to him. Made him dumb.

She took pity and smiled, reaching out and curling her fingers into his shirt and tugging him down. He caught his weight on his palms as he covered her, the layers of clothing between them a barrier he both welcomed and loathed.

He wanted her naked. He wanted her naked now. But he wanted even more to savor the journey of stripping away the fabric. Learning her, the exploration and discovery…it had been such a long seven years.

Earlier, before joining him, she'd flicked off the switch in the kitchen. The shade of the table lamp cast but a small pool of light on the other side of the room. Looking down into her eyes, however, Trey was able to see everything he needed to.

This wasn't a joke. She wasn't playing him. She was right where she wanted to be.

"I wondered when this would finally happen," he told her.

"I didn't think it ever would," was her response.

He wedged one of his legs between hers and shifted to the side, reaching up to brush her hair away from her neck before nuzzling her there. She arched to give him better access, and blew out a heady sigh. "You have no idea how good you feel."

And she had no idea that the way she tasted, like sugar and salt, the way she smelled, like warm lemons and limes, the way she felt beneath him, soft yet firm, was so much better than what he'd imagined, that he might as well have not bothered to imagine anything at all.

He raised his head again, caught her gaze again, had a brief bout of conscience telling him to go slow but ignored it. He had to believe that she would understand, that she shared his desperation. He kissed her, hard, slanting his mouth over hers with a hunger than became a craving where nothing mattered but having her.

He needed to touch her. He needed her to touch him. They had lived with this thing between them for too long already, the physical attraction, the emotional unknown. They had to get to the other side of it and sort out what came next from there.

She moved her hands to his shoulders, her fingers digging into his muscles and urging him closer. He lowered more of his weight, pressed her with his chest and his hips, slid his tongue along the length of hers when her kiss begged. They bumped teeth, bruised lips, nibbled and nipped as if they'd been starving for each other all of these years.

Trey supposed they had been. That night at Tater's kegger had been the end of Trey's time in Dahlia, but it had been the beginning of something with Cardin that had never been given a chance.

He supposed, too, that this chance wasn't a fair one. He

wasn't sticking around. She wasn't about to leave. Their engagement was a sham with a purpose. All they were doing was giving in to a lust that had grown too intense to contain.

Except…he knew that wasn't true. This was more than physical desire. It was a matter of the heart.

He lifted his head, rolled onto his elbow, looked down. Her face was flushed. Her eyes glassy with arousal. Her lips wet and swollen from his assault. She was gorgeous, and his gut tightened at the thought of having her.

"Listen, Cardin." He brushed her hair from her eyes.

She reached for his wrist and held it. "Shh. Don't talk. Not now."

Talking wasn't his first choice either, but… "I have to know. To be sure."

Her hand slid from his wrist to his fingers. She brought them down to cover her breast. "Please don't talk, Trey. I don't want to be thoughtful and logical about anything right now. I just want to feel."

She moved his fingers again, this time sliding them beneath her T-shirt. The material of her bra was a tease, the thinnest of barriers separating them. He molded her breast to fit his palm, rolled her nipple until it peaked.

When she groaned, he dipped his head, sucking her nipple between his lips, wetting both her flesh and the fabric. She raised one knee, her other caught flat beneath him, and rolled toward him as if she couldn't bear the distance anymore than he.

Neither could he bear the clothes they still wore. He lifted up, stripped off his shirt, helped her get rid of hers before unhooking her bra. Seeing her bare breasts…his heart pounded as hard as it had seven years ago when he'd looked up to find her watching him from the door.

The memory sent blood rushing south to stiffen the part of his body tired of being denied the woman he most wanted.

He crawled on top of her and lowered his head, plumping her breasts together, kissing her nipples, sucking them, laving one then the other with the flat of his tongue.

She didn't let him play long, but surged up and shoved at his shoulders, rolling him to his back on the second sleeping bag, and climbing up to straddle his thighs. The look on her face was possessive, as if now that she had him, she wouldn't be letting him go. He wasn't going to argue. This was where he wanted to be.

"My turn," she said and smiled, giving him no time to brace himself before her mouth was on his chest. She searched out his nipples in the swirls of his hair, flicking her tongue across them then nipping with the edge of her teeth. He felt more than heard the sound he made, his entire body caught up in what she was doing with her mouth.

She moved lower, the tips of her breasts dragging down his abdomen. He tucked his chin to his chest, but her head blocked his view. He could easily have closed his eyes for the ride, but she was at his waistband now, her fingers working free the buttons of his fly, and this was something he wanted to see.

She kissed the head of his cock through the cotton of his briefs, ran her tongue in a line along the elastic band on his belly. Propped up on his elbows, he lifted his hips. She skinned away his jeans; they caught at his ankles and his boots, and she left them there, lifting him free from his shorts before tugging them down his thighs.

He wasn't standing in a dark bedroom wishing Cardin were with him. Wishing had given way to reality. And nothing had ever felt so right. Smiling, she took his cock in her mouth, ringed her fingers beneath the head and closed her lips above them, using her tongue to stroke the rigid underside seam, to toy with the slit in the tip.

For several long moments she held his gaze, but finally she closed her eyes. He kept his open; he couldn't look away, not from this. Her black hair fell over her shoulder to tickle his legs and hinder his view of her breasts. But he felt them, their softness and weight as she shifted her position, her nipples grazing his thighs.

He wanted to surge into her mouth, to see her take all of him. He wanted to come, to live the fantasy that had been with him so long, it was hard to remember that it wasn't real. Real hadn't happened until now…and it was happening way too fast. He was going to be done before they really even got started.

Luckily for his pride she released his cock and came up onto her knees. While he rid himself of his shoes and pants, dug a condom from his wallet and rolled it on, Cardin stripped down to nothing.

He lay back, watching as the light played over the skin of this woman he'd wanted to take to bed for a good quarter of his life. If this was a dream, he never wanted to wake up. If it was all in his head, he wanted to stay there forever. But it wasn't, and she crawled over him, her breasts swinging to tease him, her belly sliding against his cock as it stood straight.

He could smell the salty warmth of her sex as she opened to take him in, her moisture and her warmth closing around him. He groaned, then reached for her, winding his fingers into her hair and pulling her close for a kiss.

Their tongues mated, a mimicking of the in and out motion as he thrust into her, as she raised her hips then pressed down, grinding her clit to the base of his shaft.

Later, they would make love. Later, they would take time to learn one another's bodies. When they were done here, they would spend hours finding hot spots and places to tickle and just how to touch. And they would talk. But right now, he had nothing to spare but for this.

She pulled her mouth from his and arched her spine, tossing back her head. He reached for her breasts, kneaded, sucked, biting the plump flesh and bruising her. She cried out, then brought her mouth to his neck and nipped him in return.

He pushed one of his legs through hers and flipped her over, their bodies still joined, perspiration gleaming on her skin, her pupils dilated with wicked heat that sent his body's temperature soaring, his emotions into a fever pitch of hunger.

Braced above her, his hands on the sleeping bag, her hands thrown above her head, he grit his teeth, his jaw taut, and ground his cock into her sex until her whimpers and labored breathing told him he was hitting everything just right.

She hooked her heels over his thighs beneath the cheeks of his ass, and rocked against him, squeezing and milking him as he drove deep, both of them sweating, straining, fighting to hold back and enjoy the long, hard ride.

But the crash came quickly, a fast and furious fire that consumed him body and soul. He knew she was with him, felt her following him into the spin, holding him tight as if fearing he would leave her before she was done.

He wasn't going anywhere, and he lowered himself to cover her completely so she would know that he was sticking around. And that as far as he was concerned, the night had just begun.

9

CARDIN WOKE EARLY, ALONE, and to the most blissful silence ever. Considering blissful was the last word she would have chosen to describe her life these days, the quiet was a joy, and very welcome. She didn't exactly live in a madhouse, but she no longer had anything close to this peaceful calm at home.

Now that Delta had moved out and Cardin had moved back to live with Eddie and Jeb, she had the second floor of the family house all to herself. But even from her upstairs rooms, she was constantly aware of Eddie in the kitchen banging pots and pans, or of Jeb in his garage banging car parts. Eddie found all of life's answers while cooking and her grandfather, well...

If Jeb had his druthers, he'd spend his days working at the Speedway, or on the road with any team that would take him on—though he'd always had a soft spot for Corley Motors, and for the man with whom Cardin had spent the night. Which meant hiding the truth about her relationship with Trey from her grandfather would require extraordinary skill.

And speaking of Trey...

She supposed she should get up and see where he was, what he was doing, what he wanted her to do. What he was thinking after what they'd done last night. How the tension between them had changed now that they'd scratched their itch. But she wasn't going to do anything without first injecting a whole lot of coffee into her system.

Tugging on her blue jeans, socks and sneakers, and pulling her T-shirt over her head, she made a quick stop in the bathroom to wash her face, and brush her teeth and hair. Once in the kitchen, she found Trey's coffee machine, a case of bottled water, and an unopened can of Folgers.

While the coffee brewed, she searched out sugar, powdered creamer and two mugs, then carried both out to the barn where she'd heard the sound of activity when she'd stepped onto the porch.

She had no idea how early he'd left the house—and her—to start working. He'd told her it would take weeks to sort out the mess of tools, auto parts and twenty-odd years of accumulated junk his family had stored in the outbuildings. After that he'd start on the equally cluttered house before finishing up with the acreage—the mowing, the fencing, the heavy-duty nurturing to get something to flourish besides weeds.

The morning air was deliciously cool, not quite cold enough to frost her breath, but close. The sun was just topping the ridge to the east, shooting arrows of light through the property's trees. She breathed deeply of spring coming to life, the morning's dew intensifying the heady, verdant smells.

And speaking of heady…

Twenty feet from the barn door, she came to a stop. Trey had just walked out. He had on blue jeans, work boots and a denim shirt, the sleeves rolled up his forearms, the tails untucked, the front unsnapped. The shirt teased her, the way it hung open, revealing next to nothing yet still stirring her blood.

He was frowning, looking down at a rusted piece of metal in his hands. He turned it over, held it up as if he needed the light to see. When he lowered it was when he caught sight of her and the drinks she carried. She wasn't sure which was responsible for the smile that shooed away his frown.

"Is that for me?"

She cocked her head to the side and considered how much better the day already seemed. "Good morning to you, too."

She didn't hold out the second of the coffees for him to take, but teased him with it instead. He came closer. She kept her gaze on his as she sipped from her heavy white mug, hiding her grin and her giddy rush of nerves behind it.

He stopped in front of her, and she made the mistake of lowering her gaze from his face to the exposed strip of his chest. It was either give him his cup of coffee or bury her nose against him and breathe in. She remembered so clearly how he smelled.

Their fingers brushed when he took the drink from her hand. He swallowed a gulp, then said, "Good morning, Cardin. I hope the floor wasn't too hard on you."

The floor wasn't the hardness that had made sleep difficult. She shook her head. "Are you kidding? I slept like a baby, swaddled in my sleeping bag."

"In my sleeping bag, you mean."

"Thank you. It made the floor bearable." As had the warmth of his body, she thought, then quickly changed the subject. "You must've hit town in the middle of the night. I saw the loaf of bread and eggs. Would you like me to cook breakfast? I think I can manage the hot plate."

He lowered his coffee slowly, his gaze as warm as the sun on her shoulders, as the ceramic mug heating her hands. "I didn't bring you out here to wait on me."

"You didn't bring me out here at all. I volunteered to come."

"To help me. Not to serve me."

"It's just breakfast, Trey. And coffee." Even if last night it had been more. Even if the way he was looking at her made her want more. Why had she waited so long to test the waters that had swirled around them all those years ago? "I work much better when it's not on an empty stomach. I thought it might be the same for you."

"It is, but I'll cook." He raised his mug and gave her props. "You did the coffee."

"That's because I can't work at all without caffeine."

"If I'd known that, I would've put on a pot when I got up."

"What time *did* you get up?" Judging by the sun in the sky, she swore it couldn't be any later than seven now.

"Maybe four?" he guessed, taking another sip.

"But it was almost two…" She let the sentence dangle, finishing the thought privately, quite sure he knew exactly the hour when they'd finally fallen asleep.

"There's a lot to do. And I've got a lot on my mind." He shrugged as if there was nothing more to it when she knew there was. And then he stared off toward the field behind the house full of weeds and wildflowers, and in desperate need of mowing.

She'd expected him to head toward the house. To find a skillet and scramble some eggs. To make toast in the aluminum toaster she'd seen on top of the fridge, one she was certain would still be around to brown bread and waffles and frozen streusel for any children he might one day have.

Trey with children, with an apple-of-his-eye daughter, with a strapping young son. She switched mental gears at that thought. "Can I ask you something, Trey?"

"Sure," he said, still studying the tall grass, his mug halfway to his mouth, his shirt blowing further open in the soft morning breeze.

"The other morning at the Speedway. What you said about seeing me at school." She paused, waited for a reaction, got a visible tick in his jaw for her trouble. It was better than nothing at all. "Did you never speak to me because you weren't interested? Did you think I wouldn't say anything back?"

"Why do you want to know?" he asked, slinging his mug so the dregs of his coffee flew out in a creamy brown arc.

She watched the droplets soak into the ground. "Just curious."

"I don't think so."

"What?"

This time he came around and met her gaze, his a smoky warm gold. "I think it's more than curiosity."

"What else would it be?" She wasn't looking for him to stroke her ego, or to gain any sort of upper hand. She just wanted to know. She had always wanted to know why neither one of them had made the first move. "You were older than me, but our circles of friends overlapped. We may not have shared classes, but had that in common at least. It's why we both ended up at Tater's kegger that night."

He shook his head, his mouth twisted. "I'm never going to live that down, am I?"

She didn't get it. "Why would you have to? You were in a bedroom behind a closed door. I'm the one who made the hugely embarrassing mistake of opening it."

"Were you? Embarrassed?"

Her face heated. "Yes, but I was also perversely fascinated."

"Tapped your inner voyeur, did I?"

She held her mug in both hands, staring at what remained of her drink because his gaze was bold, and disarmed her. "It wasn't about the sex. I mean, it was. I hadn't ever... watched before."

"Did you like watching?" he asked, his voice husky, thick, his breathing more rapid than moments before.

Her throat tightened. Her pulse leapt. "I liked watching your eyes, your face. The way you looked at me while...it was happening. We'd never talked, and I'd heard things about you. Girls share stuff, you know. But it was all secondhand. At least until—"

"Until you got a personal introduction to me and my friend."

He made it so easy for her to smile, to feel comfortable with a subject that wasn't. "I like your friend. I just don't understand why that moment when you backed me into the bedroom wall was it. There was nothing before. Nothing after. You left town. I worked at Headlights. And now…this. Us. Talking all the time, sleeping together. You don't find that strange?"

He took so long to react, she started to wonder if he ever would, if maybe she should let him stew and go get their breakfast started and forget working to understand how they'd reached this place with more questions than answers.

But then he headed for the house, hopping up to sit on the porch, helping her up beside him when she finally realized he was waiting for her. "I don't find it strange, no. I think we'd have connected just as strongly in high school if we'd given it a chance."

"So why didn't we?" she asked, having always felt tongue-tied just at the thought of him. He was older, knowing, forbidden.

Trey laughed softly, an awkward sound, as if he was uncomfortable with his confession. "Well, frankly, I didn't think I had anything to offer a girl like you."

She turned to look at him, frowning. "What's that supposed to mean, a girl like me?"

He shrugged with one shoulder, gave her a lopsided grin. "A girl whose last name was Worth."

Was he kidding her? They might have a bit of a Capulet and Montague thing going on now, with no one knowing the cause of the fight between Eddie, Aubrey, and Jeb. But not in high school. No way in high school.

She scooted around, sitting cross-legged, wishing for another cup of coffee as a gust of wind left her chilled. "You make it sound like we're from different sides of the tracks, or something. And Dahlia doesn't even have any tracks."

"Your family's legend, Cardin. Pillars of the community—"

"Oh, please. We're just…people. Like anyone else," she said. Her family was a local fixture, but that didn't mean they were any different from anyone else.

"My mother left without a word. My father's a mechanic—"

"And my father's a cook. So what?"

"A cook in a family owned business that's been a local landmark for what? Over forty years?" He set his mug behind him, held onto the edge of the porch and leaned forward, his brows drawn together as he stared down the long gravel drive. "When you're a guy barely out of high school, and you're pumping gas and cleaning windshields and changing oil for a living, and you hear Jeb Worth this and Jeb Worth that every time you turn around—"

"You're exaggerating."

"Not by much." He glanced over at her then, his expression kind, but curious. "You have to know that. That your family is the one family everyone in Dahlia respects."

She tried to brush it off. "All that means is that we've been here a long time."

"To you, sure. But to an eighteen-year-old kid who gets a hard-on every time he see you in the school halls—" His voice was solemn, the cockiness all tucked away. "I just didn't think I was good enough for you."

Tears welled in her eyes. To realize she could have set him

at ease with nothing but a word… "Oh, my, God. Trey. Tell me you didn't really think that."

He nodded. "I did. What can I say? I was young. Not very worldly."

"And a moron. I don't know whether to yell at you or hit you."

"Why don't you kiss me instead?" And he reached for her before she could say yes or no.

10

IT WASN'T UNTIL EDDIE WORTH hit the kitchen at dawn on Monday morning that he realized Cardin hadn't spent the night at home.

Ever since she'd moved back, and Delta had taken herself off to live in their daughter's apartment, Cardin had come downstairs each night for a glass of chocolate milk before bed.

And each day before leaving for Headlights, Eddie rinsed her glass, put it in the dishwasher, and returned the squeeze bottle of Hershey's syrup she always left out to the fridge.

Cardin was completely capable of cleaning up after herself, and when it came to the rest of her dishes, her laundry, and her rooms upstairs, she did. Hell, half the time she cleaned up after him and his father, too.

Jeb was the worst about leaving tools and scraps of wiring and electrical connectors lying around. Cardin gathered it all into a bushel basket by the back door for him to haul to the garage when he headed that way every morning.

And Eddie would have to plead guilty to kicking off his shoes wherever he happened to be when his leg started giving him hell. Cardin never complained the way her mother had. She put his shoes where they belonged, and told him how lucky they were that his accident hadn't been worse.

No, Cardin wasn't the one who was a slob. Her leaving her glass for him to rinse and the chocolate syrup for him to put away, was her telling him she remembered how as a child she would come to the kitchen and ask for a drink in the middle of the night.

A lifelong insomniac, Eddie had used the time while his father and wife slept to spoil his only child in a way he knew couldn't be healthy. But having Cardin on his lap, sipping her chocolate milk while he read the news from the day's paper aloud, had been the favorite part of his day.

Knowing she still held dear their secret had made the reason she was home again easier to bear. He missed his wife. Goddamn but he missed his wife.

It had taken every bit of his willpower this morning not to pick up the phone and call Delta to tell her their daughter had spent the night with Whip. He'd decided against it. He and Delta might be in agreement that the romance was not a good idea. But Eddie knew for a fact his wife would tell him not to do what he was doing—picking up breakfast for three from Pammy Mercer's bakery before driving out to the Davis place to say good morning to his kid.

He pulled into the parking lot of Pammy's Petals at the same time as Alex Morgan drove up in the Gran Torino she'd been restoring in her spare time. Soon enough, he figured, the body would look as good as the horses under the hood sounded.

Alex was the daughter of George who owned the garage where the fight between Eddie's father and Whip's father had happened. George was good to put up with Jeb hanging around to talk cars.

Alex smiled as Eddie rounded the front of his Dodge Charger. "I haven't seen you at the track since the accident. You doing okay these days?"

"I'm good. Thanks for asking." And for not mentioning it had been almost a year since his injury. He'd got tired of

Delta nagging about the very same thing, his becoming a homebody, a hermit. Then she'd quit nagging. Then she'd left. "I keep pretty busy in the kitchen. Not much time for anything else."

Alex reached up and smoothed the bandana tied around her long blonde hair. "Rumor has it that Jeb asked Whip Davis to drive for him in the Moonshine Run."

"Really." Eddie took a minute to open the door and usher Alex inside. He used the same minute to wonder why his father had shared nothing of his plans. *Maybe the same reason your wife left you, you ass. You're not the nicest guy to be around these days.* "Jeb's probably the biggest fan Corley Motors has, so that'll be a treat."

Breathing in a head rush of warm sugar and yeast, Eddie walked with Alex across the pink and white tiled floor to the counter where pastries, brownies and cookies were on display. Before Alex could respond, Pammy Mercer appeared to take their orders.

A schoolmate of both Alex and Cardin, the pint-sized bakery owner wore a cap shaped like her huge trademark daisy on the top of her head. "Eddie Worth! And Alex Morgan! I can't believe you two workaholics are out and about at the same time. What can I get you?"

Eddie gestured for Alex to go first. "I need three dozen donuts. Mixed. But a lot of cream-filled for Tater."

Pammy nodded, her head-hugging auburn curls bouncing, and jotted the order on a ticket that matched the green and white stripes of the apron she wore. "Feeding the boys at the garage this morning?"

Alex shoved her hands in the pockets of her denim overalls and grimaced. "I bet the shop on Friday that Butch Corley wouldn't get close to Tony Schumacher's time during the Farron Fuels. I lost, so donuts are on me."

Eddie's laugh sounded more like a snort. "You bet against Whip Davis's tuning formula?"

"Right? What was I thinking?"

Pammy turned her attention to Eddie. "And you, Eddie Worth? Did you bet against Whip Davis, too?"

He should have bet Delta that nothing they said was going to keep their daughter away from Whip, but since they were in agreement in that regard, the odds wouldn't have been worth the gamble. "Nah, I just need a half dozen Danishes. Cream cheese and apple cinnamon will do."

"Coming right up," Pammy said with a slap to the top of the glass case. She headed into the back, leaving Eddie to look around the bakery that reminded him of the fairy-tale castle five-year-old Cardin had begged for so her princesses wouldn't have to sleep on the floor.

And here twenty years later, she was the one sleeping on the floor—or so he assumed, doubting there was much in the way of furniture left in the Davis house—with a man Eddie just knew was going to break her heart.

Once he had the box of Danishes and Pammy's special blend coffee to go, he made the drive to Whip's family home in less than fifteen minutes. The Davis' property was on the other side of Dahlia than the Worth's, but nothing in the small town was more than a stone's throw away.

When he pulled onto the gravel drive, he saw Jeb's truck parked in front of the crew cab dualie Whip drove, and the two kids sitting on the porch, coffee mugs in hand.

Cardin had never been a morning person, and looked sleepy, he noticed, braking to a stop not far from where they'd both hopped down. And Whip appeared to have been hard at work already.

Eddie wasn't sure why that made him feel better, but it did.

The thought that he could've caught them otherwise engaged had him almost regretting this visit.

But only almost.

He swung his bad left leg out first, then gingerly pushed up to stand. Once upright, the pins keeping things in place gave him little discomfort. He set the coffee and pastries on the hood of his car, and called out, "I come bearing breakfast."

"Daddy, what are you doing here?" Cardin asked, walking toward him after a quick glance passed between her and Whip who followed.

Eddie blew across his cup before taking a sip. "I told you. I brought breakfast. I figured with the Farron Fuels taking up most of the weekend, that Whip here wouldn't have had time to lay in much in the way of groceries."

"I laid in a few," Whip said, holding his mug in one hand and pouring the contents of one disposable cup into it with the other. "We had coffee, but only a fool would say no to Pammy's blend. Or to anything she bakes."

Eddie reached for a Danish, as Whip added sugar and cream to his cup, and gestured toward his daughter with the pastry. "Cardin? I've never known you to say no to Pammy's, either."

She didn't look happy, but she dipped into the box as Whip did, and the two shared a look that had Eddie's chest aching as they came up holding two sides of the same one.

Whip was the gentleman and let it go. "You a cream cheese fan, too?"

"It's my fave," Cardin said, biting in without a word to Eddie for remembering.

He grabbed a napkin and licked his fingertips before wiping the glazed sugar away. "I ran into Alex Morgan at Pammy's. She told me Jeb asked you to drive White Lightning in the Moonshine Run."

His mouth full, Whip nodded, taking a swallow of coffee before he spoke. "He came out to the track late Sunday while we were making ready to roll out. He asked if I'd take a look, see what I thought about running it on the track."

"I had no idea he'd even entered this year," Cardin said to Eddie. "I thought he'd retire the car, maybe even sell it since you can't drive anymore."

Oh, he could drive. As long as he could take his time getting in and out of the vehicle, and didn't have to worry about getting clear in the case of flipping or flames.

Eddie finished off his coffee. "He's been working on the car since last year, so I'm not surprised he went looking for someone to drive it. Just surprised he didn't say anything. And that he waited so long. The race is only a couple of weeks away." Eddie stared into his empty cup, at the few grounds clinging to the Styrofoam. "I swear, the older Jeb gets, the worse he is about sharing any of what he's thinking."

At that, Whip turned to face him. "Speaking of that, I don't guess he ever said much about what went down with my father before you stepped in to stop the fight, did he?"

"Not a word," Eddie told the younger man, wondering if he would have divulged the truth had he known.

After all, accident or not, Whip's father had ruined Eddie's life. And now Whip was doing his damnedest to continue the family tradition by ruining Cardin's.

And nothing about it looked like an accident. "Would've been nice to know what I sacrificed my leg for besides a couple of tempers, but my dad's never said a word, and your dad's…"

"Dead," Whip filled in. "My dad's dead."

"And my dad can really be a jerk sometimes," Cardin added, narrowing her eyes and glaring at Eddie, all righteous indignation as she moved closer to Whip.

Taking sides already. Eddie figured at this point there

wasn't anyone he cared about that he hadn't pissed off. That didn't mean he was going to step out of his daughter's life and watch her make a magnificent mistake—no matter the cloud of tension swirling thicker here than any morning fog hanging over the ridge.

He closed up the pastry box, then moved it from the hood of his car to the hood of Jeb's borrowed truck. "I'll let you kids get back to your packing and cleaning, and head on to work myself."

"I'm sorry, Daddy. You're not a jerk. I shouldn't have said that." Cardin stepped in front of him, putting a stop to his leaving. "Especially after you went to all this trouble to bring us food."

Pammy's baked goods. Best served with a side of humble pie. Eddie dropped a kiss to the top of Cardin's head and stepped back. "I'm the one with apologies to make. Yeah, I'm angry about what went down between Aubrey and Jeb, but I'm alive. I can deal with the pain and the limitations. Like you, though," he said to Whip, "not knowing what I stepped into isn't sitting well a year later."

Whip shook his head, frustration etched in the grooves around his eyes, his hair catching the collar of his shirt. "Whatever it was sent my dad into his last spiral. I'm not saying it was anyone's fault but his own. I just want to know what happened to put him there."

"Even if you find out," Eddie assured him, seeing too much guilt on the younger man's face, "it doesn't mean you could've put a stop to your dad's fall."

"I can accept that. I have a harder time accepting there's a puzzle piece I might never find."

Eddie had sworn that he'd never press his father for the truth, that Jeb would have to make that move on his own.

But Eddie had never considered that Whip had suffered

collateral damage, too. They were the two left hurting. He wasn't going to make any promises, but helping Whip find closure wouldn't kill him.

Especially since the look on his daughter's face said she was up to her eyeballs involved. "If Jeb gets a hair and starts spilling his guts I'll definitely let you know."

"That's good enough. Thank you, sir."

He slapped Whip on the shoulder. "Just Eddie. No sir required."

"Thank you, Eddie."

"Thank you, Daddy." Cardin rubbed his arm, then raised up on her tiptoes to kiss him on the cheek. "I love you."

"I love you, too," he said, before leaning close and whispering for her hearing alone, "But I'm still gonna hurt him bad if he breaks your heart."

Before Cardin had time to respond, Eddie heard Whip clear his throat. "Listen, Eddie. Do you think Cardin and I could talk to you and Mrs. Worth tonight? At Headlights? I can be there by the time Cardin gets off work."

Eddie didn't have to see the color rise in Cardin's face to know what was going on. And what was going on was something he wasn't happy about at all. At least he had a good twelve hours warning. "Sure. We'll be there."

And before anyone else said anything else to ruin the rest of his day, he climbed into his Charger and left.

11

"WHAT IN THE WORLD did you just do?"

As Cardin's father's car disappeared in a plume of gravel dust and exhaust, Trey put his coffee cup next to the box of pastries on the hood of her grandfather's truck and headed back to the barn.

He left her with a grin he was certain would rile her further. "Hey, if we're going to be engaged, we're going to have to tell people. The sooner the better, don't you think?"

"Don't *you* think for something as important as announcing our engagement you might have checked with me first?" she called from behind him.

"I thought we were on the same page here." Though the one he'd just turned told Trey to seal this deal now—before her father made sure it never happened, and he never learned anything about the fight.

"We are on the same page" came her voice from farther away than before. "Though you're obviously reading faster than I am."

"I figured you'd like a husband who stayed one step ahead of you." He picked up the rusted pump he'd dropped earlier and walked into the barn.

Her feet scuffed over the hard-packed earth as she hurried to catch him. "Not if it means I have to walk one step behind."

"And all this time I thought that's where a woman's place was."

"Only if you're of the male chauvinist persuasion," she said, following him into the darkness of the barn.

He stopped, turned, and caught her before she slammed into him. "Hey, I've been out of the relationship game for a while. In fact, the longest one I've had has been with Butch and the guys."

"That scares me."

Trey laughed. He loved discovering that she was a good sport, that she had a sense of humor. That her mind was as incredible as her mouth. "This is probably a good time to finishing getting our story straight."

"Right," she said, swatting away a dust web. "Don't want to get caught in a lie before we even get this thing off the ground."

He figured she would see things his way. "Okay then," he began, crossing his arms as he leaned against the workbench he'd been cleaning off earlier. "Last year when I was here for the Farron Fuels, did you show up for the race? Could we have got together then?"

"Oh, yeah. It's always been a huge family affair. Up until now anyway. Last year Eddie and my mother were still living together, and he and Jeb weren't at odds."

And then came the fight that nobody seemed to know anything about, because the only one alive who did wasn't talking. "Your dad looks like he's getting around pretty good. How bad is his leg?"

From the workbench, Cardin picked up a baseball in one hand, and a conch shell Trey had never seen in the other. "Bad enough that he can't drive for Jeb anymore."

"And that's a strain between them?"

"It shouldn't be. Jeb should be happy that his son has two

working legs, not out of sorts because Eddie's bad one keeps him from racing."

Trey took the conch shell from her hand, tossing it into the burn barrel. "Wonder why Jeb never raced himself."

"Same reason he never became a lawman." She popped the baseball up and down in her palm. "The shrapnel he took in Korea. He has to be able to sit or move when he needs to."

"Too bad. Dahlia could've benefited being served by someone like Jeb, instead of Henry Buell."

"That, too, but I was thinking his own injury should make him more sympathetic to Eddie's situation."

Trey snagged the baseball midair. "Yeah, but parents tend to be harder on their kids when it comes to flaws they see in themselves."

"That would make sense if this was about his beating his wife and kicking the dog," she argued, her frustration evident. "Eddie couldn't help what happened to him anymore than Jeb could. In fact, if Eddie hadn't stepped in, Jeb might've been the one to…uh, take the fall."

"Been the one my father clocked, you mean," Trey said, striving for neutrality and hoping she would understand—and forgive—any anger that slipped through.

Her only response was to nod. "I know it was an accident. Everyone says it was. Even Eddie. I don't blame your father. But like you, I guess, it would be nice to know what happened. To make sense of it all. Because having my family fall apart doesn't make a lick of it."

Trey took a deep breath, letting the baseball roll down the workbench and off the end to the ground. "What about with your mother? What happened between Eddie and Delta?"

"I don't even know really, though I'd say it started with communication. They stopped talking. Or when they did talk, it was nothing but Delta bitching, or Eddie being a dick."

Trey smiled to himself. "Not particularly conducive to a good relationship."

"Of any sort. Parent to child, me being the child. Employer to employee, me being the employee. Even their friends have been steering clear."

"Then we'll have to make communication a number one priority. We don't want that happening to us."

Cardin snorted, then laughed as she grabbed up the baseball and lobbed it at him. "You're really getting into this, aren't you?"

He tossed it back. "Are you kidding? After last night?"

This time she blushed, running her thumb over the stitching that had faded from red to brown. "Speaking of which, I'd like to know how you expect me to sit and talk to my parents about us getting married after...all of that."

All of that. It made him laugh. "You think we wouldn't have slept together by now if we were really getting married? That you wouldn't be seeing your parents with them knowing that?"

"Well, no," she said, hesitating as if she hadn't given it much thought.

He was beginning to wonder if she'd given any thought at all to this plan. "Are you sure you're up to playing this part?"

"It's either play this one or go on playing daughter on the verge of a nervous breakdown."

"And you don't want to do that anymore, right?"

"If I have to do it another day, I'm going to go insane." She pitched the baseball into the trash; the barrel rang when it hit. "You saw Eddie this morning. Mr. Mood Swing himself."

He wrapped his arms around her waist and brought her close to his body. "Then maybe we should run some lines. Or block some action. Whatever will help you get into the role."

"I thought we were supposed to be cleaning out the barn,"

she said, though she did slide her hands around his neck and lace her fingers there.

He slipped his fingers into the waistband of her jeans and beneath the elastic of her bikini panties. "It's probably a good time for a break."

She wiggled against him, faking a frown. "A break. We haven't even done any work yet. At this rate, you won't finish up in time to get back with your team this year."

"Then I hope you're ready for a long engagement," he said, cutting off any reply she would have made with a kiss.

She squirmed beneath his questing, greedy hands, her body pressing fully against him bringing his to life in a heartbeat. Touching her made him hard. His tongue in her mouth made him hard. Hell, just thinking about her made him stiffen like a fossilized tree trunk.

Such had been the case for more years than he could remember, even before Tater's party. His holding her there against the wall and breathing her in had just been the icing on that cake.

She moved her hands to his face, holding him while she caught and tugged at his lower lip, biting him gently, groaning as she did. He groaned as well, tucking her hips into his, showing her how powerfully crazy he wanted her.

And it seemed she wanted him, too, parting the two sides of his shirt and burying her face against his chest. She licked, she kissed, she nipped softly. He swallowed hard, and stopped her from doing anything more, holding the both of them still while he found his control. And then he swept her up in his arms. She gasped, and then she giggled.

She was still giggling three minutes later when he kicked open the front door and tumbled with her to the sleeping bags stacked together on the floor.

This time they only bothered getting rid of their pants. Trey

worked his down to his ankles. Cardin pulled just one leg free
from hers, and then he was sheathed and inside of her, riding
her, grinding against her without either one of them saying a
word. Their breathing was heavy, the room was still.

He heard his own heartbeat, heard Cardin's whimpers as
she wiggled to adjust her body beneath his. She found the
place she wanted to be. He found the rhythm she needed.
They rocked together, panting, grunting, his cock sliding in
and out easily, lubed by her moisture.

Her hands gripped his shoulders and held on tight. Her
heels dug into his ass. Her pussy grabbed him, tugged, pulled,
milked him for all he was worth. He wasn't going to be able
to hold back with all of that going on.

He told himself to wait. He thought of all the things in the
barn he needed to do. He thought of ways to get more speed
out of Butch Corley's dragster. But the woman beneath him
made it hard to think of anything but her for long.

When she cried out, he focused on taking her as high as
he could. And once she was there, he followed, exploding…

Trey wondered as he came down from the blast if they
really were doing nothing but scratching an itch. Or if all this
time the attraction between them had been something more.

And what he was going to do about it—since he suspected
that he couldn't walk away and leave her here again.

12

THE FOUR TO EIGHT SHIFT at Headlights was pretty much Cardin's favorite to work. Teens came in after school for cokes, French fries, shakes and flirting. Families came in wanting a quick meal before heading off to sporting events, science fairs or band competitions.

That time period covered the regular dinner hour as well, whether folks were eating at five or at seven. She stayed busy, and staying busy kept her from thinking too much. It also made the time fly. So before she knew it, she was looking at eight o'clock—and at her mother who'd gone home earlier walking back through the door.

Delta caught her eye, curiously condemning, then headed for a far corner table, one out of the way of the dinner crowd, one the other waitresses would know to avoid. Cardin didn't know if she was up to waiting with her mother for the men.

But she did know Delta would want a Diet Coke, so she scooped up ice, filled the tumbler and carried it to the table where she set it down and added a straw, avoiding meeting— though not avoiding feeling—her mother's probing gaze.

Before she could make her escape, however, her father joined them. She couldn't look at him either, so she turned to go, saying, "I've got to clock out. I'll be right back."

Eddie grabbed her wrist before she'd taken a step. "Sit down, Cardin. Tell your mother and me what's going on."

"I'd rather wait for Trey."

"And we'd rather hear it from you," Delta said, jabbing her straw into the tightly packed ice keeping her drink a whole lot cooler than her mood.

Cardin was stuck. It would do her no good to argue that the boss wouldn't want her talking until she was off the clock when it was the boss telling her to sit.

She slid onto the bench across the table from her parents, wishing Trey were here. Wishing, strangely enough, that the lie they were about to tell was not one. Having him on her side right now, for better or for the worst she was facing, held a definitely tempting appeal.

The only thing she could think of to say was, "What do you want to hear?"

Her mother looked at her father. He looked back, then down at the picnic table's scarred surface. Neon red light from the Coors sign overhead glinted off his black hair. He picked at a gouge in the wood. He cleared his throat. "If you and Whip had something to tell us, why didn't you mention it when you asked for the schedule change?"

Oh, good. Something she and Trey had already discussed. "He hasn't had a free minute since he got here on Thursday. I wasn't going to say anything to you guys until we'd had a chance to talk."

"This has been going on a while then," her mother said, toying with her straw, no doubt wishing it were a sharp object.

Cardin wondered who it was Delta most wanted to stab—her husband, her daughter, or herself. "For about a year, yes."

Eddie's head snapped up. "Then you lied to us when we asked if there was something between you two."

"No, what I told you was that I wasn't going to let him break my heart."

"Maybe you should've thought about how you're breaking ours," Delta came back with.

Cardin looked from her mother to her father, making sure she had both her parents' attention. "And maybe the two of you should think about what you've done to mine with this ridiculous estrangement."

The tension at the table was so thick, not a single knife in Eddie's kitchen would've been able to slice it through. Cardin didn't know how long they sat there, silent, but when Trey arrived with a pitcher of beer and four frosted mugs moments later, it took everything she had not to throw herself into his arms—not as his fiancée, but as a woman at the end of her rope.

"You guys been waiting long?" he asked, settling in beside her and dropping an arm around her waist. He leaned over and kissed her cheek, giving her a quick wink before he went about pouring the beer.

If she hadn't already proposed to him, she wasn't sure she'd be able to stop herself from doing so now. Though she hated feeling as if she needed a rescue, he made a damn fine white knight.

"I haven't even clocked out yet, but the bosses don't seem to mind," Cardin teased, her joke falling flat.

She knew that when her mother said, "When payroll cuts your next check, she'll remember exactly what time you finished for the night."

Oh, yeah. This was going well. Cardin reached for the mug Trey set in front of her instead of responding to Delta's jab.

Trey looked around the table. "So what has Cardin told you so far?"

Delta was the one to respond. "Only that she lied to us not twenty-four hours ago about anything going on with you two."

He glanced over. Cardin swallowed more beer.

"It's been hard to keep it secret," he said, his voice gentle, his tone low, nearly intimate, taking her back to the hours before she'd come to work, hours when they hadn't done any cleaning or packing at all. Her body heated at the thought, only to cool as her father cursed beneath his breath.

"I'd say you've done a damn fine job of keeping it a secret," Eddie muttered. "Cardin hasn't said a thing this entire year."

Trey gave her thigh a reassuring pat. "That's my girl."

"So we've just discovered," Delta said, exchanging her diet soda for the alcohol.

"Mr. Worth. Eddie. Mrs. Worth," Trey began, and Cardin felt as if she'd swallowed a hornet's nest and was being stung to death from the inside. "I know this comes out of the blue, and if I'd had a way to give you a heads-up, I would have. But I would very much like your permission to marry your daughter."

If the mood earlier had been heavy and depressing, the one that followed Trey's request was worse. Neither one of her parents said a word. They looked from Trey to her to each other. They drank their beer. They stared at the table. They shifted restlessly on their bench.

Enough. This was ridiculous. Cardin reached out and took hold of their hands. "Mom. Dad. You can't ignore this. I know it's a shock. I know it's not what you may want for me. But I'm very very happy to be with Trey."

"Oh, sweetie." Delta squeezed Cardin's fingers. "It's not that we don't want this for you. Of course we want you to find someone and fall in love."

"That someone is right here, Mom. He's asked you for my hand." Even saying that gave Cardin chills.

"And I'm willing to answer any questions you might have," Trey put in. "Fire away."

"All right," Delta said, giving him her full attention.

"You're on the road all year, Whip. Are you planning to take her with you? Or are you planning to travel alone and leave her behind?"

Trey didn't even hesitate. "She'll be with me every day. I'm not going to let her out of my sight."

Cardin cringed. No doubt one of her parents would twist that into some sort of disturbed possessiveness.

"She'll live in a motor home, then? Or in a motel?" Delta paused for a heartbeat. "She won't have a house of her own?"

"No, Mrs. Worth. I didn't say that. Of course she'll have a house."

"Where?"

"Wherever she wants it. Right here is fine."

"I thought you were selling your place and cutting your ties with Dahlia."

Trey took a deep breath. "I'm selling the house I grew up in. That doesn't mean I can't buy or build another here for her."

"Just not for you," Eddie added.

Cardin couldn't stay out of it any longer. "Of course it will be for him, too, Daddy. When it's time. For now, though, being with Trey is all that matters. Whether that's traveling in a motor home, or staying in motel rooms. I don't care."

"What kind of life is that, Cardin?"

When Trey stiffened beside her, Cardin bit her tongue and let him answer.

"Excuse me, sir, but it's the one I live now, and I think it's a pretty damn good one."

"She's my little girl," Eddie said, his eyes darkening.

"And I respect that. But she's also a woman. One who has consented to be my wife."

"Wouldn't that make this asking permission thing a sham?"

"I proposed to Trey, Daddy." Cardin swore her head was

about to pop. "He's the one who insisted we talk to you and Mom."

Eddie sat straight, crossing his arms over his chest. "Then I guess if you've made up your mind, there's nothing much we can say."

"You can give Trey your blessing," she told her father, feeling some of Trey's tension drain.

"I don't mean to be a disappointment to you, sir."

"Oh, Whip. You're not a disappointment," Cardin's mother finally said. "This just came out of the blue. And, no, a life on the road is not exactly what we would have chosen for our daughter. But it isn't our choice, is it? As long as you make her happy…"

"That much I can guarantee you."

"In that case, I only have one other question."

Cardin waited, waited, thought she might throw up.

"Do you love her?"

One thing they hadn't talked about. Love. Cardin had assumed her parents would accept that as a given. She looked from her mother to Trey who had turned his gaze on her. She had no idea what he was going to say. No idea what she wanted to hear.

When he smiled, his dimples nearly killed her. "I have to say after a year of being apart, these last twenty-four hours have been the best of my life."

Cardin swallowed. She couldn't speak. She knew he wasn't declaring his love for her, that he was only talking about the sex, but the look in his eyes left her breathless, left her wishing that he loved her as much as she loved him. Because she did. She loved him. She loved him.

"That's not what her mother asked you, Whip," Eddie said. "She asked you if you love our daughter."

It didn't matter that they were lying about everything else,

Cardin was not going to put this burden on Trey. She looked at him, smiled, and covered his hand with hers. "He loves me. And I love him. I wouldn't have asked him to marry me if I wasn't sure of his feelings."

Delta reached to touch Cardin's hand where it lay on top of Trey's, and held Eddie's with her free one, glancing at him as if to say, *This is the man our daughter has chosen. There is nothing we can do.*

It made Cardin sad, but it also pissed her off. Even if she wasn't really marrying Trey, he was a good man. He deserved better than this from her parents. "Don't look so glum, Mom. You and Dad may not have been able to weather the hard times, but Trey and I will be fine."

At that, Delta stiffened, pulled her hand away and looked to Eddie for support. Good. That was what Cardin wanted. Getting her parents working together was the whole point of this deception. She would dig at them as often and as hard as she needed to see it happen.

Eddie said nothing, simply returning Delta's gaze. Cardin could see, however, that he was biting his tongue. She scrambled for something more to pressure them with, but at the moment was all lied out.

At the last minute, Trey saved her. "I don't know if the rest of you have eaten, but I've got to have some dinner. My treat."

"I've been here twelve hours," Eddie said, shaking his head. "I'm going to head on home. Thanks for the offer, though."

"Anytime."

Eddie splayed his hands flat on the table as if to push up, but stopped, his gaze traveling from Cardin to Trey and back. And then he held out his hand to Trey. "You take good care of her."

"I will, sir," Trey said, clasping Eddie's hand solidly and giving it a firm shake. "You can count on it."

Nodding, Eddie got to his feet. Delta followed. Trey stood

as well, leaving Cardin uncertain what to do—until she caught her mother's eye. "Aren't you going to go put in an order for Whip's dinner?"

"Oh, sure," Cardin said, climbing off the bench, already a domestic goddess failure. "What'll you have?"

"Whatever you're going to have," he told her. "Because you have to eat, too. We've still got a lot of work to do in the barn before we can even think about turning in."

Since all they'd done in the barn today was play ball. She started to walk by him, but he caught her and held her close, planting a quick kiss on her cheek, leaving her flustered and her face heated.

With Sandy Larabie, Cardin's parents and the rest of the dining room looking on, Trey had just staked his claim publicly, leaving no doubt about the nature of their relationship.

Cardin wasn't sure she'd make it to the kitchen without fainting. Was there anything more stressful than telling a lie?

She put in a rush order for two bacon cheeseburger baskets, then for the next ten minutes hid out in a restroom stall. She didn't want to be grilled by Sandy, or be caught staring at her parents and Trey, wondering what they were talking about, what questions they were asking him, what holes in their story Cardin had left that Trey was now having to fill.

She sat there on the toilet lid, and buried her face in her hands, listening as two little girls came in, giggling and whispering before flushing, chattering while washing their hands. She wanted to tell them to enjoy being ten years old. That being twenty-five sucked.

The truth, of course, was that her age had nothing to do with anything. What sucked was telling the people she loved most a big fat lie—especially when the lie itself felt as good as this one was feeling.

Before Cardin made the mistake of taking that thought any

further, she shored herself up and returned to the kitchen, picking up her order and carrying the food to Trey. He was sitting alone now, frowning, and running the pad of one finger over a gouge in the table much as her father had done.

This time she sat across from him rather than at his side. "I'm sensing some regret here."

A grin tugged at one side of his mouth. "I'm not sure regret's the right word. I'm just trying to figure out how much trouble I'm in. Your parents weren't exactly happy."

She slid their burger baskets off the serving tray and set it aside, then picked up a fresh cut steak fry and ate it. "You don't need to worry about being in any trouble. I'm the one who'll have to clean up the mess."

"Cardin," he began, but she cut him off.

"I started it, Trey. I'll finish it. All you have to do is play along."

He bit into his burger, chewed thoughtfully and swallowed, while she toyed with another fry. "I'm still trying to figure out what made me the bad guy."

"Besides the fact that you're bedding me?"

Trey arched a brow. "You really think anyone else would've got the same treatment? That this was just about our sleeping together?"

He was right. It wasn't. Her parents had reacted to her fraternizing with the enemy—exactly as she'd planned. "Sorry."

"Yeah. That's what I thought." He shook his head, then bit into his burger again.

For a moment she considered taking it all back, offering him a way out, telling the whole truth to her parents. Just as quickly, the moment passed.

Making Trey comfortable wasn't her objective. And even as the thought crossed her mind, she gave herself a bitch slap. He was doing her a huge favor. She should care about his feelings—and for even bigger reasons she wasn't ready to voice.

She looked up from her own basket of food to make him the offer, but held her tongue when she saw Tater Rawls standing right behind, his thick strawberry blonde hair tousled, a wicked gleam in his eye.

He held a finger to his lips to shush her, then brought both of his hands down hard on Trey's shoulders. "What the hell, man? You're sticking in town and you don't even tell your homeboy hello?"

"Goddamn you Tater Rawls." Trey reached for his napkin to clean up the food he'd spit all over the place. "Give a guy some warning, would ya?"

"How the hell ya been?" Tater asked, straddling the bench on Trey's side of the table, the two men shaking hands.

Cardin knew she wasn't going to eat the rest of her food, so she slid it across to Trey's best friend.

"Are you sure?" he asked. "I mean, I ate in back with Sandy before she clocked in, but I can always eat more."

"Then eat it. I'm going to duck out and let you and Trey catch up." Tater showing up like this gave her a chance to stop at home and shower, though sneaking upstairs without getting a grilling from Eddie was going to be tough.

"I'll see you later then," Trey said, grabbing her wrist and pulling her across the table for a kiss.

"Hey, hey, now. What's all this?" Tater asked, wrapping his hands around Cardin's burger and biting a quarter away.

"I guess you'll be hearing soon enough," Trey said, giving her a wink as he sat back down. "Cardin and I are engaged."

13

"YOU AND CARDIN WORTH? Engaged? What the hell?" Tater asked, having held his questions until he and Trey were alone. "Sounds like this is going to require a lot more explanation than we've got time for tonight, bro."

Trey had watched Cardin leave, then taken a bite of his burger and a gulp of his beer, ignoring the look of astonishment on Tater's face. The other man's doubts, however, he couldn't ignore. Not when Tater had been a rock through most of Trey's life.

The fact that he had made the blow sting all the more. "I figured you of all people would be happy for me. For us."

"I didn't say I wasn't happy." Tater paused as if wanting to make sure this time he was heard. "All I said was, what the hell? I mean, who wouldn't be happy?"

"Try the only other people we've told," Trey said, annoyed at too many things to name.

"I'm going to guess that's her folks."

"Bin-go." Trey reached for the pitcher to refill his mug. Tater reached for the one Cardin had left, shrugging an apology for taking something that belonged to Trey's woman.

Trey's woman. He liked the way that sounded. He liked it a lot. "Yeah. Eddie and Delta weren't too thrilled, though they finally gave us their blessing…"

Tater sputtered. "If you actually asked them, you're a braver soul than I."

Huh? "Why wouldn't I ask?"

"I'm not saying you shouldn't. But knowing her parents have been through a lot…" Gathering his thoughts, Tater screwed his mouth to one side, a motion that left him looking like a strawberry blond and freckled Popeye. "Did what Cardin tell you match up with the reality of how bad things are between them?"

Trey had to say no. So far, he hadn't seen much—if any—of the conflict between them that had driven Cardin to these lengths. "Not really, but then I've spent most of my time here with her. I gotta say, though, they did a pretty damn good job of taking sides against us."

Which was exactly what Cardin had wanted. Trey wondered if she was celebrating their response, or feeling as beat up as he was.

"Man, I don't get that at all." Tater swooped three fries through the pool of ketchup he'd poured and scarfed them down like a starving man—not one weighing the same one-eighty he had when they'd hit the football field as seniors. "I would think their siding together would be both of them jumping for joy, you know? What parents wouldn't want you for a son-in-law?"

That gave Trey a chuckle. "Thanks, but I can see where they're coming from, too. Life on the road isn't for everyone."

"It seems to suit you okay. You don't get back but once a year to say hello."

Did it suit him? Trey wondered. Or was it just what he did because he loved the work? And why was he even asking himself these questions? He and Cardin weren't really engaged. They weren't going to be living on the road, or anywhere together.

He was getting worked up over a relationship that wasn't going to have any real impact on his life. Except it already had. Over and over. Time after time. Starting in high school, long before that night when he'd leaned her into the wall, and growing so strong that when she'd come to see him the other morning in the pits, he'd felt it like the slam of a knee to his midsection.

"So," Tater started, between bites. "When *did* you guys finally hook up? And why the big hush?"

Trey pushed the rest of his burger aside, wiped his hands, and thought long and hard about telling Tater the truth, but knew he couldn't do that to Cardin. And as raw as he was feeling right now, as exposed and unsettled, this wasn't a good time to be making decisions that he might later regret.

He went with their well-rehearsed story. "Last year. At the Farron Fuels."

"What? You've been having phone sex all this time or something? Because I know you haven't been back."

His father had been living in Ohio when he'd passed, and nothing else would've brought Trey to Dahlia. "We've kept in touch by phone, yeah. And e-mail. And text messaging."

"Not my idea of a relationship, but whatever flips your switch."

Since Tater had opened the door… "And your idea of a relationship is to date Sandy Larabie?"

Tater laughed weakly. "It's all in good fun, man."

So Tater's romance was as much of a lie as Trey's. "Does Sandy know that?"

"It's not like that," Tater said, shaking his head. "We're just helping each other out. You know how these things are."

Trey knew all too well. Which made it even more interesting that the rumors of Tater and Sandy's romance had no more veracity than the ones which would soon be swirling about him and Cardin. "A man's gotta do what a man's gotta do."

"That's about the size of it," his friend said, polishing off the rest of the food in the basket Cardin had given him.

Trey wanted to ask what exactly was going on with the lanky goofball who'd been his best friend throughout school. But this wasn't the time or place, and he figured they didn't have enough beer for that conversation anyway.

Besides, even had they wanted to go there, Jeb Worth stopping by the table just then put a stop to all but shop talk.

He held his cowboy hat by the brim with both hands, and if his white shirt had had a badge pinned above the pocket, he couldn't have looked more like a lawman. "You boys mind if I join you?"

"Not at all, sir," Trey answered, though the older man had already settled across the table.

Wasting no time, he turned his attention to Trey. "Have you made up your mind?"

Apparently, this was Trey's day to be put on the spot. "Like I said yesterday, I'm going to have to take a look at the car first."

"What's this?" Tater asked, his gaze moving curiously from one man to the other. "What am I missing out on here?"

Though he spoke to Tater, Jeb kept his sharp gray gaze on Trey. "I asked Whip to drive White Lightning in the Moonshine Run."

"No kidding." Tater's hangdog expression gained him no sympathy from Trey. "If I was the type to feel sorry for myself, I'd have to dub this nobody tells me anything day."

Trey cringed. He and Cardin hadn't yet mentioned the engagement to her grandfather. He waited for Jeb to prod Tater for more, but the older man's focus was adamant. "You need to come out to the house. Take a look. The race is in a couple of weeks."

"Then how about tomorrow afternoon? Between three

and four? I can head over about the same time Cardin leaves for work."

"What's Cardin got to do with anything?"

Tater let out a loud whoop and smacked his hand against the table so hard, both his and Trey's food baskets hopped, and the two inches of beer left in the pitcher sloshed from side to side. "Then I'm not the only one who didn't know."

"Know what?" Jeb asked, and Trey could only shake his head.

Tater slapped him on the shoulder. "Ol' Whip here's about to become your grandson-in-law."

DELTA LET EDDIE TALK HER into following him home. She would've felt a whole lot better about coming here if it wasn't just the bad times that had them looking to each other for strength. Why did it take this unsettling news, this…mess to turn their conversations civil again?

It wasn't even yet ten o'clock, she realized, climbing the steps to where Eddie stood waiting, backed into the screen door and holding the front one open with his hand, and yet she felt like she could fall asleep on a dime. She chalked it up to the rollercoaster of feelings that had scooped her up yesterday and hadn't yet set her back on her feet.

Oh, who was she kidding? Exhaustion had been her constant companion since Eddie's accident over a year ago. She wasn't cut out to be the peacemaker Cardin was. She was more the type to cut and run, and hadn't even known it. All this time, she'd thought herself strong, a rock that could withstand anything.

But then she stepped into the living room she hadn't seen in four months, and the emotional pummeling she'd taken this last year came at her in one big choking fist. She couldn't draw a breath. She barely made it to the sofa before breaking down, burying her face in her hands.

She wanted to be left alone. She wanted to cry in peace. She wanted Eddie to hold her. She wanted to lay her head on his shoulder. The fact that her contradictions were the only things clear in her life had her laughing while she cried.

Eddie had been pacing in front of the sofa. At the sound of her hysterical gasps, he stopped. He tried to squat down in front of her, but his leg had him perching on the edge of the chair angled to the sofa. "You want a glass of water? A whiskey? A cup of tea?"

She shook her head, fell back and let the brown and blue plaid cushions swallow her. "I want my life back, Eddie Worth. That's what I want. Can you do that for me?"

He got up to pace again, this time his limp more noticeable as it always was when he was stressed. "Our daughter's going to marry Whip Davis, and you want me to give you back *your* life? Isn't it Cardin's life we should be trying to save?"

"Cardin's made her choice, Eddie. Anything we might have done won't do a bit of good now. She's gone."

"Goddammit, she is not gone," he said, slamming the heel of his hand against the end of the fireplace mantel. The twelve frames holding Cardin's school pictures didn't even budge. "I've got to fix this. There's got to be something I can do."

"I tried to tell you to fix things four months ago." The words were sharp, harsh, but she couldn't stop them.

Both hands braced on the mantel, he hung his head, cursed beneath his breath. "So this is my fault, too? First my father doesn't talk to me, then you leave, and now this with Cardin?"

"What's the common denominator, Eddie?" she asked, this time more softly. "There's only one thing I see."

He shoved away from the fireplace. "And yet I'm the one

with pins holding my leg together. The one who got slammed into the lube pit at Morgan and Son's garage. The one lucky to have gone out of there in an ambulance and not a wagon from the morgue."

"We all know that, Eddie. We all know exactly how bad things were." She kicked off her espadrilles, tucking her legs up under her. "But you're the only one who doesn't seem to realize that they've gotten better."

He cut a disbelieving gaze toward her. "Better?"

"Yes, better. You're not dead, and even if you do have pins in your hip, you walk. You're not in a wheelchair. Your limp's barely noticeable most of the time." She cut off his attempted interruption with a wave. "And, yes, I'm sure you still have pain. That you'll always have pain. I hate that's the way it is. I hate it more than you can imagine. But I don't understand why you can't be happy unless the rest of us are suffering, too."

"Who said I'm happy? Or that I want anyone else to suffer?"

"Nobody has to say it. We can see it. And maybe you're *not* happy. It's just that you don't seem quite as miserable when your misery has company." Could he really not be aware of that? How he had brought everyone down with him? Or was he just beyond caring, so wrapped up in his own pain?

"You don't understand," he said tiredly, scrubbing both hands through his hair that was thick, longer than she'd seen it in awhile, and as black as their daughter's.

She sat straighter, her elbow on the arm of the couch, her fingers gouging the fabric. "Then make me understand, Eddie. We've been together twenty-six years. You've always been able to make me understand."

He gave a sarcastic snort, his boot heels clicking on the hard wood as he started pacing again. "I might be able to if I understood any of it myself."

"Any of what?" she pressed, because this was farther than they'd come in a very long time, and she wasn't going to give up on him now.

"Why this had to happen."

Did he mean the accident? What had happened to their marriage? How his injury had changed him? Their daughter choosing a good man whose lifestyle would take her away from the only home she'd ever known? "I'm not sure what you're getting at. Why what had to happen?"

He rubbed at the back of his neck. "I went to the garage that day because Alex called and told me things were getting heated between Aubrey and Dad."

Delta hadn't known about Alex Morgan's phone call, or much of anything else. She was sitting in the same dark room as everyone else who wondered how the fight had started. "Then I would say the reason this happened is that you were doing your duty as a son."

"I get that," he told her. "What I don't get is what went so wrong. What was going on between Dad and Aubrey that it got so out of hand? That Aubrey would strike a man of Dad's age?"

"Aubrey had a lot of problems."

"I don't give a shit about Aubrey," Eddie shot back. "I want to know why Dad won't tell me. Why is it such a secret? Who is he protecting? If I'd hit my head instead of my hip, we wouldn't even be sitting here. Yet he doesn't think I deserve to know the truth?"

Delta sat stunned. This wasn't about the physical injury at all. Eddie was suffering because his father refused to tell him why he'd almost lost his life.

At the time of the accident, she'd been too worried about Eddie to care about the reasons for the fight. Her husband's recovery had occupied her emotions and her energy for weeks. The cause of the fight had drifted away, become unimportant, non-existent. Yet Eddie had been nursing a need to know all this time.

She'd never imagined his father's silence was behind so much of the family's grief. She didn't think her father-in-law had confided in anyone, not even Cardin. She wondered if Whip knew, if his father had told him before he died.

If it would save Delta's marriage to dig up the answer, she would. "Does your father know how you feel?"

"He doesn't care, D. He's not going to talk about it. He's got Whip to drive his car now, so all he'll tell me is to get over it and move on."

Delta didn't believe that for a minute. She knew how deeply Jeb loved his son. But she was also well acquainted with his pride, how often he let it dictate his decisions. And, unfortunately, Jeb's pride was a trait his son had inherited in spades.

If Delta wanted to put an end to what had apparently been blown out of proportion by two hardheaded men, she was going to have to do it alone.

She got up and went to him, taking hold of his hand. "Your father loves you, Eddie. Your daughter loves you. And I love you very very much. We all care if you move beyond it, but that doesn't matter because you're the one who needs to want to. And until you reach that point, I don't see anything about the status quo changing."

His mouth twisted. "Does that mean you're not going to spend the night?"

Oh, she was tempted. Four months was a long time to be without her husband, to sleep alone, to miss his body beside her in bed. "Me spending the night with you won't solve anything."

"I can think of one very big thing it would solve."

"That's because you're using the wrong head to think."

He brought up his hands to cup her face while he looked into her eyes. "I miss you. I need you."

Tempted, tempted, tempted. "You miss sex. You need to get laid."

"Same thing, sweetheart. Same thing," he said before he brought his mouth down on hers and slipped his tongue inside.

He had been her weakness for more than half of her life. Trying to find the strength to resist him now was pure futility. She didn't even try telling herself that sleeping with him would be nothing but physical pleasure. It never was that simple with them. It never had been. And he'd opened up more to her tonight than he had in a year.

Her need for him was astounding. She let him hold her, let him kiss her, but she was the one who started taking off her clothes. And when he growled like a man whose pain only she could assuage, she stripped down to her skin faster than she ever had before.

14

CARDIN HAD NEVER THOUGHT SHE WOULD miss her own apartment so dreadfully, but stepping out of the shower onto her bathmat dotted with circles of brown, pink and sea green and reaching for the matching bath sheet, she had to admit that she did.

As comfortable as she felt in the house where she'd grown up, it was nice to be home, surrounded by her own things, not having to worry about using up all the hot water, or getting caught running around in her panties and bra.

She'd headed for her parents' place after leaving the ice house, only to reach the end of the drive and find Delta's car parked outside next to Eddie's. She'd shut off the lights on Jeb's truck and backed quietly out the way she'd come in, smiling all the while.

The stress inflicted by the last few hours would be worth it if her parents' displeasure with her marriage to Trey was what got them back together.

Her marriage to Trey. She ignored the thrill the thought gave her and turned her mind to her make-believe fiancé. He had to be feeling like a punching bag.

Hopefully, getting to spend time tonight with Tater would soothe the verbal bruising her parents had left behind when he'd been so sweet as to ask for their permission to marry her. She and Trey had gone over their story a dozen times today, but he'd never told her that he was going to ask for their blessing.

He was taking so much heat, and getting so little in return, that she had to wonder why he'd agreed to her plan. She didn't believe for a minute it was only the sex. He didn't need to play her fiancé to get her into bed. That would take no more than the snap of his fingers, as had been borne out since the morning she'd visited the Corley hauler.

The attraction between them had been expected, but she was still caught off guard by the level of heat. What she was feeling for him wasn't the stuff of a fake engagement. Her emotions were engaged all the way to her soul.

And that was hard to handle when she knew he'd soon be gone.

In the meantime, while hoping their faux romance worked to get her family back together, she planned to enjoy him immensely—the conversations, the teasing and flirting and definitely the sex.

He was already at the house when she got there, but he wasn't inside. He was sitting on the open tailgate of his truck, his hands curled over the edges, his lower legs swinging. It was dark out, and she wasn't sure if that was the reason why, but her body tingled everywhere with a rush of anticipation.

"I was beginning to think you weren't coming back," he said, and she slowed her approach to make him wait even longer.

"Why would you think something like that?" she asked, her voice breathless to her own ears.

He kicked his legs, kicked, kicked… "I don't know. Maybe you decided being with me for a few months wasn't worth the cost of your parents' disapproval."

"I knew they were going to disapprove. That was the whole point." But then, he knew that.

"That doesn't mean you were ready for it," he said, and stopped kicking.

She came closer, stepped between his knees, laid her hands on his thighs. His muscles tensed. "It's not their reaction I wasn't ready for."

He hooked his ankles behind her, nudging his boots to her bottom and bringing her closer still. "I'm going to take a stab in the dark and say you're wondering the same thing I am."

"What's that?"

"Why we waited seven years to scratch this itch."

She shouldn't ask. She really shouldn't. But she couldn't help herself. She wanted to know. She ran her hands from his thighs to his waist, spreading her fingers over his rib cage, marveling at how much bigger than her he was, how much stronger, how much better.

She wasn't sure she would do for him what he was doing for her. "Is that all this is? An itch?"

"What?" He dropped back onto his elbows, distancing himself from her question. "You want to drop the fake from our engagement?"

"That's not what I said." She pulled free from the circle of his legs and made her way from his truck to the huge spreading oak that had been growing for decades in the front yard. She turned to lean against it, her hands behind her. "What are you getting out of helping me, Trey? I mean, if you're just here for the sex, that's fine. But I don't think you are."

He stayed silent, and though she couldn't see his eyes in the dark, she could tell that he'd looked away. She didn't know if that meant he hated being found out, or if his own behavior shamed him. She didn't want him to think either.

All she wanted was the truth. "Am I off base? Is this just unfinished business?"

He sat up, taking a minute to answer. "I feel like whatever

I say, it's going to be wrong. That you'll want to hear something else."

His admission caused a tightening in her belly. "Just tell me the truth. I'm not going to be mad or hurt. I'm just curious. I want to know what it is *I'm* doing for *you*."

He laughed, a deep guttural sound that sent her thoughts tumbling toward sex. It wasn't like she'd never had it before sleeping with him. She'd even had what she considered good sex. It was just that Trey went beyond that...and he took her with him.

"What you do for me, huh?" He boosted himself off the tailgate. The truck bounced, the shocks creaking. "Are you sure you want to go there?"

He was still far enough away that she felt brave. "I wouldn't have asked if I didn't."

"Even if it's sex? Just sex? Nothing but sex?"

How could hearing him say that one word make her melt? It was one word, three letters. She'd heard it spoken thousands of times. But the way it sounded when he said it, like it came from a part of him that needed to be in her or he would cease to exist, had her quivering and spineless. "I just don't want to feel like I'm the only one benefiting here."

"Trust me, sweetheart. I wouldn't be here if this arrangement wasn't mutually beneficial," he said, but that still didn't answer her question.

He had reached her now, and he braced his hands on the tree trunk, one on either side of her head. At this distance, she could see enough of his eyes to tell that this conversation wasn't easy for him. That his teasing, and his flirting, served as a mask.

She wanted to know what he was holding back. "If you tell me how you're benefiting, I'll let you have all the sex you want."

His eyes flashed. "You're a cruel woman, Cardin Worth."

If there had ever been a time to go for broke... "I'm the woman you can't wait to get naked."

"Like I said. Cruel." And then he popped the button on her jeans, opened the zipper, and slid a hand into her panties.

"If I'm cruel, that's because you've taught me well," she said, breathing hard, spreading her legs, giving him the access he needed to reach the part of her she was desperate he find.

"Your right leg. Lift it. There." He bit off a nasty word to go with his nasty laugh. "I can't believe how wet you are."

She couldn't believe how it felt for his finger to fill her, to push in and out, how it felt for him to use his thumb on her clit while they stood there in the dark beneath the moon and the tree. "You know I'm going to come."

"God, I hope so." He fairly growled out the words.

"You know I can get noisy."

"I love that you get noisy."

"Move to the left a bit. Up, down, no right there. Right there." She shivered, shuddered, sucked in a sharp breath. If all he was here for was sex—though she knew without a doubt he had more on his mind—she decided it couldn't be a bad thing.

He lowered his head, rubbed his cheek against hers, then her jaw, her neck, inhaling deeply and making her so glad she'd showered. She dug her fingers into the balls of his shoulders and held on. He nuzzled beneath her ear, sucked on the skin there, giving her the first hickey she'd had since high school.

The thought took her back, and though she didn't linger in the past—the present felt too good—she forced herself to admit that she'd never gotten over the night she'd seen him with his pants down, and what he was doing to her now was what she'd wanted from him even then.

As his middle finger entered her, his index and ring fingers slid through her folds. She wiggled against him, wished she could climb him, wanted him deeper. Wanted things from him no other man had made her crave. Things she didn't know enough to name.

He amazed her, learned her, worked her deftly, his breath hot against her neck where he said things she couldn't hear. She didn't need to hear the words he spoke to know their meaning. He was meant for her, had been made for her. They fit together too well to be a random match.

"Trey," she said, whimpering, reaching, unable to get there from here.

"C'mon, baby," he said, wedging a knee between her legs, lifting one of her thighs.

It worked. All of it. The angle, his stroke, the pressure from his thumb. She ground against him, crawled onto his hand, clawed at his shoulders and came. Sensation burst between her legs, down her thighs, up her back. She was a spring unloading, a spool unwinding. She didn't want it to stop.

Trey stroked her, gentled her, eased her back, giving her the time she needed before pulling his hand from her body, his leg from beneath her thigh.

"I'm not so sure that was the best idea," she finally said, her voice cracking, her leg muscles all wobbly jelly.

"I think it was a damn good one," Trey countered, doing her the favor of closing her jeans.

Her back scraped the tree with her movements, and she winced. "You're not the one who's never going to walk straight again."

He made a choking sound. "I'm dying here, so I'm pretty sure walking would be the least of my problems."

"That wasn't fair. We should've gone inside." God, she was selfish. "Done things right."

"Are you saying there was something wrong with that?" he asked. "Because wrong is just about the last word that comes to my mind."

She'd insulted him. Wonderful. He'd just given her the most amazing gift, and the first thing out of her mouth was a complaint. "That's not what I meant. I just feel guilty that I got all the pleasure out of that. That you—"

"I plan to get mine," he promised her. "But don't think you're the only one who enjoyed that."

Why did that make her blush? "I don't think any enjoyment you got came close to what I felt."

"And that's why you need to stop thinking," he told her, taking a step into her space, hovering close without touching her. "At least until you know me better."

She reached up, running her fingers through his caramel-colored hair where it brushed the top of his ear. "You're definitely not what I'm used to."

He turned his head, kissed her wrist. "Your previous fiancés haven't taken care of you?"

"I haven't had previous fiancés, but no. The guys I've dated haven't been as—" her fingers paused "—intent on my needs as you've been."

"That's a shame, but it does explain a few things."

"Such as?"

"Why you asked me to play your fiancé instead of tapping someone local who you'd dated."

She lowered her hand, clenched her fingers at her waist. "Tapping someone I'd dated wouldn't have made sense. I needed someone who was guaranteed to upset my parents. Besides, who would believe I was suddenly engaged to someone the whole town knew was my ex?"

"But being suddenly engaged to me was? Believable?" he asked, pressing...but for what?

Cardin ducked away from him and walked to his truck, hopping onto the tailgate where she'd found him sitting earlier. "It's not hard to imagine we'd kept in touch, developed a long-distance relationship. Especially with everyone knowing the way things were between us in high school."

He took his time moving, climbing up to sit beside her, settling in, scooting close. His pinky caught hers where their hands rested at their hips. "And here all this time I thought it was just me."

"You're kidding me, right?"

"Nope. One hundred percent serious." He slipped more of his finger through hers. "Until I saw you watching that night at Tater's, I wasn't sure you knew I was alive."

She had no idea what to say. She'd had the biggest crush on him in high school. She'd rarely had reason to drive by his house, but had always filled up at the service station where he'd worked, and made up excuses to talk to Tater whenever Trey was around. She'd cut down the hallways where his classes were, then had to rush across campus to get to her own.

How could he not have known how she felt? She'd given off so many signals, Pammy Mercer had nagged her constantly to take a class in subtle before she was put away for being a public annoyance.

"I knew you were alive. As much as you watched me on the football field, I watched you," she said, but cut herself off before adding *all the time.*

"You left quite a carbon footprint with all the gas you used."

"I took the long way everywhere," she admitted, and then admitted more. "And I let Pammy siphon from my tank for her car."

He laughed. "You didn't really use that much. I never filled it up all the way."

It felt so good to laugh, to remember, to feel that same rush of excitement she'd felt every time their eyes had met, every time she'd sneaked a peek and found him looking.

She leaned her head on his shoulder. "So why did it take us so long to hook up?"

"Neither one of us was very bright?"

"Speak for yourself."

"I am. I'm having a lot of trouble with the line between fake and real."

She didn't want to imagine what he meant. She didn't want him getting her hopes up. Not when there was a very big chance of her heart ending up broken if she gave her expectations wings.

And so all she said was, "If there is a line."

"We've been at this for less than two days. I imagine it will take time to figure out a lot of things." He wrapped an arm around her shoulders and hugged her close. "Communication, remember?"

What she remembered was that their engagement had never been anything but a lie. That didn't stop her from cuddling close. "One day you're going to make some lucky woman a great fiancé."

She could only hope he met the woman on the road and never brought her back to Dahlia. She didn't think she'd survive seeing him as part of a happy couple that didn't include her.

"You're assuming that I plan to get married."

"I guess I am, yeah."

He ran his hand up and down her arm. "The things your mother said earlier about taking a wife on the road? I've thought those same things before. About the type of husband I'd be. The kind of life I could give to a woman. She's not the only one with those concerns."

And yet, Cardin couldn't imagine being apart from him if they were really a couple. "Whither thou goest, I will go."

"What's that?"

She hadn't been aware she'd spoken aloud. "I was just thinking."

"About?"

"How I would feel picking up and following a husband. Leaving my life behind to live his."

"If we were really engaged, you mean," he said, and it almost sounded as if he were testing the waters, sounding her out, wanting to know what she would say if he asked her to be his wife.

She was imagining it. She had to be. "If I were in love with someone who asked me to."

"That would be a huge thing to ask of someone, wouldn't it?" He sighed, and held her close as together they stared off into the dark. "Especially someone you loved."

15

TREY LAY AWAKE BESIDE Cardin long after he should've been asleep. He couldn't get their near-midnight discussion out of his mind. Especially since they were here in his house, lying naked, as if their being together was the most natural thing in the world.

He'd felt more awkward in relationships that were supposed to be real. He didn't like what that said about him, but had no idea what it said about this thing with Cardin. They were not engaged. That much he did know. But as for everything else…

He eased away from her, taking care to be as silent as possible, finding his jeans and tugging them on, then exiting the house, leaving the front door propped open. The ground was cold beneath his bare feet, and the nip in the air frosting the wee hours chilled his skin.

He found a pair of work boots in the passenger floor of his truck, and a balled up denim workshirt in the seat. He put them on, then headed for the barn where he had yet to get anything done.

The sooner he took care of his business here in Dahlia, the sooner he'd get back to his team. He figured a couple of months on the barn and outbuildings, a month on the property, two months at least on the house. Maybe another to take care of the legal matters—bank accounts, insurance settlements, etc.—he'd been putting off since his father's death.

Six months max spent finishing up things here, and then he'd get back to work with his team. He wasn't on a strict schedule, and since he'd planned to do all the work himself, he'd known he was looking at several weeks. But he'd never planned for Cardin time. He'd had no reason to.

He sure as hell had reason now.

He pulled the string, and the single bulb dangling on a wire from the ceiling flickered on, lighting only a small part of the barn, and illuminating the corners just enough to give life to the shadows. The barn was a small one, with only two stalls, and it hadn't sheltered animals at any time during Trey's life.

The stalls were used for storage, while work benches and multidrawer chests lined the opposite wall. As careless as Trey's father had been about so many things, including marital fidelity, he'd been meticulous with his tools—power, precision or otherwise.

Trey had been twelve when his parents had split—old enough to understand that his mother was leaving, too young to understand it wasn't somehow his fault.

Years later, he had discovered the reason. That his fine up-standing father had slipped. Just once. But far enough and hard enough that Trey was left bewildered. For so long he'd felt that his mother had wronged him and his father both, and he'd hated her for leaving.

But learning of his father's indiscretion, and that his mother's younger sister was the one it was with, had Trey thinking a whole lot less of the man who'd reared him. Still, until Aubrey's gambling had spun out of control, Trey had been the only one to hold him in less than high regard.

Which is why his father fighting with Jeb Worth made no sense. It was like two white hats duking it out.

The only explanation that Trey had come up with was that his father had asked Jeb for money. And even that was thin.

For one thing, everyone in town knew that Jeb pinched every penny he had. For another, Aubrey would never borrow money from the people he knew. A bank, sure. A loan shark, maybe. His son, definitely.

But not friends or acquaintances. So, if it wasn't money, what had it been? It had to be big. It had to be personal. The stakes had to be huge. And Trey was at a complete loss.

"Did you decide the only way to get any work done was to do it when I was sleeping? Since I always seem to be in your way?"

He looked down at the worn brake shoes in his hands, and smiled to himself before he turned. He'd heard Cardin come into the barn, but had to wrap up his thoughts before allowing her to distract him. That's what she did, each and every time. And he found that he didn't mind at all. That, in fact, he liked it.

"You asked me today what I was hoping to get out of this deal." He saw how sleepy she was when she nodded. Her eyes were puffy, squinting as she focused, her droopy lids keeping her from it. Her hair was a tangled curtain around her shoulders. He didn't have to do this now. "Why don't you go back to sleep? I'll tell you tomorrow."

"No, I want you to tell me now. Tomorrow you'll forget, or find a reason not to."

Scary how aptly she had him pegged. "I thought sticking close to you might get me closer to finding out what your grandfather and my dad fought about."

"But I don't know," she told him, hopping up to sit cross-legged on a storage chest. "I'm not even sure Eddie knows. It's a sore spot with him. One I think he's picked at too many times."

Trey chunked the brake shoes in the trash barrel. "If he did know, do you think he would tell your mother?"

"Of course." She twisted her hair into a tail and tossed it over her shoulder. "Unless it was something Jeb had sworn him to secrecy over. And even then, he'd tell her that much."

"Maybe he really doesn't know."

"I'm thinking there's only one person who does." Her head canted to one side, she considered him intently. "The person who thinks enough of you to ask you to drive White Lightning in the Moonshine Run."

Her grandfather was definitely his best bet, and if it took driving for him in the race… "I told Jeb I'd be over this afternoon to take a look at the car. I figured I'd head out about the same time you go to work."

"You know, Jeb didn't ask you to drive for him because we were engaged." She worked her way down from her perch, came close and wrapped her arms around him. "He asked you because you're Butch Corley's crew chief, and because he wants nothing more than to be a bad dog like Butch. So you already had the in you needed. You don't have to go along with my plan."

"Yeah, but our engagement makes that *in* a whole lot more valuable. And pretty much makes me privy to any family secrets."

"It also means you have to put up with the family drama, you know."

"The perks are worth it." He nuzzled the top of her head, rocking her side to side. "You smell so damned good."

"Oh, I never got a chance to tell you." She leaned back to look up at him. "When I went by the house to clean up after work, my mother's car was there. I went back to my apartment to shower. Just in case, you know? I didn't want to barge in on a reconciliation."

"I love it when a plan comes together."

"Speaking of which," she said, stepping away, "I plan to

go back to bed now. I'll be back out to help after I get my beauty sleep."

He let her go. He didn't follow. He knew if he lay down beside her again it would be hours before she got her sleep. She had work tomorrow and needed the rest, but as far as beauty went? She could get by with never sleeping again.

TREY HADN'T BEEN TO CARDIN'S house in, well, ever that he could recall.

If she'd thrown any parties here, he didn't remember. He would've come if he'd been invited. He would've crashed if he hadn't been. Not because he had a reputation to uphold, or because that was the behavior expected of him. No, he would've been here because of Cardin.

The Worth's big two-story farmhouse sat on almost two acres. Jeb's garage was hidden from street view behind it. Trey followed the driveway around, parking behind Cardin's red Mini Cooper. For all they'd used Jeb's truck so far, she needn't have gone to the trouble of borrowing it. Of course, none of that had been the plan…

He'd barely had time to climb down from his truck before Jeb was out of the house, the screen door slamming off its frame as he crossed the yard. "I was about to give up on you."

"Sorry, sir. Time got away from me." Though the truth was that Cardin hadn't let him go.

"Well, you're here now." Jeb brought his hand down on Trey's shoulder, and turned him toward the garage. "There isn't much to be done about the delay."

He said delay like they were on a deadline. Trey decided now was not the time to look for an opening in their conversation to ask about the fight. They obviously weren't going to have any conversation. At least not one that wasn't about the Moonshine Run and the car.

After lifting away the fiberglass hood, he and Jeb worked in near silence for the next hour. Near, because like a surgeon asking for instruments, Trey did the same. He had to. He was unfamiliar with what Jeb had on hand, and learned quickly Cardin's grandfather hadn't scrimped on his tools.

Neither did he scrimp on sweat equity. Jeb got up to his elbows in the motor right next to Trey. His hands were seasoned, experienced, but they were also arthritic, his joints swollen and twisted, and more than a few times he had to stop to let Trey take over.

That was when Trey asked questions about this part and that, what results Jeb had seen from a particular adjustment to the carburetor, how well the car responded to one timing tweak versus another. They ran basic tests and measurements with the computer equipment set up in the garage. And then they started it up and listened.

It was Tuesday. Two days since Trey last had his head under the hood of a car. He was surprised how much he missed the stringent smells of fluids and fuel, the staccato click of a ratchet turning, the sting of nicking a knuckle on a sharp edge.

He wasn't sure how he'd thought he'd last six months without working.

He wasn't sure how he would stand cutting short his time with Cardin to get back to what he loved to do.

He straightened, reached for a red shop rag, wiped his hands and shook his head. "I'll have to take it out to know for sure, but from what I can see here, you've got a hell of a machine."

Rather than beaming with pride as Trey would've expected from someone who'd been given a resounding *well done,* Jeb stood at the side of the Chevy Nova, his gaze lingering over the motor that appeared to have been spit-shined before Trey ever went to work.

"You know, folks'll say winners are born, not made, but I don't believe it for a minute. It's more obvious when talking about a car, because an engine born in Detroit isn't going to give the same performance as one that's been made by hands like yours or mine."

"You'll get no argument from me," Trey said. He wasn't sure what Jeb was getting at, but did know he'd be smart to keep what points he could in his favor.

Jeb leaned into his forearms where he'd braced them on the car frame. "Your father was a good man, Whip. He did his best bringing you up. He didn't have things as easy as some, but being as it was only the two of you for a lot of years, he did a fine job of making you into a winner."

Trey didn't acknowledge the compliment except to nod. He didn't say anything at all. If Jeb was getting ready to talk about the fight, a single wrongly spoken word might stop him. And if he was making his way toward another point, Trey didn't want to derail him before he did.

"I've been bobbing around here like one of those helium-filled balloons ever since you said you'd think about driving." Jeb straightened to his full height, turning to face Trey. "But when I found out you were going to marry my granddaughter, it was like someone had cut the string holding me down. I've been flying ever since."

That was not at all what Trey had expected to hear, and he was damn glad he'd kept his mouth shut. "I'm glad you approve, sir. I know it was important to Cardin that you did. I wish her parents had been as pleased with the news."

Jeb gave a dismissive wave of his hand. "Those two can't even figure out which way is up these days. Don't pay them any mind."

"If you say so, sir," Trey said, fighting a grin.

"And stop with the sir crapola. I may be close to three times your age, but we're family now, and calling me Jeb will do." He began storing away all the tools they'd used. "Now, I think a party's in order, don't you?"

Huh? "A party?"

"An engagement party. We can celebrate that and you winning the Moonshine Run at the same time."

Right. Because a race held the same gravitas as his own granddaughter's future. Cardin was going to love this. "Are you sure that's a good idea?"

Jeb snorted as he took the timing light Trey handed him. "Why the hell wouldn't it be?"

"I was under the impression that the friction in the family wasn't only between her parents."

Scowling, Jeb shook his head. "That son of mine wouldn't leave well enough alone. And I told him if he couldn't shut up, then I would. And I did."

Trey took another very careful step. "I was made to understand that the rift between you and Eddie was because of your fight with my father."

"Maybe it is. Maybe it isn't." Jeb shut and locked the tool chest's drawers, then rolled the case up against the wall. "The story of that day has never been anyone's but mine or Aubrey's to tell. I'm not much of a bard, and Aubrey took it with him when he went to meet his maker."

Trey wanted to press, but Jeb's words rang with an unarguable finality, and so he let the subject go. He didn't bury it, or sweep it under any rug. He just left it sitting where he could easily reach it when it was time to try again.

16

As SHE PULLED JEB'S TRUCK into Headlights ten minutes after four, Cardin found herself dreading the juggling act to come. The tables she could handle. Avoiding her parents was going to be the challenge, since both would be there for at least half of her shift.

She wanted her mother and father to talk to each other, not to hound and badger her—though, she supposed, their hounding and badgering was a small price to pay to see them working toward a common goal, which it seemed they just might be.

They'd spent the night under the same roof for the first time in months, and their cars were cozied up side by side in the lot. Cardin took those two signs as progress, and had just dropped Jeb's truck keys into her purse when the ice house's back door opened.

Sandy Larabie came out, folding a stick of gum into her mouth. "I was beginning to wonder if you were ever going to show up to relieve me."

Cardin looked across the parking lot. The crowd wasn't any larger than usual for this time of day. Whoever was working with Sandy wouldn't have a bit of trouble covering the tables until Cardin clocked in. "Well, I'm here now, so you can leave with a clear conscience."

Despite her earlier reprimand, Sandy didn't seem in any

hurry to move. "Tater told me your news last night. I guess congratulations are in order."

"Only if you want to offer them," Cardin said, slinging her purse strap over her shoulder.

Apparently Sandy didn't, because what she said next was, "Word's traveling pretty fast. So are the rumors and questions."

Questions Cardin was ready for. But rumors? Pregnancy was the only gossipy thing that came to mind, and her relationship with Trey being long distance—or so they'd claimed—until recently, easily squashed that. "What kind of rumors?"

"That your family is closing ranks with Whip."

"What for?"

"To keep the truth about the fight between his father and Jeb from getting out."

How ridiculous! "You're kidding me, right? That's the most stupid thing I've ever heard."

Sandy shrugged. "No one believes it was about money. So a lot of people are saying there's a secret to hide."

"Well, if you're digging to find out, you can stop. I don't know what happened. Neither does Trey. And the idea that we would close ranks over anything is just silly."

"I don't know. Jeb could've asked anyone to drive for him in the Moonshine Run. Why did he wait until the last minute and ask Whip?"

Well, that was a big fat *duh*. "Because he's the best? Because no one can do what he does with a car?"

"Maybe. Maybe not."

"Maybe people should look at the obvious instead of looking stupid," Cardin said, wondering what a nice guy like Tater Rawls could possibly see in this woman.

"Hey, don't blame the messenger," Sandy said, taking a step toward her Civic. "I just thought it would be the neighborly thing to do, giving you fair warning."

"I appreciate it," Cardin responded, telling one of the biggest lies of this whole ordeal. She didn't appreciate it at all. Not the joy she sensed Sandy taking in being the bearer of bad tidings, nor the fact that people were talking about her and Trey.

She'd expected the talk, sure; that's what happened when engagements were announced. But she hadn't expected speculation that they were together for any reason other than being in love.

If the gossip ended up making things worse between Eddie and Delta, or between Eddie and Jeb, she swore she was going to kick her own ass so hard, she would never again be able to sit without hurting.

She wanted to talk to Trey. Now. She needed to talk to Trey. Now. But he was with her grandfather, and she had a shift to get through. Talking would have to wait.

She stashed her purse in her locker in the employees' tiny break room, tied on her pocketed apron and smoothed down her skirt. She clocked in and headed for the kitchen. Her mother waylaid her in front of her office.

Once Cardin was inside, Delta shut the door. "I know you're busy. This will only take a minute. But your father and I were talking last night."

Ugh, after her run-in with Sandy, this was the last thing Cardin needed. "More objections, I guess?"

"Of a sort, yes. But we gave you our blessing, so please give me some credit," Delta said, arching a brow.

Cardin nodded. "What's up?"

"I know Whip needs to be out at his place to do the cleanup, but there's no reason for the two of you to spend your nights there, too, since you're obviously unable to spend them apart." Delta circled around her desk. "This isn't about me being a prude. I'm thinking of the lack of creature comforts."

Yeah. Not a lot of those out there, Cardin mused, though

the camping wasn't without appeal. She leaned one shoulder against the file cabinet. "It's not so bad. Besides, Trey's a bit of an insomniac. If he wakes up in the middle of the night, he heads out to the barn. If he stayed with me in the house, his coming and going might wake Daddy and Jeb."

"His comings and goings won't wake anyone if you're staying in your apartment."

Uh… "Are you moving home?"

"Yes and no. I thought I'd stay upstairs and let you and Whip have your place."

Not exactly what Cardin wanted to hear, but close enough that a huge grin spread over her face.

Her mother did her best to wipe it away. "Don't go reading anything into that. I'm not back with your father."

"Are you sure? I saw your car over there last night."

Delta's face reddened. "We were talking about you and Whip. That's all. Even if he does end up taking you on the road, there's no reason you can't be comfortable while you're here."

"Are you sure your moving back home isn't about sending a message that Daddy's not on the market?"

"Don't tell me you've been listening to those rumors."

"Listening to? I can hardly avoid them. Paying attention to? Not so much."

"Good. Because Eddie and I will work things out in our own way. And if there comes a time when he's back on the market—" she waved a hand "—well, that time's not now. That's all that matters."

Cardin started to go, but since she had her mother's ear… "There are other rumors out there, you know. Already. About me and Trey."

"I'm not surprised. Dahlia lives for rumors." Delta sat, picking up her pencil. "Are they bothering you?"

She'd only just heard about them from Sandy, so no. "Apparently people are saying that Trey and I getting married is about closing ranks to keep the secret of the fight from getting out."

Delta screwed up her face. "Well, that's ludicrous. The secret of the fight is safe with Jeb. And no doubt he'll take it to his grave just as Aubrey did."

That's what she'd thought, but just to be sure… "Then Daddy doesn't know what happened?"

"Not why it happened, no. And his coming to terms with that is what we're working on now."

"By working on, do you mean sleeping with him?" The question slipped out, and caused her mother to gasp.

"Cardin Serenity Worth. That is none of your business."

Cardin laughed, but was prevented from saying anything else by the office door opening and Eddie walking in. "D, have you seen Car— There you are. You don't feel like working today, or what?"

"You're awfully bossy for a boss," she told her father, kissing his cheek and giving him a wink before scuttling out and closing her parents inside the small room.

She wanted to lock them in, hold on to the door knob and keep it closed until she knew for certain they would come out happily married again. The fact that they were talking was such a good sign. Even if she wasn't thrilled that they were talking about her.

Oh, well, she'd made that bed, and had to lie in it. And really, it wasn't bad at all since she was sharing it with Trey.

"GUESS WHAT?" CARDIN asked, bounding into the barn where Trey had actually made progress following his afternoon with Jeb.

It was almost nine, and Cardin was still wearing her Headlights uniform. He liked her Headlights uniform. The T-shirt that showed off her breasts. The short skirt that reminded him of the things she could do with her long legs.

Then he realized what her still wearing her uniform meant. "You know there's no water to the tub in the bathroom."

"That's okay," she told him, her smile wide and excited. "We're going to spend the night at my apartment."

"I thought your mother was staying at your apartment." As great as sleeping in a bed sounded, he was not going to share one with Cardin if her mother was a closed door away on the couch.

"She was, but she's gone back home."

"So the engagement plan worked?"

"Not quite yet. She says she's only home as a courtesy so we don't have to sleep on the floor since our minds are made up about staying together."

Best news he'd had all day. "That's a courtesy I can get behind."

"I thought you might say that. Do you want to go now? Or do you have more work in here to do?"

"I have a month's worth of work in here to do. It'll keep."

Trey sent Cardin on ahead and locked up, grabbing clean clothes and the personal items he would need before tomorrow. The thought of sleeping on a bed that wasn't in a hotel room, or in the hauler, or made up of sleeping bags stacked on the floor was made even better by the fact that he wouldn't be there alone.

After the reception he'd received from Cardin's parents last night, and their less than heartfelt blessing, the gesture from her mother surprised him. A skeptical part of him wondered if Delta Worth's motivation had less to do with vacating her daughter's apartment for Cardin and her fiancé, and more to do with wanting to return home and be under the same roof as Eddie.

Not that he was looking a gift horse in the mouth, but such an abrupt about face was certainly suspect, even though it seemed to indicate Cardin's plan was panning out. His ruminations were cut short by the buzzing of his BlackBerry. "Trey Davis."

"I didn't tell you where I lived. And I left too soon for you to follow me."

He laughed, a low throaty sound that echoed in the cab around him. "What makes you think I don't know where you live?"

"That sounds like I'm being stalked," she said, her tone curious rather than accusatory.

"Could be I just did a Google query."

"I'm not listed, so I don't think a query would've returned you the information."

"Give me a minute. I'll think of something else."

"Why? Are you embarrassed to admit that you've looked me up?"

"No. But I don't want to be thought of as a stalker."

She waited a moment before responding. "So when *did* you look me up?"

He thought for a moment, noticing the lighted steeple of Dahlia First Baptist Church in the distance. "About the time you moved out of your folks' place, I guess."

"That long ago? You've been keeping tabs on me since then?"

"Not keeping tabs, no. Tater and I were talking about you during one of my visits home. He pointed it out to me when we drove by."

"He pointed it out when you drove by, or you were driving by so he could point it out?"

Trey laughed again, tickled by the endearing skepticism in her voice. "I honestly don't remember. But I can promise you that it wasn't stalking."

"I guess I'll have to take your word for that."

"If I say it, it's true. That's one thing as my fiancée you should know about me."

"You only lie when I ask you to then, is that right?"

He slowed for the stoplight ahead. "I'm not going to lie to you, okay? Does that work?"

"Thank you. It's nice to know you'll be honest with me, even though this isn't real."

It was late, it was dark. She was a voice on the other end of a call as he drove toward her. There was no one else around, nothing to distract him. No reason for him not to open up except the possibility of falling flat on his face.

He took the risk. "That line I mentioned? I'm not so sure that some of this isn't real."

She was silent for a long time. He knew she was there. He could hear her breathing. Hear the radio turned low in the truck, and the roar of Jeb's big diesel. He didn't want to nudge, or prod for a reply before she was ready. But he also didn't want the delay to give her too much time to think.

The tension in the cab of his truck had nearly strangled him by the time she spoke, her voice small and almost timid in his ear. "I'd been wondering if I was the only one thinking that. I didn't want to say anything."

His pulse began to race, his heart pounding, pistons thudding in his chest. "Why not?"

"I'm not sure," she said, and he imagined her shrugging. "I guess I thought if you didn't feel the same, and I put it out there, I would've opened a big can of worms for no reason. Pulling off a fake engagement was going to be hard enough without adding that pressure. And I didn't want to screw up this chance to get my parents back together."

He could understand that. He even admired her for being so selfless. But that left this thing between them in a crimp. "Then we're agreed that the engagement is fake."

"Yeah," she said, and he heard her cut off the truck's engine.

He wasn't too far from the entrance to her complex himself. "But the other stuff, the you and me stuff…"

"There's something there, isn't there?" she asked, and her voice broke.

"I think there might be." He was too close to panic to say more. Too close to telling her…that he loved her. God, he loved her. All this time. So many years. Thinking of her constantly, wanting her. Coming back here because he couldn't stand the distance anymore. He loved her. He loved her.

He had to get to her. He had to have her now. "What's the code to your gate?"

"Six three six seven."

He punched it in, keeping the phone call connected, and drove through when the gate rolled back.

He could hear more sounds, the keys on her chain jangling, the squeak of the door as it opened, what sounded like her purse hitting the floor. He didn't hear the door close, heard only her breathing, her waiting.

He parked his truck, got out, locked it behind him, and was halfway to Cardin's front door when he realized he'd left his duffel bag in the cab. He didn't go back for it. He didn't care.

Her building was down the sidewalk from the parking lot and to the left. Her door was the third one from the end. He saw her standing in the rectangle of light, a silhouette with long legs and a short skirt and hair feathering around her shoulders.

His body tightened. His steps grew quick, his strides fierce, and then he was there, sweeping her up, kicking the door closed behind them, and grinding his mouth to hers.

17

"WHERE'S THE BEDROOM?" TREY ASKED as she wrapped her legs around his waist, her arms around his neck.

"I only have nine hundred square feet here. You can probably figure it out." She inclined her head to his left to get him started, loving that he was finally here and was desperate, was out of breath, was barely able to speak.

The lamp she'd switched on in the living room was the only light he had to guide him, but he found his way without any trouble at all. She felt the thud as his knees and shins made contact with her bed. And then she was on her back on the mattress, Trey on top of her, pinning her down.

"What took you so long to get here?" she asked, her chest tight as she moved one hand from his nape to brush the hair from his forehead.

"Buell and his deputies," he told her, his gaze eating her up like candy. "I didn't want to chance being locked up over night for reckless driving."

He was so sweet, so silly, so practical. "I wasn't talking about tonight."

"I didn't know that you wanted me here," he said, his soft voice at odds with the fire in his eyes.

"I've always wanted you here," she said, admitting the long-denied truth.

His throat worked hard as he swallowed. "You should've let me know."

"I was afraid."

"Of what?" he asked, his brows coming together in a thoughtful V.

"That being here wasn't what *you* wanted," she told him and he smiled.

"I can see we've got our work cut out for us with this communication thing."

Her stomach fluttered. "Were you thinking of talking, or using body language?"

"Right now, I'm in the mood to talk with my hands."

He rolled to one hip and slid his palm up her thigh, finding the elastic leg hole of her panties beneath her skirt. One touch, and her control dissolved like paper in water. She was never going to make it through the night.

"I love that you're always wet," he whispered into her ear.

"You make me wet," she told him, an absolute truth. "It's like I can't wait for you. Every time. It's never been like this before. I see you, and all I can think about is you touching me."

"That's good to know, since touching you is just about my favorite thing."

"And here I thought all you liked touching was cars."

"I like touching what responds."

He'd been toying with her all this time, rubbing over her, stroking her, but now he slid a finger deep inside, and she arched her hips off the bed.

"Yeah," he murmured. "Just like that."

"It's hard not to respond when you do that," she said, twitching a bit with the movement of his finger. "And when you do that." When he put his thumb to work, she twitched harder. "And definitely when you do that."

"I can do a whole lot of other things," he told her, his mouth on her neck, his lips kissing, his tongue wetting the skin before his teeth bit. "But most of them require you getting out of your clothes."

She wanted to get naked. She just didn't want to move to do it and lose what he was doing to her. "I'll get out of mine if you'll get out of yours."

"That's the plan, sweetheart," he said, catching her earlobe and tugging, just before he turned away.

While Trey was occupied kicking out of his boots, she scooted off the bed and ran for the shower to wash away the smell of burgers and fries. She was bare, and the water running by the time he joined her in the bathroom that was as small and compact as the rest of her place.

He stood there unclothed in the tiny space, his shoulders broad, the muscles in his arms well-defined, as were those of his abdomen. His chest was covered with hair she knew to be silky soft. It was lighter in color than that on his head, and the thatch cushioning his penis was darker than both.

His legs were long and strong, the perfect thickness for wedging between hers, for rubbing against her, for holding her braced against the trunk of a tree while he got her off. With an appreciative smile, she climbed into the tub, leaving him to pull the curtain closed behind them.

While she adjusted the temperature of the water, he reached up and adjusted the angle of the spray. "What? I wasn't making you wet enough?"

She laughed. "I smell like a burger basket."

"You smell like you."

"And a burger basket."

"Here's something else you need to know as my fiancée. I like smelling you. I like tasting you. Your sweat. The salt on your skin. I don't need you to smell like a bar of soap or a field of flowers to be turned on."

He was a guy. She didn't expect him to understand about

girl things. She leaned back to wet her hair and face, then looked at him again. "What do you need?"

"Nothing more than seeing you do that," he said, and groaned.

She laughed, reached for her body wash and her sponge. "Boy, you're easy."

"It's not my fault. I was born that way."

"Easy?"

"With a dick."

"And a very nice one, I might add." She handed him the sponge and spun away.

"Ah, now the truth comes out," he said as he started in on her shoulders, scrubbing up her nape then down her spine. "You're just looking to get your back washed."

"Guilty as charged," she said, her sex tingling and swelling as he slid his hand between the cheeks of her ass. "That's not my back."

"Your back wasn't dirty," he replied, his fingers probing deeper between her legs.

She widened her stance. "And you're looking for a part of me that is?"

He pushed his thumb inside of her. "I think I found it."

She wanted to play. She wanted to tease and flirt. She wanted to have fun like this forever. But she wanted that hard, thick cock he'd been born with even more. And so she wiggled to dislodge his hand, and bent over, bracing her hands on either side of the tub's rim.

Behind her, she heard Trey groan. "I don't have a condom."

"I'm on the Pill, and the only thing I can give you is a good time. As long as you can promise me the same thing, I think we're good here."

He ran both hands over her ass, his fingers delving into the crevices and folds between her legs. "I can promise part of it. You won't catch anything from me. But as far as being on the Pill…"

She wanted to laugh, but was too desperately ready for him. "Then fuck me, Trey. Please. I want you."

"I thought you'd never ask," he said, taking hold of her hips and entering her with excruciating slowness.

She wedged her feet against the sides of the tub and came up on her toes, opening her knees to give him as much access as possible. Finally he was all the way inside, stretching her, throbbing there where he filled her. She felt his heat and his hardness as she gripped him tight.

He began to move, sliding in and out, setting a rhythm that created the perfect storm of sensation in her body. There was friction, there was tingling, there was an aching, drawing need. It pulled at her, tugged at her womb, caused her breasts to grow heavy, her nipples to tighten.

She ground against him, her clit pulsing, her opening gripping him as he drove in and out. It was everything she wanted, but it wasn't enough. She brought up a hand to stimulate the places his cock could only skate over from this angle.

He beat her to it, lacing their fingers and letting her show him how to play with her clit. She moaned when together they got it just right. And he growled like a rutting beast in answer. She rocked her hips, working his cock with her sex.

And as she came, it hit her that she had always loved him, that she would love him until she died. She cried out, and he followed, the sounds he made bestial, possessive, a mating, a staking of a claim.

They showered quickly then, washing hair and limbs and the parts of their bodies that were sticky. They rinsed. They grabbed towels, but didn't use them. They returned to the bed wet and starving for more.

And Cardin very happily in love.

18

AN EMPTY GLASS IN HIS HAND, Eddie stood at the sink in his kitchen, a jug of milk and a bottle of Hershey's chocolate syrup on the counter. Seeing through the window Cardin's Mini Cooper parked out back had stopped him from pouring either.

He wasn't even a fan of chocolate milk. He couldn't figure why he'd decided to mix up a glass. Well, he could figure. It was Cardin. Her not being here. Her sleeping with Whip Davis in her own home.

Yeah, he was glad she was sleeping in a bed instead of on the floor, but she was still his little girl, and the idea that she wasn't sleeping alone wasn't easy to swallow.

He wondered when that would change. If giving his daughter away at the altar, if the "I do's" and the rings and the vows before God and the license legalizing the bond would make it easier to let her go.

He'd enjoyed like hell having her home these last four months. It had taken him back to her days in high school when she'd scurried around between Darling practices and games and FFA meetings. It had taken him back to earlier times as well.

Having her sit on the bench in the garage while he and Jeb tinkered with White Lightning. Reading her the newspaper, answering the questions she asked, soft-coating the stories too gritty for a five-year-old.

The only downside to his daughter's homecoming was that his wife wasn't here to share it. So when Delta had walked through the door a few hours ago, told him she'd given up the apartment then gone upstairs to their daughter's rooms, Eddie hadn't known what to think.

He still didn't know what to think. But at least he was looking for answers in a glass of chocolate milk instead of one filled with Jack Daniel's Tennessee Whiskey.

"I knew about the milk and the Hershey's."

Eddie stiffened at the sound of Delta's voice, but he didn't turn.

"I would hear her get up, and I'd watch from the kitchen door while you read to her."

He listened to his estranged wife come into the kitchen. "That was such a long time ago. Twenty years. It feels like nothing."

"Twenty years ago, is this where you thought you'd be?"

"Still in Dahlia? Yes. Living in my father's house? Maybe. Separated from my wife? No. Watching my daughter choose the man she wants to marry?" He shook his head; it felt so incredibly heavy. "Never."

"I think that's what they call life, Eddie." Delta came to stand beside him. He stared at their reflection in the window. "It happens to everyone."

"I'm not sure I like it as much when it doesn't go my way."

"It wouldn't be as interesting if it did," she told him. "You'd get all soft and pudgy and lazy if you got your way all the time. And I can't imagine you as any of those."

"Can you imagine me as old?"

"Old? I don't think so." She pushed her hair from her forehead, held it back for a moment before letting it go. "We're only a few months apart, and there's no way I'm copping to being old."

Eddie wished he could share her attitude, but he hurt. He

ached. He was weary. His body as well as his soul. He'd never felt this beat up. Or this alone. "I feel old. Worn out."

She draped her arm around his shoulders, leaned her head against him. He could see her sweet smile that he loved so much in the window and their reflected gazes met. "You've been depressed for months. You've been through three surgeries. You've taken more medicine than a lot of horses could handle. That's enough to wear out the best of men."

She turned him then, forced him with her hands on his shoulders away from the window to face her. Her eyes were big and blue and damp, and her unshed tears hit him like a fist to the gut.

"You, Eddie Worth. You are the best of men. I've known you more years than I haven't. And however long it takes, I know you'll bounce back. No one and nothing will ever convince me otherwise."

He wondered what he'd ever done to deserve this woman who had more faith in him than he did in himself. And after all he'd put her through this past year. "I'm glad one of us thinks I've still got something going for me."

"You talk like you have one foot in the grave."

"Most days? It feels pretty close."

She moved her hands from his shoulders to his face, studying him, making sure of something, then taking him by one hand and leading him to the kitchen table where they'd eaten so many meals as a family.

They'd helped run Cardin through her spelling words here. Had talked about White Lightning's performance in the latest race. Decided where to take their vacations. How best to spend the money they'd made.

He sat in his usual chair, to the left of his father's at the head, and she sat beside him, turning so their knees bumped. "I think you need to slow down, Eddie. Not because of your age, but because you never took enough time off. You went back to work too soon. You didn't give yourself the mental recovery time you needed."

Staying home doing nothing had driven him crazy. He wasn't cut out to stare at the walls, or a television screen, and the pages of a book only got him through so many hours before he needed to get up and move. "Everyone says that. Take time to heal. To recover. But the ones saying it aren't the ones sitting on their butts going bonkers."

"You know, as patient as you've always been with me, with Cardin, even with your Dad, you've never been patient with yourself."

"Patience takes too long to get things done."

"And impatience burns you out."

She was right, but he was right, too. And he didn't know where that left him. "If I cut back my hours at work, what am I supposed to do with my time?"

"You could do anything you wanted to do."

That wasn't exactly true. "I can't take White Lightning down the track."

"No, but you could go back to working on the car with your father."

His father, who refused to open up and tell him the one thing he most needed to know.

That was what Eddie had to come to terms with. Things would never be the same as they were before the accident. But if he wanted any kind of relationship with his family, he had to come to grips with the past.

"So if I take some time, get my head together, work on things with Jeb, does that mean you're going to come home?"

Until now, Delta had been leaning toward him, pleading with him, touching him, her gaze imploring. Now she moved away to sit straight in her chair. "I love you, Eddie. You're the only man I've ever loved."

"But?" he asked as fear clawed at him. He wasn't going to be able to do anything if he didn't have her with him. She was his other half, his better half. He would die for her. He would die without her.

"I'm not going to desert you. But I have to know that things are going to turn around for you—for both of us— before I come back for good. I can't handle going through another separation. When I come back, that's it. I'm never leaving again."

He didn't want her leaving again. He hated that he'd driven her away in the first place, but the idea of her not returning... "Does that mean you're going to stay on at Cardin's?"

She shook her head. "Now that she's there with Whip, I don't think so. I might see about getting an apartment in the same complex, or if Cardin thinks that's too close, a room at Bristol House."

Those places were too far away. "Or you could stay here. Upstairs. Like Cardin's been doing."

"Do you think that's such a good idea?" she asked, canting her head to one side and giving him a look that said she had his number.

"I promise I won't sneak up into your bed."

"I'm not so sure I won't sneak downstairs into yours."

He wouldn't say no if she did. He wanted her there. He needed her there. But hearing that she would never abandon him...

He had to trust her. Even more so, he had to trust himself. He had to get where he needed to be under his own steam, by making his own decisions, carving out his own way.

Needing a moment, he got up and returned the milk and the chocolate syrup to the fridge. He spoke before looking back at his wife, the change of subject a trick he hoped would work to take his mind off the hard journey ahead. "I guess we should talk about wedding gifts. A trip, some cash, a reason to settle down in Dahlia."

"If Whip's going to be on the road, I don't think there's anything we can give Cardin to make her stay here, but if we had the money, I'd buy those five acres Ahsan Wazir has for sale east of town."

"I have the money," Jeb said, walking into the kitchen and surprising Eddie and Delta both.

Eddie wondered how long his father had been in the living room, if he'd heard their conversation. If this was his way of breaking the ice, making the first move Eddie hadn't yet figured out how to do.

"But there's something else for sale I think would give them both more of a reason to stay."

"What's that?" Eddie asked.

His father glanced over, his eyes glinting with mischief. "The Dahlia Speedway."

19

"I FORGOT TO TELL YOU YOUR GRANDFATHER wants to throw us a party."

"What?" Cardin rose up sharply from where she'd been cleaning out the cabinet beneath Trey's kitchen sink. She bumped her head on the edge of the frame, frowning as she rubbed at the bruise. "What do you mean, he wants to throw us a party?"

"That's what he told me. An engagement party. He wants to celebrate us, and my Moonshine Run win at the same time."

A party at Headlights to celebrate White Lightning's showing in the Moonshine Run was an annual event. But an engagement party? She sat back on her heels. "Don't tell me he means to include gifts."

Trey kept his head down, studying notes scribbled on yellow paper torn from a legal pad. "He didn't say anything about gifts."

This was bad. Oh, this was bad. She got to her feet. "We can't let people bring gifts, Trey. We just can't."

"Then we'll have to make sure that's a stipulation."

She pulled a chair from under the table and sat, burying her face in her hands. "Ugh, what a mess."

"Lies can get messy," he said, all wise and sagelike.

"I know that. And I tried to think things through. But I

never counted on an engagement party. I guess part of me figured everyone would know this was all pretend." That sounded so stupid, she groaned. Twice. "Once we're done with this one, I'm out of the lie business forever."

She finally looked over at Trey where he sat at the head of the table, paperwork from a huge file box of his father's in stacks in front of him. They'd decided to take a break from the barn and spend a day in the house; they were having trouble out there staying on track.

They'd had just as much trouble in here this morning. Her inner thighs ached. "We'll have to make sure everyone knows we haven't set a date, we don't have a place of our own, we can't store things, yadda, yadda. So no gifts. Absolutely no gifts."

He didn't look up. "Lots of folks give cash, you know. They like to walk up and slip a few bills into the pockets of the bride and groom."

Uh-uh. "No cash, either. We can't take cash." Her chin in one hand, she drummed the fingers of the other on the tabletop. "I'll just have to tell Jeb no party."

"No need to be hasty."

Hasty? "What?"

"Well…we could go along with it, accept the gifts and the cash, and call the engagement real."

He still didn't look at her. He was going through the papers one by one, placing them in the appropriate piles he'd made on the table—a filing system she was about to shove to the floor if that's what it took to get his attention.

"What did you say?" she asked, her heart choking her.

He tossed the papers he had yet to sort back into the box, then laced his hands behind his head and cocked back his chair on two legs. He gave her a devil's grin, and said, "I think you heard me."

"I did hear you. That's why I asked what you said." She

wasn't making any sense, but then he wasn't making any sense. And the way she suddenly couldn't see straight was making even less. "A real engagement would mean we were planning to get married."

One of his brows arched upward. "What if we did?"

"Got married?"

"Isn't that what we're talking about here?"

"I don't know what we're talking about, Trey Davis." She'd never thought her heart beating so hard could actually hurt. Either she was having a heart attack or this was the worst case of anxiety, and panic and waiting-by-the-phone-for-the-boy-she-most-wanted-to-hear-from-to-call nerves that she'd experienced in her life. "I do know that I'm going to knock those other two chair legs out from under you if you don't explain."

"You asked me to marry you last week." He paused, and she almost screamed before he added, "I'm saying yes."

Calm, Cardin. Stay calm. "I asked you to pretend to be my fiancé and help me pull off a fake engagement. It was about getting my parents back together."

"I know." He nodded. "And I agreed to help. But I never answered your proposal."

Calm, calm, calm. Calm, calm, calm. "So you're putting this back on me somehow."

He laughed, a huge hearty from the belly laugh. "You see, Cardin, this is why I love you. You don't take anything at face value. You dig for the good stuff beneath."

She thought he was saying something about value and digging, but all she heard was that he loved her. "Did you just say that you love me?"

"I did."

"And that you want our engagement to be real?"

"That's right."

"And that you accept my marriage proposal?"

"I do."

She just stared at him. She couldn't move. Her belly was aching along with her chest, and she swore she was going to throw up.

Trey returned his chair legs to the floor, scooted all four of them across the worn linoleum and got up. He came to where she was sitting, spun her chair around, and knelt in front of her. "You know this story we made up to tell people about our long-distance relationship?"

"You mean the lie?" she asked, needing to make even the obvious clearer.

"That's the one," he said, reaching for the fingers of her hand that were digging into her thigh. "I'm beginning to think there's a lot of truth to it. That the distance was simply across years instead of miles."

She'd been looking into his eyes as he spoke, seeing thoughtfulness, sincerity, and an emotion that looked so much like real, live, from the heart love that it scared her. She raised her gaze to the ceiling, blinking away wetness before it fell as tears.

"I haven't dated anyone seriously since leaving Dahlia. And it wasn't until you walked into the Corley hauler last week that I knew why."

She shook her head, a rapid back and forth, not because she didn't want to hear what he was saying, but because she didn't know how she was going to keep from blubbering like a fool.

"I don't know why we never got together in high school—"

"We never even talked in high school," she said, her voice breaking on an hysterical note.

"I know that. Part of me wants to laugh when I think about how stupid I was then. Another part of me is sad that we wasted so much time. But then I think that the waiting, the distance, all of it…" He stopped to clear his throat. "It was exactly what this thing between us needed to stir to life."

She kept her eyes squeezed tightly closed. She'd never expected this, never spent time wishing or longing because doing either seemed like a waste of energy better spent where there was a chance for success.

That Trey was on one knee in front of her now... A sob escaped, a hiccup she tried to hold back.

"Look at me, Cardin," he said, his fist beneath her chin lifting her head. "Look at me, sweetheart."

It was so hard to do. So very hard to do. But she did. The tears she'd tried to stop welled, spilling from her lids and rolling down her cheeks. She didn't bother wiping them away, or trying to catch them before they fell from her face to Trey's hands.

"I've been serious about you for years. I just didn't know how so until these last few days. And when I've thought about getting back to work, leaving Dahlia, leaving you..." This time it was Trey who choked up, whose voice grew husky and raw.

Even his eyes misted. "I can't do it. I want you with me. I need you with me. Whether here or on the road. I don't care where we are as long as we're together. As long as you're my wife. I love you, Cardin Worth. Will you marry me?"

It was the last straw. She fell forward, collapsing in his arms, crying there on the edge of her chair, as he held her. "I love you, too, Trey. I think I've loved you forever. It's probably why I stopped when I saw you and Kim."

"You wanted to take her place?"

"No, I wanted to flatten her."

Trey laughed, set her back in her chair, and ran his wrist over his eyes while she used her T-shirt to dry her face. Both of them were laughing, smiling, trying to catch their breath and their runaway giddiness in the face of realizing they weren't alone in their love.

Trey grabbed his chair, pulling it next to hers. "You never answered me, you know."

"Oh, my God. Yes. Yes, of course, I'll marry you." He was everything she wanted. He was who she wanted. If this was a dream, she never wanted morning to come.

"So it's okay if people bring presents," Trey said, and she smacked his shoulder.

"You just didn't want to have to give back the cash."

He screwed up his face. "The thought of doing so was making me ill."

Her stomach hurt from the laughter. Her chest ached from the joy filling her heart. "Oh, Trey, I can't believe our engagement is real. I'm going to float through work tonight, and Sandy's going to bug me, wanting to know what's going on."

"Just tell her you're high on sex."

"After the last few days? That wouldn't be much of an exaggeration. Oh, what about your place here? Do you still want to sell it?"

"Why wouldn't I?"

"I didn't know if you'd want to keep it so we'd have a home when we're here."

He shook his head. "We'll have a home of our own. If this place doesn't sell, the house will come down. I'll keep the property, and we'll put up a house just for us." He gave her a smile. "We'll get around to figuring it all out. We've got time."

Time, and so many things to talk about, she thought. Like when they were going to get married. What kind of wedding they wanted. If they were going to continue with the long engagement or if she'd get to call herself Cardin Davis soon.

"I can't believe we're going to get married."

"Just don't go telling people that since everyone already thinks that we are."

"Oh, yeah," she said, pouting.

"Sorry to knock the wind from your sails, sweetheart.

Guess next time you'll think twice about telling everyone you know a lie."

"Trust me. I'm done with the lying. Unfortunately, I'm not done with having to earn my own living. I'd better get to work." She got to her feet.

Trey stood, too. "I was thinking I'd see if Tater wanted to meet me later at Headlights for dinner, after your grandfather and I put White Lightning through a test run."

"Is it a boys' night out thing, or do you want company?"

"If the company is yours, you bet."

"I'll see you later then." She rose up on her tiptoes to kiss him, then scurried toward the front door.

"Hey," he called out, and she looked back to see him standing there with his arms stretched out to his sides. "Is that all I get?"

"You'll get a whole lot more when you finish your paperwork."

"I've put it off for six months, what's another six minutes?"

"From here, it looks like it's time you're wasting," she said, then hurried out the door, down the front steps and to her grandfather's truck, her steps and her heart as light as air.

Cardin Worth Davis. Mrs. Trey Davis. No words had ever sounded so good, or so very very right.

20

THE SIX MINUTES CARDIN told Trey not to waste weren't an issue. It was during the sixty that followed that his life began to come undone, that he made his discovery, that a scrap of newsprint he found in the box of his father's papers shut him down.

He got up from the chair where his body had grown stiff, where his emotions had petrified, where his mind had seized up like frozen gears. He couldn't see anything else. Think of anything else. At a time when he'd least expected it, and completely on his own, he'd found what he'd been looking for when he'd come here.

The reason for the fight.

A reason that had nothing to do with money.

It was all about murder.

The headline dated 1939 said it all. *Death in Dahlia Suspect.* The story gave the facts. The body of Emmett Davis, Trey's great-grandfather, had been found outside the home of his good friend, Cardin's great-grandfather, Orin Worth. Though Trey knew Orin had run moonshine with Emmett during Prohibition, the article mentioned nothing about the duo's partnership or their illicit money-making venture.

The authorities attributed the head injuries responsible for Emmett's demise to a fall—the exact story Trey had been told all his life—but the newspaper added details he'd never heard. A female witness identified only as Trixie was quoted as saying, "Emmett didn't trip so much as he had help hitting the ground. And I seen the piece of wood that done him in."

The police discounted her story that Emmett's fall had not been accidental. That he'd been struck in the head, and killed by the blow, instead. They discounted her story because she was known on the streets as unreliable with a taste for big cigars, bigger men and strong hooch.

On its own, the clipping was fairly innocuous, though certainly disconcerting to read. The story didn't point fingers or place blame, simply questioned the findings in Trey's great-grandfather's death. But it was his father's handwriting on the newsprint beneath the article that had a cold sweat dampening Trey's skin.

Aubrey had written *Trixie = Mrs. Orin Worth,* and though surprised his father had learned somehow the fate of Cardin's great-grandmother, Trey didn't find it hard to believe. He heard more than once that the woman had vanished never to be seen again.

No, it was the list Aubrey had jotted beneath the article Trey was having trouble with. As if sorting out his thoughts on paper, Trey's father had written, *Ask Jeb about murder. He knows the truth. Am certain. Think he was there.* There was no clue as to how Aubrey had come by the newspaper, or if he'd drawn his conclusions from other sources as well.

Right now, Trey didn't care where the information had come from. His father's notes implied that Cardin's great-grandmother was right, and that Jeb knew when and how Emmett had been murdered. And neither man had ever said a word.

That was what Trey cared about. The silence, the hiding the truth. The lies.

He grabbed the newspaper and the notes and stormed out of the house toward his truck. The drive to the Dahlia Speedway took him twenty minutes. As much as he'd wanted to know the truth, he was not looking forward to the confrontation to come.

Other than a construction crew working on the containment fencing behind the southern side of the stands, the few cars belonging to the office staff and the traffic at Morgan and Son's garage, the Speedway was deserted. Trey had no trouble finding Jeb.

The older man had hauled the car to the track with the pickup Eddie never used anymore, unloaded the Chevy Nova and four-wheeler from the trailer on his own.

As Trey parked and jumped down from his truck, Cardin's grandfather waved him over, patting the seat of the ATV after straddling it. "Climb aboard. Let's see if it shows as good as it sounds."

The conversation they needed to have couldn't be done over the roar of the ATV's engine. And since Trey wasn't even sure where or how to begin, he took the piece of newspaper from the pocket of his shirt, pulled it from the plastic bag he'd used for safekeeping, and held it in front of Jeb's face.

Jeb read the words Trey's father had written beneath the article, then reached for the key and turned off the ATV. Silence surrounded them, uncomfortable, angry, heavy with questions and accusations. Trey returned the paper to his pocket, while Jeb stared off into the distance, sagging in the seat.

He shook his head, a gesture that seemed to say he'd wondered long and often when this day would come. "Let's get this race out of the way before we talk about that."

Trey shook his head, a gesture that meant no. "There's not going to be a race until we talk about that."

"I was nine years old," Jeb said, running his thumb over the palm of the other hand and staring down. "And that was seventy years ago, but I can still feel the splinters I got from gripping that board."

"Wait a minute." Trey's blood pressure shot through his skull. He took a step back, felt himself shaking, struggled to find his voice. "You killed him? You're the one in the article the witness, your *mother,* is talking about? And you kept it a secret?"

"I didn't mean to do either one. I was a kid."

"Those are excuses. Not an explanation," Trey said. His temperature soared. "I think I deserve one since it was my great-grandfather who died."

The silence grew darker as Trey waited. He felt it closing in, choking, consuming. He wasn't sure how he kept from striking out—the same feelings his father must have suffered when he'd taken his findings to Jeb—but he held on until Jeb finally spoke.

"Tell me, Whip. What do you know about Emmett Davis?"

Very little, thanks to you, he wanted to say. "I know he ran moonshine with your father. I know that Diamond Dutch Boyle was sent here to stop them. I know you're the one who finally found Boyle's car in the LaBrecque ravine fifteen years later. But I know all that because it's on the plaque hanging in Headlights. Emmett Davis didn't live long enough for there to be much more to learn. He was only thirty-eight when you killed him."

Jeb swung his leg over the ATV, pressed his hand to the small of his back as he straightened, then thumbed his cowboy hat up his forehead before he said, "Maybe we could have this discussion someplace more private."

Trey looked around, seeing nobody within ear shot. "This is about as private as it gets."

"Then let's at least sit in one of the trucks. I can't stand here for the length of time it's going to take to tell this story."

That was fine with Trey. He gestured with one hand for Jeb to take the lead and choose the truck. Jeb headed for Trey's, the big crew cab dualie roomier than the one Eddie owned.

Jeb climbed up into the passenger seat, Trey behind the wheel. He noticed a sheen of sweat on the older man's face. "Do you want me to turn on the a/c? Roll down the windows?"

"The windows will be fine." Jeb pulled off his hat, finger-combed his hair, held the Stetson by the brim on one knee, and stared straight ahead through the windshield. "I'm guessing you thought your dad came to me for money to settle up his gambling debts. I know you did that for him. That he gave you the house and left Dahlia."

"I didn't come here to talk about my father."

"Yes you did. Your father's the reason you're here at all."

Semantics, Trey thought. He was here because of his father's fight with this man, because of what his father had discovered. And because Trey was the last Davis living, this man owed him answers. "I came back to Dahlia to go through his things, clean up the place, and yeah, see what I could find out about the fight. What I've found out makes me wonder why I shouldn't go to the authorities instead of sitting here with you."

"You're doing just what your father did. You're more like him than you know."

If that meant neither Trey nor his father were satisfied until they got to the bottom of things, that he could deal with. But Trey was not a man who would cheat on his woman. Neither did he bet on anything but himself. "Then you tell me what kept my father from turning you in to the law."

Jeb snorted. "For one thing, look at the law we've got around here. Henry Buell would bungle a traffic stop before getting it right."

"He could've found someone a few pay grades higher than Buell."

"If he'd wanted to bring the law into it, sure. But like you, he was more interested in hearing the story than seeing me locked up."

Trey was pretty damn sure he hadn't said that. "I may have a lot of things in common with my dad, but don't make the mistake of thinking I'm him. I will call the law."

"And what will you tell Cardin?"

He didn't have an answer for that.

"Because I can guarantee that if you put me away, there won't be a wedding."

Not for a moment did Trey doubt that Jeb was speaking the truth.

He needed to know the whole story before he screwed up a whole lot of lives. "Right now I'm leaving Cardin out of this, Eddie and Delta, too. I don't want to take this any further if you and I can settle things here and now."

"One on one? Man to man?"

Trey gave a sharp nod. He would decide what to do once he had his hands on the whole truth.

Jeb took a deep breath and started. "I was too young to know a lot about your great-granddad, but the things I'd heard were the kind of things people only whispered about. Back then, a man's sexual appetite wasn't discussed at the dinner table along with the day's news. Private things weren't talked about openly at all. At nine years old, I didn't know what sex was. Oh, I knew boy animals got on top of girl animals, and I knew girl animals gave birth to baby animals, but that was about it."

Trey wasn't exactly comfortable with this conversation, but he had to stick it out to the end. "So my great-grandfather was a philanderer. I don't remember all of my history lessons, but I'm pretty sure that wasn't against the law, even in nineteen thirty-nine."

"You're right. Philanderers weren't put behind bars, but they weren't admired for their prowess or conquests, either. Not in decent society."

Trey braced his elbow against the truck's padded door and looked off toward the Speedway's arched entrance. First his great-grandfather was a philanderer. Now he wasn't fit for decent society.

If Jeb was trying to justify what he'd done by tearing apart a dead man's reputation, he wasn't getting far with Trey. "I guess now you're going to tell me about the girls he got pregnant and abandoned. Or ones he was rumored to have raped."

Jeb shook his head. "Like I told you, I was only nine. I wouldn't have heard those rumors. But when I came home from school one day and found him in my ma's bed, with her grunting and groaning and screaming beneath him, I wanted him dead for the hurt he was causing her."

Trey turned his head toward the older man, unable to breathe, his skin prickling as he waited for Jeb to continue.

"When you're nine years old, you hear people talk about dying, about going to heaven or meeting your maker, about being in a better place with family members who passed on years before. But there's nothing there that really makes you understand what dead means. It's just a word, and all you know is that the dead person's not around anymore."

Jeb shifted in the seat, sitting a little straighter, scooting closer to the door as if he didn't want to lose that means of escape—even though Trey knew he hadn't done anything to make Cardin's grandfather feel threatened.

More than likely, because of what he'd done, Jeb had felt threatened all of his life. "So you killed him. You caught him in bed with your mother and you killed him."

"I did," Jeb admitted, giving a solemn shake of his head. "I ran out of the house to the porch and grabbed a two-by-four. There was a stack there. My pa had been repairing the railing. It was a short board, but long enough to swing. And I was known by the rest of the kids I played ball with as a slugger."

Bile rose in the back of Trey's throat. He pulled his gaze from Jeb's profile and stared out the window. As hard as this was to hear, he couldn't imagine that it was easy to tell. But the thought of a nine year old boy swinging a two-by-four at a grown man... He swallowed hard, and used the back of his hand to wipe the sweat from his upper lip.

"I'm guessing they never heard me come in, just heard me running out. Emmett ran off the porch, tugging on his shirt, his pants flapping open. I reared back behind him and swung like I was aiming for the center field fence. He fell. I'm pretty sure he was already dead, but I ran down the steps and hit him again. And again."

"Where was your mother all this time?" Trey croaked out.

"That was about when she came through the door screaming. I dropped the board and ran, hid out in the woods and waited, watching her. She sat down in all that dirt and blood and held the board in her lap, crying like I've never seen anybody cry before. I must've fallen asleep—I'd curled up inside a rotten log—because when I woke up, there was a whole passel of men hovering around. My ma was nowhere to be seen. And we never saw her again."

Trey couldn't even imagine what Cardin's great-grandmother had been thinking. "She just took off?"

Jeb nodded. "In your great-granddad's car. They did find it down toward Nashville a day or so later. And I'm guessing that's when she told the reporter that story, likely while she was drinking. But she never got in touch with my dad again and that was the last time that I saw her, sitting there in the dirt, petticoats soaking up the blood."

There was so much to ask, so much that Trey was lost. "You never told anyone that she'd been there, or what you'd done, and she never told anybody except that reporter what she saw."

"That's pretty much how it happened."

"Did the police question you?"

Jeb nodded again. "They did. I told them I'd been in the woods. I liked to play like I was Eliot Ness hunting down Al Capone. When I walked out from the trees and my pa looked over at me, I could tell by his eyes that he suspected what I'd done."

"But he didn't say anything to the police, either."

"Nope. We never talked about it. Not a word." Jeb turned his hat round and round on his knee. "To tell you the truth, I think there was a big part of him that was relieved. I didn't work that out until I was older and got to thinking back on how he'd taken Emmett's death and my mother's disappearance. I'm pretty damn sure he suspected what was going on with the two of them. But seeing as how Emmett was his partner, he didn't quite know what to do."

What the hell? "The man was screwing his wife and he didn't know what to do?"

"Things were different then, Whip. Sure, rights were right and wrongs were wrong, but folks turned a blind eye to a lot of situations and made do with the hand they'd been dealt."

"This is so wrong. So fucked up. I don't even know what to say." Though murder had no statute of limitations, Jeb had been a juvenile at the time of the crime. Now he was almost eighty years old. Trey could turn him in, let the law deal, and ruin a lot of lives. Or he could keep Jeb's secret and try to live with himself.

Jeb shifted, cocking one knee onto the seat. "I want to say one more thing to you. I'm not trying to plead my case, but this I want you to understand. I wanted Emmett dead for what he was doing to my ma, but I never meant to kill him. I thought he was hurting her. I thought I was protecting her. When I came out of those woods and found she was gone, that was when I first knew that I'd been wrong about what I'd seen."

Trey stared at the emblem in the center of his steering wheel. "Why didn't you explain to anyone what had happened?"

"Because I was the only thing my pa had left, and I feared by telling the truth, the law would take me away from him forever. It was my fault that my ma left us, and I didn't want him to be alone."

Not wanting his father to be alone had been the very reason Trey had stayed in Dahlia until he was twenty. He didn't want to empathize with the child Jeb Worth had been, but his own mother had walked out when he was twelve. She hadn't been the one to cheat on her marriage; his father had. But all those feelings Jeb had been through? Trey recognized each one and knew them well. The fact that he did made it even harder to know the right thing to do.

He leaned his head back, and rubbed at his closed eyes, feeling emotionally battered, as if he was the one who had suffered the loss of a child's innocence. He didn't look up again until Jeb opened the door.

The older man's expression was solemn. "I figure I've given you enough to chew on for awhile. I won't hold it against you, no matter what you do with the information. I only ask that you let me know first. Give me time to get my things in order."

Trey's gut was in knots. He wasn't in any kind of mood to suit up and take White Lightning down the track, but knew work would go a long way to helping him put the things he'd just learned into perspective.

Because until he did that, until he had a solid handle on the big picture of Jeb killing his great-grandfather seventy years ago, he wouldn't know which course of action would be the best to take.

21

CARDIN WAS HALFWAY TO WORK when she drove past Pammy's Petals. Giving in to an irresistible urge, she U-turned in the middle of the road and pulled into the parking lot, sitting behind the wheel of Jeb's truck and staring at the bakery's two front windows where lacy curtains framed the words Pammy's and Petals on either side of the door.

The display counter beneath "Pammy's" showed off her namesake flower-frosted cupcakes, along with brownies, cookies and the pastries that brought so many customers by first thing every day.

In the right of the cabinet beneath "Petals" were kids' birthday cakes—ones decorated to look like baseball caps, mermaid tails, fire engines and fairies, while the left side was devoted to Pammy's specialty. Weddings.

There was a two-tiered chocolate groom's cake topped with a ball and chain of dark fudge. There were tiny bite-size cupcakes frosted to look like bridal gifts, with molded strips of sparkly sugar draped across them like bows.

And taking up the corner as if on stage was the cake that made Cardin want to cry.

She was being silly. Ridiculously emotional. What she was looking at was nothing but artfully crafted cardboard and paste. But oh, the swirls and ribbons and swoops of icing and ganache would make any princess dissolve into tears.

How was a girl from small town Tennessee not supposed to?

For a moment, she hesitated going inside. It was stupid to be looking at wedding cakes when she and Trey had only just made their engagement official; for all she knew, he might want a quick civil ceremony on his way back to joining the Corley team.

But in the end, she couldn't resist, telling herself it *had* been too long since she'd seen Pammy. Too long since she'd had one of the cupcakes customers came from far and wide to enjoy. She climbed down from the truck, smoothing back her ponytail before pushing open the door and walking inside.

The chime was still playing Disney's "It's a Small World After All" when Pammy came out of the back. Her big green eyes went wide, and her bow of a mouth formed a huge round *O* as she screamed. "Oh, my God! Cardin! You're going to marry Trey Davis!"

Cardin smiled back as Pammy ran from behind the counter and wrapped her in a hug, rocking her back and forth until they were both laughing and sobbing and howling like mad girl hyenas.

Pammy was the first to pull back, holding on to Cardin's hands. "Do you remember in high school how we walked down all the halls where his classes were? Even though ours were across campus? He probably thought we were stalking him."

Giving Pammy's hands a squeeze before letting go, Cardin ran both index fingers beneath her eyes to clear away what makeup had smeared. It tickled her to think she and Trey had just talked about the very same thing. "I don't think we were the only ones. I think every girl in school stalked Trey."

"Yeah." Sighing dreamily, Pammy reached up to settle the daisy hat that had slipped from the top of her head. "Especially Kim Halton. I was so glad she never came back to Dahlia. I heard she got pregnant her sophomore year at UT."

Her friend's sources about the goings-on at the University of Tennessee—and with Kim Halton—were better than Cardin's. She hadn't heard anything at all. "If I had missed her, I might have realized that she never came back."

Pammy's laugh came out like a snort, and she quickly covered her mouth, her cheeks coloring as if she were embarrassed to be so crass. "I'm going to get us some coffee. Or do you want a soda?"

"I want a cupcake," Cardin said.

"A cupcake coming right up." Pammy turned away, all five-foot-two of her flouncing.

Cardin settled in a chair at one of the two café-style tables along the wall, and Pammy rejoined her moments later. The cupcake she set down had been centered on a China saucer, frosted in a glittery white icing and topped with what looked like a wedding corsage.

Great. Cardin felt herself choking up again. Was this how it was going to be until she said her "I Do's?" "I don't know if I can eat this. It's too gorgeous."

"Eat it." Pammy pushed the plate closer. "There's more where that came from. I promise the cake will be the lightest you've ever tasted in your life, and the scrumptious lemon mousse inside is to die for."

Cardin picked up her fork. "Who knew cupcakes would be all the rage?"

"It's having your cake and being able to eat it, too. You know. Kinda like marrying Trey Davis," Pammy said, cradling her coffee mug in both hands and waggling her brows as she brought it to her mouth to sip.

"It doesn't seem real, you know." Cardin cut into the cupcake with the side of her fork, the zing of lemon zest tingling her nose. "I keep waiting for someone to pinch me and wake me up."

"Why wouldn't it seem real?" Pammy returned her mug to the table, her expression searching. "You've been with him for what? Almost a year? It's about time you make it permanent, and really, I should smack you for keeping the relationship a secret to begin with."

Nice, Cardin. Way to almost screw up. She quickly recovered and came up with a plausible story. "Being with him in person makes it seem like the time apart was a dream, and it's only just now real. But you're right. I deserve to be smacked."

And she expected Pammy to do just that, but the other woman had grown pensive, frowning, staring down into her mug as she twisted it where it sat on the glass-topped table. "You'll go with him when he goes back on the road, won't you? You won't stay here?"

Cardin thought back to the conversation she and Trey had had with her parents, about where they would live, how they would live. Now that all of those things were real considerations, she was absolutely certain about only one. "I won't stay here unless he's here with me."

Sighing, Pammy sat back, pulling off her daisy and holding her mob of dark red curls away from her face with both hands. "You know, I never meant to make Dahlia my home forever. But then Kevin left me, and I had Boyd to take care of, and very little money for the two of us to live on."

Cardin knew how hard things had been for her friend after the divorce, and kicked herself for not staying in touch. "I haven't seen Boyd in so long. He's, what? Three now?"

Pammy nodded. "Three, and fortunately he neither looks nor acts anything like his father. That little guy's the reason I decided to make my mark right here. I knew I couldn't haul him around while I figured out what to do and where to do it. He deserves a better life than that."

"Well, your mark is amazing. *You* are amazing, and Boyd's

going to grow up to be just the same." Pressing the back of her fork into what crumbs were left on her plate, Cardin licked them away. "Pammy, seriously, that was the best cupcake I've ever eaten in my life."

"Does that mean you're going to let me do your wedding cake? I can already see a groom's cake in the shape of a dragster." Pammy's eyes widened. "Or better yet, a pair of headlights."

Cardin laughed. "Yeah, Trey would love that. A cake that looked like boobs."

"Speaking of boobs, Trey's still good friends with Tater Rawls, right?"

Cardin didn't know if Pammy was calling Tater a boob, or labeling him as another man who liked them. Unless, like everyone else, she thought he was a boob for dating Sandy Larabie. "They've been best friends since they were kids, why?"

"Does he know, or maybe you would know since you work with her, if this thing between Tater and Sandy is for real?"

There could be only one reason Pammy wanted to know. "If you're asking because you've got a thing for Tater, then it wouldn't hurt my feelings a bit if you made a move. He deserves better than Sandy Larabie."

"I think so, too. But I'm not a homewrecker. Even if what they have is casual, I'm not going to break it up."

Cardin's decision then was spur of the moment, but it seemed so right she didn't question it even once. She and Pammy had been friends forever, and she knew Trey would ask Tater to be his best man.

She reached across the table, and took Pammy's hands in hers. "Pammy, I would love it if you would be my maid of honor."

Pammy squealed. "Oh, my God, are you kidding me? I would die to be your maid of honor. I'm so honored that you would ask."

"Why wouldn't I ask? There's no one I would rather have witness my marriage to Trey, though," Cardin had to tell her, "it may be no more than standing beside me in front of a judge. We haven't even discussed when, where, how big of a wedding."

"But you're still going to let me do your cake," Pammy said, shaking her head at what seemed like a hundred miles an hour.

"Of course I'm going to let you do my cake. I'm tempted to ask you to come live with me and be my personal chef."

Pammy laughed. "I only do baked goods. You'd be a blimp in no time. An undernourished one at that."

"Probably not a good idea then, since I might be living in a motor home with a very narrow bed. I'd hate for Trey to have to sleep on the floor."

"I don't know. If there's no room beside you, Trey might have to sleep on top of you all the time. And how could that be a bad thing?" The two women giggled like fools until Pammy sat back and sighed. "I wish I had someone to sleep on top of me every night. Or even once a week, I'm not greedy."

That was it. Cardin was going to play matchmaker and see that her friend got a chance to show Winston Tate Rawls what he was missing. "You know what we should do? Go to Beverly's Closet and see what Beverly knows about what's hot in wedding dresses. I swear, her ear is pressed harder to the ground than my grandpa's. I'll bet she'll have the scoop on Sandy and Tater."

Pammy scrunched up her freckled nose. "Ooh, I like the way your devious mind works."

Little did the other woman know how Cardin's devious mind had gotten her into trouble. "I need to get something to wear to the engagement party my grandpa's throwing us, anyway."

"Is this some kind of private party? Because your maid of honor has not heard about it."

"I only heard about it today. Jeb told Trey that as long as everyone's going to be at Headlights to celebrate the winner of the Moonshine Run, we might as well make it an engagement party."

"Tater will be there, right? Though I guess Sandy will, too."

"Don't worry about Sandy. We'll get Beverly to fix both of us up."

"I may have to shop upstairs," Pammy said, looking sad. "I'm a little short on cash right now."

"I'm right there with you. I've cut my hours so I'll have more time to spend with Trey. But you know Miz Beverly. The secondhand clothes in Beverly's Attic are better than a lot of things on the racks in department stores." Cardin gave her girlfriend her biggest grin ever. "We'll knock the socks off Trey and Tater both."

22

LATER THAT EVENING found Trey in Headlights sitting across the table from Tater. He held a longneck in one hand, and a basket of fresh roasted peanuts sat half empty in front of them; the hulls of those they'd eaten lay scattered on the floor at their feet.

If Trey hadn't already arranged to meet his friend for their long overdue boy's night out to catch up, he would've skipped dinner and headed home, busying himself in the barn, or in the house, or even in the fields. Anything to keep from having to socialize. It had been a bitch of a long day, and he was not in the mood.

White Lightning had made the helluva showing he'd expected this afternoon. He loved the racing, he missed the racing. He could've stayed at the Dahlia Speedway all day. He just didn't want to stay there with Jeb Worth for company. The Moonshine Run was over a week away, and if he didn't see Cardin's grandfather again until that night, well, even then it would be too soon.

"For a man who just got engaged to the hottest chick around, you're not looking so good, bro." Tater hunkered forward, leaning into his arms where he'd braced them on the table and giving Trey the eye.

Trey shook his head. "My not looking so good doesn't have anything to do with Cardin or the engagement." Though that wasn't exactly true. With what he'd learned this afternoon, there might be no engagement, which meant there would be no Cardin. And the thought of giving her up... "I just think I need another beer."

"Not to poop on your party, but if you're planning to drive home from here, you'd better get some food in you first."

They'd placed their order with Sandy who'd clocked in early as Headlights was seeing an unusual weeknight rush. Trey hadn't done more than wave at Cardin, catching her eye as she scurried between tables, aching with the need to hold her close.

Since he was all clogged up with the things he'd learned this afternoon from her grandfather, he figured their not talking right now was for the best. He didn't know what he'd say—though he did know that keeping his discovery a secret was tantamount to telling her a lie.

Not exactly the open communication they'd swore would be a part of their relationship, even before their relationship was real. "I'll be fine," he finally told Tater, realizing his friend was staring. "I just need to work out some kinks in my head."

"Ones Cardin can't work out for you?"

"Yeah, pretty much."

"In that case, what can a bro do?"

Trey felt the stirrings of a smile. He had missed this man. Tater's common sense, his no bullshit way of looking at life. His ability to laugh in the face of things that just weren't that funny.

Talking specifics was out of the question, but Trey was of a mind to seek his friend's advice. "If I ask you something straight up will you answer me?"

"If I can."

A swallow of beer, a deep breath, a quick backhanding of the moisture from his mouth and Trey was ready. "The other day, you told me your being with Sandy was a man doing what a man had to do."

Tater, who'd been slumped forward slowly sat up. "You're not going to try and tell me that you being out of sorts is related to what I have going on with Sandy, are you?"

"No. There's just something I might have to do."

"Something you don't want to do?"

"Something I'd rather cut off my left nut than do."

Tater reached for his beer. "Sounds pretty serious."

A massive understatement. "I have a feeling it's going to be the most important decision I make in my life, and I don't want to screw it up."

"It's not about you and Cardin."

Trey shook his head. "Not directly, no."

Tater sat nodding, a delay that gave Sandy time to deliver their food.

"Here ya go, boys. Got your hot wings and corn on the cob. I had Albert throw in an extra half order of both while Eddie wasn't looking. You two looked like you were ready for some chow time."

"What a gal, eh, Whip?" Tater grabbed Sandy by the waist and pulled her close. "Always got her eye on her man's needs."

"Keeping appetites satisfied is just one of my many talents," she said, draping her arm around Tater and patting his shoulder. "You boys enjoy."

Once she was gone, Trey grabbed for a wing and tugged most of the meat off in one bite. He gestured with the bone. "If you tell me your relationship with her is all about sex, I'm going to be really disappointed."

"I told you. A man's gotta do—"

"—what a man's gotta do. I know." Trey's frustration was mounting fast. "But a man doesn't need a commitment to have sex."

Tater gnawed his way through half an ear of corn before he answered. "This-is-sworn-to-secrecy stuff, so you'd damn well better keep your trap shut."

"Not even an open sesame will pry it out."

Tater rolled his eyes. "That was lame, bro."

"Yeah, well." Trey grabbed another wing. He needed Tater to tell the story before Cardin clocked out and joined them. "You know me. I'm a vault."

"Too much of one, I'd say. You don't even call to shoot the shit."

Trey couldn't say why he hadn't kept in touch, though he'd likely been putting distance between his past and his present, until the past hit home with his father's death. "It's not going to happen again. Trust me on that."

Tater nodded, finished off his corn, and grabbed a wing with each hand. "It's not that big of a deal, really. Sandy got into some trouble with a guy in Nashville. A stalker type. He wouldn't leave her alone. And Sandy, well, you know her. She doesn't have a lot of friends."

For a good reason, Trey thought to himself,

"She had her car in the shop one day, and we got to talking. Seems this guy liked to mess with it, make sure she got stranded, then conveniently be there to pick her up. And by picking her up, I mean taking her back to his place and not letting her go until he was ready to."

Jesus. "Did she report him to Buell? Or the cops in Nashville?" Trey added, when Tater cursed loudly at the mention of the local law.

"A restraining order's really not much of a threat. It's just a piece of paper. By the time the cops respond to a violation, it's too late."

"So you're her flesh and blood restraining order."

"More or less."

"With perks."

"It's been known to happen."

"But it's not a long-term deal with you two."

"Nah. We're pretty much wrapping things up. No one's seen or heard from the guy in six months. Figure he's moved on to someone else, in another town, maybe even another state." Tater stopped to butter more corn. "Does any of that help you?"

What it did was remind Trey what a good man his friend was. But as far as the situation he found himself in… "You did the right thing. My right and wrong choices aren't so clear cut."

"You know, I've kinda come to believe that those shades of gray between the black and the white are more about what we can live with, maybe even what we're comfortable with. And I don't mean comfortable like a recliner and a big screen TV, but like being comfortable with what our actions mean to others, to our conscience." He shrugged. "Maybe even to society. Kinda depends on how big the picture is."

Trey took a deep breath, then blew it out. "This one's big enough."

"And you're trying to decide what to do about it."

Trey gave his friend a nod.

"Then I'd say you've gotta look at whether what you do is gonna bring more good than it causes harm."

"If I do what I'm thinking is right, it's gonna cause a whole lotta harm."

Tater studied him closely. "And the good?"

That was what Trey didn't know. He polished off the rest of his beer, raised the bottle overhead and waved at Sandy to bring him another. When he looked back at Tater, the other man was shaking his head. "My last one. I swear."

"This thing. Does it have anything to do with your dad?"

Trey's stomach lurched. "What makes you ask that?"

"I talked to Cardin when I came in earlier. She told me you'd spent the day going through his papers. That you had some meetings with his lawyer and the bank coming up."

"It was in a box of his paperwork, yeah. I found something that can mess up some people I like in a really big way. I don't want that to happen. But I'm not sure I can just let it go."

"Why not? What would happen if you did?"

"Nothing would happen if I did. Things would go on as they have been for everyone involved." An everyone that since his father's death had numbered one.

"Then unless you're talking about a crime or something…"

"I am."

"Hmm. That puts a spin on things, doesn't it?"

It did. A spin that had been making Trey dizzy all day. "I've come at it from every angle I can think of, and every time I wind up at the same place."

"Which is?"

"That well enough is probably best left alone."

"Then what's the problem?"

"I'm not so sure well enough is enough for me."

"Do you want justice? Or do you want revenge?"

Leave it to Tater to hit the head of the nail Trey had been avoiding. Jeb Worth had lived with what he had done all his life. He would take it to his grave. A seventy-year sentence of carrying that burden…

Was that punishment enough? If Trey sought more, would it be about revenge? The circumstances being what they were, it was unlikely Jeb would suffer anything beyond the humiliation of having his private deeds publicly known.

Yes, Trey wanted justice. But he didn't want that. He shook his head, ran his hands down his thighs, left them braced there. "I don't want revenge."

"Then that should make things easier for you."

Or not, Trey mused silently. He grabbed for the beer Sandy left on the table on her way to deliver an order. "You've given me a lot to think about at least."

"I can give you a whole lot more. Sandy says she's never known anyone to talk as much as I do about absolutely nothing."

"And you're surprised that I never called," Trey said.

The two men were blotting spilled beer off the table and laughing like goats when Cardin walked up.

"Is it safe to sit?" she asked, and the only answer Trey could give was to pat the bench beside him. Tater patted the bench beside him, too, and Trey reached across the table to sock him in the shoulder.

Instead of sitting next to either of them, Cardin grabbed a chair from one of the patio tables, brought it in and sat at the head of theirs. She looked from Trey to Tater to what was left of the food and back to Trey. "I don't even know why I'm here."

"You're here because this party needs some class," Trey said.

"Class. Is that like a division of racing?" Tater shot back.

"I think you two have been hitting the juice a little too hard."

Tater looked aghast. "We've got a lot of years to catch up on. Don't be keeping your man down."

"Yeah, don't be keeping your man down," Trey said, realizing as he did that he had no business driving home. Home. Cardin's home. Cardin's bed. A place he'd never sleep again if he took her grandfather down.

He got to his feet. "C'mon. We'll get your food to go. I need you to take me home before I do something really stupid. And end up regretting every beer I just drank."

23

AT 12:00 A.M. ON THE NIGHT of the Moonshine Run, Cardin sat beneath the Dahlia Speedway's blinding stadium lights wishing she hadn't forgotten her earplugs. Her whole body vibrated as the cars roared to life.

In years past, she'd sat here with Delta because Eddie had been the one in Jeb's car. Tonight, both of her parents sat on the bench behind her because it was Trey behind the wheel.

Trey, who loved her, who was going to make her his wife...unless his behavior of late meant he was getting cold feet.

She'd hardly spent any time with him this last week. In fact, since the night they'd eaten dinner with Tater, Trey hadn't been himself. And all she could think was that he regretted making their engagement real.

Another part of her, the part that was more sensible, knew he'd had a lot on his mind. He'd been going through his father's things, his family's things. That had to bring back years' worth of memories—of his childhood, his mother's abandonment, his father's death.

It couldn't be easy, and she hadn't exactly been sympathetic. No, she'd been a selfish brat, focused on wedding cakes, party dresses and living plans. That was no way to support the man she loved at a time when he needed her to be his rock.

She thought of all the things he'd told her that she should

know as his fiancée. He hadn't said anything about needing time to himself. She supposed for communication's sake, the smart thing to do would be to ask if that's all that his silence meant.

She wouldn't have time before the race, and really, she wasn't stupid enough to bother him now with her fears that things weren't as fairy-tale perfect as she'd thought. But she wanted to see him, to wish him good luck. To tell him how much she loved him. That she could do, that she *would* do.

She got to her feet, only to have her mother grab at her hand, and shout, "Where are you going?"

"I want to wish Trey good luck," she shouted back.

"Didn't you do that already?"

She shook her head. "I couldn't find him in the pits. I came straight up here."

"That's strange." Her mother frowned.

Her father frowned, too. "Did you see Jeb?"

Cardin nodded. "Yeah, he was talking to Beau Stillwell and Tater."

"But no Whip?" Eddie asked, both his voice and his expression taut.

Now Cardin was worried. "I'm sure he's around somewhere. He is driving, right?"

Eddie stood. "I'll walk on down to the pits with you. Make sure nothing's gone wrong with the car."

"Hey, you guys seen Whip?"

Cardin and Eddie both turned to see Tater climbing the stands toward them. Delta stood, too. "He's not with Jeb?"

"Jeb hasn't seen him. He's staged and ready to go." Tater gestured with one thumb over his shoulder. "But he's out a driver."

"No, he's not," Eddie said, pushing by Tater before Cardin or Delta could stop him.

"Eddie Worth! You are not driving that car," Cardin's

mother called after him, scrambling to follow and offering apologies when she stepped on the feet of other seated fans.

Oh, God. Where could he be? What was wrong? Had something happened? Her heart pounding, Cardin shoved at Tater to hurry, and the two of them crawled over the gathering crowd, following her parents to the pits.

They found Jeb on his four-wheeler, White Lightning tethered behind him, queued up in the staging lanes, waiting his turn to race. Cardin, Tater, Eddie and Delta converged on him in a rush.

Jeb scowled from beneath the brim of his cowboy hat. "What the hell are you all doing down here?"

"You're missing something, Dad," Eddie said, walking along the side of the ATV. "Where's Whip?"

Jeb shrugged. "I haven't seen him, but he said he'll be here, and I take that to mean that he will."

"I'm going to grab my gear," Eddie said, and turned.

Delta reached for his arm. "Eddie, no. You can't race. Your leg. What if you wreck and can't get out of the car?"

"If the boy wants to race, let him race," Jeb said, climbing off the four-wheeler and stepping into the fray. "He knows his own limits."

But Delta wasn't having it. "I swear to you, Eddie Worth. If you get behind the wheel of that car, that's it."

"Mom!" Cardin yelled. "What are you saying?"

Delta crossed her arms, her posture defensive. "Your father's trying to prove to his father than he's worthy of being a Worth."

Jeb and Eddie both turned on Delta, Eddie striking out first. "I'm not trying to prove anything, D. I'm only doing what I have to do."

"And that right there proves my son is a better man than I'll ever be," Jeb said, his hand coming down hard on Eddie's shoulder in a squeeze. "He's the best Worth there's ever been."

As Eddie stood dumbstruck and Delta stood shaking her head, Cardin took a step away, looking off toward the cars and the crowd in the pits, and ignoring the drama her family seemed bent on stirring. Her stomach was a knot of emotion and nerves.

She should've known nothing she could do would get her parents back together; just look at them! They were only making progress if arguing counted as talking things out. Why Trey would ever want to marry into this madhouse was beyond her comprehension.

He'd be smart to run far far away. She turned to go, tears of sadness threatening to spill—and ran smack into Trey's solid chest.

The relief overwhelmed her. She jumped up, yelped, then wrapped her arms around his neck. "Where have you been? Everybody's been worried about you. I came to wish you good luck, and you weren't here and my family's going insane."

Trey glanced over her head to where her family was still gesturing wildly. "You want to cut out of here and let your father drive?"

"You don't know how much I want that. But, even more so, I don't want him behind the wheel of Jeb's car. Not going a hundred and fifty miles an hour and being unable to get out fast should he need to."

"C'mon, then," Trey said, pulling her with him. "Let's make sure that doesn't happen."

"Where were you anyway?" she asked, as they hurried to catch up with Jeb.

"I left my boots at the house. I didn't realize it until I was halfway here." He smiled down at her, his dimples carved deep. "You didn't want me to risk burning my toes, did you?"

She looped her arm through his. He felt *so* good at her side. "No, but a phone call would've been nice."

"Yeah, well, about that," he said. "Seems I left my Black-Berry's charger in the Corley hauler. I'm outta juice until I pick up a new one."

Cardin laughed. "I was wondering how you were going to fit in with the Worths."

"And your verdict?"

"Perfectly. In an absent-minded way." They slowed down as they reached the others, staying just out of earshot. "As my fiancé, I want you to know something."

"What's that?"

"If you're not already crazy, my family's going to make you that way. I mean, look at them." She waved one hand, an encompassing gesture taking in the three people besides Trey she loved most in the world. "My mother not wanting my father to drive. My grandpa saying it's up to Eddie, while being well aware of his son's condition. And Eddie trying to prove God knows what to the both of them."

"They're all talking. Isn't that what you wanted?"

"I keep telling myself that it is," she said, leaning her head against his shoulder.

"Then I'd say your job here is done. Whatever happens with your family's going to happen. Time to focus on you now."

Trey's comment brought her back to what she'd been thinking earlier, and she shared her chagrin. "I think all I have been doing is focusing on me. I haven't been a very good fiancée."

"What do you mean? You're the best fiancée I've ever had."

"I thought I was the only fiancée you'd ever had."

"Oh, yeah. You are."

She pulled back, thought about punching him, and instead cuddled close again—a display of affection for her benefit alone. "I know this is no time to talk, that you've got to get your head in the race, but I worry that we rushed into this and didn't really think it through."

"Which part did we rush into?" he asked, tucking his boots tighter beneath his arm. "Your fake engagement, or my real one?"

It wasn't one or the other, it was the whole thing. "You came here to pack up your place and leave, and now you're tying yourself to the town. To me. To my lovable but lunatic family."

"Cardin, look at me," he said, stepping in front of her, his knuckles beneath her chin nudging her head up, bringing her gaze to meet his. "I'm not tying myself to anybody or anything. Not in the way you're making it sound. Making things official. Making them real…" He paused, brushing her bangs from her forehead. "That was my choice. My want. My need. I love you, Cardin. Being with you for the rest of my life is going to be an adventure. And I plan to enjoy every minute of it."

He made her so happy. God, he made her happy. But she still had to know. "Even with my family butting in and wanting everything to go their way?"

"Hey, every good story needs some crazy sidekicks."

She glanced toward her family, surprised to see things had calmed, and that all of them were looking at her—Jeb leaning on the four-wheeler seat, and her parents side by side, Eddie's arm over Delta's shoulders, Delta's around his waist.

Crazy sidekicks just about covered it. Arguing one minute, loving the next. They made her smile.

Trey swatted her on the bottom. "I think they're waiting for me."

"They can wait another second or two." She grabbed hold of both sides of his jacket, making sure she had his attention. "You go out there and win, Trey Davis. You forget everything

except being safe and taking that car down the track as straight
and as fast as you can."

"Yes, ma'am," he said before dropping a hard kiss on her
mouth, then jogging over to where Jeb and the others
waited.

She followed more slowly, watching him snap on his neck
brace, pull on his helmet and his gloves. He gave her a wink,
most of his face hidden behind the protective gear, then
climbed into the driver's cage and fastened the harness that
would keep him in his seat.

Eddie hopped on to the back of Jeb's ATV and they
advanced in the staging lanes. While Cardin and her mother
rushed back to watch from behind the cement barrier separating the track from the stands, Trey rolled White Lightning
into the burnout box.

Tater, acting as crew chief, stood in front of Trey on the
track, using hand signals to guide him into the grooves left
by the cars that had run before. The smell of scorched rubber
that rose as the drivers spun their tires in water for traction
left Cardin feeling as if she'd swallowed a charcoal briquette.

Trey eased the car forward, breaking the prestage beam, and
the prestage bulbs lit up to indicate his distance to the starting
line. Once his tires were positioned, the yellow stage lights on
his side of the Christmas Tree lit up. The second driver did the
same. With their crews out of the way, having given them the
thumbs up, the two drivers revved their engines.

Cardin held her breath. The large amber lights flashed,
followed by the green, and the cars blasted forward. The
crowd around her roared, and Cardin slammed her hands
over her ears as the cars exploded down the quarter mile
track. Seconds later, the parachutes deployed, the drivers cut
the engines, and the cars coasted to a stop.

She looked up the signs at the end of the track, saw that Trey had reached a speed of 158.02 miles per hour and run the quarter mile in 4.686 seconds—the best time of the night so far.

Cardin whooped and hollered, jumping up and down, waving her arms in the air. She watched as at the end of the track, Eddie and Jeb tethered White Lightning to the ATV and pulled it back to the pits.

Leaving her mother to follow, Cardin hurried from the barrier in front of the stands back to the pits to join them. She didn't care about the numbers the remaining cars would post. She didn't care if another car beat him. She just wanted to get to Trey.

By the time she reached him, his helmet was off, his jacket hanging open, and he was surrounded by autograph-seeking fans. Eddie and Jeb were already wrapped up discussing the car's performance, and all Cardin had a care for was the man who had driven it.

She couldn't wait to get him home.

24

TREY DIDN'T WIN THE Moonshine Run. Artie Buell, the sheriff's son, did. Though the loss stung, Trey hadn't expected to come away with the best time of the night. He'd spent an afternoon under the Nova's hood, but wasn't familiar enough with the motor to test its limits.

He'd first agreed to drive because Jeb was Cardin's grandfather, and at the time he'd been asked, he wasn't above scoring points. Working with Jeb would put Trey closer to finding out the truth about the fight—or so had been his thinking at the time.

He'd decided to drive in the end because he missed racing. He *really* missed racing. The smells, the sounds, the feel of an engine firing. And because Jeb was still Cardin's grandfather, and stepping up was a way to have everything he loved— two birds with one stone, and all that.

But, winning? Well, it just wasn't in the cards. That didn't make the Moonshine Run party any less fun. It did, however, make Artie Buell that much more annoying.

Leaning a shoulder into one of Headlights' support columns while listening to the band playing from the corner stage, Trey watched Artie show off the trophy Jeb had reluctantly awarded him. If Trey had lost to anyone else, he doubted Jeb would've been so peeved at turning over the title, but it was no secret that he didn't think much of the Buells.

Lifting the longneck he'd been toying with more than drinking, Trey turned his attention to the rest of the crowd, most who'd gathered to celebrate his and Cardin's engagement more than the race. There was music, there was food, there was drink and all of it on Jeb's tab.

To the right of the stage, where the picnic tables had been pushed aside, Eddie and Delta Worth were dancing as if they were the only people in the room…her eyes closed as she rested her head against his chest, his eyes cast down to where he stroked a hand over her hair. If they hadn't already reconciled, it looked to Trey like they were headed down that road, and it was a good thing to see.

Wondering if Cardin was watching her parents, he sought her out, finding her near the ice house's kitchen with Tater and Pammy Mercer, who'd gotten real cozy real quick the last hour. It appeared Tater had finished up his thing with Sandy, too. Trey had seen her tell Tater goodbye earlier with a kiss on the cheek, her fingers lingering on his before she'd walked out the door.

As he looked around at the crowd trying to make themselves heard above the band and the din of their own conversation, Trey was struck with the realization of how things had changed since he'd first arrived in Dahlia. Learning what fueled the fight between his father and Jeb Worth had let him finally forgive himself for not keeping in touch with his father.

But the biggest change was from admitting how much he loved Cardin. That he'd always loved her. That he always would. How he had done without her all this time, why it had taken him so long to figure things out… He raised his beer to his mouth and emptied the bottle, thinking he was one slow son of a bitch, and the luckiest one alive.

"It's going to be hard for folks here to see Cardin go. Her own folks especially."

Trey glanced to his side, and took in Jeb Worth standing there, his hands in the pockets of his suit pants, the tails of his western cut jacket flaring behind him. "I'm sure it will be."

"They'll understand, of course. They love their girl, and know being with you is what she wants. What makes her happy."

Trey kept quiet as he'd learned to do with Jeb. The older man took his time getting around to his point. Even now, he rocked back on his bootheels as if it helped him order his words. "'Course, should you want to stay in Dahlia, I can think of a good reason."

"What's that?"

"Andrew Fisk has put the Speedway up for sale."

Trey snorted, tossing his beer bottle in the garbage cans set aside for empties. "Like I can afford to buy that."

"You can with a little help from Diamond Dutch Boyle." Jeb pulled his right hand from his pocket and offered Trey an aged red velvet drawstring bag with the word "Hopscotch" in faded gold lettering across the front.

Trey hesitated. The bag was weighty, bulky, filled with what felt like marbles. Frowning, he opened it up and peered inside. Not marbles. Diamonds. Small, large, dozens, if not hundreds. "What the hell, Jeb?"

Jeb gave a brisk nod, went back to rocking on his heels. "I found 'em when I found the car. They were jammed in the casings of the Plymouth's headlights."

"You've had them all this time? And have never done anything with them?"

"Once in awhile I'll head over to Knoxville, or ride up to Lexington, or even down to Huntsville and sell one if I'm running low on funds, but I've kept the biggest. Figured to put them to good use some day."

"And buying the Dahlia Speedway is good use?"

"It is if it gives you and my granddaughter a way to make a living and a reason to stick around. Since they belonged to a gangster, I never saw the need to turn them over to their rightful owner. A law and order type might do just that, but I figure you using them to buy the Speedway works for the common good."

Trey didn't even know what to say. Since asking Cardin to marry him, he'd thought more than once about staying in Dahlia, settling down to raise a family where the two of them had grown up.

But giving up his crew chief position with the Corley team? Losing that connection to drag racing? Yet as owner of the Dahlia Speedway he wouldn't have to lose the latter, and he could probably convince "Bad Dog" Butch to give the town a second chance.

"I'll have to think about this. Talk to Cardin…" He tightened the bag's drawstring, too stunned to finish the thought.

Jeb cleared his throat, his gaze cast down. "Did you do any thinking about what I told you the other day?"

Trey nodded. "I did."

"And?"

It hadn't been an easy decision to reach. Trey had turned over his options and weighed the possible outcomes more times than he could count. In the end, it had been Tater's questions about justice and revenge that had made up his mind.

He didn't want revenge, and justice wasn't his to mete out. "I found what I came for, the cause of the fight. It's not my place to turn you over to the authorities. The rights and wrongs here you'll have to decide for yourself, and do what you need to accordingly."

"Well, then," Jeb said, taking a deep breath. "I'd best get this party started." He brought a shaking hand down on Trey's shoulder. "Thank you."

"Thank *you*." Trey bounced the bag on his palm before

tucking it into his pocket, then headed for the tub of iced long-necks. He needed another beer, needed to talk to Cardin, and had just pried off the bottle cap when Jeb slashed his finger across his throat to stop the band.

The music wound down, and the crowd hushed, turning as one to face the stage. Jeb settled his hat before speaking, his gaze sweeping from one side of the ice house to the other. "Tonight was supposed to be about celebrating Whip Davis driving White Lightning to a win in the Moonshine Run. But we've got something even better to celebrate—"

"Since Whip didn't win," came a heckle from Artie Buell's corner.

Jeb ignored the outburst. "Tonight, we celebrate the best news this old man has had in awhile. Whip, come on up here. And where's Cardin? Eddie? You and Delta, too."

The crowd applauded as Trey made his way to the stage, shaking Jeb's hand but staying on the main floor and waiting for Cardin. She came behind her parents who were holding hands, peeking at him over her mother's shoulder, and grinning.

Finally she was beside him, and he kept her there with an arm around her waist and a quick kiss she couldn't escape. Tears welled in Delta's eyes, and Eddie's weren't much drier. When Trey looked up at Jeb, he saw a man content at last, a feeling the two of them shared.

"For any of you dumb enough not to know why we're really here, let me tell you. Whip Davis is engaged to marry my granddaughter Cardin." Cheers rose from all corners, along with whistles, whoops, hoots and hollers.

It took Jeb a good three minutes to quiet the room. "I can't think of a man I'd rather welcome to the family, or one better suited to being my grandson-in-law. Now, let's do some dancing and some drinking and turn this shindig into a party worthy of Dahlia, Tennessee!"

The raucous cacophony started up before Jeb even got off the stage. The band began playing "I Fooled Around And Fell In Love," the singer crooning how he'd gone through a million girls, but since meeting his baby, that love had him in its hold. For Trey, it sure as hell did, and he wouldn't have it any other way.

Cardin looked stunning. Her hair was down from the ponytail she usually wore, her fringed bangs as dark and thick as her eyelashes. He didn't think he'd ever seen her in a dress, and this one was pure temptation, her waist cinched in with what looked like a cummerbund between the beaded halter top and the skirt that flowed around her knees.

When she looped her arms around his neck and pressed her body to his, he swore there hadn't been a more perfect moment in his life. He didn't even care how cheesy it sounded. He was a man in love.

"You clean up nice," she told him, nuzzling his tie where it lay in the center of his chest.

He wanted to groan. So he did. "You clean up so nice, I can't think of anything that's not dirty."

"Trey! We're on a dance floor. In public. I'm not sure this is the time and place for dirty."

"There's a Dumpster out back."

She giggled. "There's also an office. With a door that locks."

He wondered how fast they could get there. "If you keep up the teasing, I'm going to need the walk-in cooler."

"We can't do that," she said, swaying with him side to side. "We'd melt everything."

"I wasn't going to take you with me."

"Uh-huh." She gave the reprimand with a laugh and a shake of her head. "From now on, you'll be taking me everywhere you go."

Now was as good a time as any… "What if we just stay here?"

"Dancing?"

"In Dahlia."

She slowed, frowned, her dark brows coming down in a V. "What're you talking about?"

They needed privacy for this conversation. "I'll show you. If you show me."

"Show you what?"

"Where the office with the locking door is."

"We can't…do that here. Not now. This is our party. People expect us to be here."

"We're not going to do that here. Now. We can do it here later, but this is something else."

She gave in, letting him dance them to the corner nearest the service window. When the singer stopped to introduce the musicians behind him, Cardin grabbed Trey's hand, and ducked into the hallway that ran between the kitchen and the restrooms, then through the office door.

She closed it, and leaned against it, breathing as if she'd just run a marathon. "Now, tell me what you're talking about. Wouldn't staying here keep you from working with Corley Motors? And wouldn't that make 'Bad Dog'…mad?"

Trey moved to stand between her and the desk. "Your grandfather told me that the Dahlia Speedway is up for sale."

"And he's going to buy it?"

This was where it got good. "He wants me to buy it."

"You have that kind of money? I'm marrying a wealthy man?"

"You are now," he said, and pulled the bag Jeb had given him from his pocket. "You know the speculation about how Diamond Dutch Boyle got his name?"

Cardin walked closer as he loosened the drawstring, watching as he poured out the diamonds in the middle of her mother's desk.

She gasped, quickly covering her mouth with one hand as if she feared the sound would give away their secret. "Jeb had the gangster's diamonds? All these years?"

"Yep. He said they were hidden in the car's headlights."

"And he gave them to us?"

"He did. There's no way to find out or prove who they ever belonged to, so…" Trey shrugged. "Finders keepers."

Cardin finally looked at him, her eyes twinkling, her voice soft and low. "We could do anything with that money, Trey. We could probably live off of it for the rest of our lives. We could go anywhere."

He nodded. "Or we could stay right here. We could look into buying the Speedway. It would give me something to do every day before I came home every night to you."

She looked back at the diamonds, shaking her head, her hands on her cheeks, then her heart. "You know, Tater would be thrilled to have you stay here."

"And your parents would be thrilled to have *you* stay here."

"Is that what you want to do? Buy the Speedway?"

"We don't have to decide tonight, though there is something we should do while we're here."

"No way," she said, pulling the visitor chair between them, using it as a barrier the way she'd used the trash can the other day. "I'm not having sex with you in my mother's office."

"I wasn't thinking about sex. Well, I was thinking about sex," he said, moving the chair out of the way and reaching for her hand. "But mostly I was thinking we should pick out a diamond for your ring."

"My ring?" She echoed his words, let him pull her close.

He tucked her hair behind her ear, trailed his fingers along her jaw, loving the feel of her skin. He would never tire of touching her. "I wasn't exactly prepared when I proposed. I didn't even offer you a cigar band or a soda can pull top."

"You offered me yourself, Trey Davis. You told me that you loved me. You're the only thing I need, the only man I've ever wanted, or loved," she said, throwing her arms around his neck and kissing him, sliding her tongue into his mouth as soon as her lips met his.

Minutes later, she was the one who suggested they have sex in her mother's office.

He didn't say no.

* * * * *

HARD TO RESIST

BY
SAMANTHA HUNTER

Samantha Hunter lives in Syracuse, New York, where she writes full-time. When she's not plotting her next story, Sam likes to work in her garden, quilt, cook, read and spend time with her husband and their dogs. Most days you can find Sam chatting on the Harlequin Blaze boards at eHarlequin.com, or you can check out what's new, enter contests, or drop her a note at her website, www.samanthahunter.com.

For all my friends at Love Is an
Exploding Cigar, who make every day,
even tough writing days, fun.

1

"I THINK WE REALLY might have found the twelve sexiest men in America," Lacey Graham's assistant, Jackie, sighed as they took in the photographic buffet of gorgeous men before them on the project board. The final selections for the "Sexiest American Heroes" calendar had been made the week before. As photographer for the project, these gorgeous guys were all now in Lacey's capable hands.

Lacey stood back, one arm wrapped across her middle with her other elbow balancing on it, her chin resting in her fingers as she assessed the blowups of the hunks with a cool, experienced eye.

Too many blondes in a row in March, April and May—she'd switch April with August. Since they were in October now, she'd reversed the schedule, starting with Mr. December, who was set to arrive tomorrow, and November a few days later. She wanted to take them one at a time, calling them back at a later date for group cover shots.

She and Jackie had been juggling these promo shots all day, most of which were not professionally done but were good enough for roughs. Actually, it was impres-

sive how incredible these men looked in the bad lighting and overly bright PR poses. Her hands itched to get
to work, to get them in the right setting, good light.

"I don't think I've ever seen such a collection of
perfect men all in one place." Jackie sighed. "I want
them all, and not necessarily one at a time."

Lacey chuckled. "Down, girl. Don't you have a
steady boyfriend?"

"Well, sure, but I can window-shop, can't I? K.C. is
my guy, and he knows it, but frankly, he's not above
checking out some beautiful woman when she walks
by and turnaround is fair play. So if you had to
choose…?" Jackie prompted Lacey mischievously.

Lacey shook her head, not interested. She looked at
the men on the board in the only way she could, as
professional modeling subjects and that was all. She
rubbed her right forearm, knowing it was healed, but a
shadow of an ache lingered anyway. Her last lover had
not taken her attempts to break up very well, leaving
her with a broken forearm as a parting gift, along with
an assortment of bruises and a nasty laceration that
had taken several stitches. Broken hearts were something you could get over most of the time, but having
someone break your arm wasn't easily forgotten.

Swallowing deeply, she studied the board, fighting
the sick feeling in her stomach that she got whenever
she thought about being with a man. It would pass.
She'd get back in the game at some point. When *she*
was ready and not before, not even for guys like the
ones lined up in front of her. Until then, she'd keep to
herself and focus on her work. That was what mattered.

No one here knew her secret.

Jackie didn't know and no one was going to know about what had happened with Scott, her ex. On the advice of the doctor who treated her arm, Lacey had made one visit to an abuse counselor when she'd arrived in the city. Once she saw the haunted expressions of the women sitting in the lobby, she'd walked back out. That wasn't her. She'd handle it on her own.

What Scott had done to her had been a onetime thing, a huge, incredibly stupid mistake. But Lacey hadn't waited around for more and wouldn't allow it to happen again. She wasn't like the women who were trapped or who wouldn't leave.

Still, the memory pinched at her as much as the residual ache in her arm. On a certain level, she was irritated with herself for not being able to enjoy the beauty of the men as she once would have done. Like Jackie said, there was nothing wrong with looking.

There was no doubt that the array of males she'd be working with were prime fantasy material. She also knew she shouldn't change her perception of all men because of one bad apple. She *knew* that—in her head.

Her heart, however, was still playing "keep away," and so was her body. She'd made a few small forays into a normal dating life—tried to go out to clubs with friends—but it hadn't worked out. The thought of a man touching her, even to dance…well…not yet.

"I'm a professional. I don't have a favorite," she said primly, breaking the spell of her thoughts.

Jackie wasn't buying it. "Ha. Give me a break. Check

out Mr. November and tell me he's not absolutely perfect."

Lacey glanced up, relenting just slightly. "No one is perfect."

"Cynic."

"Groupie."

They grinned at each other, and Lacey relented a little. "It is hard to resist an honest-to-goodness cowboy."

"Not a cowboy, a Texas Ranger," Jackie corrected with flourish. "Rough, rugged, and they always get their man."

"Isn't that the Mounties?"

"Whatever. I bet they always get their girl, too."

Lacey studied the man staring out from the Ranger's PR photo and smiled. "He's got good eyes. Dark hair, dark eyes. That straight jawline could be on a statue at the Met, but he's so serious. All the rest are smiling."

"Maybe he doesn't like having his picture taken."

"We'll have to change that right quick," Lacey said in a mock Western accent, slipping out of her serious self for a moment, though she couldn't joke about the facts in front of her.

"This guy is the real deal. Look at his bio. Very single, career cop, has more awards and recognitions than I can count. He was nominated for the calendar by his community after he stopped a school shooter single-handedly. He found the guy targeting a local migrant school before the shooting happened. Tracked him through the Texas desert for five days and brought him back. Alive."

"Wow," Jackie breathed the word, fanning her face, and Lacey had to agree. *Wow* indeed.

Lacey couldn't help but be impressed with the stories of the twelve men on her wall. They were good men. Men who put their lives on the line to help others. The one thing all of the calendar candidates had in common was that they'd pitched in to help during the weeks of 9/11, one of the criteria for the application.

The *Bliss* calendar this year was going to be a smash, a celebration of the best of the best. It was also going to be a very visible leap for Lacey into the world of commercial photography. It could push her to the top. That was what she was counting on, anyway.

Lacey had given up several other opportunities to land the deal. The women's magazine equivalent of the *Sports Illustrated Swimsuit Issue,* the *Bliss* project was the chance of a lifetime.

She wasn't going to let the past get the best of her.

Eyeing Mr. November again, she allowed herself to imagine the possibilities, just for a second.

"His eyes *are* good," Jackie agreed, "but I can't wait to see him with his shirt off. I bet he has great abs, naturally defined, not gym-machine generated."

Lacey agreed. "I love the slope of the croup…"

"The…*what?*" Jackie frowned at her as if she was nuts.

Lacey laughed. "Sorry. My parents raised horses back in Nevada, and sometimes I can't help thinking about people's bodies in equine terms. Especially men."

"I'll bet he's hung like a—"

"Jackie!" Lacey admonished, laughing. "We're not taking *those* kinds of pictures."

"Hey, gotta show some skin for *Bliss*. But what's the slope of the— What was it again?"

"Croup. On a horse, it's the curve that follows the hip to the tip of the tail—right about here on our handsome model," she said, leaning in to trace the masculine line from hip over his hindquarters.

"Oh. Yeah. I *love* that part," Jackie said approvingly. "Very important for good thrust, yes?"

Lacey choked on a shocked laugh, pulling her hand back as she realized she hadn't withdrawn her finger from the photograph yet, her cheeks catching fire. Maybe she wasn't quite as detached as she thought she was.

"Yes, I suppose it would be. Thanks for the visual. I guess Mr. December should be here tomorrow, right?"

Jackie snapped to attention. "Oh, crap, I meant to tell you—I had to change up the first two appointments. November is coming in first because December's wife went into labor, so he won't be in for a week or so."

"Oh, well, good for them. We should send something, congratulations, flowers, whatever," Lacey commented absently, still studying the pictures.

"Already done."

"You're the best."

"So, Mr. Luscious should be arriving at LaGuardia around 10:00 a.m.—I'll meet him, of course." Jackie grinned like a cat swallowing a whole flock of canaries. "And then after lunch you'll meet him for an afternoon planning session, some studio time, and get out on the shoot day after tomorrow. He's single. No babies to worry about, thank the heavens."

"Sounds good. Thanks so much for all of your help. I've never had a full-time assistant before. I could get used to it."

"Hit a bull's-eye with this job, and you'll need one to keep up with all the projects that will be coming your way," Jackie said sincerely, patting Lacey's arm. "Oh, I have to go. I'm meeting Kenny at the rib place he's been insisting on going to. You want to come along? He's into photography, too, and was hoping to talk shop with you at some point."

"Really? I didn't know that—what's he do?"

Jackie shrugged. "He's been doing all kinds of things for a while. He had a small gallery show, and he's been picking up some brochure work, catalogs, that kind of thing."

"Everyone has to start somewhere."

"He's really good—I could show you some of his stuff sometime."

Lacey smiled, but always felt awkward in situations where up-and-coming photographers wanted to make contact, but it was how the game was played, and Jackie was her assistant.

"Sure—but you go ahead for dinner. I have work to finish up here. Thanks, though."

"Okay, I'll have your hunk here for you safe and sound tomorrow."

"Don't take a bite out of him before you get here."

Jackie stuck her tongue out. "Spoilsport."

Lacey grinned, then was left alone to quietly study

the men. They were all amazing, although Jackie was right. November stood out. Maybe slightly older than the others, he had more presence, more...*something*. Manliness, charisma... Those steady brown eyes might have been staring down a suspect as much as a camera as he peered out from the picture. *Dangerous*. Not to be messed with.

Would he look at her that way? Did his eyes soften when he was with a lover? Naked, tangled in silky sheets, skin to skin? Was he still all hard edges and intense eyes then?

A shiver skidded over her skin. She didn't need to be around any man with the capacity to be dangerous. Still, she wondered what it would take to make him smile. Reaching out to draw her finger along his outline again, she stopped when her fingers met his lips.

Maybe Mr. November could remind her how good being with a real man could be, not some jerk who got off on hurting women. They would be working alone for several days, moving around the city. Almost nothing was as intimate to Lacey as staring down the barrel of her lens at someone, closing in, finding the shot.

It was New York City. Anything could happen.

SLOPE OF HIS CROUP, HUH? Would she be asking to check his teeth or feeling him up for spavins and thorough-pins and other physical faults before they were done? Jarod Wyatt shook his head, mostly amused. The idea of her feeling him up wasn't an entirely unappealing one, and at least she knew something about horses. He hadn't expected that from a city girl.

He stood in the dark corner of the *Bliss* studio, fascinated by the conversations he'd overheard, and more so with the woman who couldn't seem to keep her hands off him—or off his picture, anyway.

The smaller, dark-haired girl with the lusty sense of humor walked out the back, leaving the blonde—the photographer—standing alone in perfect silhouette against the white wall. She was lanky and somewhat coltish in build, but she moved gracefully. Her fingers were long and thin like the rest of her, though beneath the khakis and black T-shirt, he could see she had her share of curves.

Jarod had only been to New York once before, on the day after the bombings. The empty spot on the skyline still kicked him in the chest because he'd stood in the middle of it for several days and those were memories he wasn't likely to ever forget. He wasn't sure what he expected to feel coming back. Mostly it was good to see the city had recovered, that it was busy and teeming with life, the way it should be.

On the approach, he hadn't been able to take his eyes off the spot where the Towers used to be, but he noted driving in that there was so much life here, nothing could ever completely erase it. New York was a place unique unto itself, and if he wasn't here for such a ridiculous reason, he might enjoy the visit. He loved the scrub desert and wide-open spaces of Texas. His home was a part of his soul. Still, he enjoyed getting away every now and then, just like anyone else. Cities had their advantages.

He'd also been told there was a decent place that did

Texas barbecue better than he could find in his home state. He didn't want to believe it, but he had the address in his PDA and hoped to find out for himself.

Feeling a little like a Peeping Tom, he figured he should make himself known. He'd stayed to the back when he'd walked in, not wanting to interrupt, but now there wasn't any reason to lurk, except that he was enjoying the view.

Clearing his throat gently to signal his presence, he stepped forward from the hallway where he'd been standing. She whipped around, obviously startled, and he froze. Her posture signaled fright to him. Not a jump or a gasp of broken concentration, but her big eyes landed on him with a look that he'd seen far too often. Fear. Momentary panic.

He put his hands up, calming, showing he was no threat.

"Sorry, didn't mean to scare you, ma'am. I'm Lt. Jarod Wyatt, Texas Rangers, El Paso division— November, as you have me up on your board there," he said with a healthy dose of Texas charm and sincere chagrin. The picture reminded him why he was here, and it made his eyes roll every time he thought about it.

"You're not due until tomorrow," she said starkly, sounding a bit choked, as if trying to breathe correctly. Was she always this jumpy? She'd mentioned Nevada. Maybe she wasn't a city girl as he'd assumed.

"I took an early flight. Thought I'd stop by and check the place out. The door was open, and a secre-tary pushed me in this direction," he explained with just a hint of apology, then held out his hand. "Nice to meet you. I guess you're the photographer?"

Her eyes narrowed. "Why would you assume that?"

Whoops. He didn't want to let her know he'd been skulking in the corner for the past fifteen minutes. From the glare in her eyes, he wasn't sure that would go over too well.

Lacey Graham was a prickly number. *Pretty as could be, though,* he thought, taking in fine, almost porcelain features. Her eyes snapped dark green, and her mouth formed a perfectly pink rosebud, bare of any lipstick. Just what he preferred.

"Well, ma'am, it doesn't take much to figure out. You're here, in the studio, checking out the pictures on this big board, and speaking matter-of-factly, I heard you and your assistant talking when I first came in. Didn't want to interrupt," he offered by way of explanation and was glad to see her shoulders relax, her frame softening as she nodded.

"Sorry. It's not a good idea to sneak up on someone like that, especially after hours. I'm Lacey Graham, but I guess you already knew that."

Her hand was small in his, but strong. She had a firm grip, which triggered a small dart of unexpected arousal that he firmly pushed to the back of his mind.

"So this is the calendar spread, huh?" he said, scrutinizing the wall, trying to ignore his own picture among the others. He recognized one or two of the other guys, men he respected, and it helped him to not feel quite so cheesy about doing this. Not that he'd had much choice in the matter.

"Yep. These are just the PR shots we're using to play with. It will all change when we have the actual photos we choose for the final, but this gives me some idea what I want to do with each model."

"All due respect, but I'm not a model, and I'm betting none of these other guys are either."

He saw the corners of her lips twitch. "With all due respect back, Lieutenant, you *are* a model for the next week. It'll be fun, don't worry."

He frowned. "A week? I thought we'd spend a day taking pictures and I'd be on my way?"

She shook her head. "It will take more than that. We're shooting around the city, so I had to arrange for permissions to use various locations for each model. Some we have to get to at crazy times of day, they have to clear them out for a few hours, and that needs planning. Then I'd like to do some unposed, candid shots. The letter we sent stated the time requirements clearly."

He took a breath, shoved his hands in his pockets. He wasn't going to admit he'd been in a bitch of a mood about having been ordered to do this in the first place, and when the letter had come in the mail he'd ditched it, thinking he'd get out of the whole deal. His superiors had made him realize differently. Even law enforcement cared about public image these days. Far too much, in his view.

"I guess I figured it wouldn't take that long," he said, wincing slightly at the idea of this taking up so much time. "It's just a few pictures."

She laughed then, and he was struck by the sound, how

lively and natural it was. He had a feeling she used it a lot.

"It's much more than that. We need to cover a lot of ground, and I want to cover all four seasons from all models, since I may change my mind as to who gets placed where in the final analysis. This is a big deal, Lieutenant. I want this calendar to be a wild success."

"Good for your career, huh?"

Her posture stiffened again, and she tipped up her chin, nodding shortly. "Absolutely. Probably won't hurt yours any, either."

He didn't answer that. This had nothing to do with his career, but he wasn't going to get into a pissing match with the pretty lady.

"We'll be doing a group shot at the end at Ground Zero. You'll have to come back up for that, probably. Any problems there?"

"I guess not. Should there be?"

"Some of the guys weren't sure they could go back, to the site, I mean."

"I'm fine. Unless I happen to be out in the scrub chasing down felons, getting back here for a day shouldn't be difficult. As long as it's only a day," he warned. His supervisors had told him to do whatever the magazine needed, and this didn't come off his vacation time, so he found it hard to argue.

She peered up at him through thick lashes. "You hungry, Lieutenant?"

"Call me Jarod. And, yeah, I could go for something."

"If you want, I know some good places. Let me

close up here, and we can have our initial consult over some pizza or whatever you prefer. My treat."

His blood warmed more than it should, but there was no way he was turning down her invitation. He was curious about this beautiful photographer. No doubt she was smart. She was cagey, too, and she also had no qualms about meeting him eye to eye. She had a well-used laugh. All in all, an intriguing package.

"Sure, sounds good. I have to check in at my hotel, though."

"Where'd you book?"

"The Affinia. Not far from here."

"You'll like it. I'll meet you in the lobby in an hour, then?"

He reached up, tipped his hat. Her eyes followed his gesture so closely, as if she was already mentally taking him apart frame by frame. It was disconcerting.

"See you in an hour."

2

LACEY COULDN'T QUITE stifle the riff of excitement that hastened her movements as she rushed back to her loft and jumped in the shower to get ready to meet Lieutenant Wyatt in thirty minutes.

She'd nearly had a coronary when he'd walked up behind her in the studio. The man moved like a big cat. She hadn't heard a step on the hard acrylic floors, but how long had he been there? How much had he heard of Jackie's conversation with her? She shrugged. She'd said nothing that she felt ashamed of…well, there was the *thrusting* thing…but Jackie had come up with that one.

Lt. Jarod Wyatt was astounding in real life. The picture had muted the overall effect of absolutely radiant masculinity. She'd completely forgotten everything else—who she was, where she was—when he'd reached up, tipped the brim of his hat and smiled at her….

Oh, my.

She wasn't prone to fluttering around men, but Jarod Wyatt was fully deserving of it. He was stunning in person.

He also touched something deeper, a chord of comfort and familiarity. It seemed odd, having just met him, but he reminded her of the men she'd grown up with in Nevada. Big, capable men who put a premium on being gentlemanly, and who could be gentle. Like her dad, her uncles and cousins. Lacey had known plenty of good men, and only one bad, so she counted herself fortunate.

There was a sense of polish about Jarod Wyatt, too, though. He'd gone to college, for one thing. She knew from his profile that he had a master's in criminology, and he had some background in forensics. It was probably why they'd pulled him in on 9/11, beyond the sheer need for manpower. He wasn't just any cowboy cop.

It was why she'd asked him to dinner. That, and because she wanted to look at him more, to study him the way an artist would study any subject. He would be pure joy to photograph. Her mind was already placing him in poses, in settings.

A few of which were X-rated and included her bedroom.

She smiled, reaching for a towel and wiping down briskly. God, it was *good* to feel this way, if only for a moment. To look forward to a man's company again, even though it was only business over pizza. Maybe this was a good sign.

Grabbing black, formfitting pants, she tugged on a pair of heels and a hot-pink T-shirt with a colorful, fringed vest, assessing herself in the mirror.

If she were honest, she knew it was an outfit meant to draw a man's eye. A particular man's eye in this case. She nibbled her lip, suddenly apprehensive. So he was a good-looking guy—she should still be careful. Was it smart to have agreed to meet him, a stranger, for dinner? What did she really know about him, after all?

She shook off the doubts and their chilling effect. It was just business, some pizza and conversation. She'd wear this same outfit if anyone had suggested meeting her for dinner that evening. A lot of her clothes were colorful and funky and often drew attention. She wasn't going to second-guess it. This was who she was.

The phone rang, and she contemplated not bothering with it. She had to meet Jarod, and contrary to popular wisdom about keeping men waiting, Lacey was never late. She was obsessively punctual, in fact.

Making sure she had her wallet, she dug around to transfer her stuff to a smaller purse as she answered the phone.

"Hello?"

"Lacey?"

"Yes?"

"This is Gena, from Legal Aid in L.A.?"

She froze in place. Legal Aid had handled her case back in Los Angeles, since she couldn't afford a high-priced lawyer. Her family would have paid, but she didn't want them to know what happened. She told them she'd changed her name for business reasons, to maintain privacy from her work. She hated lying to them, but it was better than having them worry about her.

"Hi, Gena, what's up?" She tried to sound casual, cheerful, but it felt as if her stomach was in her throat.

"Listen, there's no need to worry, I want to emphasize that first. You should know that Scott Myers was released from his sentence to finish his probation on house arrest. He's out of prison, but he's still in California, and he won't be able to leave a predetermined schedule of home and work for fourteen more months."

"No," was all Lacey could breathe before Gena continued.

"Please, don't worry. He's wearing a personal monitoring device. He won't be able to find you, and probably won't bother, given his profile, the steps you've taken and your history. Still, if he attempts to contact you in any way, your restraining order is still in force, even under your new name, so let us know, okay? I don't want to upset you, but we like to make sure you know what's going on."

Lacey's breathing seemed cut off and she swallowed, her previous cheer evaporating as she found the air to mumble an answer before she hung up.

Scott was free.

He shouldn't have been released for another eighteen months, she recalled. The night he left Lacey unconscious on her kitchen floor he'd gone to a local bar and started a fight there, causing several thousand dollars of damage and other injuries. Luckily, the combined charges had sent him away for a while.

Lacey breathed deeply, calming herself. She had to listen to Gena, who wouldn't bullshit her. Scott wouldn't come after her. Still, when he'd left her lying there, broken and bruised, he'd made it clear he thought she was dead. His only comment upon finding out she wasn't was relief that he wouldn't be charged with murder.

She was far away now, new city, new name. The calendar project didn't really put her in the public eye—she was behind the scenes. *Bliss* wouldn't give out her personal details. She was safe, she reassured herself, standing frozen with the phone in her hand for several minutes.

Eyeing the door, the dark city streets that she usually loved so much suddenly seemed ominous. Anxiety gripped her at the thought of going out. With a stranger, no less.

What had she been thinking? Hadn't she learned anything from her previous mistakes?

She had no idea who Jarod Wyatt was, and just because he had an impressive official record, that didn't mean squat. Plenty of cops, firemen, doctors—all kinds of men—were closet crazies. More dangerous because of their outward appearance, because they had power and liked to use it. That's how it had been with Scott. Witty, handsome, successful…with all of that violence hiding under the surface.

She put her purse down, started to take her vest off, but stopped, pausing in the center of her living room.

This was important, her heart told her. She had a big choice to make.

Was she going to hide in her apartment and her studio for the rest of her life?

No. She didn't want to be that person.

The fear was just an emotional response, a *good* response, so the counselor at the hospital had reassured her. It would keep her alert and keep her safe, but she couldn't let it run her life. Good fear, bad fear. She had to remember the difference.

Jarod Wyatt was a man she'd be working with

closely, and she couldn't let her personal demons get in the way of her success on this job. His record was impeccable, and she'd been alone with him earlier and hadn't felt the least bit afraid. She'd been excited about seeing him tonight—maybe a little too excited—so now she knew to throttle that back so she didn't give the wrong impression. But she would still go.

She'd meet him in a populated, well-lit place for some pizza, talk work and welcome him to the city. Enjoy having his company for a few hours. She'd be friendly, professional and keep clear boundaries. Then she'd come home and put this all out of her mind.

She needed to keep things in perspective—it wasn't as if Jarod had asked her out, and he hadn't indicated anything other than casual friendliness. He was just a guy, another model.

No big deal.

JAROD STEPPED OUT of the elevator of the very nicely appointed hotel and smiled at a group of older women who watched him walk by. He smiled at them and touched his fingers to the brim of his hat. The group seemed to get a kick out of it.

He saw the beacon of Lacey's fuchsia shirt immediately as she stood poised by the entrance, looking around furtively. A glance at his watch told him he was five minutes early, and she'd obviously changed her clothes, so she couldn't have been waiting long. After his surprise appearance earlier, he approached carefully, making sure she had ample time to see him. She turned, smiling falsely, overbrightly.

Did she regret making plans with him?

He was perfectly happy to explore the city on his own, but he also looked forward to some company, someone to share the sights with for an evening. She'd seemed interested and friendly at the studio. He wondered what had changed.

"Hi there," he said casually, looking out at the streets bustling with early-evening traffic. The noises were muted here in the lobby. Though he could spend long days and nights in the desert enjoying nothing but the silence of the sand and the stars, he found the energy of the city stimulating, as well.

Or maybe it was the woman standing just a foot away, in spite of the tension stiffening her very nicely built form. Something about her had his blood circulating with a low, warm hum through his system, but he wasn't sure she was having the same reaction.

"You okay?" he found himself asking.

"Sure. Why do you ask?"

"You seem…strung a little tight."

She frowned, and shrugged. "Just distracted. Busy day, a lot on my mind."

The message underneath the cool reply really said "mind your own business" and wasn't lost on him. If this was going to be the mode of conversation, he was in for a long evening.

"How about a drink first? I could use something to warm up. Chilly out there tonight."

"I think it's going to be an early winter this year."

"You said you wanted to shoot seasonal photos— how is that possible when it's already October?" he asked as they walked to the bar. She hadn't said yes or no to the idea of a drink, but he wasn't lying about wanting one. She didn't object as they headed in that direction.

"Mostly we'll use props, how you're dressed, that kind of thing. Then the postproduction guys can work their magic, too. The photo will be mostly you and not so much background. So for a July shot you might wear trunks, and we'll work it that it looks summery."

"Even if I'm freezing my ass off in reality?"

"Yeah." She smiled then, and laughed. "Welcome to the cruel world of modeling."

He ordered a whiskey, neat, and asked her if she wanted anything, surprised when she ordered the same. His eyebrows lifted as they tilted their glasses toward each other and she swallowed hers in one throw, closing her eyes as if she'd needed it more than he did. He hadn't realized how pale she was until the warmth from the whiskey infused her skin with a pink glow.

Something had happened between the time he'd left and now, but he didn't feel free to inquire. He was a stranger, a visitor that she was nice enough to spend some time with because they had to work together. That was it.

Maybe not, maybe more, whispered the hum in his body. He ignored it. He wasn't opposed to having some fun with a willing woman while he was here, but he wasn't about to complicate matters with the prickly photog—unless she offered an invitation—but she wasn't being too inviting at the moment.

So why was he enjoying the view of the very feminine swell beneath the stylish top, taking advantage while her eyes were closed?

"You want to get some pizza? I know a place that has the best in the city," she said, opening her eyes just as he looked back up. *Almost caught staring,* he thought, feeling about seventeen.

Her green eyes were luminous, maybe in part from the whiskey, but she was a natural beauty, indeed. He waited before answering, questioning whether this was a good idea, but he'd already agreed. Jarod wasn't in the habit of backing out on a woman when he promised to spend an evening with her.

"Pizza? That sounds good. Must be a hundred pizza places here, but you know the best one, huh?"

He winced internally. Small talk was not his strength.

She grinned, seeming more relaxed. "Yes, I do, as a matter of fact. It's an amazing experience that will shift your entire perspective on what the dish means. The place is a hole-in-the-wall that tourists never find, so you're in for a treat. We'll pick up a bottle of vino on the way because they don't serve drinks. You have to bring your own."

"I like a lady with a plan," he agreed, glad she seemed to be loosening up.

"If you want to go up the Empire State Building at night, we could do that, too, after dinner—we'll be shooting up there. You afraid of heights?"

He shook his head as they walked out into the cool evening. "No. Heights aren't a problem. But you don't have to take me sightseeing. I figured this was a business dinner."

Her cheeks became warmer, and he realized his statement didn't quite come out the way he meant it.

"I meant—"

"No, no, you're right—this is a business dinner," she said easily, but didn't meet his eyes.

How could things be so weird and awkward, hot and cold, with a woman he'd just met two hours ago? Jarod was usually good with women. He enjoyed them as friends and lovers, and never had such tension or foot-in-mouth disease before. This one had him tripping over himself, and it wasn't a great experience.

They popped into a liquor store where Lacey seemed to be on a first-name basis with the owner and he handed her a Chianti that he knew she liked. Jarod insisted on paying.

"Fine, but the pie is on me," she said, and while it wasn't his habit to let women pay for a date, he agreed. It was her city, her pizza place, her expense account, he figured.

They walked a few blocks and turned in through a glass door painted white in order to be opaque into a deep, narrow room that was brightly lit, but nothing fancy. Small, round plastic tables hugged a stark white wall that featured signed pictures of various New Yorkers, many famous, others he didn't know.

"Interesting spot. I would never have guessed from the street this was even here."

"Best-kept secret."

She must be right as they had to navigate the narrow space between the counter and the tables to the far end to find an open table. The place was packed, and the rich aromas and sizzling pies he spotted on people's tables had his mouth watering.

Locating an empty table, they sat in plastic chairs that he hoped were sturdy as he settled his large frame into one. The napkins were paper, from a metal dispenser next to a small vase with some fake flowers. He wasn't a fancy guy, but he had to assume all of the money and talent in the place went into the food, not the decor.

"So this is your favorite place, huh?"

"Isn't it great?" She was all smiles again. If he were prone to it, her mercurial changes would make him seasick, she seemed to shift back and forth so often.

"I found it completely by accident. I was just passing by one night and someone opened the door. The smell of the sauce and spices had me making a U-turn to come in and see where it was coming from. It's bare bones, but cozy. Warm. And the owners are really nice people."

"Probably a gold mine, as well. Can't be much overhead," he commented.

"I bet you're right. Locals call it the Pizza Room, though I don't think it actually has an official name. If you get takeout, it's just a plain brown box, no logo. They don't do delivery and aren't in the directory."

He grinned, liking the simplicity of it. Lack of marketing was probably the best marketing of all in a world drowning in logos.

"I'm glad you decided to show me one of the city's secrets," he said, meaning it. This was much more his speed than some froufrou bistro or someplace where food arrived under silver domes.

"How hungry are you? One pie or two?"

"Are you going to eat?"

She stared at him, dumbfounded. "What? Of course I'm going to eat. Why do you think I'm here?"

"I meant, you're so thin, and given your profession, I thought you might be an 'eat salad and smell the real food' type."

She looked as if she couldn't believe his brashness, and then burst out laughing. At least he hadn't upset her.

"Ranger, I can put it away. Don't underestimate me there. I am blessed with what my father used to call a hummingbird's metabolism—small animal, eats a lot. No animal has a faster metabolism. I can probably eat damned near my own weight in this pizza."

"Is that right?"

She nodded and gave the waitress their order—two pies—after grabbing a few plastic cups from the counter for their wine and a conversation about the owner's new grandchildren.

"You seem to know everyone—I always thought New Yorkers were cold and distant."

"C'mon, you've been here before, so you know different. But anyway, I'm not a native. It's a big city, and it has its share of attitude, but I've found the people here to be some of the friendliest I've ever met. It's huge and intimidating, but you find your own corner and settle in. I've known small towns a lot less friendly."

He had to admit that was true. "Where do you come from originally?"

"Nevada. My parents owned a ranch there."

"Seriously?" He sounded surprised, even though

he'd heard her reveal that fact earlier. She seemed tickled by his feigned reaction.

"Yep. Grew up with the desert, rattlesnakes, horses and cattle—probably not unlike you, huh?"

"I actually didn't grow up on a ranch. Just a small house outside Corpus Christi. I didn't learn to ride until I took a summer job on a local cattle ranch and got hooked."

"I thought everyone in Texas was born in a saddle," she said, obviously teasing.

"My father was a good horseman, but he was all cop."

"Law enforcement runs in the family?"

"Yep. My sister is a Federal Marshall, Dad's a lifelong Ranger, though he'll be set to retire next year. He's not taking that well."

"Your file said you were in the El Paso Division?"

"Yeah. I was transferred a few years ago. Dad is still over in Corpus Christi. My sister is based in Dallas, but she's constantly traveling."

"That's a lot. How does your mother handle it?"

"She didn't. She took off when I was about thirteen after putting up with it for as long as she could. I can't blame her, not entirely."

"Really?"

"The job is tough, comes with a lot of risks, makes having a family hard, just like any cop's life does. My mother couldn't take the stress. It happens."

"I suppose. I'm sorry to hear it, though. Are you still in touch?"

"You writing an exposé or taking pictures?" he

snapped back, and noticed too late that he shouldn't have. She'd just hit a nerve.

He'd always felt responsible for his parents' breakup, though as an adult he knew it wasn't true. Still, it was hard for him as a boy to ignore that his mother had taken off shortly after he'd said he wanted to be a Ranger, just like his father. Hard to convince a kid it wasn't his fault, even though his dad had tried.

"It helps me take better pictures if I get to know you," she said evenly, but her eyes didn't meet his.

"Apologies, Lacey. Sore spot. Shouldn't take it out on you," he said, and she looked up again, her eyes forgiving him. "But, no, we lost contact with her a few years after she left. She stayed in touch for a while, but I guess her new life took her elsewhere."

"I'm sorry about that. And I didn't mean to pry."

"I know."

Thankfully their pizzas arrived, taking up all of the space on the table and capturing their attention for a good while.

"Wow, this is amazing," he said, his senses in heaven between the pizza and the wine. "I mean, my God...what do they do? I could eat only this for the rest of my days," he crooned, meaning it.

"Told ya." She smiled, as she kept her promise and put away her share of pizza. He couldn't figure out where she fit it all.

"So, you want to talk about work?" he reminded her as they poured more wine. She wasn't tipsy by any means, but she was more relaxed and he liked it. The glow she had was real now, and the buzz of attraction in his head became a little louder. She was fun, and good company when she wasn't acting like something was about to bite her. Whatever cloud had been hanging over her earlier seemed to have lifted.

"That's what we've been doing. I like to get to know subjects before I shoot them, so I can put you into places, settings, poses that are going to really show the real you, not arrange you in some contrived position."

"I see. That's interesting." He was unsure of what else to say, slightly uncomfortable at being analyzed in this manner. He'd thought they were just having a good time. He sighed. "I'm not quite sure how all this model, photographer stuff works. It's a first, and hopefully a last, for me."

She grinned. "Maybe you'll get hooked. You could get catalog ads, newspaper, maybe even hit the catwalks," she teased. She was playful, something he liked in a woman, and in a bed partner. How playful would his pretty photographer be in the sack? He watched her lick some sauce from her fingers and thought about those long, thin fingers wrapping around him.

He had to stop or he wouldn't be able to stand up safely, and grabbed his drink and took a long swallow.

"I said it's time to go, dammit. I gotta get to work," a rough voice growled, interrupting them. The jovial conversation in the place dulled to a murmur. Everyone looked toward a tall twentysomething guy who stood and grabbed the woman with him by the wrist, pulling her up. She tugged her arm loose, telling him she wanted to stay and pack the rest of the pizza for takeout.

There were several beer bottles on his side of the table and his words were slurred as he objected again. It was obvious he'd had too much to drink.

When the guy lifted his hand toward her, Lacey went very still. Jarod, on the other hand, moved so quickly the guy didn't seem to realize he was there until he'd grabbed the man's arms and pinned them behind his back before he managed to deliver the blow.

"This is a nice place, and we're all enjoying a nice meal. You, however, are not behaving nicely," Jarod said in a voice that was dead calm.

"Let me go, you moth—"

"Uh-uh." Jarod yanked harder on the guy's arms, choking off the curse. "There are kids in here. Watch your words."

"Let him *go*," the girlfriend demanded, her hands on her hips as she stared at Jarod as if he were the enemy.

"Ma'am, are you okay?"

While the guy had gone still, the woman didn't seem to be intimidated by Jarod at all, and walked up as close as she could get to him.

"Why don't you mind your own damned business? Let him go so we can get out of here."

"He looked like he was about to slap you. You sure about me letting him go?" Jarod asked.

She glared at him as if he were nuts. "Don't I look sure? He don't mean no harm. He just gets worked up." She blew off Jarod's concern with a dirty look that brooked no argument.

Others sat down and Jarod let the guy's arms go, putting his hands up, backing off. When the thug turned on him with fiery eyes and appeared as if he might try throwing a punch, Jarod didn't move a muscle, but just stared. Something in his posture made the kid think twice. He and his girlfriend charged out the door, cursing. They left their pizza behind.

Jarod returned to the table, shaking his head.

"Unbelievable. I kept him from possibly hitting her and she defends him."

He sat down, eyes landing on Lacey. It was clear that something had changed. She was white as a sheet. Her irises were open and dark—a classic fight-or-flight response.

"Hey, you okay?"

She nodded, but when she put her fork down, her hand was shaking. Jarod reached across the table, put his hand over hers. It was ice-cold, he noticed, before she snatched it back.

"Want to talk about it? I can be a good listener."

That woke her up, and she blinked, as if coming alive. "No, I don't. I should get home," she stated flatly, and he felt properly put in his place. Thing was, he'd been put in his place plenty of times, and he pretty much knew when he didn't want to stay there.

"I'll walk you to your apartment," he offered, throwing down a few dollars to cover the bill.

"No!" she objected too strongly, and when she glanced at him he could swear she was afraid of *him*. Where had that come from?

"I just want to make sure you're safe, is all."

"I'll be fine. I'm just tired and have a bad headache, from the wine," she explained, standing and walking rapidly toward the door. When they got outside, she took several deep breaths and seemed to steady. He wasn't quite sure what to do or say.

"I'm sorry," she said, sounding more normal, though she examined the narrow street, up and down, as if she were expecting someone. "I guess I was a bit thrown by that episode. I'm not great with confrontation. It was good of you to step in, though."

"It's my job."

"Not here."

"Doesn't matter where I am. It's still my job."

She focused on his face, and studied him for a few long moments with those perfect green eyes.

He knew he wanted her. He didn't know how he'd manage it, but he was going to make it happen.

"You sure you don't want me to walk you back?"

She paused, but then nodded.

"I'm sure. I'll be fine."

It hit him then that she didn't want him knowing where she lived. She was afraid of him—or afraid of men, in general.

There were only a few good reasons women had for this kind of reaction, and thinking about any of them made Jarod's blood boil. The lady had some serious fear, and he knew he had to find out why. Then he'd make sure she had no reason to fear anything, least of all him.

"Fair enough, then," he said, knowing when to give in and when not to. "I guess I'll see you tomorrow for that appointment, and you can let me know more of what's expected of me?"

"Yes. Thanks," she said, though he wasn't exactly sure what she was thanking him for. He just nodded.

She walked off without another word, and he veered off in the direction of his hotel—at first.

Within a minute he looped back, caught sight of that hot-pink shirt and didn't take his eyes away from her the rest of the way. He kept his distance and watched. She checked her surroundings constantly, as if the devil himself were after her.

Jarod stayed with her until he saw her turn into a building. He waited, saw a light come on, didn't see her come out. Walking up closer, he noted the address, the spot, and committed it to memory. Only then did he walk back through the dark street to his own place, quietly planning to find out what had Lacey Graham so spooked.

3

JAROD SAT IN THE SUNLIGHT of the large hotel window, the city sprawled out below him while he perused the Net, making good use of the wireless connection that came with the room. He enjoyed touching base with law enforcement colleagues on various boards and Web sites, and he was taking an online course in further forensics study.

He didn't particularly want to become a forensics expert. He was more interested in chasing down perps directly, rather than investigating the mess they left behind; still, he found the material interesting.

Mostly.

Today, no matter how intently his eyes traveled over the words on the screen, his mind kept returning to the image of Lacey's green eyes. He loved her eyes, and the way she pushed her hands through her short blond hair every five minutes. She had hair like corn silk, soft-looking in spite of the blunt edges of the style she wore. He flexed his fingers unconsciously, thinking about touching it. The ring of his cell phone jostled him out of his fantasy, and he recognized the number as his captain's.

"Hey, Cap."

"Jarod. How are things in the big city?"

"Noisy. Busy. Damned good pizza, though."

Tom chuckled. Jarod liked him. He was a good man, no-nonsense, and had as much tolerance for political bullshit as Jarod did.

"Thought you might be out somewhere with twenty half-naked women draped over you for this calendar thing," Tom said lightly, razzing him. There would be no end to that when he got home.

"Nope, no women, just eleven other guys, unfortunately, except for the photographer, and she's pretty tough."

"Would have to be to deal with the likes of you." Tom laughed again. "Anyway, I'm calling about Darren Hill."

"What about him?"

"He jumped bail last night, thought you'd want to know."

Jarod cursed. Darren Hill was the worst of the worst, selling everything he could get his hands on to pay for drugs, including his six-year-old daughter. Jarod had intervened, and the girl had escaped serious harm in the nick of time, taken away and placed in a foster home. No one knew if she'd been born on American soil or not, but Hill claimed she was. Meanwhile, the mother was long gone. *Poor kid.* Jarod still felt a twist when he thought about it. Still, she had a real chance now, placed with a good family in Houston. Hopefully they would keep her permanently.

Jarod had a feeling they needed to be looking for the mother's body, unfortunately. Hill was scum.

"How the hell did he even make bail?"

"It was set high, but his drug-dealing friends must have come up with the cash."

"Great. That's just great." Jarod narrowed his eyes, peering out through the window. "Any idea which way he headed?"

"Pretty sure he wouldn't go back over the border— he wouldn't take that chance. And he has a bone to pick with you taking away the kid. We wouldn't want to ignore that."

"Oh, yeah, he was a really devoted father."

"It's about the power and control. You know that. You damaged his rep. He might be looking for revenge."

"Yeah, well, he can bring it on. I'll get the first flight back."

"No, you're out there until this calendar thing is finished—brass made no bones about that."

"Dammit, Tom, if Hill's looking for me, the easiest way for me to bring him in is to be there, not here."

"It's being handled, Jarod. Stay there, and enjoy being out of the line of fire for a bit."

"Tom—"

"Jarod, you know I don't care about this PR crap any more than you do, but the brass does care and you're supposed to be doing this. So do it."

"Aren't you the brass?"

"You know what I mean. We'll find Darren. The place does tend to run without you, you know," Tom added jokingly, and Jarod blew out a breath.

"Fine. Keep me up-to-date on what's happening?"

"You bet. By the way, you put any more thought toward taking that captain's position that's opening up? You're the perfect candidate. You'd have no problem getting through the interviews. I'd be happy to write you a rec."

Something nasty squeezed at Jarod's temples, and he told Tom the truth. "All due respect, and believe me, being asked to fill your shoes is an honor, but I don't know if I want that, Tom. I like where I am now. Too much paperwork comes with being a captain."

"Ain't that the truth," Tom agreed, laughing good-naturedly. "Still, there are more guys who can do your job, and not many as well suited as you are to this chair. You're a natural leader, Jarod. And captains are still hands-on much of the time. Better pay, too. Maybe a chance of living a little longer," Tom joked, having been in the captain's seat for ten years before recently being promoted to assistant chief.

Jarod knew Tom wanted him to take the spot, and it was getting harder to resist. "I'll think some more on it."

"Think faster. This has to be decided sooner than later."

"Will do."

They hung up, and Jarod rubbed his eyes, feeling tired. A restless night's sleep had done him no favors. He was going to have to make some decisions. His father wouldn't be happy if he turned down the promotion, yet it just didn't feel right. He should be excited, but for whatever reason, he wasn't. He liked what he did, and had never really thought about climbing the political ladder. He just wasn't ambitious that way.

Shaking his head, he set the thoughts aside and sat back down at his computer, distracting himself by typing Lacey's name into the search engine.

His conscience pricked at him a bit, but what of it? He was going to be working with the woman, and he was curious.

Surprisingly, he didn't find much. Wouldn't a person in her line of work have more Internet presence? Promotions, articles, displays of their work, a Web page? She did have a Web page connected to *Bliss,* but it was basic info, a few samples of her previous work—impressive—but most notably, no pictures of herself. Wasn't that odd, for a photographer?

He shrugged. Maybe he was off base. However, following an instinct, he accessed a database used by law enforcement to do background checks and paused before typing in her name. He had no call to do this, no professional reason.

No, his reasons were personal. The lady had been seriously stressed about something. Jarod didn't think for a minute that she was a criminal, but she was hiding something; he could smell it. And he wanted to know why she was so afraid, and of what.

He wouldn't dig too deep, only see if anything curious came up. Then he'd leave it at that. There was a fine line between curiosity and concern, and invasion of privacy.

He didn't know if he was relieved or not to find that on the surface query nothing came up. Not even a speeding ticket or a court date. However, Lacey Brown had changed her name to her mother's maiden name,

Graham, upon arriving in New York City. She'd renewed all of her official IDs, license, Social Security, etcetera, all at once.

When she'd come here, she'd reinvented herself—it piqued Jarod's attention as to why. It could be as simple as her not liking her last name for starting a new career, or perhaps she'd been married, and returned to her mother's name when she'd left the relationship.

Lacey Brown. He couldn't see where that was such an objectionable name—why wouldn't she want her father's name? She'd sounded happy with her childhood from what Jarod could tell when he'd heard her talking about growing up on the ranch in Nevada, and so why the switch?

Some people did business by adopting a business name, a DBA, "doing business as" but Lacey had changed her entire identity, officially. When someone took such a drastic step, there was usually a big reason why.

The need to know was balanced by the need to stick to professional ethics. He'd already crossed the line slightly, and he wouldn't pry any further, regardless of the temptation. Closing the database and the computer before he gave in to his baser impulses, he sat quietly, wondering.

Other than criminal activity, the other obvious option was that she was hiding or running away from something or someone who scared her. It brought him to simmering anger to think about that, and he almost opened the database again, wanting to know. If Lacey was afraid of something, he could help. What would he find if he checked into Lacey Brown's past?

If she wanted him to know, she'd tell him, he reminded himself sternly. He had no compelling reason to pry into her business. None at all.

Standing up, he headed for the shower, needing to get out of the room. He was meeting with Lacey in two hours, and he was looking forward to it a little more than he should be.

IN GOOD TIME Lacey finished two of her interview consultations, one with a member of their own FDNY and another with a member of the California Highway Patrol. Things were moving ahead and a spirit of excitement was only dimmed by the black cloud of knowing Scott was out of jail. She'd barely slept all night, paranoid and stressed, and feeling like an idiot for how she'd acted with the Ranger in the pizza place.

She glanced at Jackie, who was across the studio, but it was hopeless. Jackie was far too busy flirting with one of New York's best to notice Lacey. Lacey frowned—Jackie was a free spirit and probably just used to playing the game at work, but it was hard to believe she was in much of a relationship if she was acting like that….

And look at me, little Miss Critical, who hasn't been near a man in months, Lacey chastised herself.

To say she was feeling out of sorts was an understatement, her day full of surprises so far. The execs from *Bliss* had wanted her to walk them through the current setup, and though she'd tried to explain that it could change once she had all the early photos in, they had seemed happy, if not thrilled, with the early work.

Her stomach turned; she needed them to be thrilled, ecstatic even, but Lacey was sure that the female exec in Marketing, Nina, would never like anything she did completely. There was an innate animosity there that Lacey didn't understand, but it happened sometimes. Personalities clashed for whatever reason.

Lacey was determined to do better than her best, and wow them no matter what.

It wasn't going to be a smooth morning by the looks of things. Jackie was busy and had messed up a few scheduling details. Assisting Lacey wasn't her only duty at the magazine, so Lacey tried to be understanding. Now there was a very annoyed California Highway Patrol officer demanding to know why his appointment had changed—again.

Lacey tried to placate him, but she just couldn't fit him in at the moment, and needed to push his shoot back until she was done with Jarod. The patrol officer wasn't happy about it. The guy was not Mr. Sunshine, and Lacey couldn't blame him for being irritated, but there was nothing else to be done.

Jarod was due here any second, and she needed time to prepare. She wanted to start by taking some studio shots of Jarod, to get a feel for him, so to speak. She'd thought about that in more ways than one the evening before, until the incident in the café had thrown her.

She couldn't help it, but seeing someone manhandled just brought back flashes of Scott. Seeing Jarod step in had been both exciting and frightening. She didn't know what to think of it.

Left to handle it all on her own for the time being,

Lacey turned back to the disgruntled highway patrol officer and offered a friendly smile, hoping it would dim his temper. It did, maybe too well. She realized while she'd been looking toward Jackie, the guy's eyes hadn't moved from her chest.

Great. Like she needed this.

"Listen, Officer Bridges, if you go talk to my assistant—"

"She looks busy," he said, not even glancing at Jackie. He stepped closer, turned on a little charm of his own. "I'd rather talk to you. Maybe we could have dinner, work this out, find some time to squeeze me in. I'm not opposed to a private session, you know?"

The suggestive way he said the words and leaned in made Lacey reflexively pull back, his intimidating closeness unwelcome. Her back was, however, literally against the wall, and he planted a big hand just a few inches to the right of her head.

Panic was reflexive.

She tried to keep her cool in spite of her racing heart, but wanted to draw the line at his suggestive tone and mannerisms. She was in a public place, and in no danger. "Back off, please."

He grinned. "Aw, c'mon, sweetheart. Surely you and I can work something out that's good for both of us? I came all the way across the country to be here…can't we make it worth my while?"

She weighed her options quickly, and decided she wouldn't stand much chance of pushing him away, his chest was massive. She started to duck under his arm, when a cool voice stopped her mid duck.

"The lady said back off. I suggest you listen."

She looked underneath the officer's massive arm to see a pair of well-fitted jeans…and cowboy boots.

Straightening, she met Jarod's eyes, and was shocked that the warm brown of his gaze could turn so cold.

"Why don't you get in line, Tex," the California officer said dismissively over his shoulder.

Lacey found herself suddenly standing alone, free from the arm that had been by her head. The next thing she knew, two large and extremely agitated men were facing off with each other just six feet in front of her nose, seething at each other like large, angry bulls. She moved quickly, keeping her distance, her heart pounding, and she made it to Jackie's side.

"Call security," she said, her voice tight. She noted with relief the fireman who'd been talking to Jackie heading toward the two men with calming gestures.

"That won't be necessary," Jarod said, overhearing her, and acknowledging the fireman. "Everything is under control, and Chippie here is just leaving."

The young Californian started to object, but took in the measure of the Texas Ranger and fireman standing before him and broke eye contact first. He cursed, pointing a finger in Lacey's direction.

"Fine, I'm outta here and not coming back to this hole of a city. You can find someone else for this stupid calendar," he said, spitting and sending red-faced looks toward all of them as he stormed out. "You had me too late in the lineup anyway. Don't know what the hell you're doing."

Jackie's voice broke through Lacey's haze, but her eyes remained glued to the men.

"Hey, what's up? You're shaking like a leaf."

Lacey blinked a few times, and realized everyone was staring at *her* now, not the men. Awareness kicked in.

"I'm fine," she said automatically.

"You don't seem fine. That guy really got to you, huh?"

"He was just being stupid," she said, her throat feeling dry.

"Well, Mr. November took care of him just fine, with a little help from Mr. April, who, by the way, is perfectly single and lives here in New York," Jackie said playfully. Lacey barely heard, her eyes still on Jarod as he spoke with the firefighter.

"They make quite a pair, huh?"

"Uh, yeah, sure."

"Mr. November sure seems interested in impressing you—he looked like he wanted to wallop that guy."

Which is exactly what bothered Lacey. She liked Jarod, as much as she knew about him, but he had an aggressive streak and wasn't the type of guy to hold back. This was New York, not the Wild West.

"You should ask him out," Jackie added.

"I can't date these guys, Jackie. It's not professional. At least until their shoot is done. The magazine must have some kind of policy about that."

"For regular staff, yes, but not regarding contract and freelance employees, which includes you and those two gorgeous hunks over there. So it's fair game."

"I need to get November into the studio for some inside shots," Lacey said, dropping the subject and focusing on work again.

"Hey, do you want to tell me what has you so freaked out, Lace?" Jackie inquired.

Frowning more deeply, Lacey studied her lens as she polished it. "I'm just tired and stressed. I need this to go perfectly. We're off to a bumpy start and we need to get this under control."

Jackie's expression soured, and Lacey regretted sounding so harsh.

"No problem. I'll get back on it."

Lacey closed her eyes.

"Jackie, wait. I'm sorry. I just hate getting rattled when I really need to concentrate. This calendar is my big break, and I want it to be perfect," she explained.

"I get it, and I'm sorry, too. I've been enjoying the fringe benefits too much. But Ken's been such a crank lately, it's a relief to come to work, you know?"

Lacey wasn't sure if Jackie wanted to say more about her troubles with her boyfriend, but now wasn't the time, and she wasn't exactly someone to hand out romantic advice anyway.

"I hope it works out," she offered and lifted her camera, studying the serious profiles, angular features, and sharp eyes of the two men. She snapped a few quick shots of them as they talked. Candid shots, when people weren't posing or looking, had always been her favorites to take. A moment captured in time that often showed the truth about the person being photographed.

"Well, you have no shortage of material to work

with, that's for sure. Just let me know what you need to make it happen." Jackie slipped back into her professional role, and Lacey felt her shoulders relax.

"I'm moving to studio one—could you tell Jarod to join me in about ten minutes? I'll be ready for him then."

"Sure. You got it," Jackie said, though Lacey could feel her assistant staring as she left the room.

She needed the few minutes of quiet before being around anyone again, to get her bearings, to distance herself from her churning stomach and riled nerves. The cop wouldn't have hurt her, he was just being obnoxious. Lacey had come across worse in her dating life, and had usually laughed it off. This time, she hadn't. Was it always going to be this way?

No. She wouldn't allow it. It was simply the aftereffect of the news about Scott. And it had to stop. Now.

Taking a deep breath, she cleared her mind and stepped backward, finding herself up against a solid wall of muscle.

"Whoa, careful there. You okay?"

Jarod's hands were on her shoulders, the rest of him warm and hard against her back as her nervous system sparked to life like a car battery with a new charge.

Warmth from his touch traveled over her skin. He leaned in, speaking by her ear, and she closed her eyes as his voice filled her senses.

"Lacey, are you okay? You seemed upset out there."

The reminder had her pulling away, rubbing her hands over her arms and meeting his gaze furtively.

"I'm fine. I just… I don't like… Nothing. I'm fine. Let's get to work."

She looked away from Jarod's curious gaze and set to messing with lights and her camera, placing a small wooden stool at the center of the room, in front of a few gray-and-white screens.

"Can you please sit there? Don't pose or do anything particular. Hang out and let me get a sense of shooting you."

Jarod agreeably made his way to the seat and turned to her with a smile.

"This okay?"

"Sure," she said, shrugging and taking a few preliminary shots.

She fell into her groove easily, everything else taking a backseat as she studied him through the lens, taking in his features as if she'd never seen him before. Zooming in, she noted the lush fringe of lashes and framed his eyes only, liking the laugh lines carved into tanned skin and the flecks of color in his cocoa irises that only her camera would pick up.

Click.

Moving down, she saw the beginnings of his beard and realized his nose had been broken.

"How'd you break your nose?" she asked, her fingers navigating the camera's controls quickly and naturally as she readjusted her shots. The space between them dissolved through the closeness of the focus, and she could have been touching him as much as touching the machine in her hands.

Click.

"Which time?" he asked with a sardonic slant to his lips.

"The last time."

"Kidnapping standoff. A guy held a woman and her daughter in their apartment with a shotgun for eighteen hours. When we went in, some of us went for him, drew the fire, while others got the victims out. Turned out the gun wasn't loaded. The guy was strung out, though, and it took six of us to get him out of there. I caught his knee to the face while restraining him."

Jarod's eyes became so serious as he spoke, the irises expanding and the brighter flecks of gold seeming to disappear momentarily, swallowed by his memories. She widened out the shot.

Click, Click, click.

Amazing.

Her blood sizzled the longer she listened, the closer she looked.

"Knee to the face, sounds fairly painful," she commented briefly to keep him going.

To that, he smiled more widely, and the camera responded with an explosion of action that took her to the end of the roll. She held her breath the entire time.

Finding she needed to catch her breath, she stood and reached for some more film.

"You can relax for a second," she said, not looking up, needing to get hold of an emotional response she didn't understand. She loved to shoot and always enjoyed the rush, but it had never affected her physically, never like this. With Jarod, the necessary distance between photographer and subject was made of gossamer, thin and fading.

"No digital?" he asked casually, standing, but not

joining her. She could feel him watching her and it was disconcerting. Normally, the positions were reversed, the subject of her shoots being the one studied and explored.

"I like film. *Bliss* has supplied me with a digital, and I'll do some sessions with that, too. Part of my agreement to do the calendar was based on being able to work in film. Digital is just not the same."

"How so?"

"With film you have to be aware of your limits, of how many shots you have, and then it takes physical maneuvering to make them work. They can still be manipulated on a computer, of course, but I like developing myself, and it's just more…"

"Personal," he supplied.

"Real." She spoke at the same time.

She glanced up and met his knowing look. She shuffled her step a little, trying to work away the warmth that gathered low in the pit of her abdomen, signaling how long it had been since she'd felt the things he was causing her to feel.

"Yes. Personal. Anyway, just do what comes naturally, and we'll be finished in a few minutes," she said somewhat breathlessly, to her dismay.

"Sure." He shoved his hands in his pockets and simply noted her with a steadiness that made her pull back the zoom, taking more comfortable, wide-angle shots.

God, he was gorgeous. The thought would not be denied, and the heat inside picked up intensity. She was in some kind of trouble.

"When do we start doing this for real?"

"Tomorrow."

"Here?"

"No, our first stop is Central Park."

"Do I get to keep my clothes on?" he asked cheekily, with a naughty sparkle in his eyes. She fumbled the camera, messing up the shot and frowning.

"Depends on whether you mean during or after the shoot," she said off the cuff, shocking herself. It was something the "old" her would have said without a second thought, and she couldn't repress a smile as she watched his rapid reaction.

Score one for Lacey. She still had it, apparently.

He didn't say anything else, and she finished the last roll of film, pleased with herself for the shots and for finding her own spark. Temptation quelled doubt for the moment.

Lieutenant Wyatt had something special, a mysterious quality that reached past her fears and sparked her former, playful spirit to life.

Did she dare?

This tall Texas cop might be good for her after all. He might be worth the chance, she thought, focusing hard on her camera, but she wasn't really paying attention to what she was doing; her hands moved automatically.

Maybe. Just maybe.

4

"THAT'S PERFECT, thanks," Lacey said, giving the thumbs-up on the props put in place by the small crew the magazine had sent out to get their first official calendar session under way.

It wasn't complex; she wanted natural photos that emphasized the masculine power of the models. The most handsome heroes in the country against the backdrop of the most powerful city in the world. She didn't want a lot of hokey items drawing attention away from Jarod. As if they could.

She noticed he hadn't arrived yet and peeked at her watch. He still had a few minutes, but he did like to cut it close, making her punctuality nerves bristle.

She wondered if he'd been as affected by their time in the studio the day before as she'd been, then chastised herself for the thought. How could he have been? She was the one with the camera, watching his every movement up close and personal through her lens. The details of his eyes, the shape of his mouth had followed into her dreams that night.

She'd almost called him, but had talked herself out of it. Instead, she stayed up late developing the pictures she'd taken, memorizing each one, telling herself they were no different than what she did for any other model, any other shoot. Details were her business, and Jarod happened to have particularly nice ones.

"We're all set," one of the prop guys told her after they'd set up some barricades fencing off the area to keep bystanders out of the shot and had raked colorful leaves into strategic positions. Thank God there wasn't any wind today.

A colorful blanket was positioned on the ground among the leaves, two wineglasses and a bottle poised perfectly, waiting for Jarod to complete the picture. A fall picnic in the park with a handsome Texas Ranger. It had been Jackie's idea, and pure genius. He'd sit alone, as if waiting for someone—and millions of women looking at the calendar would imagine they were the one he was waiting for. Exactly what Lacey intended. She wasn't sure if it was her own fantasy driving her direction, but as long as the shot worked, that's all that mattered. She wanted every woman in America thinking about joining Jarod on that blanket.

She played with the fantasy of sitting down there with him, herself, sheltered from view by the trees and the large boulder, the skyscrapers looming in the background sky... What would happen?

"A few of the prop guys are grabbing lunch. The stylist will prep Jarod as soon as he gets here, and we should be okay. Did he know the way? Should we have sent a car?" asked Jackie.

Lacey shrugged. "I offered. He said he'd get here on his own power—oh, wait—there. In the nick of time."

Both women turned to watch Jarod striding down the walk, emerging from one of the park's many tunnels into the dappled sunlight, looking like...well, Lacey wasn't sure she had the right words. Good thing she took pictures for a living.

"Wow," was all Jackie said, and turned back to tell the stylist their model had arrived.

You're a professional, cool it, Lacey lectured herself silently, her hormones begging to stand up and salute.

She'd asked Jarod to wear his official uniform today, and he'd informed her that unlike other police or fire departments, there really wasn't any official Ranger uniform. So, he'd come in the clothes he used as a dress uniform. Western-cut white shirt, dark tie, gray pants, belt and cowboy boots. A white hat. The clothes weren't that unusual, but the man who wore them made them seem more...elegant.

Powerful.

Lacey's fingers itched, and she lifted her camera, taking a few shots of him as he crossed the grass.

There wasn't a set of female eyes in the park that could turn away, and several guys looked on, too, for that matter. Some whistled. Several started gathering around the edges of the shoot as he arrived.

He seemed to have eyes only for her, though, and she had to admit that set her on fire, especially when he smiled. She might have smiled back, but couldn't risk it.

"Hi, there. Didn't know there'd be an audience," he said casually enough, hands on hips, peering at the gathering crowd through narrow eyes.

Lacey grinned a little wider. "It's New York. Something's always going on, and someone always wants to watch."

He laughed and shook his head. "Whatever you say. So how does this work?"

"We have the set put together, we'll use that first, with you in your dress uniform and then your casuals. Later, we can walk around the park and I'll get some candid shots. It will give me a variety to select from later."

"Casual?" He frowned. "I didn't bring any change of clothes."

"No problem—we have stuff we want you to wear, designer labels that paid to be in the calendar. Product placement, you know. You can see Jen, the stylist, for any last-minute touch-ups, and then we'll get started. You can change after."

"Stylist?"

"Yeah. Hair, makeup, clothes—she'll get you all set." Lacey felt a twinge of jealousy as she thought about the young, pretty stylist with her hands all over Jarod, and squelched it. Stupid.

"Makeup? I am not wearing makeup."

Blinking at him, she frowned. "Why not?"

He looked down at her, but didn't say a word.

Lacey stared in the face of his stalwart refusal to wear makeup, her aggravation rising—what was the big deal? But as she saw Jackie behind Jarod pointing to her watch, and then upward toward the sun, Lacey let it go. They were going to be dealing with shadows crawling across the scene if they waited much longer.

"Don't blame me if you look blotchy," she warned. "I'll deal with it."

Actually, she knew he wouldn't look blotchy at all, which was why she hadn't insisted more strenuously. The studio light had been more controlled, but she knew that the soft, indirect sunlight would be kind to Jarod's desert-tanned skin.

She watched Jackie instruct him about the shot, and cursed as her cell phone buzzed in her pocket. She'd forgotten to shut it off, as was her habit when she was shooting.

Unknown name and number. Again.

Her fingers turned cold as she ignored it, only to have the phone ring again a few seconds later, with the same result. Finally, she answered it. Nothing. Someone hanging on the line, not saying a word. Then, a soft male laugh, and a click. Her knees felt watery, and she turned her back to Jackie and Jarod. She took a minute, pretending to be on the phone, but really getting her bearings.

It was hard to tell from just a laugh, and the scratchy connection of what was probably a cheap, disposable cell phone didn't help. It could be anyone, but it was most likely Scott. It had to be.

It was only a phone call, she reassured herself. He was far away, under house arrest, and he couldn't do anything to her over the phone. If it continued, she'd call her lawyer and make it stop.

She didn't want to start anything, or give Scott any more reason to come back at her, so she'd wait and see. He was just baiting her. Letting her know he was out there. That was all. As if she'd ever forget.

She turned back around, blowing out a breath that teased her bangs, and shot a bright smile at Jarod, who was watching a little too closely with those hawklike eyes. She glanced around, gave a short nod.

"Okay, everyone, let's get to work."

JAROD HAD ONCE SPENT eighteen hours with his leg jammed in between rocks when he'd slipped while he'd been searching for a fugitive. His dad always said it was the little things that could kill you. Like slipping at the wrong moment while climbing rocks you'd been scaling since you were a kid.

He'd had enough water to keep himself going, but had dropped his radio about ten feet away and crushed his cell phone when he'd fallen. Basically, he'd been completely screwed; if not for keeping his gun, he might have been snake or wildcat bait, as well. Luckily, when he hadn't checked in, they came looking for him, saving him from death or having to do something unspeakable to free himself. He'd been hot, sunburned, dirty, sore, hungry and nearly dehydrated when they brought him back.

Still, that had been more fun than he was having right now, being primped and poked in public, bent this way and that, holding up a champagne glass to the camera and having to look…well, deserving of the wolf whistles and other comments that floated over from the crowd.

Lacey had actually used the phrase "come hither" until she realized it made him glare, not smile.

He'd have to get his gun and go shoot something when this was done, just to get his self-respect back.

"You're doing great," Lacey reassured him, changing out her film again and then switching over to her digital camera. How the hell many pictures did she need to take just to find one good one?

"Can you change clothes, and we'll finish up here and then head out around the park?"

"Sure," he half growled and thought he might have seen her smother a grin. She'd done that a few times and it was pretty enough to distract him from his pain.

Actually, in the few moments when he could focus only on Lacey and forget everything else around them, he didn't much care what she did, as long as she was focused on him, too. He'd had several imaginative thoughts about his pretty photographer in response to the command, "You're waiting for your date. You're anxious for her to arrive. You haven't seen her for a while, and you're thinking about what you'd like to do when she gets here."

He wondered what *she'd* do if she knew what he was thinking he'd like to do to *her.* That he'd like to stretch her out on the blanket he sat on alone, and maybe take some of the honey in the picnic basket and drizzle it over her breasts, sucking the sweetness off the dusky nipples that were just barely visible under the thin cotton of her top. That he'd like to work his way down from there, stripping off those sexy, low-cut army pants she was wearing, and taste the secrets she held between her thighs.

Her camera started making noise, and she smiled. "Oh, that's good, just like that, Jarod," and he nearly exploded with a boner right then. Did she have any idea how sexy she sounded, urging him on, and how she was feeding into his fantasy as if she could read his mind?

Still, there were question marks, he reminded himself, trying to get his desire and his body's response under control. Her rigid body posture when she'd turned, pretending she was taking a phone call. Half of knowing what was coming at you was being able to read body position, expressions…and Lacey had not been happy or relaxed as she had pretended to be when she'd returned. In fact, he'd say whatever she'd picked up on that call had scared her.

Who did she think she was fooling, and why was she trying?

On her signal for a break, he ducked into a small changing station, stripping out of his dress clothes and putting on the designer duds that they provided, surprised when they fit. Thank God they let him keep his boots on.

When he reemerged, he was a little surprised to see the prop guys already throwing their stuff in the back of a small car. The shoot was completely torn down and everyone was leaving. They came over and took down the changing tent almost as soon as he stepped foot out of it. He was glad that they had given him time to get his pants on.

"They're on their way to another shoot, and have to hustle," she said, as if reading his mind. "It's just you and me, now, cowboy."

"What about my clothes?" He looked down at the getup he was in.

"They'll leave them back at the studio, don't worry."

The urban metrosexual look wasn't his usual taste, but he supposed he could live with it for the afternoon. He felt naked without his hat, though, and gazed wistfully at the car that was leaving with his clothes.

"More pictures?" He wasn't sure if he growled, but maybe.

"It will be easy now. You don't have to do anything. I just want some natural shots, nothing formal, so relax. We'll grab a hot dog and enjoy what's left of this gorgeous afternoon, okay? My treat—you were a good sport back there."

"It was easy with you taking the pictures," he said tactfully. It was true in part, because watching her work had been a pleasure. Pure pleasure. "What if I drop mustard on this shirt?"

"You'll owe *Bliss* about fifteen-hundred bucks," she said seriously, making his eyes bulge before she grinned and said, "Gotcha."

He shook his head, laughing, unsure what to make of her. "Does this seriously cost that much? It's just a...*shirt*."

"Yeah, it would go for that much retail, but it's given to *Bliss* so they can use it in shoots. The price is because of the designer's name, and the way it fits, the quality of the material, which is pure silk, by the way. If you could see yourself in it, you'd see how it affects the contours of your body, and even changes the effect when you move, when you walk... That's what people pay big bucks for." She grinned as she watched some women watching him. "That shirt with those jeans makes you sex on legs, cowboy."

"I think I feel objectified," he grumped humorously, but he didn't mind in the least if she wanted to make him into her sex object.

"That's what sexy calendars are all about," she said, laughing. "Though the proceeds from this one will go to a worthy cause, too, so you can take comfort in that."

"It's the only reason I'm here," he said honestly. Well, that and he was under orders to be here.

"I can understand that," she agreed. "For someone who's not used to being in the limelight, and who doesn't look for recognition from his work, this must be kind of awkward, but that's what makes a hero a hero, right? And you guys deserve to be recognized. It's good for people to know there are still heroes in the world, Jarod. People need them."

As they walked underneath a tunnel, he didn't answer, hardly considering himself a hero for doing the job he was trained to do. But was Lacey talking about herself, too? Did she need to believe there were heroes out there? If she knew the thoughts he had about her with her clothes off, she might think him less than heroic.

He was willing to risk it.

As they emerged from the other side of the tunnel under one of the park's many bridges, he saw a yellow ball go rolling across the road. A young girl, no more than four, raced after the ball. Jarod, however, saw the bike rider whipping around the corner toward her, the cyclist hitting his brakes, veering, wheels screeching on the pavement.

Jarod acted on reflex, lunging forward to step in

front of the little girl, her mother calling her name in a panic from the grassy lawn. Jarod scooped the child up, though he couldn't get out of the way fast enough, and the cyclist grazed him as he screeched to a halt, nearly riding into the stone curve of the bridge.

The little girl wiggled in his arms. "My baaaaalllll," she cried, struggling furiously to be let loose.

Jarod set her down, but didn't let go as her mother rushed to them, apologizing, and white as a sheet.

"Delilah! You know better than to ever run off on me like that, ever!" she scolded. The mom's eyes brimmed with tears in delayed reaction to her daughter's close call.

Jarod spotted Lacey talking to the cyclist, and made sure Delilah was firmly attached to her mother before jogging away and retrieving the ball.

"Is he okay?" Jarod asked.

She nodded. "Just shaken up. It was a close call for everyone, but he's fine. You?"

"I'm good," he responded, turning back to give the crying child her toy.

The mother, much calmer, smiled gratefully. "Thank you so much. You could have been hurt, too. You might have saved her life, thank you so much."

Out of habit, he went to touch his hat, but it wasn't there, and he smiled wryly. "No problem, ma'am."

"Play?"

He looked down, and Delilah held her ball up. "Play." She giggled, running off into the grassy lawn, beckoning him.

"Do you mind?" he asked the mom.

"Not in the least. Her dad is in Afghanistan, and I think she misses him playing ball with her. She says he throws it different than I do," the woman said, smiling warmly. Jarod's jaw clenched against the surge of emotion he felt, the respect he couldn't help but feel for the sacrifices others made. He was no hero, not compared to what others were doing in the world.

He was suddenly aware of the whirring sound of the camera, and felt his muscles tighten, then relax again. It was just Lacey doing her thing. He still wasn't used to it.

He caught the ball one last time and brought it to the little girl, smiling. He hoped to hell her dad made it back to play ball with her soon.

"Delilah, I have to go now, but you stay away from the roads, okay? If your ball goes there again, wait for your mom to get it."

She nodded solemnly. "'Kay." She then toddled off to her mother, promptly forgetting him. Jarod returned to where Lacey stood, packing her camera away.

"Done for the day?"

When she looked up, he was caught for a minute by the bare emotion in her eyes. He wasn't sure, but he thought she might have shed a few tears, too.

"Are you okay?" she asked, and her eyes widened, drawing attention to his shirt. "You did get hit. Let me see. Why didn't you say something?"

To be honest, he hadn't even realized it. The shirt hadn't torn but apparently he had picked up a scrape from the bike's handles and there was a small bloody patch on the expensive silk.

"Lacey, I'm sorry—" he started, and then sucked in a breath as she lifted the edge of the material and ran her fingers over the spot where he was injured.

"You should clean this up. It's not deep, but it's bruising."

"Can't even feel it," he said hoarsely, telling the truth, because all he could feel were the cool tips of her fingers on his hot skin. Damn.

She was obviously concerned. So worried about a little scrape, it made him smile.

"Yeah, I'm fine. The shirt's probably ruined, though."

"Who cares about the shirt?"

The vibe between them had changed tangibly as she straightened and they found themselves standing very close. Her expression went from worried to sultry as her eyes drifted to his mouth. The look shot desire through him, and his cock swelled in response—pure male reaction. And if she could do that with just a look, what else could happen between them?

"That was the most amazing thing I ever saw," she said.

"It was just—"

She put a finger to his lips, and the softness of the touch stopped him cold.

"Not 'just' anything. You reacted so fast, without thought. And then playing with that young girl... I don't think I've ever seen anything so brave or so kind in my whole life, Jarod." Her hand moved from where it had been poised on his lips to rub her thumb along his cheek. "You're the real deal, a real hero."

"Lacey," he tried to object again, not wanting her to put him on too high a pedestal, especially with the erection from her touch straining at his jeans. Thank goodness the shirt hung over the front of his pants.

She pushed up on tiptoe and pulled him down as she wrapped her arms around his neck, taking his mouth in a hot and desperate kiss. He responded on instinct, wrapping his arms around her and crushing her up against him.

Her kiss was intense, and her passion equaled his, her tongue rubbing on his invitingly, her hands gripping his back as they strained to be closer than was physically possible.

When giggling cut through the lusty haze of his thoughts, he remembered they were out in the open. As he pulled gently away, he spied a group of teenage girls with knowing eyes, still giggling. He smiled, tilting his forehead against Lacey's, both of them catching their breath.

"That was some kiss," was all he could say.

She laughed, and pressed her lips to his one more time before slipping her hands away to put a few inches between them.

He hadn't seen her glow, not really, until this moment. It was as if a light had turned on inside of her—the sun and the moon and stars all shining through her at once.

"We should go back to your room and wash up that scrape," she said, her voice hitching slightly, her eyes unsure.

He took her hand and brought it to his lips, his own

heart hammering hard as he realized what she was really saying. She didn't have to be unsure with him. He was certain enough for both of them.

"It does sting a bit, now that you mention it."

They walked quickly toward the subway station, their hands mingling, his thumb rubbing the center of her palm.

He let his eyes travel over her body as she stretched upward to grip the handrail. Hanging on, jostling against each other every few seconds, they moved with the sway of the train until it screeched to a halt. He wished he'd brought his handcuffs, imagining her stretched out on a bed like that, her arms secured above her head, while he enjoyed her any way he pleased.

They just about made it inside the apartment before desire exploded between them.

5

LACEY WAS PRETTY SURE she was going to lose her mind by the time he was sliding the small white card into the lock, though she'd been ready for him since they left the park. It had been the longest subway ride of her life. Who knew that a man pressing his thumb to the center of her palm could have her wet and ready so easily?

Jarod was all lean, hard male animal. Pressed up against him, she wound her arms around him, pulling him in, opening her lips and letting him explore to his, and her, delight. She didn't want to think or talk; she wanted to burn the slate of her memories clean and start new right here, right now, with this man.

To move things along, she slid her hands down and around, pressing her palm along the hard ridge between his legs. He moaned his approval, and she reached to undo his belt. She was surprised when he gently nudged her hands away.

"What are you doing?" she asked on a gulp of breath.

"Just slowing us down a little, sweetheart." His gaze burned into hers as he trailed a finger from her cheek to the line of her jaw and shoulder, finally brushing over her left nipple in a touch that made her catch her breath. "I plan to take my time and enjoy you."

She shook her head. "Fast the first time. Then slow after that. Please, just fuck me," she said on a quivering breath, holding his gaze.

She didn't want to tell him that slow would give her too much time to think. Even now, she was afraid that if she stopped looking at him, if he stopped touching her for too long, the chill would settle in when all she wanted was his heat.

She held her breath as they shared a silent look for several heartbeats, and when he moved his hands down to his belt, loosening it, she almost thanked the heavens aloud.

It only took her a minute to catch up, stripping off her clothes, and then they were both naked and wrapped around each other, just as she'd hoped they would be.

The branding of his hot flesh on hers was a welcome mark she'd never forget. She pressed in, wanting it all, touching gently, cupping his balls in her hand, squeezing in a way that pulled a moan from deep inside of him.

She smiled into the kiss as she stroked his rock-hard shaft, rolling her thumb over the head and feeling him shudder. He filled her hand, and she wanted him filling *her*. The thought of him inside her had her muscles aching and clenching, begging for contact after having been empty for so long.

His hands palmed her breasts, alternately rubbing and pinching her nipples.

She levered herself up to slide her legs around his hips, and in turn he slid his hands around her backside to lift her as he carried her, never breaking their kiss until he had to speak.

"Protection," he said, nodding toward his suitcase on the chair and setting her down long enough to search inside.

She drank the sight of him in, all taut muscle and golden skin. Later, she'd have to ask him why, exactly, he didn't show any tan lines. He leaned down and grabbed a box from the suitcase. A big box.

She smiled. "You thought ahead. Figured a cowboy might get lucky in the big city?"

The look he shot her direction was pure sex. "I never could have imagined getting *this* lucky," he said, sweeping a look down over her body and back to her face. "You're perfect," he said roughly.

She blushed from the intensity of his inspection, watching him as he slipped the transparent latex over a very lovely, thick erection. She might have licked her lips.

"I need you," she whispered, walking to him, needing to finish what they started. "Now."

"You've got me." He pulled her into his arms. Wasting no time finding her core, he slid deep inside, one sure thrust linking them together, chasing her demons away. He swallowed her gasp and moved them to a spot where nothing hung on the wall, pushing her up against it.

"Hang on, honey," he warned on a raspy breath, making her laugh even as her entire body seemed to clutch in ecstasy.

Oh, how she'd missed this. She tried to hold on to all the sensations assaulting her, to the feeling of being completely connected to someone, to all this raw male power throbbing inside of her. Soon, though, there was too much, and she gave herself over. Jarod braced her against the wall and thrust into her, hard and fast, just as she'd asked for. Her mind blanked completely.

Yes.

"More, more, more, harder, *please*." She wasn't sure if she was begging or demanding as she chanted in time with the staccato rhythm of his thrusts. Her body stretched and expanded to accommodate him as he seemed to push even deeper, touching her where no one had ever touched, taking her places she hadn't been.

Big, sure hands cupped her bottom, holding her in place firmly, and she cried out when his fingertips brushed over the sensitive bud between her cheeks, igniting a hard climax so unexpected that she felt tears on her cheeks as the sweetness of it claimed her.

When she opened her eyes, it was to find him watching her, his face close to hers, features taut, irises dilated. He was wild and yet completely in control. She could probably ask him to stop right now, and somehow, she knew he would.

Her muscles tightened around him as he seemed to get even thicker and heavier inside of her, and she knew he was probably close. His breath was labored, his back turning rock-hard under her fingers.

"I want you to come with me, darlin'."

"I don't know if I can again. That was so good," she said on a half gasp, half laugh.

Something primal and deliberate gleamed in his eyes, and she knew her admission had been received as a challenge. It made her shiver.

"I think we can do better," he said, teasing, but sounding completely serious all the same.

She squeaked as he pushed her legs up higher, his hips widening the space between her legs. He opened her completely and pushed the velvety hardness of his pelvis fully against the soft folds of her sex.

He literally touched her everywhere, inside and out, and she dug her nails into his shoulder blades reflexively. Her head fell forward from the onslaught of pleasure, seeking more. She couldn't move, literally pinned against the wall, but he was moving in all the right ways.

"That's it, sweetheart," he crooned as his chest rubbed against her breasts, as the hard muscle of his abdomen ground against her clit relentlessly. She took her hands from his shoulders and pushed her breasts together, letting him suck both nipples simultaneously, a move that had her spiraling out of control.

Within seconds, she felt him shudder and buck against her while she melted in his arms, coming apart so completely she lost all sense of where she was. For several long moments there was nothing except for heat, waves of pulsating pleasure and Jarod.

They stayed together against the wall, catching their breath and coming back down. When she felt him move, felt his body leave hers, he didn't put her down on the floor. Instead, he flipped her around easily and carried her with him to the bed. Laying her down and moving over her, he stretched out beside her and pulled her onto his chest.

The protective, gentle gesture moved her and tears threatened again for very different reasons. When one slipped down and splashed on his chest, he pulled back, looking at her in concern.

"Hey, you okay?" he asked, studying her intently. But the panic or discomfort she was accustomed to seeing when men were faced with women's tears was absent. He was too much man to be scared by tears.

She nodded, smiling, crying, and feeling like a complete, naked idiot.

"I'm good…better than good. It's just that was so good, and you're so…nice," she said lamely. The emotions she was experiencing defied words.

"It was good," he agreed easily, still watching her. "And you're pretty easy to be nice to, Lacey."

She didn't know what to say and buried her face in his chest again, loving the texture of his skin, how he smelled and how fantastic he felt, too.

"Hey, we forgot to fix up your scrape," she said softly.

"We can do that later. I think it's okay," he replied and she could hear the smile in his voice.

He mindlessly stroked her arm, and then brought her fingers up to his mouth for a kiss, and she sighed in bliss. Anxiety and tears disappeared in a relaxed after-glow that she hadn't felt for ages. Though really, had she ever felt this? This exact combination of satisfaction, warmth and ease? It was as close to heaven as she could imagine.

"What's this?" he asked, and she realized he'd been inspecting the arm he'd been kissing. She'd completely forgotten the scars there. Reality crashed in hard, and she yanked her arm back.

"Nothing. Just an old injury."

"Not that old."

She looked at him apprehensively. He read the question in her eyes and answered simply, "I have a few scars of my own, and I've seen plenty more. Those seem pretty recent. How does a photographer end up with that many stitches?"

She had to think fast, and shrugged, hoping she sounded casual. "I fell in my bathtub about a year ago. Broke my arm, and sliced that part below the elbow on the faucet."

"Sounds bad."

"It wasn't fun, but it's healed now," she said easily, amazed at how the lie fell out, and not liking that she'd become used to hiding the truth. But it was about survival and privacy. She was entitled.

She certainly didn't feel threatened by Jarod. She wouldn't be here with him if she did, but no way would she tell him the truth. Especially now—he'd never look at her the same way if he knew. She'd found out quickly that once you admitted to being a victim, people changed how they saw you, and not for the better. So she simply wouldn't admit it.

"Good thing, since you're going to need every bit of strength you have," he said, kissing her hair. He then moved out from beneath her, letting her slip onto the pile of pillows. He was, truly, the most handsome man she'd ever laid eyes on, and even more so here in his naked, tousled, sleepy-eyed state. She pushed up on one elbow when he shifted from the mattress, and leaned over to pick up her camera bag.

"What are you doing?"

"How complicated is this camera to operate?"

"Not bad. I mean, it's up to the photographer to know how to take a good picture. The camera is just a tool."

His eyes remained on hers steadily. "Could I handle it?"

It took her a minute before what he was suggesting landed in her mind, and she felt herself physically pull back.

"I'm sure you could, but we're not going there," she said definitively.

His eyebrows quirked up. "Why not? You've had this thing trained on me all day, even when I wasn't aware of it. Don't you think turnaround is fair play?"

"You weren't naked. It wasn't sex."

"I felt more exposed than that, at some points," he confessed.

She blinked. "Why?"

"I'm not used to being watched like that. I don't know what you're homing in on. What you're seeing. You're in complete control."

Settling into the pillows, she had to admit that she'd never thought about it that way. Most of the subjects she'd shot were models, and were used to being in the limelight. She hadn't considered how vulnerable it could make someone, like Jarod, feel—a man who was always used to being in control.

"Okay, I get that, but this is different."

"How? It's another way I can get to know you…and it's your camera, your film. You can just destroy it later if you want to. Though I'd love to see the photos first," he added in a voice like warm honey.

Like many photographers, Lacey preferred being on the working end of the camera for a reason, but she had to admit, the look on Jarod's face was compelling. And the idea of giving him that gift was seductive.

She smiled. "What if you don't like what you see?"

He shook his head resolutely. "No chance of that," he promised, his eyes drifting over her as she lounged on the bed.

She paused, considering. He'd let her demand what she wanted earlier, given her what she needed without holding back. He had only showed her passion, consideration, kindness. She knew if she told him no, he'd listen.

So maybe it was a moment for her to give him something.

"Okay, there's only a dozen or so pictures left on there anyway, but let me show you what to do."

Heat and something else—admiration?—flared in his eyes when she agreed. Her own breath became a little short at the thought of what they were about to do.

After a few quick instructions, she wasn't sure if she was more nervous about being photographed nude or him handling her expensive camera. But his hands were sure, and he took a position at the end of the bed.

As he lifted the camera to his eye, she froze for a second, wondering what to do. The barrel of the lens seemed to zero in on her, tagging her to the spot. She'd never realized how it felt to be so tightly zoomed in on, explored—exposed.

But her frozen posture gave way to heat as he spoke.

"Relax on those pillows…think about what we did a few minutes ago. Think about me inside of you, fucking you up against the wall."

How did he know so easily what to say, what turned her on? She loved sex talk, hard, raw and honest. It was how she liked sex, as well, and Jarod seemed of a like mind.

"Open up your legs…let me see what you're hiding there," he continued playfully, his tone light and teasing, and she did as he asked.

She dealt with her nerves by hamming it up at first, mocking a sexy pose against the pillows, letting her thighs fall only so far apart, teasing, and lifting her arms up to jut her breasts out for his view. She imagined she looked ridiculous. She was confident in her body, but wasn't built to pull off the sexy poses her more voluptuous models could. She was more…made for modeling running clothes or sports equipment.

When she heard him suck in a breath, bite off a short curse and saw his cock spring forward with interest as he took the shot, she reconsidered. Doing what he said, she looked over at the spot where he'd held her against the wall, buried inside of her, and pushed up on all fours, looking back at him over her shoulder. The click of the camera and his harsh breathing egged her on.

"You're so incredibly hot," he said, his voice rough,

telling her he was not unaffected. "Touch yourself for me."

The lens connected them; model and photographer were always linked in an intimate way, even more so in this kind of situation. She did as he asked, catching her breath as her hand slipped between her legs and found her skin sensitive and soft. She knew how to make herself feel good, and didn't hold back. Hearing the soft hum of the zoom focusing, she knew he was making it a tighter shot. As liquid warmth seemed to move through her limbs, she lost her self-consciousness and let her eyes rest on his sex. It was perfectly built, like the rest of him, and it strained toward her.

"You have the most beautiful cock. I want to suck you," she said softly, trembling as her own touch brought her to the edge.

"I'd love to see that, Lacey. I want to see your mouth moving on me, making me come," he growled as he took the shot, and his words, the image they built in her mind, pushed gentle cries of pleasure past her lips.

She opened her eyes as he set the camera on the dresser and turned to her, his body set in rigid, sensual tension.

"Can we set this on remote?"

She told him how and a minute or two later he was back on the bed with her, the camera watching them from its lonely post on the dresser. As he moved down, stretching out at her side, she was moved by the dark emotion, the passion and the need in his expression.

"Thank you for sharing this with me, for being so open with me," he said simply, his fingers stroking the inside of her thigh.

"It was…intense," she said, propping up on one elbow and meeting his eyes for a moment before she shimmied down and closed her lips over his cock, sucking off the dew there. She moaned in soft approval as he lay back, arching up into her mouth.

She reached over and hit the remote snap without looking.

"I want to taste you, too," he whispered, and she swung her legs over, straddling him as she explored his sex with her mouth. He broke her concentration, opening her with his hands and prodding her clit more insistently with this tongue.

Gasping, she forgot all about the camera, following the steady current of pleasure that his strokes created, making her crazy with the tricks of his fingers and the talent of his mouth. It became a game between them. He would find a way to drive her one bit further, and then she would go down deeper, suck harder, find a sensitive spot with her tongue, until they were both convulsing with the pleasure of mutual victory.

She pushed back on the pillows, and he followed, sinking down next to her.

She brushed her fingers tenderly over his onyx hair, silently drawing his attention upward to the camera.

Her head rested in the crook of his shoulder, his arms around her, one finding its way up into her hair, holding her head against him in a gesture so intimate she thought she wouldn't be able to breathe. They lay there, snuggling quietly, replete for the moment.

Spotting the remote on the mattress where she'd

dropped it, she reached it without moving, and with a
lazy, satisfied smile, she stopped time with a press of
her finger, capturing them both.

6

LACEY WALKED BACK to her apartment feeling loose and well exercised—and she was smiling. Considering they hadn't slept more than a couple of hours combined, she should be worried about her model having rings under his eyes and her ability to stay awake, and…she wasn't worried about any of it. She could barely keep herself from grinning ear to ear.

She felt like her old self again, and it was wonderful.

Jarod was wonderful, too. Considerate, adventurous…and with stamina women dreamed about. She didn't know if they'd continue to spend their nights together, but she also wasn't sure how she'd be able to function if she didn't have a way to deal with the inevitable turn-on of working with him. Incredibly, after everything they'd done, she wanted more. The very idea of looking at him through a camera made her lick her lips.

And today was beach day. He'd be taking off his shirt, and she couldn't wait. Fortunately it was minimal crew, wardrobe was simple and the formal part of the day wouldn't take long. He'd seemed agreeable with the same schedule as before—do the staged shoots, then move around the area taking some candids.

Of course, she thought, placing her hand over the spot in her camera bag where she kept her film, nothing quite as candid as the shots they'd taken last night.

Would she develop them?

She grinned more widely. Life was good. Lacey hummed to herself as she turned up the steps to her apartment, taking the stairs and doing a little jog all the way down the hall. She was running a bit late, and had to—

Stopping in her tracks, she noticed the door was open. Just a crack, but it was open. She tried not to panic as her heart began to hammer and she fumbled reaching for her cell phone.

She suddenly understood why the seemingly stupid heroines always rushed in to the house when they knew there was danger waiting inside—she had to make herself step back, remembering the general advice to call police in such a situation, not rush in.

But underneath the fear was anger. Someone had intruded in her space, in her world. She wanted desperately to burst through the door and answer the question *who*. To stop it, to know why.

The driving need to know nearly pushed her into the apartment, regardless of the danger that was possibly inside.

Instead, she dialed 911 and waited, reported the break-in, and moved back down to the stairway, never taking her eyes off the door, even though the operator had told her to meet the police at the entry. She was determined to know if someone came out of her place.

Nothing happened. The hall was silent, and she didn't hear anything coming from the room, either. Her neighbors were mostly professionals like herself and had likely left for work. She was alone.

Doubt wheedled itself into the cracks of her panicked thoughts. Had she forgotten to lock the apartment? Could her super have gone in for some reason and failed to shut the door completely?

Too late for second guesses as she heard the police come through the door downstairs. She looked at them in both relief and worry as they climbed the stairs toward her.

"You reported a break-in, ma'am?" one guy who could have been a candidate for the calendar asked her.

"Yes, I mean, I don't know, but the door was open, and I'm sure I locked it, but I—"

"You stay right here. You did the right thing by not going in. Let us check it out. I'd recommend you go outside just in case."

Lacey nodded, although she didn't actually go anywhere. Her feet seemed to be frozen to the spot as the two officers moved carefully down the hall toward her apartment, standing at each side, covering each other as they nudged the door open, and went in.

Nothing.

Lacey didn't realize she was holding her breath until she let it go when one of the policemen came out and waved her down the hall toward the apartment.

"You can come in now, ma'am, but I have to warn you, it's a shock. Someone was here," he said with a stern expression. She walked past him, wanting to know what on earth he was talking about. Then she stopped cold in her doorway, sucking in a breath, her world tilting a little.

"Oh, my God..."

Everything was a wreck. The entire contents of her apartment had been upended, and whoever it was had written *BITCH* in huge black letters with spray paint across one wall, where she was sure to see it first thing through the door.

"Lacey, what...what the *hell?*"

She jumped as she recognized Jarod's voice beside her and faced off with him. The adrenaline was pushing through her system so violently she didn't know where to aim her anger first. He grabbed her by the shoulders, leveling her a look.

"What happened here? Are you okay?"

She wrestled away. Her breath coming harshly, she eyed him warily. "How did you know where I live?"

It was impossible for her to separate all of the conflicting emotions coursing through her at the moment, so she targeted them all in his direction. The cop stepped forward, not quite between her and Jarod, but almost.

"Step back, sir," he said in warning. Jarod nodded, stepping back, but only slightly.

"I'm just...a concerned friend," Jarod explained, "You can pull my wallet—and my badge—from my left pocket. I'm a cop, too. Texas Ranger, El Paso."

The second officer joined them to see what the fuss was about, and Lacey's mind cleared. She started to tell them that Jarod wasn't the one she was worried about just as they took his wallet and flipped open his badge.

"Ranger, huh? Well, you aren't from around here, and the lady doesn't seem happy to see you, so maybe we should walk you out."

Jarod looked at her, making her look at him.

"Is that what you want, Lacey? You want me to leave?"

Lacey didn't know what to think, but casting a glance at her apartment, she shook her head.

"No, I want you to stay. I'm sorry, officers, I…was shocked," she finished lamely, and the NYPD men watched her carefully for a few moments before finally relenting.

"I'll call this in and we'll need a report," one said, and they all nodded, flanking Lacey as they walked deeper into the apartment. Jarod was closest to her. She welcomed his presence as much as she questioned it. She knew he couldn't be responsible for this, but how he showed up when he did, and how he found her address…they'd talk about that before this was over.

As she scanned the mess in her apartment, she reached for something to hang on to and Jarod's firm, warm grip was there. When she turned into his chest, he was there. It gave her the strength she needed to turn back around and face what she had to.

"Have you received any threats lately, Ms. Graham? We would chalk it up to breaking and entering, but this—" the cop's eyes traveled to the scrawl "—seems pretty directed. Personal. And it doesn't look like the usual stuff was taken. Your television, even your laptop, is still here."

"I—I can't imagine who would do this," she said, though she didn't meet their eyes.

She'd call Gena, the secretary from Legal Aid, and find out what was going on, if Scott was where he was supposed to be. But who else would have done something like this? The police were right. There wasn't anything missing, although several things were broken. The break-in was definitely a message of some sort.

"Or they were searching for something, and it wasn't here," Jarod offered reasonably.

"I can't imagine what," she responded as the officers took notes.

"You didn't spend the night here, last night, Ms. Graham. Did anyone know that?"

"No, it was...a last-minute decision." Her cheeks flamed and she refused to look at Jarod.

"It's just as well you weren't here, but did you have anything with you that the intruder might have been looking for?"

She shook her head. "All I had was my camera bag, my film, my lenses...undeveloped shots from the past few days. Nothing anyone would want."

"Hard to say. What kinds of photos?"

Her cheeks turned hotter as this time she did meet Jarod's gaze, thinking of their private photo session. "They're modeling shots for *Bliss Magazine*. That's it..."

"Maybe someone was up to something they shouldn't have been, and you caught it on film," the other officer speculated, and Lacey blinked. Did things like that happen in real life? Could she have gathered some kind of evidence against someone in the park or in her candids that they'd later come looking for?

"Well, the pictures aren't developed yet, and I'll check through them carefully, but how would some stranger know I took the picture, or where I lived?"

Jarod nodded in agreement. "And why the message? Why go to the trouble? They'd want to get in, get the film, and get out—ideally without being seen or noticed."

"True," the officer agreed. "Well, then, as nothing was stolen and no other harm was done, I guess that's all we can do here. But if you have any more trouble, be sure to call us," he said.

"Thank you, I will." Lacey closed the door behind them, and turned toward her apartment again, the day shot down the tubes. She'd had to cancel the session, and now she had to deal with this mess.

"So do you want to tell me what's going on?" Jarod asked calmly, standing in the middle of her living room, looking big and imposing among the disaster, looking at her as if he could see right through her.

"Excuse me?"

"Listen, Lacey, normally I mind my own business, but you've been as jumpy as a jackrabbit since I laid eyes on you, and now this? I saw your face when he asked you if you'd had any problems recently. You're not as good a liar as you think you are. Who's bothering you? Why would they do *this*?"

She stepped forward, eyes blazing as her heart thudded in her chest. He was too close, and she pushed back, hard.

"It's really none of your business! Just because we had sex it's not an invitation into my life. How did you show up here anyway? You've never come to my apartment, you couldn't possibly know where I lived unless you…" The answer dawned, and she put her hand to the edge of a table near the door to steady herself. "You've been following me?"

The sick feeling in the pit of her stomach increased as she saw the truth on his face, and she didn't bother holding back tears, but they were mostly from anger at herself, for being so stupid as to let her guard down. Thank God she had the pictures, she realized. Regret was a second blow, and she leaned harder on the edge of the table for support.

"Just get out before I call the police back. Forget about the shoot, leave me alone. I mean it."

For a second, they were both still, and she didn't know what was going to happen. He didn't seem angry; he didn't step forward. When he spoke, she could hardly believe her ears.

"Sorry, darlin', but that just isn't happening until you tell me what's going on."

JAROD FELT as if he'd already stepped over a line, but there was no way he was going anywhere. Lacey was in trouble, and he wanted to know the source of it. He wanted to help.

He'd do anything for this woman. He didn't know how he knew that, but he knew. In the same way he knew she was wounded, and frightened of something she was too stubborn to admit.

"Lacey, listen for a moment."

She started to protest, her eyes wild, arms wrapped

so tightly around her slim frame that he had to hold himself back from going to her and holding her himself. But now wasn't the time for that.

"I did follow you, but not to scare you. I... Oh, hell," he cursed, throwing his hands up. "I like you. I really like you, but there's been something going on here. I can see the fear on your face, the way you react to things like a sudden movement or someone crowding your space. It's as if you're poised to run. People don't normally react that way unless they've been given a reason to."

She looked away, and he knew he'd hit on the truth. But could he convince her to share? To trust?

"Then there was that phone call, and now this. I'm not stupid, Lacey. I knew something spooked you the other day, and so I simply followed you back to your apartment so I could make sure you got there safely. That's all. Then today, I saw the cops arrive, and I lost it. I had to make sure you were okay.

"Lacey, I hope you know I'd never hurt you—not a hair on your head. Not after what we shared, and I, well..." He blew out an exasperated breath, unfamiliar and uneasy with sharing his thoughts this way. "I hope you wouldn't have slept with me in the first place if you thought you couldn't trust me. I'm sorry if following you scared you. That's the last thing I would ever do."

She didn't say anything, but he could see her processing the information. He took a step closer, then another, until he was standing beside her, and lifted his hand to brush some of the hair from her eyes. Hell, the worst she could do was hit him and tell him to leave again, but the fight seemed to have gone out of her.

He wasn't sure if that was a good thing or not.

"Lacey—" he started, but she didn't say anything; pressed her fingers to his lips, silencing him.

"I believe you, Jarod, and I guess I have been jumpy. I just never expected anything like this," she whispered, looking around at the apartment.

He closed his eyes, relieved about her accepting his apology.

"I know, and I'll help you clean up. I'd like it if you'd stay with me again tonight, at my hotel." He said the words on a smoky note as her form pressed against his. Protectiveness wasn't the only thing he was feeling for this woman.

"No, I won't be driven out of my own apartment. They probably won't even come back."

"They?"

She shook her head. "Generic pronoun. I don't know who it is, I really don't. I did get a weird call, and sometimes I have the feeling someone is watching me, but I thought that was my imagination."

"This isn't imaginary."

"I know. Jarod, I have to make another phone call. Privately," she said, and he nodded. She still wasn't telling him what was going on, but this wasn't a time to push.

"Sure, I'll go check out your kitchen and start setting things to rights."

"You don't have to do that," she protested.

"I want to. I want to be here, with you, Lacey. Okay?"

She almost smiled, and seemed to relax slightly, and Jarod did, too. He walked through louvered French doors to the kitchen and was tempted to hang close, but he said he'd give her privacy, and he did.

The kitchen was less untidy. He picked up the garbage, and straightened out a few other things, listening to Lacey's voice as she spoke to someone in low tones, although he couldn't make out the words.

As he put the garbage pail back in the corner, his eye caught sight of a crunched sheet of paper on top. He couldn't help but see the name underneath the letterhead, "Domestic Abuse Counseling."

The scar on Lacey's arm, the way she'd panicked when the CHIP guy had gotten too aggressive… An ugly picture was forming in his mind. Yet, this could be junk mail and have nothing to do with her at all.

As his fingers touched the edges, he hesitated again. No.

If Lacey had been abused, if she had one man violating her life, he wouldn't be another one, no matter how much he wanted to know.

It was up to her to tell him about her past if she wanted to, if she could trust him enough. He pushed the paper back down into the garbage and turned away.

But in his heart, the details had started to form a truth he hadn't really considered. The protectiveness he'd felt before blossomed into something much, much more powerful.

When Lacey walked in, he'd just dumped a dustpan of broken glass into the garbage pail and had the place almost looking normal again. She seemed relieved.

Whether it was finding the kitchen not as wrecked as the living room, or the phone calls she'd made, the color was back in her cheeks, her eyes were less panicked.

"I'm sorry that took so long, I just had to check on something."

Like an ex-spouse or boyfriend?

"No problem. Apparently the kitchen wasn't a huge draw for your intruder—not so bad in here."

"Thank you, Jarod, and thanks for staying. I know I...reacted badly to you showing up, but I'm really glad you're here."

He took a deep breath. It was something. More than he'd expected, maybe more than he deserved, considering the circumstances.

"I'm glad I'm here, too," he said, smiling. Crossing the kitchen to pull her close, he was happy when she came willingly into his arms. "I thought I'd go get some paint and take care of your wall art in there. Any color you like in particular? New paint job? I don't offer often, so take advantage," he teased, rubbing his hands over her back, and feeling her body expand and contract with a sigh.

"You definitely don't have to do that. Seriously. The super will send someone to take care of it," she said, leaning back and looking up. "But thanks."

"I don't want you having to see it one minute longer than you have to. I don't mind," he insisted, liking how when she leaned back from him their hips met, his groin snuggling against hers.

"I guess I would be a fool to turn down more help."

"Let's put things to rights, and then I'm taking you to dinner. If the day is lost for work, we might as well find some small enjoyment in the meantime, huh?"

"Sounds like a plan."

They worked in tandem for several hours, and before long, the apartment was put back together again. Still, it bothered him to see her so controlled, so measured, as she picked up broken objects that were obviously important to her, and put them in the garbage. She didn't cry once, but repressed emotion strained every muscle in her lithe body, and he knew from his own experience the mental and physical toll something like this took.

Jarod didn't plan to leave her alone. If she wouldn't stay with him, he'd find a way to convince her he should stay here. Admiring the pout of pretty breasts under her T-shirt and remembering how her soft skin tasted, he didn't think it would be a sacrifice.

"There. Not bad," she announced, gesturing at her room, studiously avoiding the wall where the first coat of paint was drying. He'd used a stain-blocker, but the black was tough to cover against a light wall, and it still showed slightly. He would put on the second coat in a few hours.

Jarod walked up behind her, massaging her neck, playing along. Sometimes it was necessary to just act normally even when things obviously weren't normal at all.

She turned, and he was leveled by the emotion in her eyes when she looked up at him.

"Thank you, Jarod," she said simply.

He felt like the richest man on earth. *I am in so much*

trouble with this woman, he thought, as he leaned down to kiss her, wondering how he'd gotten in so deep, so fast.

7

OVER STEAMING PLATES of Chinese food at a tiny place downtown, Lacey laughed hysterically as she watched Jarod, one of the most capable men she could imagine, fumble with chopsticks until he finally gave up and signaled the waiter for a fork.

"The food smells great. I'd actually like to eat some of it," he said, smiling at the waiter who offered him utensils. "I don't know how you manage those things," he said, eyeing her chopsticks with malice.

She wiggled her fingers at him after popping a succulent straw mushroom into her mouth.

"Nimble fingers, I guess," she replied.

He snatched the fingers of her other hand gently and brought them to his mouth. "Don't I know it."

Heat shot up her arm and swept away any other thought. In fact, though this had been close to one of her top-ten worst days ever, in the past half hour she hadn't even thought about her apartment. Sitting here amid the colorful sights and sounds of the bustling neighborhood, she sighed, actually feeling happy.

It was completely incongruous. How could she be *happy* when she'd just suffered a break-in, and Scott was out of jail? Not that the two were connected, but they could be. Who else would do this to her? Who else would make it so personal?

"Hey. What's going on in there?" Jarod asked, a concerned expression on his face.

"Just thinking how nice it is to sit here and forget everything, which of course made me remember it all."

He reached over, and squeezed her hand. "I'm here if you want to talk about it, and even if you don't."

She smiled, grateful, but apprehensive. Whatever it was between them had the telltale signs of turning into something far more complicated than a fling, and that worried her. It was too fast, for one thing, and he was going back home soon, for another.

Sleeping with a guy for some mutual fun, fine—starting a relationship with him—that she wasn't sure she was ready for. Jarod was incredible, but the way he was getting so close was making her uncomfortable, so she went to a more comfortable topic: work.

"Listen, we have to make up the beach shots in studio, which should take a day, and then another day around the city. We're scheduled for the Empire State Building tomorrow, so we could wrap this up sooner than we thought. You could probably be back tracking down bad guys in Texas by next week."

His eyes narrowed. "Really? Well…that's good to know, I guess."

"Yes, I'm sure you want to get back."

"That was before—"

He was cut off by the ringing of his cell, and she tried to hold off a visible sigh of relief. The call must not have been good news, though, but she couldn't tell much from his regular nods and grunts of acknowledgment to someone named Tom.

"No problem, Tom. I'll go now."

He hung up, but something had changed. The lines of his face seemed harder drawn, and he didn't look at her, not right away.

"Is everything okay?"

"That was my captain. There's a guy we've been tracking—bad case—and he jumped bail a few days ago. A small-town policeman just north of here grabbed someone on a DWI with the same name, and they want me to check if it's him, and if so, send him home. I may have to go with him."

Her eyes widened. "But the calendar!"

He blinked, and she wasn't sure if she saw disappointment flash across his face. She felt like an ass. He'd been so good to her, and all she could think about was her work. Talk about messed up. She was definitely not in shape for a relationship, and she grimaced. He replied calmly, but set down his fork.

"Let me see what the story is. It might not even be him, but we have to make sure. This is important."

She couldn't help feeling stung at that. "This job is important, as well."

"We're talking about a guy who kills people. And technically, while I'm up here on the department's request, I'm not on vacation. If they tell me to do something, it has to take precedence."

She knew he was right. Obviously tracking down a felon was more important than a magazine's calendar, but disappointment stabbed at her, as well, and that was not a good sign. She didn't want him to leave, but there was no way she could admit that.

She nodded. "Sorry, that was uncalled-for. I know you have to do this. It's been one thing after another with this shoot, and just…life. We can reschedule. It's not like we haven't been jostling everything around lately anyway."

She signaled for the check, feeling like an idiot—when had she ever been this needy or this stupid?

"Lacey," Jarod began, but paused as he took the bill from the waiter, though she'd grabbed for it first. "This isn't just work, and it's on me."

"Uh, sure. Okay."

She felt awkward and restless, and just wanted to get out of the restaurant.

"I'll be back by morning if I can. Will you be okay?"

"Sure. I'll try to get one of the local guys for the sky-scraper shots, and—"

"I didn't mean will the shoot work out. I meant will *you* be okay?"

She swallowed. "I'm fine. In fact, I'm going to head to the studio now and make up for some lost time."

He frowned. "Tonight?"

"I often work late into the night. It's not unusual for us artsy types," she said lightly, but secretly the real truth was that she couldn't go back to her apartment. Not yet. Not at night, alone.

"I'll walk you there."

"Not necessary. Really, go. I'm fine," she stressed again.

"It will make me feel better to walk you to the studio."

She paused. She hadn't considered that he could be worried, too. He shouldn't be worried. She didn't want that. His concern for her triggered guilt about her lack of honesty concerning her past, and Scott, but she also couldn't help the relief she felt at Jarod's insistence.

She didn't tell anyone about Scott, and Jarod wasn't the exception to that rule. She didn't want ugliness from her past coloring what she was enjoying with him. They were having fun together, everything was good, and if it would make him feel better to make sure she was safe, what was the harm? It would give her a few more minutes of his company, too.

"That would be nice, thanks," she acknowledged, and they fell into step together, heading to the subway. "We'll catch a train and it won't take long."

As he grabbed her arm, she felt herself spun around in front of him, and gasped in surprise. He pulled her up tight against him, the granite planes of his chest feeling all-too-good. They ignored a few wolf whistles and comments by passersby as he leaned in and kissed her in a way that assured her he wasn't entirely in a hurry.

"I don't want you feeling pressured, but I like you," he said once he broke the kiss, getting right to the point. "I *really* like you. I don't know what that means, but let's not rush to the end of this, okay?"

He didn't give her a chance to answer. Instead, he wound his hand in her hair and tilted her head back so that her breasts pressed into his chest. Her nipples sensitized and peaked as arousal coursed through her. His tongue rubbed against hers in a lazy, mating motion that reminded her what it was like when he was inside of her.

When he released her and looked down askance, all she could do was whisper, "Okay."

He smiled, and her knees went a little weak. She'd yell at herself for being such a sap later. Right now, all she wanted was for him to go, come back, and kiss her again.

PARANOID ABOUT leaving anything at her apartment, she'd dragged her camera bag along with her to dinner, and that included the roll of film containing the pictures of her and Jarod from the hotel.

Soon, she was lost in her own world, ensconced in the basement labs of the *Bliss* building. The rooms were still functional, though not used as much as they used to be now that everything was going digital. It made her sad. She was a romantic at heart, and she loved the tangible experience of bringing a photograph to life.

The photos she was working on now had nothing to do with her project, though. She watched with an analytical eye as the first image came forward, Jarod's strong features slowly emerging, and her jaw dropped as she saw what he'd photographed. There were some ultrasexy shots of herself that had made her chuckle, slightly embarrassed but privately pleased at how he'd viewed her through the camera. Then she came to the images of them together.

As a photographer, she was impressed, and couldn't

ignore the chemistry leaping from the images of them.
As a woman, she…she wasn't sure what she felt as she
took in Jarod with his face turned into her thigh,
looking for all the world as if he was worshipping her,
his eyes shuttered, his concentration complete.

A thrill shimmied its way through to her core,
making her inner muscles heat and clench as she remembered what it was like as he had slowly made his
way upward, to fasten those amazing lips on her clit and
suck her into sheer oblivion. And how she'd returned the
favor.

Her heart hammered as she revealed one shot after
another documenting the progress of the raw desire
between them. When she reached the final shot, the
one of them cuddled together afterward, their arms
wrapped around each other, faces mirroring the satisfaction of the climax they'd just shared, something
settled deep inside her heart.

This was not just any man. Not a fling. The images
revealed so much more than that.

Her hands shook as she hung the prints to dry, her
eyes following the photo story of their lovemaking
from start to finish.

She noticed she was rubbing her arm as she admired
the photos. He didn't know about her past. Maybe he
suspected, but he didn't know. Would it change how he
looked at her? Shouldn't she give him more credit? He
was obviously an extraordinary man.

He hadn't called yet. Would he be back in the
morning, or off to Texas, leaving her in the lurch?
Jackie's message had said that Mr. July was out, having

suffered a serious injury in the line of duty. Now they might be losing another model, or at least having the schedule disrupted. Mr. April, however, of the FDNY, would be coming in to take Jarod's place for the day, so at least she'd get something done.

Lacey had to wait for the prints to dry before she could leave. Very likely no one used these darkrooms much any more, but she couldn't take a chance with material that was so personal.

Her eyes were tired, and there was a cot in the corner. More than one magazine photog had put in long hours here in the past.

Several hours later, a noise pulled her sharply from her sleep, and she sat up, her heart beating hard. She was momentarily disoriented. Something was wrong.

Gathering her wits, she realized what it was in a flash of shock—the pictures. None of them were hanging where she'd left them. Unbidden panic burbled in her chest as she heard a shuffling noise by the door and she stood on shaky legs, trying to cross the room quietly, grabbing a jar of developing chemicals, the only weapon available to her.

"Who's there? I've called the police," she warned loudly, grabbing her cell phone from her pocket, but grimacing when she saw she had no signal down here.

"Too late. Time for payback, bitch," a sneering and definitely male voice said; though it was muffled through the door, hard to recognize, the sentiment was clear.

She knew what had happened as she heard the man laugh, and footsteps walking away. Whoever it was must have followed her from the restaurant, but how could he have gotten inside the building? He was leaving—with her pictures!

"Oh, no, you aren't," she said with a burst of determination—she couldn't stand the idea of someone else having those pictures. It could ruin her career, or Jarod's.

She grabbed the door handle, feeling the heat building up on the other side. An acrid smell assaulted her, and her heart sank in fear.

Fire.

She couldn't see anything, the room was locked and tightly sealed against light, but some smoke was finding its way under the door. She was trapped.

It had to be Scott.

She fought to keep her breathing steady, her mind clear as the room seemed to close in around her.

Options?

She took a blanket from the cot and jammed it into the crack under the door, stemming the progress of the smoke. She pulled her shirt up over her face, and hit the hard door, yelling, "Help! I'm in here!"

Someone had to hear—they had to.

She looked at her watch. The sun was coming up, and there would be people arriving for work. She heard the fire alarm ring, and relief washed through her. Help would come; she just had to sit tight.

Easier said than done, she thought, pacing. Smoke was filtering in, and she had to get out, soon. Taking a breath, she started banging on the door again, shouting, and hoping someone heard her soon.

8

JAROD WALKED OUT of the police station in Walden, NY, both relieved and disappointed. Disappointed because the man they'd apprehended was not the Darren Hill they were after, but another guy with the same name. Relieved because this meant he'd be able to have more time with Lacey.

He stood silently, taking in the quiet street of the village. It was the quaint kind of upstate New York that everyone imagined on postcards. Narrow streets, trees and a picturesque white church at the center of town. Unlikely Hill would have ended up here, but every lead had to be chased down.

Jarod looked around, thinking of the small town he grew up in, and imagining he could live in a pretty town like this. Get to know his neighbors, volunteer at the school, the local fire department. His mind immediately jumped to Lacey, thinking about sharing that kind of life with her.

He shook his head, smiling to himself as he walked to the car. Lacey may have grown up on a ranch, but she was a city girl through and through. What would she do in a place like this? And why was he even thinking about it? He had no interest in leaving his home state, or his job, either.

His only interest right now, he thought with anticipation as he got into the car, was getting back to the city, and to Lacey.

LACEY STRODE out of the E.R., happy to escape. She asked the cab driver to take her directly back to the *Bliss* offices, her mind spinning. They'd insisted she be checked for smoke inhalation and other injuries even though she was fine.

The smoke had set off the sprinkler system, and she was rescued about twenty minutes after she discovered she was locked in. She'd been scared, and smelled horrible, but that was about it. She was also a wreck about her missing pictures. Intimate photos in the hands of someone who wanted to hurt her wasn't good, but who could she tell?

Only Jarod, and he wasn't here, hadn't called.

It had been complete chaos. The fire hadn't had time to do much damage, but the water had soaked things considerably, though only on the basement floor, where the damage had been contained. Still, whoever had set it meant business—the place reeked of gasoline, and if the fire had traveled much farther, catching the floor above, Lacey might not have gotten out alive.

Unfortunately, the bastard had taken all of her other work, too. The calendar shots were gone, along with everything else. How could she have slept through that? Exhausted, she knew, but still....

How could she explain this to the *Bliss* board? Her

stomach bottomed out, and she thought she'd be sick. She was due to start studio shots of Ryan Murphy, FDNY, in two hours.

Taking a deep breath, she resolved to go home, get cleaned up and deal with it when she had to. Right now, she'd save the calendar project from going up in flames, and that meant getting back here and doing what she could with Ryan today, as well as making sure she had enough pictures of Jarod.

The police were investigating motives for the fire. Coupled with what happened at her apartment and the phone calls, it was clear that someone was working out a grudge. She told them, albeit haltingly, about Scott, and they made that their first check, though she hadn't heard anything confirming or denying her ex's where-abouts.

While this was hardly her fault, she had a feeling the *Bliss* project board might not care. They were business-people, and if she cost them too much money, too much time, or brought in negative press, they would can her and bring in another photographer to take over. She had a meeting with them after her session with Ryan, and she needed a plan to approach them confidently, to assure them things would be fine.

If only she believed that herself.

WHEN JAROD FINALLY caught up with Lacey, he was on the edge of his patience. He'd spent his last nerve hours ago when he'd brought the car back to the police garage, and a guy he'd talked with, Lt. Ward, about Hill had told him about the *Bliss* fire.

He hadn't been able to get Lacey on the phone and something very close to fear ate at him until he spotted Jackie as he entered the *Bliss* offices.

"Is Lacey here? Is she all right?" he asked Jackie.

"She's fine. She's in a session that she rescheduled over yours."

"Where?"

Jackie shook her head. "Nope, sorry. You can't just bust in there in the middle of—"

"Jackie, I need to talk to her. Where is she?"

Jackie looked at him speculatively. "You two have quite a thing going, huh?"

Jarod wasn't going to talk about his relationship with Lacey, especially not with her assistant. "I really just want to see if she's okay. That's all. Let her know I'm back."

"She's in 3-b, the same place you had your studio— Hey!"

Jarod took off. He didn't bolt into the studio, but walked in quietly, and waited, watching Lacey, letting his eyes take in the reality that she was, in fact, all in one piece.

Why hadn't she called him? Why hadn't she let him know?

"Satisfied?" Jackie said, hands on hips.

"Not quite. When will she be done?"

"When she decides she's done," the assistant said smartly.

Jarod ignored the jibe and studied Lacey, ever the professional, taking pictures of the shirtless fireman who smiled at her as if he meant it—and Jarod found a new reason for his blood to simmer. Lacey was smiling, too, laughing and flirting, like she had done with him, and taking shot after shot.

Impatience and maybe a little bit of the green-eyed monster bit at him. He'd been worried sick, but she really was fine. He was glad for that, of course, but he wanted to touch her, and to make sure she was okay for himself. The cops said she'd gotten lucky, not to have been hurt in that fire.

When she put down the camera, whether she was done or not, he moved in, taking in her surprised expression. She was tired, too, he could see, and clearly under stress for all of her professionalism.

"Jarod—what are you doing here?"

It wasn't exactly what he expected to hear. "I've been trying to call, trying to find out if you were okay after I heard what happened. Why didn't you call me?"

She glanced from where Jackie was talking to Ryan, back to Jarod. "Why would I call you? Why didn't you call me?"

"Lacey," he started, keeping his ire in check.

"No. Don't come into my studio workplace making demands of me like you have a right to. Who do you think you are?"

Everyone had gone silent, and Jarod pulled back, wondering what was behind the defensiveness of her stance, but seeing the shadows in her eyes, he lowered his voice. "I'm the guy who's been half out of his mind hoping you were okay, that's who. I was worried sick, thinking I was gone, and someone tried to hurt you."

She closed her eyes and nodded, running a hand over her face.

"Jackie, why don't you take Ryan to get a coffee and a wardrobe change, and leave us alone for a minute?"

Jackie's gaze went to Jarod, and back to Lacey. "You sure?"

"Yeah, go ahead. See you in about thirty."

"Okay," her assistant agreed and led the fireman from the studio.

"I'm sorry, Lacey. I was just imagining every awful thing when I couldn't get you on the phone. Lt. Ward told me he didn't know what happened after you went to the hospital, and the hospital wouldn't tell me anything, of course."

"I'm sorry, too. I didn't hear from you, and then there was so much to deal with, and I knew you were in the middle of your own stuff—"

"You could have called me. Should have called me," he said, pulling her in close, hugging it out, feeling the tension drain from her body as she wrapped her arms around him, too.

She shrugged. "I didn't want to bother you. I knew you were working, and I was okay."

Her pretty lips turned down as she pulled away, wrapping her arms around herself and crossing the room. When she was hurting, he realized, she pulled in, distanced herself, instead of leaning on anyone.

"Someone tried to kill you, and that's not okay. I need you to level with me, Lacey. I need to know what's going on, why someone would be doing this to you. Do you have any idea who it is? Why?"

She looked up at him, and he could see she was struggling with something, as if wondering what she should say and what she shouldn't. He didn't press anymore.

"The only person I can think of is in California, an ex of mine, and they're looking into it. I don't know who else it could be."

"Tell me about him," Jarod said gently.

She shook her head. "Not here, not now. I have to work. This is more of a mess than you know. I could lose the calendar project."

"Why? You're the victim here."

"This calendar shoot hasn't gone well from the start—people keep canceling or schedules are missing. Then there was the problem with my apartment, that cost me time, and now this fire and—" she took a deep breath, meeting his eyes "—the pictures I was developing last night were the ones of us, from the other night. But the guy took my camera bag, the digital and all of the negatives—all of them. From the shoot and from the hotel. No one knows about the, uh, personal pictures, but I'm going to have to tell *Bliss* about the rest. And why would someone take our pictures, unless they were going to try to use them somehow?"

It took a minute for her meaning to strike him. "You were developing our pictures last night?"

"Yes."

"Your ex, in California. Could he have hired someone to harass you here?"

He saw the last question had taken her by surprise, and she seemed to consider it. She faced him, a quiet determination in her eyes that made her even more beautiful to him. He wanted to touch her, protect her, and God knew what else. He wanted all of it, but there wasn't time to think about that now. Probably a good thing.

"Let me finish this session, and I'll tell you, okay? But I have to get through this, and I have to talk with the project board. There's just too much right now, Jarod."

He understood more than she realized, thinking back to the letter in the trash. He wished she could trust him more, but they'd only known each other a couple days, and he would let her have as much room as she needed.

"Sure. But I'll stay here all the same. Is there somewhere I can catch a nap? It was a long night."

She nodded. "Yes, of course, there's a break room next door. I'm sorry, I didn't ask—but since you're back, I guess you didn't get the man you're after?"

"No, we didn't. But I'm glad, or I wouldn't be here with you."

She didn't have time to answer, as Jackie and the fireman returned. Jarod watched Lacey smile, putting her professional face back on.

"I'll come get you when we're done, after my meeting, okay?"

Jarod nodded and found his way next door, though he would have rather stayed with Lacey. But soon, he planned to have his answers, and he'd make sure she was safe, one way or the other.

LACEY FACED the four-person project board hoping she appeared more confident than she was. The session with Mr. April had gone great. Ryan was an easy, fun guy who liked being photographed, but she hadn't been able to get into the groove as well as she usually did.

It was hard to look through the lens of the camera without thinking about Jarod. He was in her thoughts constantly, interfering in everything, even her work. She thought about his face, and the possessive way he'd stood there when she was working with Ryan. She didn't like jealousy, and she didn't like anything screwing with her head, but she had more pressing problems at the moment.

How did you talk to your employer about the fact that there could be compromising pictures of you floating around New York City?

She could kick herself for taking them in the first place, she thought as they all settled in, but then, as the images from the photos played in her memory, she realized she didn't regret it at all. She did, however, regret being careless and having the negatives stolen.

While honesty had always been her best policy, she decided that maybe it was best if she worked with Jarod behind the scenes to try to find out who was behind all the trouble.

However, for all she knew, it could be someone connected to one of the people in front of her—Nina, for instance, head of PR, had seemed to dislike Lacey from the start. Lacey had the distinct feeling that her hiring was not a unanimous vote.

She explained about the harassment she'd been suffering, the break-in at her apartment, and then the fire in the darkroom. Lacey didn't regret her lie of omission as much when she saw they were more concerned about their timeline and bottom line than her safety.

"If you look at the schedule, you can see we're still on the mark. We've lost some pictures, and the camera—"

"A twelve-thousand-dollar camera, Lacey," Nina said, as if Lacey had stolen it and she was too tired not to bite back.

"Yes, an expensive camera that was stolen out of a *Bliss* darkroom that I had left locked. I'm sure you have insurance to cover it," she said, and thought she saw a glint of admiration in Theo Harris's eyes. He was the head of the project board; she liked the older man who had thus far sat quietly.

"You don't need to worry about that, Lacey. We're glad you weren't hurt, but we are concerned that someone seems to be harassing you, and it could hurt the project or the magazine."

"I'm sure it won't. I won't allow that to happen, Theo. This project means everything to me, and it's really coming together well, even with the bumpy start. The police are looking into it, and I'll be careful. Please, I can finish this without any more problems. I promise. I have it under control," she assured them, meeting their eyes and hoping they bought it.

She knew she'd made the right decision not to tell them about the photos. If they found out from whoever stole them, fine—there was nothing she could do about that, but she wasn't about to dig her own grave.

"Okay, Lacey, let's table this for now. We'll see what the police say, and you keep up with the project, but I'd like daily progress reports to the board."

Lacey took a breath. "Absolutely, Theo, no problem."

She sat for a moment as the board members vacated the conference room, and thought about her close call. If she was booted from this project, word would get around, and she'd find herself taking kids' pictures with Santa. Whoever was doing this, it had to stop.

She told Jarod she'd tell him the truth. And she'd do it, too, even if it damaged what was growing between them. Lacey dropped her head into her hands, and closed her eyes, feeling trapped. Still, she didn't realize that she'd started to doze off, she was so tired.

"Hey, taking a nap?"

Lacey almost jumped out of her skin as Jackie walked into the conference room.

"You scared the life out of me," Lacey said, wiping her eyes.

"Jeez, sorry. I was just kidding," she said, "I don't care if you sneak a nap."

"Not sleeping, not really, only thinking." She noted the bandage on Jackie's hand that she must have missed earlier. "What did you do to yourself?"

Jackie smirked. "Got crazy slicing an onion the other night—five stitches, but I'm functional."

"Ouch. Onion is one mean vegetable."

Jackie grinned.

"Can I trust you with something personal?"

Jackie nodded. "Sure. Shoot."

"I need a favor."

"I'm your girl."

"Don't agree too fast and feel free to tell me to stuff it, okay?"

"Always."

"I need a list of names of people who applied for my assignment, the portfolios the board reviewed."

Jackie's eyes went wide. She obviously hadn't anticipated that. She might have thought Lacey needed something more normal, like having Jackie grab her some lunch or pick up her laundry, not corporate theft.

"I need to see the list because someone has been…giving me a hard time, and it hit me that it could be someone who wanted this job, or maybe someone who is trying to discredit me, or sabotage the project. I thought the list might be a place to start."

She told Jackie about the break-in and the pictures, and watched the shock and surprise cross Jackie's face. Lacey wrung her hands a bit, embarrassed.

"I know I shouldn't have let him take pictures like that in the first place, and I certainly shouldn't have given in to temptation and developed them here, but—"

Jackie waved her off. "Puh-lease. That's some tame stuff. Is there a couple in America that hasn't brought out the old camcorder or digital camera at least once? C'mon…this is not your fault. But I can see where you're worried. Those things could pop up anywhere, anytime, huh?"

Lacey agreed, miserable. "Pretty much. And while I might deserve to get fired, Jarod doesn't. He's really an innocent bystander in all of this."

"Not so innocent, since it was his idea to take pictures. Lucky you, I might add," said Jackie, grinning, and Lacey felt the corners of her mouth twitch.

"True, which is why I don't want him getting

screwed over by my mistake. Why I developed those here...dumb move."

"Stop beating yourself up. Let me see what I can do."

"Thanks, Jackie. I know it's asking a lot."

"Hey, I'm your go-to girl," Jackie said, though her voice sounded strained. Lacey paused on her way out of the room. "You okay?"

"Oh, yeah, I'm fine. Just a late night at the emergency room getting those stitches."

"I hear you. Take the rest of the day off. We'll start early tomorrow."

"Sure, thanks."

Lacey made her way back to her office, where Jarod had closed the window shades and was dozing on the sofa, barely big enough for him. She looked down at him sleeping, and her heart seemed to recognize his. He was gorgeous, and good through to his bones.

Still, she had to deal with the problem at hand, rather than the nasty what-ifs that were haunting her. It was why she had to tell him everything. She wanted it all to just go away, but it was never really going to, was it?

He had the resources and the know-how to track down whoever might have done this, and while it might not be Scott, it could be someone connected to him.

"Hey, Lacey."

She jumped. He was awake and looking at her.

"I thought you were still sleeping. I didn't know if I should wake you."

"C'mere," he said, holding his arms out, but she stayed back.

"I don't think it's such a good idea here."

"I'm willing to risk it," he replied with a hint of a chuckle.

She lay down over him, and admitted he was right. She needed this, too, his warmth, his strength. Everything felt better the second his arms wrapped around her. As she nestled against him she also felt a little something extra poking against her hip and wiggled appreciatively.

"There's time for that later, you vixen," he said, sounding more awake. "As tempting as you are, I haven't had a shower since yesterday, and I'm starving."

"It's three in the afternoon."

"Feels like breakfast time to me. Any place we can manage that?"

"It's New York. You can get anything any time you want it," she said.

"Sounds like my kind of place."

After some snuggling and kissing she was grateful for the reprieve as they made their way out of the building and down the street to a diner that she liked.

"So how did it go?"

"Let's eat, and I'll tell you what you want to know. We have to figure out who would be doing this, and why," she said briskly, determined to stop moping and start acting.

They sat, and as she kept herself busy for a few minutes with her flapjacks and butter, syrup and bacon, fixing her plate as he fixed his, she finally ran out of things to do and had to face the music.

"Okay. It's not a huge deal, but I do like to keep it private, especially in my work. I need to maintain a certain image…" Her voice drifted off, and she cut a bite of pancake on her plate, but then laid her fork down.

Jarod reached a long arm across the table and gently touched her hand.

"I know we haven't known each other long, and this is hard for you, but you can tell me anything, I promise. This will never go further than me."

She looked out the window at the passersby. It was getting dark earlier by small degrees, but on a cloudy day, even more so.

"Thanks. The long and the short of it is that my ex-boyfriend, Scott Myers, is the guy in California. We met when I was doing some brochure work for his company, and sort of hit it off. He was a classic California guy, looked like he spent all his time on the beach, you know?"

Jarod nodded, but added, "Eat while you talk."

Reluctantly, she picked up her fork. She was hungry and took a bite. The soothing sweetness of the comfort food helped.

"Anyway, we dated, had some fun, but a few months into it he started getting possessive, and kind of mean. It was small stuff at first, but then he actually showed up at one of my shoots and threatened a male model he thought was flirting with me. I had no idea, but he'd hired a private detective to follow me, to take pictures. I had no idea."

Jarod didn't say a word, but she noticed how his grip tightened around his fork.

"So, I told him that was it, to get lost. He claimed he was just worried about me spending all that time with male models and such, and apologized, so I thought, you know, we get along so well. I wanted to give him one more chance. It's not like I'm Miss Perfect. And up to that point, he'd never done anything to hurt me."

"But then that changed?" Jarod prompted easily when she paused, lingering over another bite.

"Yeah. It was okay for a while, seemed like it was back to how we were at first. I thought he'd just been stressed from work or whatever. But then he came home drunk as a skunk one night, and he wanted to, uh…" She stuttered, blushing and uncomfortable talking about having sex with Scott with the man she was having sex with at the moment, and Jarod seemed to get it, waving her on.

"I hear ya, and I don't need details, either."

Thank goodness.

"So I put him off. I wasn't about to deal with him in that condition. I told him to take a shower and go to bed, and when he was sober, we'd talk. The next thing I knew, I was seeing stars. It really came out of nowhere. He accused me of having sex with my models, and that's why I didn't want him. And let me assure you, though you have been an exception, you're the only one—I do not sleep with my models."

"I'm glad you made an exception, then," Jarod said, smiling, but the smile didn't reach his eyes.

"I won't detail the whole episode, but I ended up with a broken arm, and a few other cuts and bruises. It might have been worse. However I managed to get hold of a meat hammer and caught him unawares in the face. It wasn't much, but it stunned him at least. Luckily, before he came at me again, I passed out. I think maybe he thought he'd killed me because he took off. He got into a few other fights that night, he was finally arrested and tested positive for alcohol and cocaine. On combined charges, he was supposed to be away for a while, but he was recently let out on parole to home detainment for 'good behavior,'" she said with a snarl. "Good behavior, my ass."

"So that's where the scar on your arm actually came from."

"I guess I just got so used to keeping it to myself that it feels strange to talk about it. I also wanted to forget it, just let it be part of the past. No matter how I try, though, it keeps coming back up."

Jarod's expression was serious. "Did you talk to a counselor at the hospital?"

Lacey stared at her food and disentangled her fingers from his.

"I spoke to one. I went back, but it just wasn't…for me. I wanted to handle it on my own."

"I get where you're coming from."

She hadn't expected that response, and her surprise showed.

"You do?"

"Sure. I've been forced into my share of shrink appointments—it's SOP after certain things, like the first time I had to shoot someone and they died in front of me. The first time I lost a friend, a fellow Ranger—that one was harder. Sometimes it helps, sometimes it doesn't. What I do know is you have to be open to it for it to do any good, and no one can force you into it. If you're not ready, you're not ready."

Relief thrummed through her. "So you just dealt with it on your own?"

"For a while. I was able to handle the fact that I'd had to use my gun. I grew up in a house with a Ranger, and I knew that carrying that weapon meant probably having to use it. But, when my friend Matt was killed, that was tough. I thought I could shake it, but I couldn't."

"How did he die?"

"We were having a beer after a bad day—you know, winding down? We'd just caught a guy who'd been causing some pretty serious trouble around town for a while."

Jarod picked up a piece of bacon then put it down again. Her heart hurt at his carefully controlled expression, the way he didn't let much show, when there was so much going on inside.

"Turns out his younger brother was his partner in crime, not that the kid had much choice. He was barely out of his teens. We didn't even know about him. As we left the bar, the kid walked up to us and shot Matt. There was no talk, no warning, nothing. Just a gunshot, point-blank in the chest. Matt was dead before he hit the ground."

"Oh, my God," Lacey breathed, horrified. "And then?"

"The kid was dead a second later."

Lacey stared, unable to get her mind around what he was saying. How was it possible he dealt with ordeals like that on a regular basis?

"I—I don't know what to say, Jarod. It's unthinkable." She stood, crossed to him and slid into the booth on his side and wrapped her arms around his shoulders. "How do you deal with that? How can anyone deal with that?"

"That's kind of the point," he said calmly, taking her hands and kissing them. "I couldn't. I had gone through the motions with the shrink before, and made out okay. I thought I could handle this, too, and I crashed, big-time. Got in a tight spot a few weeks later and almost shot an innocent person, and that's when I knew something was fried in my brain from what had happened with Matt. So I went for counseling. It took a while, but I made peace with it."

"How?"

"Talking it through, reliving it, saying what I had to say—realizing there wasn't anything I could have done to stop it."

Lacey felt tears prick her eyelids. She couldn't say anything. She felt like a coward, whining about her onetime altercation with Scott when others went through so much worse. She said as much, and Jarod dislodged her hold, pulled away.

"Lacey, that's not why I told you that story, because it's not something I share often, either, and it wasn't meant to make what happened to you smaller."

"But it seems so—"

"No. What I'm trying to say is that if you can't quite get away from this, it's because you haven't let it go.

You won't be able to let it go until you figure out a way to work through it."

She went back to her seat. "You do think I should see a counselor."

"I didn't say that. I don't know what's right for you. You need to figure it out. You were attacked, but you also fought back. You hit him and you kept yourself from likely being killed. That's huge. You're a fighter. Don't let him win now by letting it eat you up inside. By being afraid all the time."

Lacey listened, took in what he was saying, though she didn't know what to do. She didn't know if counseling was the answer. But what he said about letting it go made sense. Still…how?

"You've helped," she said in a whisper, her gaze meeting his. "I knew, somehow, when I saw you with that little girl—maybe before that—that you were the complete opposite of him. That I could…be with you."

"I'm glad about that," he said, smiling, and this time the smile did fill his eyes.

She took a deep breath. "I suppose it felt good to finally tell someone, too—you—and to hear your story. Everyone has their stories, I guess."

"Yes. But that doesn't make yours any less important."

"Maybe." She picked up a bite of pancake and though it was now just lukewarm, it tasted much better than before, when she hadn't been able to taste anything. She caught the spark of heat in Jarod's gaze as he followed her progress, watching her slip the morsel between her lips. She warmed inside, but with more than desire.

He still wanted her. He didn't see her as weak, or less sexy, or as a victim. Nothing she told him had turned him off. In fact, she was pretty sure from the light in his eyes that he was very much the opposite of turned off. She looked at the syrup on the table, and said, "You know, I wonder if they do takeout?"

He groaned and shook his head, smiling.

Later. Definitely later. She planned to lick him clean.

"I know it's not Scott," she said, switching gears and returning to their original problem. "I called Legal Aid today and spoke to their assistant, Gena, who said he's still in California under house arrest."

"That makes it harder to figure out who it could be, but we'll find him."

"I asked Jackie to get me the list of people who were in line for this project. Maybe I'll recognize a name, or we might find someone who wanted to sabotage the project, or something."

"That's smart."

She smiled, the praise igniting a warm glow inside. "Thanks for listening, Jarod, and thanks for not seeing me as a victim."

"Are you kidding me? With your spirit? No way. You're one of the strongest women I've ever met, and one of the most gorgeous."

"You're not so bad yourself."

"Oh, honey, I have yet to show you just how bad I can be," he said smoothly, a wicked promise in his eyes.

She hoped he planned to, and bought the extra bottle of syrup, just in case.

9

THE NEXT DAY, atop the Empire State Building, the second shoot wasn't going as well as the Central Park work. The problems of the past few days were taking their toll. Jarod wanted to help, but he wasn't sure how. Lacey had done okay with Ryan, who went before him so that he could still make his shift at the firehouse on time, but now she seemed to be having a hard time. Jarod wondered if it was him, or the cumulative stress.

He tried distracting himself by watching the amazing vista of the city laid out below him, but his mind would only travel back to Lacey.

She'd already broken one lens. Her clumsy fingers were probably caused by lack of sleep and nerves, and she was cursing as she couldn't get the shots she wanted just the way she wanted them. Which meant he was bent and folded into yet more ridiculous poses and fluffed and primped even more. It grated on his own bad mood, but he put up with it because it was Lacey, and she didn't need him complaining.

"Shit, shit, shit!" she shouted in frustration, and put the camera down, he figured, so that she didn't end up throwing it.

He pushed past the stylist and crossed the platform, took her by the arm and led her into the lobby through the doors where they could be alone for a few minutes. He saw her cast a concerned glance back at the crew, who watched them curiously as they disappeared from view, but he didn't give a rat's ass what anyone else thought at the moment.

"Hey, come here," he said, pulling her in and rubbing his hands over the stress-hardened muscles of her back until he felt her relax and soften against him. "Not such a good day, huh?"

"Work usually distracts me from anything bothering me, but today, I just can't seem to clinch it. Everything is swirling in my head and I can't focus," she said, banging her forehead softly against his chest. "I felt like I rushed Ryan through, and I can't get these shots right, either, and I have to get a progress report in by four," she said in exasperation.

The scent of her shampoo wafted up, and he found himself thinking about more erotic things than comforting her. He'd love to get back in the shower with her, work soap through those short, silky locks and move his hands down the length of her body, touching every inch of water-slick skin. He'd make sure she was relaxed.

"Let's see if I can't settle down some of the things spinning around in there," he said seductively, leaning down to capture her mouth in a soft kiss. She stiffened in surprise at first, probably worried about someone seeing them, but only for a second before a wildfire erupted between them. All of the emotions they both had bottled up channeled through the kiss until his hands were inside her shirt, thumbs caressing her nipples into tight peaks. In return she was slowly rocking her pelvis into his erection.

Another minute of this and he was going to haul her up and have her on the spot; instead, he lowered his hands and exerted some self-control. Truth be told, he'd needed to touch her pretty badly, and the short tryst had helped his own mood considerably. Just being near her seemed to help, soothing his worries and frustrations. He couldn't remember any other woman having that effect on him before. He wasn't sure he was the same guy who'd landed in the city just a few days ago, when his job had been the center of his universe.

"Still thinking too much?" he asked against the delicate shell of her ear, planting a kiss there and enjoying her gasp of a response. Encouraged, he slipped his fingers under the top of her pants and caressed the soft, secret spots just below the small of her back.

"Only about getting you out of your pants," she said baldly, her breath quickening at his touch, and he laughed.

"Hold on to that thought. Any chance we can hang back here for a bit when they leave?"

She looked at him in surprise, and he loved how her eyes sparked with pleasure and adventure as she realized what he was asking. Whatever had happened to her in the past with the bastard who had broken her arm, she hadn't lost who she was. Jarod was just glad that he got to be the man who helped her learn that, as well.

"I think we might be able to arrange that. Not for

long, their security is pretty strict, but I bet I could wrangle enough time for...a quickie."

"Sounds fun. Something to look forward to. Let's get back out there and finish this, then, huh?"

She smiled at him, nodding, and his heart did an untrustworthy flip that he purposely ignored.

Feeling considerably better, they both went back out to the deck, noticing the crew's determination not to make eye contact. Jarod took his position against the rails again, and watched as she lost the stiffness that had held her before. Her moves were more fluid now as she captured him through the camera.

When she aimed the camera at him, it was like a touch. The memory of her taste came back to him, her scent. He thought about her face when he was inside of her, how her irises darkened. Sometimes her lashes fell down as she came, her mouth forming a soundless O, and other times she looked straight through him, letting him see and hear every nuance of the pleasure he gave her. Thinking about Lacey's expressions during orgasm, he could barely hold back his body's response.

He followed her instructions, happy to do whatever pleased her. After a while he started to focus on the way her skin took on a fine sheen of perspiration from the physicality of her work with the camera. She squatted down and leaned in, the scoop of her low-cut tee revealing tender flesh. His fingers flexed, wanting to rediscover the velvety texture of her nipples. How much longer did they have to do this? How many pictures could she possibly need?

When he heard the slight hum of the zoom, he concentrated, hoping she could read everything he wanted to do to her in his eyes. And that he didn't think he could wait much longer. Thankfully the pants he was wearing were baggy, because he had a boner that would challenge the tower rising above them. He smiled in satisfaction when he saw her pink lips part below the camera's edge. She was as turned on as he was.

They were both on edge by the time she called it quits—two wardrobe changes and about a million pictures later. No one would be able to tell except for him. She went through all the professional motions, wrapping it up, excusing the crew, telling security they were staying to do some extra shots.

Jarod didn't waste time when he saw the security team accompany the crew to the elevator, leaving them alone until a guard came back to escort them out.

"We have about ten minutes, give or take, by the time he gets back up here," she said, taking Jarod by the hand and pulling him over to one side of the observation deck overlooking the Chrysler Building.

"No problem. I want you so much I've been ready to come for the past twenty minutes."

He had her low-rise capris unbuttoned and unzipped before she could answer, his fingers dipping under the delicate material of her thong and in between soft folds of flesh. She was already wet, hot and ready for him. He'd never been so thankful in his life.

"Jarod," she panted, and he thought maybe she was going to protest, but she just broke their kiss to say, "Get these off." She pulled at his jeans, releasing his cock with nimble hands.

"Good thinking," he said, turning her so that they were both propped against the ledge, looking down over the city. He slid inside from behind in a hot thrust that had him closing his eyes to the amazing view.

She gasped, moving back against him, and he lifted her tee, closing his hands over her breasts. He could barely wait to explode inside of her.

"That photo session was so hot…the way you were looking at me," she said, her tone husky and trembling with desire, "I couldn't wait for them to leave so I could fuck you."

He loved how she talked dirty, and he found his desire pushed up a few more notches, if that were possible.

"Good. Tell me more, what you want, just like that," he said, wanting to hear her demands, her needs, and wanting to meet every single one of them.

She would always surprise him, and he welcomed it.

"You want to hear how I love feeling you get harder when you're inside me? How it was all I thought about while I was taking those pictures?"

"Yes," he said roughly, increasing his pace. "I wondered if you were getting wet as you were looking at me through the lens, and I remembered how you taste, how hot, sweet…"

She groaned and moved her hips in rhythm with his thrusts. It was heaven.

Until he realized they didn't have protection and his mind screamed in protest. How could he have forgotten?

"*Lacey,*" he panted, fighting for control at the way she was writhing against him. "I'm not wearing anything," he said, although the heated silky flesh of her sex felt tight around his shaft and he didn't want to leave. But he would if he had to, even if it killed him.

She paused slightly, and surprised him again. "It's okay, we're good, I'm on the pill, I just wanted to be extra careful before…just don't stop, please," she begged in the sweetest way possible, pushing her hips up and rotating her ass in a way that made him tremble.

LACEY WAS MORE THAN HAPPY to forget everything in the world except the wonderful, wet, gliding sensation of Jarod's cock as she looked out over the dizzying view.

Power rippled through her, emotional freedom mixing with physical pleasure. He'd set loose her true nature. This was *her*. She was wild, willing to do anything he wanted, anywhere, and she reveled in the feeling. Staring at the sky and the expanse of the world below, she knew she'd never felt more free in her life.

His eyes had telegraphed one sexual promise after another as she'd snapped the pictures, and nearly had her coming before they'd even finished the session. She was halfway there before he even touched her, and it pleased her that she could tell him what she wanted, how she wanted it, and her lack of inhibition only seemed to drive him further.

They didn't have time for inhibition—the guard could be back any moment, catching them, and the idea just made her hotter, made her want it more. When she imagined what someone would see, how they looked going at it here in the open, a low moan worked its way up from her chest, the arousal almost too much.

He held her tight around the waist, and she savored every second of it as the sizzling sensation set off a myriad of others. Her inner muscles then gripped him in spasms of pleasure against his thrusts until he was so deep she was sure he was touching her soul. She'd never cared for being done from the back, the facelessness of it bothered her, but with Jarod, she was fully aware of whom she was with, and only wanted more.

His body took its cue from hers, the heat of his own orgasm throbbing and flooding inside of her. He bucked hard, his hands grasping the soft skin of her bottom as he pushed harder, deeper, which sent another spike of release rocketing through her.

Finally, they stilled, but the pleasure was so complete and so lingering she didn't want to let go. The residual sensations traveled everywhere in her body, even to the ends of her fingers and toes. She didn't want to return to the real world, to thinking.

She wanted to stay up here with him and keep feeling this way... or stay anywhere with him and keep feeling this way? *Maybe,* she thought fuzzily.

"Mmm..." She turned and nuzzled his mouth with her lips, sharing lazy, satisfied kisses. If she waited a little, she knew the embers settling between them would spark again.

Until they heard the buzz—the elevator was back.

"Oh, no," they said in unison, laughing and pushing

apart, shuffling to a far spot where they quickly got their clothes in order.

Lacey grabbed her camera in a desperate attempt to look as if they were finishing up a few pictures, but instead, she collapsed, chuckling at the fun of it. Her heart hammered at almost being caught, literally, with her pants down. She could only grin at Jarod as the guard appeared, looking bored and stoic.

She took a few shots, and for fun, grabbed a couple of the surprised guard, as well, before they headed back down to the ground and back to reality.

10

"I SHOULD HAVE GONE back to the labs. You know, to make up for the time I lost," Lacey said, staring at the ceiling and catching her breath after another bout of amazing sex with Jarod. She rolled over, covering him with her body, loving how big and warm he was. She threaded her fingers through his chest hair, leaning in to nibble a flat, brown male nipple until he moaned for mercy.

"There's always time for work."

"Maybe. I feel like I need to do double time these days, to make up for all the problems."

"Has anyone said anything else?"

"No. I just e-mail in a progress report, and everything seems okay. There hasn't been anything said about the pictures. Maybe you're right, and whoever took them had no idea, or didn't think they were worthwhile, or whatever. I have no idea."

The reminder was a splash of cold water. She really should have gone back to work, but the lovemaking up on the Empire State Building had been so exhilarating they'd been unable to take their hands off each other after, and had barely made it back to her apartment for more.

Lacey had had several lovers in her life—nice guys, great guys and some obviously lackluster ones, too—but she'd never been as voraciously hungry for anyone as she was for Jarod. Just looking at him lounging in her bed was enough to make her throw all of her priorities out the window and…what?

They hadn't talked about anything. They didn't have any kind of relationship or plans or promises. All they had was this, what they were doing right now.

"Hey…you're clouding up. What's wrong?"

"Oh, I'm sorry. I guess it's just back to reality with a thud. I really should have worked—tomorrow is Saturday, and maybe I can make up some time this weekend, because Monday will be the last shoot we'll be doing…"

She let the thought drift, and felt a slight pang when he didn't fill the void. So that was that, apparently. Come Monday, this little fling would be done.

What had she expected?

"Listen, Lacey, there's something you need to know, and I guess I should have told you before now, but…well, I guess I was pretty happy being distracted from reality, too."

Lacey took a deep breath. *Here it comes,* she thought. His gentle letdown, the reminder that they never had more than sex, the long goodbye.

"There's an APB out on Scott. Apparently he found a way to hack the ankle alarm so that it didn't go off, or he paid someone who knew how to do it. It's been reading as if he's there in the house. No one checked until he didn't show up for work. He could have gone anytime the night before, so he has a good lead."

Lacey was stunned. That wasn't what she'd expected at all.

"When did you find out?" she asked in a whisper. "How can that be? I called…"

"You called your Legal Aid office, and you spoke to the assistant Gena, right?" he asked gently, reaching for her hand and squeezing.

"Yes."

"She's missing now, too. They think she's been working with him, using her position to help him out. She was probably covering for him when you called."

"Gena? She's involved with Scott?" It was too bizarre.

"Apparently they got together during your case, and kept it under wraps, but they found letters from her in his house, indicating an affair."

Lacey processed what he was telling her, and as the picture clarified, so did her anger. "She knew where I was, and she told him. He was probably using her to find me, knowing him. He's not stupid."

"Possibly, which means she'd be in danger now, too."

She shook her head. The whole thing was surreal. Gena had always been such a doll to her, so sincere and convincing. But then, Scott could put on a good act, too. *Poor Gena,* Lacey thought, feeling sorry for the woman, and fearful for what could have happened to her.

"Why didn't you tell me right away?" she asked, unable to keep the accusation from her voice.

"At first, I didn't want to disturb your work. You

were having such a hard time. And I figured, as long as you were with me, you're safe. I wouldn't let him get within ten feet of you, you know that," Jarod said seriously, sitting up and edging close.

"So he's here," she said flatly. "Fine. Let him find me. Then it will be settled."

"Yes, it will be because I'm not leaving your side until it is."

"Jarod, we'll be done with work on Monday, and you have to go back, and—"

"I have vacation time coming, and I'm not going back until I know you're safe—already told you that. Unless…you'd like me to leave?"

She wouldn't have believed it if she hadn't seen it herself, the speck of uncertainty that flickered in his gorgeous eyes as he asked the question. And leaned down to kiss her fingers where their hands were folded together. She shook her head.

"No, I don't want you to go. That's kind of a problem, too, don't you think?"

"I don't know. It's certainly not something I counted on, getting in this deep this fast, but I can't say I regret it," he said, sliding a hand under her chin and leaning in for a kiss.

"Me, either," she admitted, noting how the heated desire that was automatic between them was picking up a warmth that it lacked before. A deeper sense of connection as they admitted, just a little, that what they had might be more than a fling.

"Good. We'll do this together. You're not alone," he promised, drawing her against him so tenderly that her eyes pricked with tears, but she blinked them back. This was good. Jarod was good, and things were going to be okay. She had to believe that.

She ran a hand along the inside of his thigh, marveling at his strength, inside and out.

"If he's watching, then the best thing to do, the fastest way to end this, is to take control of the game. It's the weekend. Let's go out. We'll be tourists, we'll be visible, we'll make it clear we're lovers, which won't be an effort at all," Jarod murmured against her skin.

"You want to flush him out?" she asked, shivering, but not from fear. The idea of taking control, of ending this on her terms—their terms—was appealing.

He kissed her shoulder, tasting her lightly with his tongue all the way down to her elbow.

Her professional life was at risk, and her crazy ex was on the loose, and yes, all she could do was admire how gorgeous Jarod's body was. The mutual agreement that they had something special between them, regardless of where it was leading, was a definite turn-on. She shifted a little, letting her hand move higher on his thigh, her palm closing over his cock, stroking him to hardness.

Nestled in his lap, his hand wound in her hair, the sheets tangled warmly around them, she sighed against his skin, knowing a moment of perfect connection and happiness unlike any she had known before. Right now, here with him, she didn't want to think about anything but Jarod. The rest would come soon enough.

He smelled great, musky and male. Their scents mingled, seducing her, and she shifted a little more until she could rub her lips over the head of his erection in a way she knew he liked. She smiled at the murmur of approval, the shudder that worked its way down his long body.

Using her hands and her mouth, she wanted to bring him more pleasure than he could imagine. She set about the task with steady purpose, inventive in her kisses as she kept him in her throat, curling her soft tongue along his length like a lazy cat. She continued teasing the tender skin of his sex until he was gasping mindless exclamations, his body hard and rigid, held taut under her own.

Her fingers gently stroked his legs, stomach and sac, keeping him on edge. When she sensed he was about to come, she pressed firmly on the area below his scrotum while sucking him to orgasm once, and holding back his ejaculation successfully.

He pushed up on his elbows, panting, as she slid her mouth down over him again and erotically met his gaze.

"How…?"

She released him from her sexy kiss and smiled. "Little tantric secret I learned…it makes it so you can come more than once, and it's more intense. Was it?"

"My head nearly came off my shoulders," he confessed, shaking his head in amazement.

"How about we try it again?"

"Sure. You can join me this time," he said with a sexy growl. Suddenly, he rolled her over into the mattress, his knee pushing her thighs apart as he pulled her calves over his shoulders and his cock found the slick entrance to her body.

"You're close, too," he said, sliding a finger down between her legs and she couldn't help but cry out.

"Sucking you makes me hot," she admitted plainly, and was rewarded as he took her mouth in a deep kiss, fucking her mouth with his tongue as he thrust into her body, both of them starving in spite of all the previous loving.

He moved her legs down off his shoulders, staying inside her, but he gentled and slowed his strokes, making her wait, making them both wait as he framed her face with his hands.

"I can't seem to get enough of you…"

"I feel the same way," she said, even though her heart was crying out words that were too soon to say—right?

All words quickly became unimportant as they held on for as long as they could. They moved more quickly, then slowed—a few times stopping altogether to see how long they could take it. He also showed her a few of his own tricks to prolong their anticipation and their pleasure. Finally, need took over and drove them both to release; hands clasped, they were connecting even more deeply than perhaps they knew, or were ready for.

Jarod collapsed over her, and then moved to cuddle her into his side.

Lacey was limp from satisfaction, and maybe a little sore, but that even felt okay. Dozing, it took her a minute to realize the sound she heard in the background was the ringing of her phone.

Pushing herself up, she grabbed her cell from the table with a sense of trepidation, but saw Jackie's name show on the screen and felt relief instead. "It's just Jackie."

At the same time, Jarod's phone rang, and they smirked, their peaceful moment well and truly intruded upon.

"It's Tom, my captain—it's still afternoon there, work hours—I have to take this."

"No problem, I need to call Jackie back, too. She was getting the list of other applicants for us, but I don't know if we'll need it."

"Get it anyway. Can't hurt to cover all the bases."

"Sure," she said with a sigh, hoping that no matter what, this would all be over soon.

"Jackie? Hi, yeah, Lacey. If you're calling about the list—what? Oh, no…"

Jackie was calling from the hospital. Someone had attacked her, and Lacey had a terrible feeling that Scott had found yet another victim.

JAROD PINCHED the bridge of his nose between his thumb and forefinger, staving off a headache. He had to get off the phone and go with Lacey to the hospital, but he'd gotten a dose of his own bad news. Although it wasn't as bad as it could have been.

"Tom, any chance we can dust that envelope for prints?" Jarod asked.

"Already sent it—left the pictures in my desk drawer, of course."

"Dammit all to hell. I understand if you have to report—"

He didn't get any further.

"Jarod, there's no way I'd tell anyone about this, and with any luck, we can clean it up quietly. You think this is the same guy who's stalking the, uh, woman in the photos? And I'm sorry that I looked at them, it just took me a few minutes to process what it was I was looking at, until the note dropped out. Seems like someone is taking a serious shot at your reputation, and there's no way I'm letting that happen to any of my officers, least of all you."

"Well, we think we know who's behind it. A man named Scott Myers. He was Lacey's boyfriend, broke her arm, hurt her some before he got sent away."

"Son of a bitch."

"Yeah. She's the photographer on the shoot, so this could cost her her job, as well. I want this guy as soon as possible so we're going to try to flush him out."

"You watch your step, Jarod, and maybe bring the local guys in on this, especially if you're involved with this woman."

Jarod took a deep breath, knowing Tom was right. "I'll contact a guy."

"Is this thing serious?"

"Hell, yeah, this guy is—"

"Not the case, the girl," Tom said, laughing.

Jarod paused, feeling foolish. He looked up when he heard the shower turn on. "Yes, I think it's getting there."

"Then taking this promotion might be good for you—keep you alive longer, home more—unless you're thinking of moving to New York?"

"No, no, nothing like that."

"So you want the job? I have to know if you're going for it."

"What about the pictures?"

"What about them? Some asshole is trying to ruin your reputation, and I'm not letting that get in the way of my best man moving up. You didn't do anything illegal there, well, maybe in Texas, but as you're in New York…" Tom teased, and Jarod found himself grinning. Some of the stuff he'd done with Lacey, and what he wanted to do, was probably illegal in several states.

"Thanks, Tom. But, yeah, put my name in and I'll go through the paperwork when I get back this week."

"Good news, Jarod. I was worried there for a bit."

"I have to go, Tom. Later," Jarod said, hanging up.

He couldn't think about this now. Lacey had mentioned something about her assistant, Jackie, being hurt, and he needed to get cleaned up to go with Lacey to the hospital. He knew she feared it was her ex, but why go after the assistant?

Pulling the shower door aside, he let his eyes wander over her supple, soapy form. He joined her under the spray and couldn't imagine not seeing Lacey like this, in his shower, in his bed, in his life, every day.

But that was a long leap from where they were now, and he wasn't sure how they'd get it to work. First things first, he thought, planting a light kiss on her lips, and hoping that soon all they had to worry about was how they'd manage to be together.

LACEY'S HANDS SHOOK as she walked down the hospital hallway, searching for Jackie's room, so she stuffed them in the pockets of her pants. She didn't want Jarod to see how freaked out she was.

When they'd been making love and talking about how they could pull Scott out of hiding, she'd felt all fired up by adrenaline and desire. However, as she turned the corner and saw her friend's bruised face, she had to maintain her composure—for Jackie's sake—but was reminded of how dangerous Scott was. This was no game.

Lacey walked to Jackie's bedside, taking her hand gently.

"Oh, Jackie, I am so sorry. Who did this?"

Jackie shook her head. "I don't know. Some guy. He jumped me on the way out of the office, by the alley on Third. I thought he was a mugger, but he grabbed me and asked me where you were."

"Where I was? But how could he expect you to know?"

"I didn't know...I h-had no idea," Jackie said, tears filling her eyes.

"Shh. You don't have to talk about it."

"No, it's okay. Thank God someone saw him, called for help, and when I looked later, I saw that the list was gone. He took everything in my bag, including the list."

"The list?"

"With the names of the other people who had applied for the calendar project. He took that, though who knows why..."

Jarod spoke softly. "He probably figured you had contact information in there somewhere. I'll talk to the NYPD, explain, and see if they can get someone on your door in case he comes back."

Jackie's eyes opened wide in fear. Lacey shot Jarod

a look, but she knew he was right. Abusive men were often so determined to find their exes that they didn't even care what happened to themselves, or to others, as long as they achieved some kind of vengeance for being denied.

Which meant she was going to do just as Jarod said, and make it easy for the bastard—he'd gone too far this time, and she wasn't going to let anyone else she cared about be hurt.

She squeezed Jackie's hand as Jarod went outside to make his call.

"Don't worry. This will be over soon."

Jackie tried to smile with a cut lip. "I know. You two… He's pretty amazing, huh?"

Lacey felt her cheeks warm, and couldn't resist a smile. "Yeah, he really is."

"I'm glad. You deserve it after what you've been through."

Lacey stilled. "What do you mean?"

Jackie paused at her tone, shrugging. "Just that with all the harassment, your apartment, the horrible thing on your wall, the pictures being stolen… It's good that there's something positive coming out of this for you."

Lacey relaxed.

"Thanks. I'm just so sorry this happened to you."

"Hey, a few days of rest and watching TV. It'll be fine, until the painkillers wear off. This is some great stuff," Jackie joked bravely, and Lacey forced herself to laugh, though she felt like doing quite the opposite.

"Where's Kenny?"

"He was here earlier, but he had to work."

Jarod appeared in the doorway, and Jackie's eyes fluttered shut. Lacey squeezed Jackie's hand again. "I'm going to go now, but you don't worry—and get some rest. I'll be back. Call me if you need anything, or just to talk."

"Thanks," Jackie murmured sleepily, dozing off before Lacey reached the door.

She looked Jarod in the eye. "This has to end."

"It will. They're going to notify hospital security and get the floor guard to make more stops. It's the best they can do. They can't post a cop up here if they aren't even sure it was Scott."

"I'm sure," Lacey said resolutely.

"Jackie didn't have a good description. It could have been anyone."

"Of course it wasn't just anyone—who would attack my assistant and take her work bag? He didn't even take her money!"

"The police can't spare the resources unless they have more compelling evidence, is all. It's the way of things," Jarod explained, steering her down the hall.

"So what do we do now?"

"We get some food, get some sleep, and tomorrow, we play tourist until we flush out the creep. With the APB it won't be easy for him to walk around. He's a wanted man."

Lacey nodded. Walking out into the humid night, she tried to feel better, but as they headed down the dark street, she wondered if they were being watched.

In case they were, she stopped and pushed up on tiptoes, wrapping her arms around Jarod's neck. She then delivered a kiss that was worthy of stopping in the middle of a busy New York thoroughfare.

"Wow. What was that for?" Jarod asked as she drew away.

"Just because," she answered lightly, planting another quick kiss before falling back into step at his side, hoping Scott was watching and that he got the point.

11

"RELAX, LACEY. You're strung as tight as a bow wire," Jarod said, slinging an arm around her shoulders to pull her close and plant a kiss atop her head.

"I know. It's just so weird to be walking out here, pretending to have a good time, enjoying a Saturday stroll in the park. As bait."

"You're not bait. Not really. You're really the hunter, remember. We're in control because he doesn't know we're setting a trap. Besides, I'm here, and everything will be fine, okay?"

He reassured her while his eyes covertly scanned the scene around them. He wanted to make sure of two things: that Scott Myers had ample opportunity to see them, and that they passed by enough less-populated parts of the park that if the guy decided to make his move, he'd do it, thinking Jarod was completely distracted and unaware.

Surprise.

His forty-five was snug against his hip on the opposite side of where Lacey snuggled in, and Jarod wouldn't hesitate to use it, if that's what it came to. Her safety was first. Jarod would make sure that Scott never bothered her again, one way or the other.

"Do you like museums?" she asked.

"Some."

"There's the Met ahead of us, which is awesome, and the natural history museum is farther up. There's also the zoo, and the Conservatory Garden…"

"This park is so vast. I never really had a chance to appreciate it until now," he observed, getting into the spirit. Children played, running down slopes of shallow rises. In another spot, a small dog chased a ball, running happily back to its owner. Lovers found a more private spot, setting up camp for the day under a large tree, the city towering in the backdrop. People carried coffees and books, looking for a place to lounge, and runners and bikers came into view as if appearing from thin air.

Saturday morning in the park was an event all its own.

"I wasn't here to sightsee the last time I was here, of course."

"That must have been horrible. I saw it on the news. I was in California then, but I have a new understanding of it, being here, even now."

"Yeah, it was…overwhelming."

She looked up at him, her beautiful eyes hidden behind enormous, purple-shaded sunglasses.

"I can't imagine you being overwhelmed by anything."

He pondered telling her just how much she pulled the rug right out from under him every time she looked his way, but shrugged instead.

"I don't think anyone walked away from that situation the same person they were when they walked into it." He found he really didn't want to talk about it, not here in the sunshine and on such a beautiful day. "But no more of that. I vote for the zoo. I haven't been to a zoo since I was a kid."

"Really? I usually make it a point to visit them whatever city I'm in."

"I always felt sorry for the animals, cooped up instead of out, roaming freely."

"Where poachers and lack of habitat threaten them daily?"

"True. The world's not the same for anyone anymore, is it? Not even the lions, tigers and bears."

"No, but the world's also filled with people who protect all of us—like you, for instance."

He didn't have anything to say in response to the blatant admiration in her voice, and it touched something deep inside of him when she held on to his arm more tightly and pressed her cheek against him.

"I guess it's a little bent to say I'm enjoying myself, even considering the circumstances," she said with a rueful laugh as they made their way to the zoo. "Pretty sad when even luring out a felon is a way for us to spend time together," she joked, but didn't really think it was funny.

"No way, I'm enjoying this, too. In fact," he said playfully, pulling her over against a huge boulder to their left, "let me show you how much."

He removed her sunglasses and shoved them in his pocket, pushing hair back from her face. He looked at her closely, noticing faded freckles across her cheeks, adding interest to porcelain skin. She had some bright flecks in the green of her eyes, and as he studied her, he smiled as pink tinted her cheeks.

He took his time, able to see their surroundings, so he could take a moment to commit every feature to his memory.

Mindful of a nearby family, he leaned in, bracing his hands on the rock behind Lacey, pressing soft kisses all over her face until she was laughing, but also breathing a little more quickly. He found her mouth and slid his tongue lightly over her upper and bottom lip, no other parts of their bodies touching at all, though they were begging to.

"It would take forever for me to kiss you in all the ways I think about doing," he said, balancing his forehead against hers. "You know this isn't the end of this, right?"

She cupped her small hand around his face in a gesture so sweet that he was embarrassed to admit he turned to mush.

"I'd like that, but you know, maybe it's just the circumstances, the urgency of it all. I don't expect any promises, Jarod," she said, but he held his hand up to stop her.

"I've had my share of one-night stands, and in fact it's all I've known, more or less. I figured that's what we were doing, too, but I know better now. I want more. I don't know how, but we'll work it out, won't we?"

Her face became radiant in the sunlight, and while he knew marriage to a cop was a stupid bet—thinking about his parents' relationship disintegrating—there was no way he could live without Lacey. He'd go for the captain's position, and get it. It would give him a more normal schedule, and he could find more weekends, vacation time, to make it to New York, if that's what it took.

"I'm just so glad none of this touched you."

"You've touched me," he said, feeling silly, but it was true. There was no way he was telling her about the pictures reaching Tom—with any luck, that wouldn't amount to anything. Except some embarrassment that his friend and his boss had seen some pretty intimate moments in his life.

The thought reminded him of why they were there, and he pushed back from the rock, handing her glasses to her.

"To the zoo?"

She smiled, full on, and Jarod realized he was going to have to get used to a whole new set of emotions being around this woman.

"Lead the way," he said, grabbing her hand as he did a quick check of their surroundings. Nothing.

Could they be completely off base? He reminded himself to be patient. It was still early. Maybe their stalker was off to a slow start.

LACEY COULDN'T BELIEVE what a fantastic time she was having. She felt on top of the world as they made their way slowly through the zoo, watching the animals, sneaking into secret places to steal kisses and sometimes a little bit more.

This was real, she thought. It had come out of nowhere when she'd least expected it, but what she felt for Jarod was growing in leaps and bounds every second, and it was real.

So what did that mean? Did she give up everything she'd worked for and move to a small town in Texas to be a wife and mother?

No. That wasn't her style.

Did he come to New York? He hadn't mentioned anything specific, just that he didn't want what they had to end. But she had a feeling Texas was a part of him, just like his job.

So, a long-term, long-distance relationship?

She had friends who made it work, in fact, who flourished in those situations, but she'd never considered it for herself. She wanted the whole enchilada, her career, and the man in her life to be around to cuddle up with at night, to discuss the events of the day, and not on the phone.

But she also wanted Jarod and she supposed she'd do what she must to have him.

In spite of the complications, she felt ridiculously light. It was midafternoon, and they strolled slowly from the zoo, taking the long way, stopping to sit in the stretch of shadows created by trees as the sun passed overhead. Casually touching, they were always making some contact.

It was good.

She had almost completely forgotten about why they'd come there in the first place, and it seemed that maybe they'd made a mistake. Scott wasn't stupid, and perhaps he wasn't going to be lured out while she was with Jarod—he'd wait until she was alone. She shared as much with Jarod as they walked.

"If you're saying I should leave you alone to deal with him, forget it," Jarod said resolutely, his expression hardening.

It tweaked her a little. She appreciated his protection, and she certainly didn't want to take on Scott by herself, but she was still an independent person, making her own decisions.

"I'm just saying, you have to go back to Texas this week, and he's probably waiting for that."

"He doesn't have the time—he's an escaped felon, and all of those circumstances are going to push him to act fast, and make a mistake. Trust me, I've been here a million times."

"I know, but I know Scott. He's not stupid."

Picking up on her tone, he nodded. "So what are you saying?"

"Maybe we could part ways? I'll walk home on my own, you could go to pick up some food or something? I'll stay out in the open, among people, so I'll be safe, and I have my phone. We can see if he shows then."

"I don't like it. It makes you too vulnerable. He's desperate, and desperate men do crazy things."

"Jarod, I'd be perfectly safe on midtown streets, and maybe you could follow behind, then, or we could have a signal."

"A signal?"

The way that he asked that made her feel as if he wasn't taking her seriously. She didn't like it and said as much.

"Listen, I get your point, but do I tell you how to take pictures?"

"What? What does that have to do with anything?"

"You have your area of expertise, and I have mine. I've seen what can go wrong with the best-laid plans, when we send in civilian volunteers with wire taps, Kevlar and a SWAT team backing them up and things can still go wrong. It's never predictable."

"But here we are, walking around trying to get him to notice us. Isn't that just as dangerous?"

"Not with me standing here with you."

She had to smile, knowing she was beating her head against a wall, but she really liked the wall, so it was hard to fault him.

"Okay, but can we duck in here? I have to use the ladies' room," she said, nodding to the diner they were passing.

"Sure. I could use a little something anyway."

"We just had lunch a while ago."

"Man needs to eat, and I'm curious about knish…I saw someone order them yesterday and they looked good."

Lacey laughed, and offered a kiss as they found a booth. "I'll make a New Yorker out of you yet," she vowed, heading to the ladies' room.

On her way out of the bathroom, she stopped to check her phone to make sure she hadn't missed any calls, and stiffened as the hairs on the back of her neck stood—someone was right behind her.

Something hard and sharp was pressing into her back, and coldness ran over her skin, chasing away anything but panic and numbing fear as the point dug in.

He'd found her.

JAROD LOOKED AT THE CLOCK. He knew women could take a few minutes in the bathroom, but his instincts were buzzing. Something was wrong. Cursing and throwing some money on the table just as the waitress brought the food he'd ordered for himself and Lacey, he got up and made his way to the back.

Dammit, he should have known. She was right. Myers had waited for her to be alone—and Jarod had let his guard down, thinking they were safe. He should have known better.

Striding along the narrow hallway, he knew he was right as he saw Lacey's sunglasses thrown recklessly on the floor. He picked them up, pushing down the fury and tangle of emotions that threatened to cloud his thinking.

Spotting something else out of the corner of his eye, he saw her lipstick—he knew it was hers, recognizing the case she'd used earlier in the day—lying on the floor near the back door of the diner. She was leaving him a trail, and he just hoped he was in time.

LACEY DIDN'T KNOW what was going on. The man who had her clearly wasn't Scott, and that had rattled her more than if it had been her ex. She struggled, having taken a self-defense course when she moved to the city, and she knew she had to fight for herself. Fighting back was often enough to discourage a would-be attacker.

Luckily her bag was open as she'd left the bathroom, and she'd been dropping stuff left and right, but there was no telling if anyone would notice.

"Just take my bag. There's cash and credit cards, and you can…"

"Shut up, and keep walking." The voice was smooth, almost polished in her ear, his breath warm, but there was the lingering odor of something. As he tightened his grip and she lifted her foot to try to stomp down, pulling at his arms or trying to angle her head so she could bite, she felt the sharp point against the side of her neck and froze. "I don't want your money. I want your man."

"What are you talking about?"

"You be a good girl, you might just make it out of this. It's not you I want, so I don't care if he finds you alive or dying, as long as he comes after you. You should keep that in mind," the soft voice warned.

Her mind finally comprehended his words—she wasn't being mugged or robbed or attacked. At least, not in the way she thought. She was bait.

"Who are you?"

"An old friend of your Ranger's… He's taken something I want back, and he'll tell me where to find it as long as I have something he wants. You," he said and she could hear the smile in his voice, shuddering from revulsion as he buried his head in her neck and sniffed.

"You smell good. Maybe we could have some fun after the Ranger's dead."

"I thought you said you just wanted something from him?"

She had to keep him talking. Maybe someone would hear, she thought, her eyes traveling up the narrow brick walls of the alley behind the diner. The windows were small and high, and if she screamed to get attention, he'd strike. Of that she had no doubt.

"I do. And I plan to get it. And then I plan to make sure he can't follow me where I'm going. Though I have to thank you for dropping things out of your purse to lead him to us—that was helpful," the man said, laughing against her hair.

Her stomach flipped. She'd inadvertently led Jarod into danger. How could he know that this maniac was after him and not her? The man who held her had all the advantages.

"What did he take that you want back?"

"My daughter."

"Jarod won't give you what you want, not even for me."

"*Jarod won't give you what you want,*" he mimicked her in a high-pitched tone, laughing again. "You had better pray that he will. But maybe you like dangerous men? Maybe you like the excitement?" he said seductively, and she held back a cry as his free hand snaked around and covered her breast.

It had been about a minute, and it seemed like a year. Her logical thoughts seemed to have been replaced by fear and hopelessness. Maybe Jarod thought she'd ditched him? Maybe he'd never gone to look for her, or he missed her path of dumped items, or he just couldn't find her, and she was going to die, and probably suffer worse, here in a back alley at the hands of a criminal.

"Darren Hill." The name popped to her lips—the man Jarod had had to identify, the one who had escaped custody in Texas.

"How do you know who I am?" he asked, pressing the knife harder against her throat, and she realized her error. If she knew who he was, he'd never let her walk away.

"My name is Lacey," she said, not answering his question, hoping to buy herself more time.

"So the Ranger told you about me, Lacey. I'm flattered," he said, laughing one moment, and gripping her even harder the next. His tone was angry. "Where the hell are you, Ranger?" he shouted into the alley. "You're sure taking your time, and I might just decide to enjoy myself a little more with your girl here," he said, his hand digging into her tender flesh as she whimpered.

His tone softened again. "You call him. You tell him how you feel with my hands on you, and you beg him to save you," he said and jerked her backward. *"Now."*

"J-Jarod," she called, her voice weak, and then she repeated it more strongly, praying that someone heard if not Jarod. "Jarod—I'm okay. Do what you have to and shoot this sonofabitch between the eyes if you c—"

"Puta!" Hill spat, and pushed her to the ground. The wind was knocked out of her, but she managed to keep from hitting her head. He towered over her, pulling a gun out from his jacket and she froze as he aimed it at her and then both of them were distracted by another voice. Jarod stepped forward out of the converging alley.

Lacey forgot her stone-cold fear, unable to see anything except for her captor swinging the gun in Jarod's direction. White-hot anger took hold and all her walls of fear came crashing down with blind rage. She lashed out, knowing this time she was going to win.

JAROD HEARD THE ECHO of voices and a muffled struggle as he made his way along the alley. Backup was coming, but it wouldn't be here soon enough. The alleys merged and his head snapped up when he heard Lacey's cry, then her shout. He rushed to turn the corner just in time to see Hill shove her to the ground and pull his gun. Jarod shouted instinctively to draw Hills attention his way as he reached for his gun, but Hill had the jump.

He wasn't prepared to see Darren Hill, and he certainly wasn't prepared for what came next.

Lacey, yelling loudly, blindly grabbed onto a bottle lying near a garbage can and swung hard at Darren's crotch, nailing him perfectly. Darren's gun went off, ricocheting wildly around the brick and pavement. Jarod saw him lunge for Lacey, and called out a warning as she skittered away, but then Darren's body arched in surprise and fell to the ground. He groaned in pain. Jarod saw two of New York's finest in an upper window, and three more charging down the alley.

He raced toward where Lacey sat, staring at Darren, who was cursing a blue streak. The NYPD officers dealt with him while Jarod helped Lacey to her feet.

"You okay?" he asked as he searched her for serious injury. The short question was all he could manage as the emotions needed to stay at bay for the moment.

She looked at him steadily and nodded. "Good."

One of the officers approached Jarod. "This the guy you were looking for?"

Jarod nodded, exchanging looks with Hill, who was now cuffed and put in an upright position against the wall while being read his rights, an ambulance screaming in the background.

Turning back to Lacey, he looked her over again, making sure all was well.

"It wasn't Scott," she said to him, sounding confused.

"No. I have to admit, I never seriously thought Darren would have come after me here."

And with that bit of miscalculation, he'd put Lacey in danger. Had almost gotten her killed. Something cold settled down in his gut as he watched the paramedics escort her to the ambulance to check her out, a cop close behind her.

Someone shook him out of his haze, as well, and he realized Lacey was being asked to give a statement. He went with her, keeping a close eye.

She was holding up well, all things considered, and he was proud of her. One tough cookie, his photographer. If not for hitting Hill with that bottle Jarod knew he might be dead.

"Wait—how come you're here now and not over there?" he said, signaling the paramedic, but Lacey grabbed his arm, stopping him.

"They looked me over, and I'm fine. Just some dents and bruises," she joked, even smiled, but he didn't laugh, his gaze focused on her. His hand came up to hold her face.

"You should go to the hospital. I can come with you," he offered.

Her hand covered his. "I'm fine, Jarod. Really. Please, the last thing I need is one more hospital visit."

"He hurt you," Jarod said softly, and touched the bandage at her neck, noticed the bruises.

"Yes, but he won't be able to do that again," she said, stepping closer. "You saved my life. I don't know how you thank someone for that, but—"

"I put you in danger," he said gruffly, still scrutinizing her injuries.

"What?" She was incredulous.

"Tom told me there was a chance Hill would head this way. If he had—"

She put her arms around him, squeezing tightly. "But he didn't. I'm *fine*."

Tenderness that threatened to swallow him whole took hold, and he had to suck a deep breath just to speak.

"Nice shot with the bottle, by the way."

"I know," she said, shaking her head. "After having that scumbag touch me, threaten me, and then he turned that gun on you, I just… Something gave way. No how was he going to win."

"Most people would have let the fear get to them," he said, knowing it was true, and how extraordinary she was.

"I know it probably doesn't make sense, but I feel…good. Really gross, from this alley, and a little sore, but…better than I have in a long time."

"It's the adrenaline, and the relief," Jarod said, wishing he could say the same. She'd apparently faced some demons and put them to rest, but his had just awakened.

Regardless of her disclaimers, she never would have

been in danger if it hadn't been for him, his work, his past. Who was he to think of a future with this woman, any woman? And children, or a life…the kinds of things that men like Darren Hill could hold against him, threaten him with. Unless he stopped being what he was, and that couldn't happen, either.

"Jarod?"

"Huh? Sorry," he said, pushing his hand through his hair.

"Can you please take me home? I'm dirty, and…I just need to be with you right now."

"The hospital—"

"I don't need the hospital. I need you," she said vehemently, and he realized he needed her, too. Needed to forget all the problems and all the reasons it wouldn't work, couldn't work, and enjoy what time they had. It couldn't be forever, but it would have to be enough.

_12_

SUNDAY PASSED in a haze of sex and sleep, both of them wanting nothing more than to be with the other. Lacey was hesitant to take her clothes off, not wanting Jarod to see where Darren's harsh grip had bruised her, but there was no hiding the fact.

Jarod saw everything, absorbed everything and made it all right. He kissed the bruises, replacing the memories of the felon's hard grip with a lover's warm lips and gentle hands. Their lovemaking was just as passionate, but sweeter than before, and Jarod went from tender and loving to playful and teasing as the morning wore on.

"Sunday rule, nothing serious today. We're not leaving the apartment, and we're not thinking about anything else but us. We'll order in, and just enjoy."

She grinned, playing along. She needed the lightness. They ordered pizzas, drinks, salads and desserts, and leftovers filled the kitchen counters and refrigerator. Her stereo played soft renditions of Norah Jones's tunes in the background, and they'd actually danced in her living room. Naked. It was a first.

There were a lot of firsts with Jarod. At the moment,

they were laughing hysterically as bubbles flew every-where in her bathroom, both of them barely fitting in her clawfoot tub.

The water was lukewarm as they washed and touched each other until the kidding was chased away by desire, and Lacey turned, poised over him, and took his shaft deep inside as she lay back against his chest.

"I've never had a bath quite like *this* before," she said, her voice catching. His arms came around front to apply fragrant bath gel to a sponge before he started sweeping it gently, erotically over her thighs, stomach and breasts. Her breath came faster, and she felt his heart slamming in his chest. She pushed her feet against the bottom of the tub, rocking slightly, drawing a moan from them both.

"Can't say I've ever been much of a bubble bath guy, myself," he said huskily, continuing to wash her as he continued to fill her. He thrust up gently in response to her rocking motions, and water sloshed around them and over the tub's edge onto the tile. "But it's definitely an experience I'd like to repeat."

"Can you repeat that little thing you just did with the sponge?" she asked breathlessly. Her head dropped back when he did, pressing the rough-textured sponge down between her thighs and drawing slowly upward. He applied the right pressure, and she gasped, sensation cascading through her as he leaned down and found her mouth with his, swallowing her cries of release.

As her orgasm spent itself, rippling through her muscles much like the warm water did around her, she planted her hands on the side of the tub. Lifting herself up just enough, she drove down on him harder, then again, knowing what he needed.

"Oh, yeah…like that, just like that," he said, groaning his approval as she complied, his hands splaying over her hips and supporting her and helping her balance. "You're so damned tight…I love when you squeeze me hard inside," he panted, knowing it excited her when he told her what he liked.

His excitement was hard to deny when after only a few more hard thrusts he grabbed her hips and held her down, with a long, guttural sound that told her exactly how satisfied he was.

She wasn't sure she could get enough of him. Her body should be sated, but hearing him come, feeling him come, had her worked up all over again. She was almost embarrassed to admit it, but somehow he knew, and reached down with his hand instead of the sponge and stroked her to a quick, mindless climax that had her trembling.

Getting out, he grabbed a big towel and dried her limp, well-loved form and carried her back to bed. They slept for a while, ate cold pizza, and couldn't help but be aware that the day was ticking to an end, and tomorrow would have to be dealt with.

She woke first, sometime in the middle of the night, and watched him sleep. Tomorrow was their last day working together, and they hadn't said a single word about what came after that.

"Deep thoughts going around in that pretty head?" he murmured, surprising her. She hadn't known he was awake.

some of the tension dissolve. "But I do want to protect you. I can't help it, it's who I am. But what about the time that I can't? What about the next nutcase or freak out for revenge that—"

"Then I guess you trust me to handle it myself and hope for the best," she interrupted, reaching up to touch his face.

He was so handsome, but that wasn't the thing that made her heart contract inside her chest. He touched her more deeply than she thought anyone could. "I'm falling for you, too, but there's no need to rush things. We have time," she reassured him, suddenly finding herself in the position of quelling his fears.

Everything inside of her warmed when he smiled.

"You're an amazing woman, you know that?"

"I suspected," she said teasingly, and they laughed, but then he became serious again.

"I don't know, Lacey. I always said I'd never put anyone in the same position my mom was in, and I have this good shot at a promotion, even though the pictures we lost, uh—"

"What about the pictures?" Her senses sharpened. "Did those pictures show up somewhere?"

"My captain got them, yeah."

She slid down to the mattress again, staring at the ceiling.

"You didn't tell me."

"You had enough to worry about, and it wasn't an issue. Tom is my captain, but he's also a friend, and he knew what was going on—he brushed them for prints, but whoever it was, was careful."

"It could have cost you your job."

"Not really. Well, it might have raised some eyebrows, but I technically wasn't on duty, and there's nothing unethical about me being involved with you, so except for making it somewhat awkward, I don't know what anyone hoped to gain by sending them. I would have thought they'd send them to your bosses."

"If they did, I never heard a word about it."

She could see the cop emerge as he slipped into pensive mode.

"So maybe someone was trying to piss me off, to get me to have to leave, to separate us...to leave you unprotected?"

She sighed. They were back to that.

"I suppose, but why force issues? You'd be going home eventually anyway."

"That's true. I don't know. None of it makes sense." He leaned over, planted a hot kiss on her lips. "I'm sorry I didn't tell you, but honestly, at the time, it didn't seem like the most important thing. And I didn't want you to worry."

"You know, if we stay in this, if we make this...more, then I will worry. How could I not? But I don't think that's a reason for us not to be together," she said, then frowned. "We have more practical problems."

"Such as?"

"Well, the fact that we live in two pretty distant places, and we're both building careers, that are kind of geographically challenging?"

He sighed. "I know. I've tried to find a way around it, too."

"I don't know what will happen after the calendar is done. I might stay here, I could be back on freelance, and that sends me all over the place for varying amounts of time. What was the promotion you were mentioning?"

His fingers started trailing up and down her arm, and she shivered, but not from cold.

"Tom is moving up, and wants me to take his spot. It's a test, some interviews, but he thinks I'd get the job. It's more desk time, more office work—"

She snorted. "That doesn't sound like you at all. Why would you even consider it?"

"I don't know. Better pay, more regular hours, less chance of dying out in the desert. The basics, really."

He joked, but what she knew in her heart was that he was considering it for her, for them. And it was too much—too much that he'd consider such a sacrifice when they'd only known each other for a week and couldn't predict how things would be a week from now.

She sighed, reaching up and pulling him down next to her, and he didn't argue, leaning in to trail kisses over her face and neck, moving down to her stomach.

"Let's just take it a day at a time, okay? Can we not make any big decisions? Let's just…enjoy this," she said, sucking in a breath as his lips closed around her nipple and drew sweetly on the sensitive bud.

"Fine by me," he whispered, his breath feathering over the spot his mouth had made wet, creating more sensation.

Levering over her, he parted her thighs with his

shoulders and settled in, kissing her intimately, laving her soft flesh with his tongue until she was writhing and begging for him to fill her, a command he was happy to follow.

Settling down on top of her slender form, he entered her gently. He rained kisses down her neck, her chest while he moved slowly and tantalizingly back and forth, rocking them to a climax that had them both shuddering in each other's arms.

Later, as dawn peeked over the windowsill of her apartment, they looked at each other quietly and made no promises. How they touched each other was promise enough for now.

JAROD TURNED HIS GAZE from the view of Lower Manhattan, to the people setting up his last bunch of shots. Oddly, he no longer felt strange being made up, his clothes changed, as he got ready for the shoot. Maybe it was because anything that allowed him to be close to Lacey right now was okay with him.

"Did you know the Brooklyn Bridge is the only place on earth where an airplane can fly overhead while you are walking over a car that is driving over a boat that is floating over a train?" she asked with a smile, camera in hand.

After their talk last night, they hadn't mentioned any future plans again, but he still was uncomfortable leaving her until everything was settled. He'd promised he wouldn't, but work demands dictated his presence back home. He was being asked to travel with a marshall to bring Hill back to Texas, and it wouldn't wait.

Jarod smiled, wanting to pull her close, but resisting, as they were on work time. "I hadn't thought of that before. Makes me consider the people who built all of this. Utterly amazing."

"I'm always freaked out by the pictures of the men sitting on the girders back in the twenties, eating their lunch—no ropes, nothing attaching them. Incredible."

"A lot of lives lost over the decades, building this place," he said, his eyes drifting back to the island.

"Yes, but as much happiness, too, I'd like to think."

"Is that why you came here? To find happiness?"

She took a deep breath. "No. I wasn't even thinking about happiness, then." She studied him from under her lashes, blushing slightly before turning her gaze out over the river. "I came here to escape. It was far enough away, big enough, and different enough, and I thought no one could find me here. I guess I was wrong."

"People have gone to the desert for exactly the same reason. They're really not all that different in the basic sense—both big and threatening if you don't know your way around, and both beautiful."

"You have some poetry in you, Ranger," she teased, turning when someone called to her.

"We're all set. Ready to make love to the camera, stud?"

"Always ready to make love to the woman handling it," he said just as playfully, loving her smile.

She hadn't done the things other women might have done. She didn't pressure him to stay, or complain that he had to leave, even though he'd wanted to remain until Myers was caught. All in all, she seemed okay with things the way they were. He wasn't as sure that he was.

"There's still no word on Myers or Gena—they don't even know if she's still alive."

"I realize that," she said softly. "But there have been no more calls, no more problems."

"Somehow it seems like if he was here, he would have popped up by now."

"I can't think of anyone else who'd be calling me or who would have broken into my apartment."

Jarod took his position at the bridge railing and leaned back as she fiddled with his shirt and posture.

"Maybe he figured out he couldn't get to you and left. Those guys are basically cowards. They like to exert their power, and when they can't win, they take off."

"I guess. It would make me feel better if they found him, though."

He had to say it. It wasn't the best time, but the words came out. "I know I said I'd be here until we straightened that out, and I don't feel right leaving you, but I don't have a choice."

Her eyes flickered with various emotions, and he knew she wasn't exactly in the best position to talk at the moment, but it had to be said.

"I'll be fine. I'll be careful. I'm going to stay at Jackie's for a few days anyway. She needs help getting home from the hospital tomorrow, and she'll need someone there for a day or two. Maybe by then we'll hear something."

"I'll talk to a cop here who I've gotten to know a bit. He can stop by, or check things out for you, too."

"Thanks. I'm sure I'll be fine," she said.

"I want to come back as soon as I can swing it, and…I'm not taking the promotion. I talked to Tom this morning."

"Good for you, Ranger," she said approvingly, and not caring who saw, pulled at his collar, bringing him down for a quick kiss, to his surprise. "Now look pretty for the pictures," she ordered, joining her crew who had discreetly averted their eyes.

"Very funny," he replied, but watching her work was fun, and he got through the final shots with ease.

"I'm treating everyone to pizza at Grimaldi's," she announced, and he was disappointed not to have her to himself.

"Pizza sounds great," he agreed and focused on the festive mood as they packed up and made their way from the bridge into Brooklyn, pleased as she snaked her hand into his.

As she said, they had time. He didn't know how, but he knew he wasn't going to let Lacey Graham out of his life, one way or the other.

THE AIRPORT WAS HELL, and Lacey didn't mean the traffic, the crowds or the delays. She'd rented a car to pick up Jackie from the hospital, not wanting to subject her bruised friend to a possibly adventurous cab ride, and take Jarod to the airport, which gave her extra time with him, too.

"You're a good driver," he observed as she made her way off the Expressway heading toward the airport.

"It's been so long since I've driven, I almost forgot if

I could do it. It's actually not quite as bad here as I thought."

They arrived at the airport, and she hadn't anticipated how difficult it would be to say goodbye, even though she knew it was temporary. She'd felt so confident and adult the night before, telling *him* not to worry. And that they'd work things out and find a way to be together. Not to rush things. But now she felt like the neediest Nellie on the planet.

Good Lord, how she didn't want him getting on that plane. She stopped herself short of telling him she didn't want him to go because she was an independent woman, and doing so was clingy and unattractive and—

"God, I wish I didn't have to go," he said roughly, and she bit her lip to hold back the emotion that welled up. He gathered her in close to comfort her.

"I'll be back as soon as I can. I'll come up here until you're done with the calendar, and after that's over, maybe you can take a break and come down to my neck of the woods?"

He gently tipped her chin up and looked into her eyes, and it did her good to know he hated this as much as she did.

"Sounds like a plan," she said, forcing a smile that he scooped up in a hot kiss. He checked his watch and reluctantly pulled back. "You be careful. And call me if you need me. You've got Ward's direct number, too, remember," he said. Ward was the NYPD officer he'd dealt with on the Hill shooting.

"I will. I'll be fine. You stay safe, too," she said, realizing the reality of what he had been talking about as he got out of the car with his bag and walked away.

It was the first moment that she really understood why he had such serious doubts. On a daily basis, Jarod's life could be in danger. They had plans, but it was really a day-by-day thing. Who knew if he'd come back, if she'd ever see him again? He was getting on that plane with a Federal Marshall and the man who had tried to kill them both.

No. She couldn't think that way. Jarod was good at what he did. He'd be back.

Watching him disappear as he entered the aiport, she waited until her vision stopped being so blurry and started the car. She had work, and she had to take care of Jackie. She loved Jarod, but she had her life, too, and she was going to get back to it.

13

"I'M SORRY YOU HAD to miss the pizza wrap-up lunch. It was fun, and I think we got things back on track, so we're off and running again," Lacey said to Jackie as they waited for the nurse to come with a wheelchair. Jackie grumped.

"It's so stupid to have to be wheeled out of these places. I'm perfectly fine to walk. I just want to get home."

"I don't blame you, but enjoy the rest while you're getting it. I'm doubling up the schedule over the next few weeks so we can get more finished. Now that Jarod's pictures are done, and I've got plenty of Ryan and another guy coming in tomorrow, I have a much better idea of what I need from everyone else. We're actually ahead of schedule. I think we can cut through it all much faster, thankfully."

Lacey was particularly motivated to stay on schedule because when she was done she was taking a few weeks off to visit Jarod. That was the advantage of freelance work, and she was going to enjoy it.

"Execs will be happy about that. Nothing like being on track," Jackie said and let out a small whoop of happiness when the nurse appeared in the doorway.

"Yay, time to go," her assistant gushed, and Lacey chuckled as they all headed for the entrance. Soon she and Jackie were making their way to Hoboken, where Jackie lived.

"So…how are you doing?" Jackie asked, once she'd settled into her place.

"Me? I'm fine. You're the one recovering."

"You know what I mean. Jarod had to go home, and Sally came in and mentioned to me that you two were pretty hot and heavy at the shoot, not that I didn't know something was going on before. You two could start fires just by looking across a room at each other," Jackie said.

Lacey couldn't help but grin. "He's a great guy."

"C'mon! That's all you're going to give me?" Jackie let her head fall back against the seat's headrest, rolling her eyes in disgust. "I'm an injured woman, I need details."

Lacey laughed again. "Well…he's coming back, maybe in a few weeks, and I'm going there at the end of the project…"

"And?"

"And what?"

"You're killin' me here. What's he like in the sack? What do you like most about him? Are you guys in something serious, or what?"

"We're taking our time—it's only been a week. But I'd say we both agree it could be something serious, and because of that, I'm not telling you about the other stuff. Except to say that I think I pulled several all-nighters in the past week, and I enjoyed every single second of them."

"Yesss!" Jackie said, clapping.

"I know. I never thought there would be a guy like him out there. Decent, sexy, caring… I mean, he has his faults—he's a little bossy, a little, um, not arrogant, but you know, he kind of likes to take over if you let him—"

"Which you don't."

"No, but he listens, too. Even when we disagreed, we could actually talk, and he *heard* what I had to say, you know?"

Jackie didn't say anything, and Lacey looked over as they stopped at a light, seeing her friend sitting, staring down into her lap at her fingers.

"Hey, what's the matter? You feeling all right?"

Jackie sniffed and shook her head. "Yeah, I'm fine. I'm just happy for you. You deserve it."

"How about you and Kenny?"

"I, uh, I don't think it's going to work out."

"I'm sorry to hear that. But take it from me there are many, and better, fish. Maybe that fireman who was flirting with you last week? What was his name? Mr. April. I can remember their month, but forget their names. Except for Jarod, of course."

Jackie smiled weakly. "Ryan Murphy. He was nice. Maybe. Right now, I don't know if I want anything to do with men at all."

Lacey remained quiet for a moment. "I know how you feel. That's where I was before I met Jarod."

"Really?"

"I know it's different, but a man attacked you, Jackie, maybe the same man who attacked me once."

There, she said it.

"Is that what you guys were talking about that day, and why they sent security to my hospital room?"

"That's right. We were afraid he'd come back, that he was trying to get to me through my friends, through Jarod—he sent the pictures of us to Jarod's boss."

"Oh, no! Is he in trouble?"

"No, it sounds like his captain kept it quiet. Jarod hadn't crossed any ethical lines by being with me. But obviously someone was trying to mess with us. Maybe make him think I was too much trouble, or get him to leave." Lacey shrugged.

"You said you were attacked, too?"

"My ex-boyfriend was a maniac, and beat me before he took off. It was why I came here, and it ate away at me until I settled some things recently, I guess."

Jackie's voice was thin. "He hit you?"

"He broke my arm, threw me around… I think he might have done worse if I hadn't passed out."

"Oh, my God," Jackie said. "I'm so sorry."

Lacey felt a knot loosen in her gut. This was easier to talk about than she thought, and it felt good to get it out, especially as maybe it could help Jackie.

"Thing is, I didn't want to deal with it or talk to anyone. I told Jarod, and you, and somewhere in all of it, I started to work through it. That's my point, really. You were hurt, too, and you might need to talk about it, or do something to get past it. Just don't lock it up inside like I did because it eats at you. It doesn't go away on its own."

Jackie said nothing, and Lacey worried. It was so

unlike Jackie to be so quiet or moody, but then again, she'd been through so much recently.

"Jackie, I'm sorry if you didn't need to hear all that right now. I know I hated people preaching at me to talk about it, or to tell someone… I had to come around to it in my own good time, so I'm sorry I pushed."

Jackie shook her head. "It's not that."

"We're almost there. Just relax, okay?"

"Lacey, there's something I really need to tell you," Jackie started, but Lacey inadvertently cut her off when someone cut her off, taking a turn far too fast.

"Damn, that guy nearly took our front end off! What were you about to say?"

"Um, nothing, maybe later. Thanks for telling me all this. Do you really think it was the same guy?"

"I don't know. I really have no idea anymore what's going on. Things have been calm for a few days, and so Jarod thought maybe Scott went away. You didn't see him?"

Jackie went back to looking out the window.

"Well, listen, we'll keep each other company, and we'll be perfectly safe. And if you want, I can even grab more stuff from my place and keep you company for a few days."

"You don't have to do that."

"It's what friends do for each other, Jackie, and I hope we are friends."

"I hope we are, too."

"Okay, here we are. Where can I park?"

Jackie directed her to a space on the street, and Lacey helped her out of the car, noticing a pizza place close by, her heart squeezing a little. Ordinary as it might be, pizza was now kind of a special thing, having been the first date she had with Jarod, even if she hadn't thought of it that way at the time.

"That place serves a piece of pizza almost as big as a whole pie—they're kind of known for it. There's a great bagel shop, as well. Kinda funky," Jackie said, noticing her staring down the street.

They made their way up to the teeny third-floor apartment, and Lacey was delighted to find that there was a roof garden and a patio accessible from Jackie's loft.

"This is so cute! I should look for a place over here, if I stay in the city long-term."

"It is nice—quieter, more like a small town, in some ways. Nice neighbors."

They settled in, and Lacey went out to bring back a couple of the huge pizza slices, figuring Jackie might need a few minutes alone. She was acting a little strangely, and Lacey knew she just had to be patient, and be a friend. It was something she'd been lacking after her own ordeal.

Returning up the building's steps, she realized that in a few weeks, she'd developed more close relationships than she had in months before, just by opening up. She didn't feel alone anymore, and the future looked brighter than it had in a long while.

LACEY WAS EXHAUSTED and slightly uncomfortable on Jackie's sofa. She missed Jarod and figured being here on the lumpy couch was better than being home alone in her bed. She jumped when her phone rang, hoping it was him.

"Hello?"

"Hey, sweetheart, you awake?"

"Yes, I was just reading and missing you like crazy. Good flight?"

"Boring. Long. The usual. But they got Hill where they needed him to be, and tomorrow it's business as usual for me. I miss you, too."

"I take it there's been no information on Scott?" she asked.

"Nothing. He seems to have evaporated. Maybe he went over the border, who knows? A friend of mine said it wouldn't be typical of his profile to come back after you, so that's a comfort, I guess."

"Although it doesn't explain any of the stuff that has been happening."

"You alone there?"

"Jackie's in the next room, sleeping, though her TV is on. Why?"

She smiled to herself, able to tell from the tone of his voice that something was on his mind—something sexy, for sure.

"Because just hearing your voice is turning me on, and I figured, since we're giving this long-distance thing a shot, we'll have to get creative once in a while. Are you feeling creative?"

"Sure, but let me get to a more private spot. There's a nice patio on the roof, I can go up there. It's a little muggy outside, but I'm feeling kind of hot anyway," she said teasingly, and heard him groan appreciatively.

Making her way up the steep metal fire escape steps to the roof, she was relieved to discover that she was alone. Her heart picked up a little as she contemplated what she and Jarod might say to each other with her sitting out here in the open.

"It's gorgeous up here, Jarod. They even planted a small patch of lawn on half of the roof, with flower boxes and benches, a swing and a grill. I guess everyone uses it, the eight people who rent here."

"So that means you could get caught." His tone was low and naughty. "Does that bother you?"

"Not really...I can be discreet."

She could hardly believe that she was getting breathless from just talking to him about sex. Although she had a feeling it was going to go a lot further than talk very shortly.

"Where are you sitting? The bench or the swing?"

"The swing. It looked inviting and has a canopy. The cushion is soft and I can stretch out. In fact, it's pretty warm outside, so I think I'm going to lose my top, do you mind?"

Another groan. "Are you seriously taking off your shirt?"

She had a very sturdy running bra on underneath, but Jarod didn't need to know that, she decided with wicked glee.

"I am, and I did. There's a soft breeze, and my nipples are very hard because I'm hearing your voice, and thinking about your mouth," she said, and that much was true. She was already on fire for him.

"I thought I was supposed to be seducing you," he said roughly, but with a laugh.

"You are. You tell me anything you want me to do,

or what you'd do to me if you were here…and I'll do the same," she instructed, loving this new way to play.

"You know I love it when you talk dirty, sweetheart, so don't hold back."

"I don't intend to. All I've been thinking about is how I'd like to—"

A sharp noise from below her made her stop and frown.

"Lacey?"

"I'm sorry—I heard a loud noise, and it sounded like it came from directly below, which would be Jackie's room."

"You should go check. Keep me on the line."

"Okay," she agreed, and heard another loud bang, along with a yelp, and moved faster. "Jarod, something's wrong. I think I just heard her scream."

"Lacey, stop! Forget it, don't go in there. Get off the line and call for help, but stay out of there, okay?"

"Okay," she said, hanging up and dialing 911 at the top of the steps, but as she heard another cry, she flinched and peeped around the edge of the door leading to the escape, and saw Jackie's apartment door flung open.

She quickly gave the emergency operator the info and moved carefully down the steps. She had to see if she could help. If Jackie was already hurt, and in there alone, Lacey wouldn't forgive herself if all she'd done was just wait outside.

Sliding along the wall, she saw an older lady down the hall poke her head out and yell, "What the hell is going on down there?"

Lacey put her finger to her lips and frantically motioned her back inside. The woman glared, and muttered something, but ducked inside her door. Probably to call the police. Fine—the more the merrier.

It was silent in the apartment. Not a good sign, and Lacey stopped just outside the door. Suddenly assailed by a million doubts, she wondered if she was really going to be able to help Jackie, or if she was making a horrible error in judgment.

She took a deep breath. Too late now. She stepped into the apartment, pushing the door back and saw nothing, but then heard a noise from the bedroom.

Jackie.

Heart slamming in her chest, Lacey reached out and grabbed a baseball bat Jackie kept by the door—she called it her "burglar bat," which Lacey had found funny at the time. Now, the solid wood felt good in her hands. It was something.

Moving farther in, she heard papers shuffling, and a drawer closing. Could this be a robbery? There was no way Scott could know she was here, unless he had followed them.

She failed to breathe when her ringtone chimed from her pocket and she realized she hadn't shut her cell phone off. It had to be Jarod calling back.

Shit.

She turned, heading for the door, but didn't quite make it.

14

"WHOA THERE, HONEY. You hold up. And you can put down that bat, too," commanded a male voice she didn't recognize. It was an inebriated male voice, as well. She could tell from the slurring of his words.

She faced a tall blond man who looked rough around the edges and didn't fit her idea of a burglar at all. Her phone stopped ringing, and went to voice mail. Jarod must be crazed, she imagined, but she didn't have time to worry about that now.

"Like hell I will. Where's Jackie?" Lacey asked calmly, and noted the man's eyes flare.

"She shouldn't-a brought you here…she knows how you piss me off. She told me to get lost. Do you believe that? Picked you over me," he said with incredulity, his gaze turning mean. "But I showed her."

Lacey then realized whom she was talking to.

"Kenny? You're Jackie's boyfriend?"

"I was…until the ungrateful bitch dumped me, refused to keep helping me get what I deserved."

Lacey heard a soft moan from the other room, behind Kenny, and homed in on his words.

"How was Jackie helping you do that?"

"She was helping me get to you, you know? I asked her to mess up a few things. Just enough to make you look bad, but she wasn't doing a good job, so I had to *help*," he said, throwing his hands up, which made Lacey jump. And he laughed more loudly.

"Why would you want me off the project?"

He shoved his hand in his pocket and pulled out a wad of paper. "See this? This is the list. She wouldn't give it to me before, she said she was going to tell you it was me, turn me in."

"So you took it and put her in the hospital? It was you?"

"Dumb bitch," he muttered. "You're all bitches. You come in from wherever, flashing your tits and your baby blues and get whatever you want. Do you know how long I have worked in this stupid city, barely scraping by, and you just walk right in?"

"That's not my fault, and it's not Jackie's fault, either."

"It is her fault!" he roared, and Lacey fought a cringe, trying to keep him talking. What was taking the police so long? "She was on the inside, she could have put in a word for me, she could have gotten rid of you! She coulda done a million things, but she wouldn't do it, wouldn't help me, she said. Until I made her." He took a knife from his jacket pocket, smiling.

Lacey's mind traveled back along the timeline, remembering Jackie's hand.

Five stitches, Jackie had said, from cutting an onion. Jackie didn't even like onions. She always told the lunch guy to leave them off her sandwich.

"You *cut* her?"

He shrugged. "She had to learn not to say no to me when I needed her. Not to put some bitch at work above her man, or there would be consequences. The cut was just enough to get the message across. I could do much worse. Wanna see?"

He waved the knife and Lacey felt a shiver run down her body. It had blood on it.

Oh, God. Jackie....

She raised the bat, more afraid than she ever had been, and looked him in the eye. She wasn't taking any chances.

Where are the cops?

"What did you do, you lousy, cowardly sonofa-bitch?" she growled at him. He wiggled his eyebrows, grinning madly.

"Weeha, you have some spunk, don't you? This will be fun," he said with relish, swiping the knife in an arc and moving from one foot to the other. Lacey moved quickly and put a chair between them, a wall at her back, and held the bat poised.

"I've called the police, and so did the lady next door," she spat, hoping the latter was true. "They'll be here any minute. You'll never make it out of here."

"Aw, this won't take more than a minute," he teased. "I'm so sick of rich, privileged bitches taking everything from the people who work hard for it. Let's see how well you do in the world if your face ain't so pretty."

The world whittled down to just the small space containing the two of them. He moved closer, swinging and feinting, laughing again, and Lacey held the bat high. She heard sirens wail and car doors slam, but the sounds seemed far away.

Kenny's face was fierce as he came closer, moving faster, and she might have screamed, but wasn't sure. He looked to the side, distracted by something, and she took her chance, swinging forward, fast and hard.

Home freakin' run.

She wasn't aiming for anything specifically, but hit him somewhere in the gut. The knife went flying, someone shouted, and Kenny fell to the floor with a grunt.

He started to get back up, and Lacey drew the bat high a second time, but someone grabbed it and people crowded her vision. She fought to free herself, her eyes trained on Kenny.

"Calm down, ma'am, it's okay. Lacey? Calm down. We're here, and we've got him."

She dared to take her eyes from Kenny when she realized officers had entered the room, the one next to her holding the bat with one hand, waiting for her to recognize him.

"Officer Ward," she said, remembering the name from Jarod, and he nodded.

"That's me. How about you relax now? We've got him," he said.

"My friend…Jackie, she's in there," she cried, tears, relief and adrenaline all hitting at once. "She's hurt…he hurt her, again. He attacked her before. He— he cut her hand…"

Suddenly her phone rang and the cop in front of her glanced toward her pocket.

"I think that's for you. Why don't you answer it, and then we'll take a statement, okay?"

She nodded, reaching for her phone, watching two

other officers drag Kenny from the room as he cursed left and right.

She put the phone to her ear, looking toward Jackie's room, where police had gone in but hadn't come out. She could hardly breathe as the paramedics raced into the apartment. She pointed and they went into Jackie's room, too.

"Lacey? Is that you? You're there?"

Jarod's voice broke through the fog.

"I'm here. I'm…okay."

"Oh, God, honey, you near gave me a heart attack when you didn't answer the phone. What the hell is happening?"

She started to tell him, but then she saw Jackie being wheeled out by the paramedics. Lacey ran to her side, so happy to see her eyes open.

"Jackie," she whispered, taking her hand as they wheeled her through the apartment.

Jackie looked at her but didn't respond. She tried to say something Lacey thought might have been "sorry" but she couldn't tell.

Jarod was saying something, asking what was happening. Lacey told him she was there, asked the paramedics if Jackie was okay.

"Lacey, goddammit, what—"

Lacey fell into a chair, her knees trembling. "It's okay, Jarod. It was Kenny, Jackie's boyfriend. He was doing it all, the pictures, the apartment, the fires, the calls… He wanted the calendar project. He made her help. He was the one who hurt her."

"Is Jackie okay?"

"He came after her, but I guess I interrupted him doing anything really bad, and so, yeah, she'll be okay. Physically. He's done a job on her mentally. I don't understand…I never would have guessed. She never showed any sign of a problem like this, but maybe I wasn't paying attention."

"You saved her life. And risked your own, which we are going to have a long talk about…"

She smiled, and started to laugh and cry at the same time. "There's a policeman here who wants to talk to me, Jarod."

"Okay. Do what you have to. Remember I love you."

It was the first time he'd said it just like that, and it put the world to rights.

"I love you, too," she said, meaning it. "I'll call you back as soon as we're done."

"Promise?"

"Promise."

JAROD LEFT LACEY a message, unable to wait for her to call back. Talking on the phone just wasn't going to cut it. He had to be there.

Turning around almost as soon as he'd gotten home, he got a ridiculously expensive last-minute business flight and took off. Five hours later, the sun was just short of coming up, and he was jumping out of a cab in front of Lacey's apartment. He was nearly crazy with the need to see her, touch her, and make sure she was okay.

She opened the door to his furious knocking, sleepy-eyed and standing there wearing a shirt—his shirt that he left behind, and he couldn't get her in his arms fast enough. Closing the door behind him, he pulled her in tight, running his hands over her, making sure everything really was all right.

When he finally loosened his hold and she looked up, he just captured her mouth in a kiss, soaking in her touch, her scent, her taste, even though it had only been a little more than twelve hours since he had last seen her.

"I had to be here. I shouldn't have left in the first place," he said against her mouth, now starting to believe that she really was okay.

Lacey shook her head, making some utterly female, comforting noise that wrapped right around his heart.

"I can't believe you came back. Did you get any sleep at all?"

"I don't need sleep. Like I could sleep. Do you have any idea what it felt like to hear you and know that you were in danger, and to not be there? The things that went through my mind, sweetheart, when you didn't pick up that phone—"

"I'm sorry. I just… I couldn't let Jackie be hurt. It was rough, but it worked out okay."

"You could have been killed," he said flatly.

She nodded. "Twice in a week, that must be some kind of record, even for a New Yorker," she said wryly.

"How can you joke about this? And Myers is still missing. No way am I moving from this spot until he's found."

She moved back, looking partly amused, partly turned on, and partly consternated.

"Jarod, you can't do that. You have your job, remember? The one you are supposed to report to in—" she slid a look to the clock "—about an hour?"

"They can fire me."

"Be serious."

"I'm completely serious. In everything I ever faced in the course of my work, I don't think I was ever as afraid as I was when you didn't pick up that phone."

She frowned. "You're focusing on the wrong thing."

"What?"

Sitting on the sofa and pulling her lovely legs up under her, she yawned and patted the seat next to her. He went and sat close, his fingers finding her nape and stroking the silky hair there, still needing to touch her and reassure himself she was okay.

"You're focusing on the problem, on the fact that you weren't here to protect me, but what you aren't focusing on is that I was able to protect myself," she said with a sort of fierce look in her eye that surprised Jarod, but shouldn't have.

"I know. I know that. Rationally," he said. "But in here—" he took her hand and put it up against his heart "—I wanted to be the one to make sure you're safe. That you don't ever have to do that, ever again. I don't know how I can do that with us far apart. Or how my job figures in, or what I—"

She shook her head. "You can't. You have to be who you are, and let me be who I am, and we just have to have faith it will be okay. Seeing what Jackie went through with Kenny, and realizing I could have helped sooner, I could have maybe avoided the entire thing—"

"Wait—how? You aren't to blame here."

"No, not to blame, exactly. I know it's Kenny's fault. But I was so wrapped up in my own issues, wanting to hide and pretend nothing had ever happened to me, that I couldn't see what was happening to someone standing right in front of me. Maybe if I had…opened up, you know, gone to the counseling, allowed myself to heal sooner, Jackie would have told me what was happening to her."

"That's a lot of maybes. How is she doing?"

"She's okay."

Lacey looked down, taking a breath, her words coming out quickly, as if she had to muster the courage to say them.

"I'm going to go talk to someone later—an abuse counselor—to work through my own stuff, but also hoping it will encourage Jackie to do the same."

Jarod felt his own throat tighten and swallowed hard. "You are the bravest woman I have ever known in my life, I swear," he said huskily, bringing her fingers to his lips.

"You helped me get there. You made me believe again," she said, and he knew no matter what the hardships, they couldn't abandon what they had. They'd just find a way to make it work.

Pulling her up against him, he kissed her more lazily this time, his tongue touching hers in a slow, mating motion. His body reacted sharply with relief and desire as she pressed into him wearing nothing but the shirt.

"Let me call Tom and give him the rundown. I'll go

back as soon as I can get a flight out tomorrow but for now maybe we should go to bed for a few hours...get some rest or something," he said, tasting the warm, soft skin of her neck.

"Or something," she agreed, as his large hand massaged her breast.

THE FURTHEST THING from Lacey's mind was sleep. It had taken hours for the adrenaline to wear off. As he touched her intimately, everything inside of her body seemed to melt. In spite of the stress and lack of sleep, she wanted him.

She'd been surprised, though overjoyed, to get his message that he was coming back. The news had kept her awake for hours as she waited to see him again, and to feel his hands on her. However, it didn't look as though either one of them was going to leave the couch until they'd had their fill. She smiled as he unbuttoned the shirt.

It was, of course, the moment her cell phone rang.

"Mmm...might be about Jackie. I asked them to call me," she said, breaking away.

"Answer it. Then meet me in the bedroom."

The words were wickedly delicious coming from him, and she watched him walk away rather than looking at the caller ID on her phone.

Her warm mood and fuzzy feelings crystallized into something cold and sharp when she heard a familiar voice.

"Lacey, don't hang up."

Hang up? She was so stunned she couldn't move.

She tried to breathe normally, her heart hammering as she ran down the hall and grabbed Jarod by the arm, silently mouthing to him who was on the phone.

Like magic, his expression went from molten sexuality to granite. He made a hand motion for her to keep her caller talking and she nodded.

"I'm not hanging up, Scott. How did you find me? Are you in the city?"

Jarod gave her the thumbs-up as he grabbed his own phone.

"That's why I'm calling, I, uh… Gena heard that you were having a bad time with someone, and they were looking for me, and it's not me. I'm calling to say I'm, uh, sorry. But I haven't been following you. I've changed, Lacey, or at least, I'm trying to."

"I know it wasn't you, Scott, but that doesn't explain why you're calling me. The restraining order is still—"

"Listen, I'm in love with Gena. I took off because I needed to get to her, not to come after you. We had a fight, and I was locked up in that house. She wouldn't answer my calls, so I had to risk going to find her."

Lacey's blood ran cold. "Is Gena okay? Did you hurt her?"

"Hurt her? No! I would never hurt her. She's here with me. She's the one who told me to call you. I…wanted to say I'm sorry for what happened, for what I did to you. Part of it was the drugs, the booze, but my counselors said I can't use that as an excuse, and they're right."

Lacey listened, and felt more or less as if she'd fallen down the rabbit hole.

"Scott, I don't know what game you're playing, but

you'd be better off to turn yourself in. At the very least, you've broken house arrest."

"I know. I had to do it. When I told her I'd taken off, she met me here and told me to turn myself in. I guess I'll have to do extra time, but maybe if I give myself up, they'll let me finish at home in L.A."

She grabbed a pen and wrote "Reno" on the pad. Jarod started to dial but she motioned for him to stop.

"If you're lying, you should know I'm not alone, and they're looking for you—you won't get away with this."

"I'm not playing games, not anymore. I—I had a lot of problems, and I didn't know how to handle them. I'm learning now. I'm trying."

"If what you're saying is true, and I hope it is, for Gena's sake, then I'll wish you well," she said, feeling something spring loose inside of her. "You can't ever call me again, Scott. You hurt me badly, and I want you out of my life, completely, forever."

"Thanks, Lacey. You'll never hear from me again, I promise."

He hung up, and that was that.

Jarod was on the phone and though she paced for twenty minutes while he checked, eventually he hung up, shaking his head incredulously.

"It's true. He's turned himself in to the Reno police. He says he's in love with Gena. She's there with him, confirming his story. He escaped, called her, and she left to find him, to try to get him to turn himself in."

"He…apologized." The idea hit her as so strange that she couldn't quite get her mind around it yet.

"It gets weirder. They want to get married, so that they could legally see each other while he's finishing his sentence. You okay?"

She nodded. "I just feel…strange. I don't know what I expected, but it wasn't that. I can't really forgive him, but at the same time, I kind of hope he makes it. For her sake, anyway."

"That's a kind of forgiveness…it's healthy, but confusing, I know. I've seen victims forgive their attackers, or those who killed loved ones. I've never been able to imagine doing the same, but they tend to say it sets them free in a way."

Lacey nodded. "Yes…there is that feeling, I think. Like it's finally, really over."

Jarod extended his hand. "It is over, but we're just beginning," he murmured.

She smiled against his lips, laughing as he picked her up and carried her to the bedroom, not letting anything get in their way.

Epilogue

Three months later

LACEY SLIPPED HER FOOT out of her sandal and slid the pads of her bare toes along the length of his calf, her subtle flirting hidden under the table. When Jarod coughed abruptly as her foot flirted higher up his thigh, sneaking inside the loose material of his shorts, she laughed and enjoyed the mix of playful censure and desire in his eyes.

"You're bad, you know that?" he said. "I could have scalded myself on that slice of pizza, or dumped my beer down the front of my clothes, and then what would we have done?"

"I guess we'd have to go somewhere and get those clothes off, or I'd have to kiss it and make it better," she said, not the least bit repentant. In fact, her making him dump that beer was sounding like a good idea. It was a perfectly sunny, seventy-degree December day in Texas, but suddenly she was feeling a bit overheated.

"Hey, you two, this is a public area. Stop before I have to make up some new version of the fire code," Ryan Murphy joked, holding out a chair for Jackie as they arrived.

"This is great. Wearing summer clothes in winter. I may have to move here," Jackie commented, stretching bare arms above her head. Ryan caught one and kissed it, making her blush.

"And leave the best city in the world?" Ryan said in his heavy Brooklyn accent.

"Maybe. Maybe not," Jackie flirted. Her friend seemed happier and more herself than Lacey had seen her be in a while. Ryan was a good man, and exactly what Jackie deserved.

Lacey smiled at them, happy to be here, basking in the sun, the company, and the free time she was enjoying at the end of a very busy several months. Jackie lifted the beer that the waitress delivered to their riverside table, as people walked by the restaurant's patio.

"To the end of a successful project, and to our fearless leader for making it all come together in the end," she said, focusing on Lacey, making it her turn to blush.

"Hey, I could never have done it without you, Jackie, not to mention twelve sexy, barely clothed men," she joked, though she was only interested in one of the dozen, and he knew it. Things were good.

"To barely clothed men, then," Jackie repeated gustily, but only hers and Lacey's bottles met. Ryan and Jarod both put their beers down, comically refusing to join that particular toast.

"This was a fabulous idea, though, Jarod. A minivacation for all of us," Lacey added.

"I never spent much time in San Antonio…but we'll be changing that," he said, his foot finding its way over to nudge at Lacey's. "My transfer went through," he announced, and a hail of cheers went up.

Lacey was happiest of all. Three months of traveling back and forth from New York to El Paso were at an end. She could move to San Antonio, and she was sure she could find work in Texas, especially with the recommendations and exposure *Bliss* had offered her.

"Hey. Wait. I thought the only position open in San Antonio was the captain's?"

"That's right," he said calmly, leaning back in his chair. He looked at her from underneath that hat, those gorgeous brown eyes telegraphing her all kinds of wicked messages.

"But you didn't want to be captain. You wanted to be out in the field."

"Um, honey," Ryan spoke up, "why don't we go take a look at the river for a moment, until the food gets here? When we go home, all there will be is snow and slush," he said tactfully, taking Jackie's hand as they left the table.

"Jarod, I don't want you taking a job you'll be miserable in just to be near me."

As much as she wanted to be with him, he'd never asked her to give up her career, and she couldn't ask the same of him.

"Happy means being near you, in case you haven't noticed. Spending days on the road, tracking fugitives and drug-runners through the desert, has lost some of its charm, to say the least. I'll be busy in the new job, it'll be different, but I'll be coming home every night to you."

Convinced, she leaned in to kiss him. "I guess I can't argue with that," she said huskily. "No long-term assignments for me, either, at least, not in the near future."

"Speaking of long-term, there was something else I wanted to ask you about," he said, wrapping her hand in his.

"What's that?"

Reaching into his pocket with his other hand, he pulled out a small blue box. Tiffany's. Oh, my.

Oh, my, oh, my, oh, my, was all she could think, as he released her hand to open the box to reveal a glittering platinum-set diamond.

"I know it's only been a few months, and there's no rush, you can take your time, but—"

"Yes! Are you kidding me? Absolutely yes!" She jumped up, nearly overturning the table as she threw herself into his arms. She branded him with a long, scorching kiss that only broke when they drew applause. He looked deep into her eyes.

"I'll always be there for you. Always."

"I know. I'll be there for you, too," she promised, tears welling as he slipped the gorgeous ring on her left ring finger. "You really are a hero, Jarod."

"As long as you see me that way, that's all I care about, sweetheart."

Jackie and Ryan returned to the table, hooting, and congratulating them.

"Leave the table for a minute and see what happens," Ryan teased, slapping Jarod on the back and taking the seat he'd left earlier.

"Hmm, who knows who will be next?" Jarod quipped, watching Ryan's face, but he simply smiled, revealing nothing. The women were bent over the ring, sighing and talking animatedly, and Ryan shook his head.

"They might be at it for a while."

Jarod grinned, enjoying every second of it.

"Yeah, but that's okay. We have time."

* * * * *

Romeo and Juliet, Outback-style.
Teague Quinn has loved Hayley Fraser since they were both kids. But time and feuding families got in the way. Now Teague and Hayley are both back home – and back in bed with each other. Can they make first love last a second time around?

Turn the page for a sneak preview of

The Mighty Quinns: Teague
by
Kate Hoffmann

The Mighty Quinns: Teague
by
Kate Hoffmann

Queensland, Australia—August 1996

TEAGUE QUINN STRETCHED his arms over his head and closed his eyes against the sun, the warm rays heating the big rock beneath him. The wind rustled in the dry brush. The sounds of the outback were so familiar they were almost like music to him.

He'd managed to escape the house before anyone noticed he was gone, saddling his horse and riding out in a cloud of dust, the shoe box tucked under his arm. When he wasn't working the stock with his father and brothers, he was tending to some other job his mother had conjured out of thin air. He wondered what it might be like to live a normal life, in a grand house in Brisbane, where daily chores didn't exist.

There'd be girls and parties and school and sports—all the things fourteen-year-old boys were supposed to enjoy. Teague sighed. Most boys his age didn't like school, but real classrooms with real teachers, chemistry and biology and physics and math, these were things he'd never experienced.

Instead, Teague was stuck on a cattle station in Queensland, with his parents, his two brothers and a rowdy bunch of jackaroos. Classes took place at the kitchen table, him and his brothers gathered around the radio listening to School of the Air. The closest town, Bilbarra, had a library and a small school, but that was a two-hour drive, much too far to make it practical day to day. Some of the kids on the more profitable stations were sent away to boarding school, but Kerry Creek wasn't exactly swimming in cash. Though the Quinn family wasn't poor, they weren't in the big bickies, either.

Teague heard the sound of hoofbeats and pushed up on his elbows, scanning the approach to the big rock and cursing to himself. Would he ever be able to get away from his brothers, or would they be following him around the rest of his life?

When he didn't see a rider coming from the direction of the homestead, he glanced over his shoulder and watched as a horse galloped full bore from the opposite direction, its rider hunched low in the saddle. Scrambling to his feet, Teague stood on the rock, ready to defend his territory against the interloper.

The boy drew his horse to a stop, the animal breathing heavily. From beneath the brim of a battered stockman's hat, he stared at Teague, a grim expression on his face. He wasn't very big, Teague mused, sizing up his chances if it came down to a fistfight.

But then suddenly, the boy smiled. "Did I scare you?" In one smooth motion, he brushed his hat from his head and a tumble of wavy blond hair revealed not a boy, but a girl. His breath caught in his throat as he stared into her pale blue eyes. Teague swallowed hard. She was the most beautiful girl he'd ever seen.

"I scared the piss out of you, didn't I? You should see your face. You're as pale as a ghost."

Teague scowled, embarrassed that she'd noticed his reaction. "Nick off. I wasn't scared. Why would I be scared of a mite like you? You couldn't knock the skin off a rice pudding."

She slid off her horse. "Oh, yeah. Well, you're so stupid, you couldn't tell your arse from a hole in the ground."

Teague opened his mouth, shocked to hear that kind of language from a girl. But then, he really had no experience talking to girls. With no sisters, he wasn't sure how girls were supposed to talk. On the telly, they always seemed to act so proper and prissy. This girl was acting more like his brothers.

She hitched her hands on her waist and stared up at him. "Well, are you going to give me a hand up or are you going to be mingy about the view?"

Teague studied her for a long moment. There wasn't much to fear from her. She was at least a head shorter than him and a few stone lighter. Though, in a verbal sparring match, she'd probably slice him into dinner for the dingoes. He reluctantly held out his hand and pulled her up beside him.

She scrambled to her feet and took a good look around. A frown wrinkled her brow, then she plopped down and sighed deeply.

"You don't like the view?"

She shook her head. "I thought I might be able to see the ocean."

Teague laughed, but when he saw the hurt in her eyes, he realized the depth of her disappointment. "Sorry," he mumbled as he sat down beside her. "You can't see the ocean from anywhere on this station. Even if you get up to the highest point. It's too far away."

She cursed beneath her breath before turning away from him. "I used to live near the ocean. I could see the water every day. I wish I could see it again."

A long silence grew between them. "That must have been nice," he finally ventured.

"It was better than living out here. Everything is so…dusty. And there are flies everywhere."

"Yeah, but you don't get to ride horses in the city," Teague offered, surprised to find himself defending the outback. "Or keep cattle. Or have a lot of dogs. And you don't see lizards and 'roos like you do here."

"You like animals?" she asked, her disappointment forgotten as suddenly as it had appeared.

Teague nodded. "Last month I found a bird with a broken wing. And I healed it." He pointed to the box beside him. "I'm going to let it go today."

"Can I see?" she asked, bending over the box.

Teague picked the box up, said a silent prayer, then lifted the lid. The sparrow immediately took flight and the girl clapped her hands as it flew into the distance. He felt his cheeks warm. "Maybe it healed itself. It's only a sparrow, but I kept it alive until it could fly again. I find hurt animals all the time and I know how to make them well again." He paused. "I like doing that."

A tiny smile tugged at her lips. "All right, there is one good thing about living on Wallaroo."

Teague swallowed hard, wondering if she'd just paid him a compliment. Then her words sank in. "You live on Wallaroo?" He hadn't even considered the possibility. But now that he thought about it, this was the girl his parents had had been talking about. "You're Hayley Fraser, then."

She seemed surprised he knew her name. "Maybe," she replied.

He'd heard the story by way of eavesdropping. Hayley's parents had been killed in an auto wreck when she was eight years old. She'd been moved from foster home to foster home, until her grandfather had finally agreed to take her. According to Teague's mum, old man Fraser hadn't been on speaking terms with his only child since Jake Fraser had run away from home at age eighteen. And now, his poor granddaughter was forced to live with a cold, unfeeling man who'd never wanted her on Wallaroo in the first place.

Teague's mum had insisted that Wallaroo was no place for a troubled young girl to grow up, without any women on the station at all, and with only rowdy men to serve as an example. Yet there was nothing anyone could do for her. Except him, Teague mused.

"You ride pretty good," he said. "Who taught you?"

"I taught myself. It doesn't take much skill. You hop on the horse and hang on."

"You know your granddad and my father are ene-
mies. They hate each other."

Hayley blinked as she glanced over at him. "No
surprise. Harry hates everyone, including me."

"You call him Harry?"

She shrugged. "That's his name."

Teague felt an odd lurch in his stomach as his eyes
met hers. She had the longest eyelashes he'd ever seen.
His gaze drifted down to her mouth and suddenly, he
found himself wondering what it might be like to kiss
such a bold and brave girl.

© Peggy A. Hoffmann 2009

millsandboon.co.uk Community

Join Us!

The Community is the perfect place to meet and chat to kindred spirits who love books and reading as much as you do, but it's also the place to:

- **Get the inside scoop from authors about their latest books**
- **Learn how to write a romance book with advice from our editors**
- **Help us to continue publishing the best in women's fiction**
- **Share your thoughts on the books we publish**
- **Befriend other users**

Forums: Interact with each other as well as authors, editors and a whole host of other users worldwide.

Blogs: Every registered community member has their own blog to tell the world what they're up to and what's on their mind.

Book Challenge: We're aiming to read 5,000 books and have joined forces with The Reading Agency in our inaugural Book Challenge.

Profile Page: Showcase yourself and keep a record of your recent community activity.

Social Networking: We've added buttons at the end of every post to share via digg, Facebook, Google, Yahoo, technorati and de.licio.us.

www.millsandboon.co.uk

2 FREE BOOKS
AND A SURPRISE GIFT

We would like to take this opportunity to thank you for reading this Mills & Boon® book by offering you the chance to take TWO more specially selected titles from the Blaze® series absolutely FREE! We're also making this offer to introduce you to the benefits of the Mills & Boon® Book Club™—

- **FREE home delivery**
- **FREE gifts and competitions**
- **FREE monthly Newsletter**
- **Exclusive Mills & Boon Book Club offers**
- **Books available before they're in the shops**

Accepting these FREE books and gift places you under no obligation to buy, you may cancel at any time, even after receiving your free books. Simply complete your details below and return the entire page to the address below. You don't even need a stamp!

YES Please send me 2 free Blaze books and a surprise gift. I understand that unless you hear from me, I will receive 3 superb new books every month, including a 2-in-1 book priced at £4.99 and two single books priced at £3.19 each, postage and packing free. I am under no obligation to purchase any books and may cancel my subscription at any time. The free books and gift will be mine to keep in any case.

Ms/Mrs/Miss/Mr _____ Initials _____

Surname _____

Address _____

_____

_____ Postcode _____

Send this whole page to: Mills & Boon Book Club, Free Book Offer, FREEPOST NAT 10298, Richmond, TW9 1BR